Also by this author

THE WOLF CHRONICLES: Promise of the Wolves

THE WOLF CHRONICLES

SECRETS

OF THE

WOLVES

DOROTHY HEARST

SIMON & SCHUSTER

NEW YORK   LONDON   TORONTO   SYDNEY

Simon & Schuster
1230 Avenue of the Americas
New York, NY 10020

First Simon & Schuster hardcover edition August 2011

SIMON & SCHUSTER and colophon are registered trademarks of Simon & Schuster, Inc.

For information about special discounts for bulk purchases, please contact Simon & Schuster Special Sales at 1-866-506-1949 or business@simonandschuster.com.

The Simon & Schuster Speakers Bureau can bring authors to your live event. For more information or to book an event, contact the Simon & Schuster Speakers Bureau at 1-866-248-3049 or visit our website at www.simonspeakers.com.

Manufactured in the United States of America

10 9 8 7 6 5 4 3 2 1

Library of Congress Cataloging-in-Publication Data

Hearst, Dorothy, 1966–
    Secrets of the wolves : a novel / Dorothy Hearst.
        p. cm.
    ISBN 978-1-4165-7000-4 (alk. paper)
    1. Wolves—Fiction. I. Title.
    PS3608.E27S43 2011
    813'.6—dc22   2010028204

ISBN 978-1-4165-7000-4
ISBN 978-1-4165-7022-6 (ebook)

Dedicated to
Jean Hearst
with love and gratitude
and many thanks for all of the words

SECRETS
OF THE
WOLVES

Prologue

I was not the first wolf to promise to be the guardian of the humans. That pledge was made many years ago in a time of great hunger, when a wolf named Indru met a tribe of starving humans. It was so long ago that wolves had just become wolf and humans were not yet quite human. The humans stood on two legs as they do now but had not yet lost their fur. They had not learned to control fire or build sturdy dens, and they had not learned to make throwing sticks that could kill beasts many times their own size. They were not nearly as good at surviving as were Indru and his pack.

The humans that Indru met at the edge of a great desert were so thin and hungry-looking that it seemed certain they would die. They should have made good prey for his pack, but Indru did not hear the call to the hunt. He felt pulled to the humans, as he would to his own packmates. He felt so drawn to them, so protective, that he could not let them die. He wanted to help them live. So Indru and his pack taught the humans the secrets of wolfkind: how to hunt rather than just scavenge what others had killed, how to find the best prey, and how a pack can work together to be stronger than any one individual. The humans survived.

Indru's wolves and the newly vigorous humans hunted together and slept side by side. The bond between them strengthened until it was as much a part of the wolves as their own heartbeats. Wolf and human might have become one pack, one family, but as the humans gained strength and knowledge, they grew proud. They did not stop learning after mastering the skills the wolves had taught them, but gained more and more knowledge, until they were stronger than many other creatures. They said that they were better than other creatures and they demanded that the wolves serve them. When the wolves refused, the humans became so angry that they used their newfound knowledge to destroy everything within their reach. They killed whatever could not escape them and, when they learned the secrets of fire, even burned their own lands.

What happened next, our legends tell us, is that when the Ancients—Sun, Moon, Earth, and Grandmother Sky—saw what havoc the humans caused, they prepared to destroy both wolf and humankind. In other times, there had been creatures who had grown too powerful, and the Ancients had killed them, too. The legends say that one time they hurled a huge rock from the sky that caused a night that would not end, and that many creatures perished.

Indru climbed to the top of a high mountain and pleaded with the Ancients. He was so eloquent in his supplication that he convinced the Ancients to spare wolf and humankind. In exchange, the Ancients demanded a promise from Indru. They told him that the humans, when left on their own with their newfound knowledge, would continue to believe that they were different from other creatures, better than any others, and thus would find it easy to destroy everything around them. Indru promised that wolves would become guardians of the humans. They would teach the humans of the Balance— how all creatures are part of the world and must not destroy that which they depend upon to survive. They would forever watch over the humans to ensure that they never again grew too proud and destructive.

Indru and his packmates taught the humans how to be a part of nature, and how one must never take Earth, Sun, Moon, Sky, and the bounty they provide for granted. They taught them about family and taking care of one's pack. They taught them how to be part of everything around them. And they showed the humans how to cherish the Balance. For generation upon generation, wolves tried to keep humans in touch with the world around them. But the humans, who bred faster than wolves ever had, began to want more than they had. They once again grew proud, and once again tried to make the wolves their slaves. The wolves—who could be as proud as any human—once again refused. There was a great war, with humans killing wolves and wolves killing humans. The wolves, angry and resentful, forsook their promise. The legends say that the Ancients then sent a winter three years long to end the lives of wolves and humans. That other creatures would die, too, apparently didn't matter to them. Throughout the land, humans and wolves starved. Throughout the land, wolves and humans died.

The second time wolves and humans hunted together, the long winter ended. A youngwolf named Lydda, who lived in the Wide Valley generations before I was born there, found a hungry human boy weeping against a rock. She felt drawn to him, as Indru had been drawn to his humans, and lay down beside him. Then Lydda and the young human killed a weakened elk. The meat saved both Lydda's pack and the young human's tribe, and the wolves and humans of the Wide Valley began to hunt as one pack, bringing the two clans together once more. The Ancients, pleased that the wolves had remembered their promise, ended the long winter. But it was not long before wolves and humans began to fight once again.

That was when the Greatwolves came to the Wide Valley, and as soon as they arrived, they began to tell lies.

They came down from the eastern mountains and found Lydda and her boy watching, bereft, as their families fought one another. No one had ever seen such huge wolves before, and when they told Lydda that they had been sent down from the sky by the Ancients, she believed them. They forced her to leave the valley, telling her she was a danger to wolfkind.

Then they invented a false legend: that when Indru had spoken to the Ancients, he had promised not to watch over the humans, but rather to stay forever away from them so that humans would not continue to learn so many new things. They said that they had been sent by the Ancients to teach the humans of the Balance from afar and that someday, when the weakness that made the Wide Valley wolves love the humans so much had been bred out of them, the Greatwolves would let them take over this task. Lydda believed them. She took her human boy and left the Wide Valley. Only after her death did she learn the truth. She discovered a way to return to the world of life. And she came to me.

By the time she did so, I was already an outcast from my pack. My mother had mated with a wolf from outside the valley. The Greatwolves carefully controlled the breeding of the Wide Valley wolves, and only they could give permission for mixed-blood pups. Wolves with Outsider blood were considered unlucky, and I had almost been killed as a smallpup because of it. When I grew fascinated by the humans, it only made things worse. I was told that being with the humans was wrong and that my inability to stay away from them made me a danger to my pack and to wolfkind, that it was proof that I was an aberrant wolf. When I saved the life of a human child, I kept it secret from my pack, believing that I was unnatural.

Lydda found me and told me the truth, that wolves and humans were meant to be together—that our survival depended on it. She helped me learn of the Greatwolves' lies, so that I could stop a battle between wolves and humans that would have led to war. She gave me the confidence to convince my pack that we were to be the guardians of the humans and the strength to take on the promise of wolfkind. Then she left me.

She came to me one last time, a quarter moon after I had stopped the battle. I was crouched against a stout oak, sheltering myself from a sudden windstorm. She spoke urgently, as if she expected any moment to be set upon by a larger hunter.

"You've done so well, Kaala," she had said, touching her nose to mine. "But I can no longer come here to you."

"Why not?" I needed her. I had promised to take on responsibility for the humans at least in part because she had told me to, because she had made me promise to succeed in the task that she had failed in. She couldn't leave me to face the consequences alone.

"The leaderwolves of the spirit realm forbade me to come here, and now they know I have disobeyed them," she said, looking over her shoulder. "They will be watching me carefully. But it's not just that. Wolves of the spirit realm are not meant to return to the world of life. We cannot endure here for long. If I continue to come, I will not be able to live in either world."

It was then that I noticed how thin she was, how frail. It had been less than a moon since I'd last seen her, and then she had been sleek and healthy.

"But I need you," I had said. "I'm supposed to keep wolf and humankind together. I can't do it alone."

"I know, Kaala. You have done more than I could have hoped, and I will not abandon you. I have heard of a place where the worlds of life and of death come together. You must find that place."

She might as well have told me to hunt a herd of elkryn on my own.

"How?" I asked.

"I don't know, Kaala. The leaderwolves of the spirit realm don't tell me things, but I have overheard them speaking of such a place, and of one who can travel between the world of life and death to get there. Perhaps you can find this one who travels."

I heard an angry howl, echoing through the valley. Lydda

cringed. "I must go. Will you promise me to try to find this place?"

"Yes," I said, blinking against the wind.

"Good. Then I know I will see you again soon."

She spoke to me quickly then, telling me everything she could before she had to go. Then she licked the top of my head, and disappeared into the thick underbrush.

I was not the first wolf to hunt with the humans, but I might very well be the last. It was one of the last things Lydda told me before she had to return to the spirit world: that this time, there would be no more chances.

1

I caught the delicate scent of distant prey and stopped, digging my paws into the earth. Lifting my muzzle to the wind, I inhaled, allowing the distinctive ice-and-hoof aroma to sink to the back of my throat. Snow deer, in our territory and on the move. All at once, blood rushed to the sensitive spot just behind my ears. My mouth moistened, and every muscle in my body hungered for the chase. Next to me, Ázzuen stood as still as I was, only his ears twitching. Then his dark gray head began to sway, pulled between the lure of prey and our task.

"We can't go after them," I said. "We have to get to Tall Grass."

"I know that," he replied, panting hard. We'd run most of the way across our territory at full pelt. "I'm coming."

Neither of us moved. I could, just barely, restrain myself from following the prey-scent, but I couldn't bring myself to move away from it. Neither could Ázzuen. The small cluster of pine trees in which we stood blocked out the early morning sun, allowing thick drops of moisture to form on Ázzuen's fur. His entire body now strained toward the prey. As a fresh gust of deer-scent washed over us, I closed my eyes.

A painful yank on the fur of my chest made me yelp. I glared down to see dark eyes peering at me out of a gleaming black feathered head and a sharp beak poised to jab at my paw. I stepped back. Tlitoo raised his wings as if to take flight, then strode forward to stand under my chin, staying within stabbing distance. His winter plumage made him seem larger than a not-yet-year-old raven should, and his tail and back were speckled with the snow he'd been rolling in. He stared a beady challenge at me, and then at Ázzuen, who jumped aside to get out of beak range and buried his nose in the snow, trying to freeze away the deer-scent.

When Tlitoo saw that he had our attention, he quorked softly.

"The Grimwolves are exactly fourteen minutes behind you, wolflets, and their legs are much longer than yours. They will catch up."

My throat tightened. I'd thought we had more time. The Greatwolves had ruled the Wide Valley for as long as any wolf could remember, and all wolves were required to obey them.

An angry howl made all three of us cringe. *Stop!* The command in the Greatwolf Frandra's voice was clear. *And wait for us. Stay at the pine grove. We will come for you.*

"How do they know where we are?" I demanded. "Their noses can't be all that good." We'd heard rumors that the Greatwolves could read the minds of other wolves. Ázzuen claimed the Greatwolves made up those stories themselves.

"They smell us and they smell pine," he said firmly. "And they're guessing."

"It doesn't matter, wolves!" Tlitoo rasped. "The longer you blather, the closer they get!"

I took a deep breath, calming myself. The Greatwolves would catch up with us in the end, and when they did they would be angry. But I was determined to make it to the Tall Grass plain before they found us, no matter what the consequence. For on the morning wind there rode another scent, one even more potent than that of the snow deer. A scent of sweat and flesh, of smoke and pine, of meat cooked over fire: the scent of the humans who shared our hunt. The ground beneath our paws was softening with the beginnings of the thaw, and the breeze that ruffled our fur sang of winter's weakening. For three nights, the Ice Moon had narrowed to the smallest of crescents and then faded to darkness. And with the waning of the Ice Moon, the wolves and humans of the Wide Valley could be together once again.

It had been three moons since we'd last seen our humans, on a cool autumn morning when the humans and wolves of the Wide Valley had nearly gone to war. If we had done so, every wolf and human in the valley would have been killed by order of the Greatwolves. I had stopped that war, with the help of my packmates, and in doing so had convinced the leader of the Greatwolves to spare us. In exchange I had made a promise: that for one year I would ensure that the wolves and humans of the Wide Valley did not fight. If I succeeded, the Wide Valley wolves and humans would live. If I failed, the Greatwolves would kill us all.

The next night, a heavy snowstorm howled into the Wide

Valley, warning us that the hungry days of winter neared. Wolves and humans, along with every other creature in the valley, would have to struggle to survive the harsh winter, and so the Greatwolves gave us three moons to prepare before we took on the task of keeping peace between human and wolf— as long as we stayed away from the humans during that time. Today was the day our task was to begin. But two nights ago, the Greatwolves had ordered us to come to them as soon as the Ice Moon waned. Instead, awoken by Tlitoo's warning, we'd fled.

I met Ázzuen's eyes and filled my throat with the cool morning air. The Greatwolves had lied to us too many times. With one last look in the direction of the snow deer, I leapt over Tlitoo's snowy back and sprinted toward the Tall Grass plain, folding my ears against the wrathful howls of the Greatwolves.

When we reached the Wood's Edge Gathering Place, a few steps from where the trees met the Tall Grass plain, we found Marra pacing restlessly, her pale gray fur flecked with dirt and leaves. She darted over to touch my nose and then Ázzuen's with her own, her muzzle quivering with impatience.

"Ruuqo and Rissa are on their way here with Trevegg," Marra said quickly. "The rest of the pack went after the snow deer." I had sent her on ahead to warn the leaderwolves that the Greatwolves followed us; we hadn't wanted to risk howling. Tlitoo could have flown to them more quickly than even fleet Marra could run, but he had refused to leave us. He'd been agitated since waking us at dawn. Even now, he stalked back and forth between me and Ázzuen, clacking his beak impatiently.

Marra must have run like a hare to get back to Tall Grass so quickly. She wasn't even winded. She barely took a breath before speaking again.

"MikLan and BreLan are out there," she said. They were the two males that she and Ázzuen hunted with. "And your human, too, Kaala."

I didn't need her to tell me that. The aroma of humans had grown overpowering, one human-scent in particular nearly knocking me off my paws. I felt a familiar yearning deep in my chest. TaLi and I had run the hunt together and slept side by side. She was as much my packmate as any wolf and her fragrance as much a part of my being as my own skin.

"Did Ruuqo and Rissa want us to wait for them?" Ázzuen asked, taking a few steps toward the plain, then looking back at us. His tail began to wave. Ruuqo and Rissa were the leaderwolves of the Swift River pack. All wolves must obey the will of their leaderwolves, especially wolves like Ázzuen, Marra, and me, who at nine and a half moons old were not yet quite considered adults.

"No," Marra replied, averting her eyes. "Rissa's ribs hurt her today, so the pack moves slowly." Rissa had injured her ribs in a fight with a maddened elkryn three moons before, only steps from where we now stood. It still hurt her when the weather changed.

"Ruuqo said we should try to talk to the humans before the Greatwolves get here." Marra licked a paw, still not meeting my eyes. "You could have saved me the trouble of warning the pack, Kaala, with all the noise the Greatwolves are making."

I narrowed my eyes, not entirely sure I believed Marra. She wasn't above stretching the truth from time to time, and I doubted Ruuqo and Rissa would want youngwolves like us to defy the Greatwolves without our pack leaders at our side. I had worked hard all winter to regain the leaderwolves' trust and didn't want to lose it again.

"We could wait," I said. "The pack will be here soon."

"So will the Gruntwolves!" Tlitoo retorted, slapping his wings against his back. "You did not run all this way to stop now. What is the point of making the Gripewolves angry for no reason?" He picked up half a pinecone in his beak and hurled it at me. It bounced off my shoulder. "Slugwolf!" he screeched.

"We *are* the ones who know the humans best, Kaala," Ázzuen said, sensing my indecision.

Just then a furious and startlingly nearby Greatwolf howl shook the air. My legs made up my mind for me. I was running before I realized it, bolting from the safety of Wood's Edge with Ázzuen and Marra at my tail. We broke through a line of spruce trees and onto the Tall Grass plain where we could at last see our humans again.

Six of them stood around a mound of dirt and snow, poking at it with the blunt ends of the long, deadly sharpsticks they used for hunting. We loped across the plain slowly, not wanting to startle the humans. Tall Grass was a large plain, where we often hunted horses and other grazers. The humans were halfway down the length of it and intent on their dirt mound, so they didn't notice us at first. TaLi's scent drifted more strongly than ever across the grass, but I couldn't pick her out among the humans. All three of the females had flat, dark fur like TaLi's and were dressed in bear and wolverine skins against the cold. None of them, however, was the right shape to be TaLi. Had I somehow mistaken her scent? I slowed down. Tlitoo lost what little patience he had when Ázzuen and Marra slowed, too.

"Plodwolves!" he shrieked. He flew over my head, scraping my ears with his sharp talons, beating his wings hard to reach the humans. He soared low over their heads. Several of the humans leapt back, startled, and looked up at the raven. That was when I saw her.

She was taller, even after only three moons. Her legs and arms were long and very skinny, like someone had been pulling on them, and she moved awkwardly, as if balancing on a loose rock in the river. Ázzuen had stumbled around like that earlier in the winter, when he suddenly grew taller than any of us other pups and hadn't yet accustomed himself to his new height. A small whuff of surprise escaped my throat as I realized that TaLi would not be a child much longer. When I had pulled her from the river, not six moons before, she had been smaller and much more solid-looking.

BreLan, the young male who hunted with Ázzuen, spotted us. He gave a glad shout. That was all it took for Ázzuen and Marra to charge full speed toward the humans. I hesitated, suddenly uncertain. Many humans hated and feared us. Trevegg, the elderwolf of our pack, had warned us that even if our humans liked us now, they might change their minds as they matured. I couldn't help but wonder if TaLi, now nearly grown, might no longer wish to run the hunt with me. I stole forward, watching her for signs of fear or rejection. She raised her hand to shade her eyes against the early morning sun. Then she gave her huge, bared-tooth smile, set down her sharpstick, and galloped toward me.

"Silvermoon!" she bellowed like an elk stuck in the mire. It was her name for me, because of the moon-shape of white on the light gray fur of my chest.

I broke into a run and met her before she had taken ten steps on those ridiculous legs. I placed my paws gently on her shoulders, taking care not to hurt or startle her. She threw her arms around me and hurled her weight against me. I allowed her to topple me over and she landed on my ribs. Grunting in delight, I rolled her onto her back, and we wrestled in the dirt until I stood atop her chest, panting. The scent of her filled me, bringing back in a rush the memory of the day I first found her. She had been struggling for her life in the unforgiving waters of the Swift River, and I had pulled her to safety. It was forbidden by ancient laws for the wolves of the Wide Valley to have contact with the humans, and I should have left her there on the riverbank to live or not. But I couldn't. Within moments of looking into her dark eyes, I knew that leaving her to die would be like abandoning part of myself in that river mud. Ázzuen and I returned her to her home, an act that some in the valley claimed had led to the battle at autumn's end.

I pressed my nose against TaLi's soft skin, inhaling as much of her scent as I could.

"Silvermoon, you stink," the girl said, pushing me off her chest and sitting up.

I wasn't sure what she meant. Ázzuen, Marra, and I had dug up one of our old caches of horse meat and had eaten some of it the night before, which should have made my breath smell good. But you could never tell with humans. I cocked my head, considering what she might mean.

"You smell like you rolled in something dead!" she accused.

I panted happily. I had indeed rolled in something dead. The old horse meat from our cache. All three of us had rolled in it so we could let our pack know we'd eaten it and that there was some left over for them. Horse meat was good eating. I pressed myself against TaLi to share the scent with her.

A look of horror crossed her face. "Silvermoon! You reek! Get away." She shoved me again, hard. Those scrawny arms were stronger than they looked.

"She means you smell very bad," Tlitoo offered, settling himself beside me and running his beak through his wing feathers. He plucked out one feather, examined it, and threw it aside. He was calmer, now that we were with the humans. It infuriated me. He had been frantic when he had awoken us. He told us we had to convince our humans to go into hiding until he found out what the Greatwolves were doing. He wouldn't tell me why, only that we and our humans might be in danger if we didn't.

"I know what she means," I snapped. But I wasn't entirely sure I did. Once, wolves and humans could communicate as easily as one wolf speaks to another, but no more. Most creatures can understand one another at least a little. We can speak to ravens as if they are packmates, and to dholes and rock bears almost as well. We can even understand some prey. Somehow, though, almost all of the humans had lost the ability to understand other creatures. A few could converse in

Oldspeak, the ancient language that all creatures once spoke. Even fewer could understand us when we spoke normally. Ta-Li's grandmother could understand both Oldspeak and our normal language, but she had spent a lifetime learning from the wolves. TaLi and I were both learning Oldspeak, but neither of us knew it well. Most of the time I understood TaLi when she spoke, but I could rarely make her understand me. And I *had* to make her understand me. It was the reason we'd risked provoking the Greatwolves. I paced in a tight circle, desperate to find a way to communicate our message to TaLi.

"Too late, wolflet," Tlitoo quorked, twisting his head almost all the way around to look behind him.

I followed his gaze. At the edge of the forest, about two hundred wolflengths down the plain, the bushes trembled. A moment later, two huge, shaggy wolves stalked onto Tall Grass. Even from a distance, I could see their gaze sweeping arrogantly over us and all six of the humans. Jandru and Frandra were the Greatwolves the Swift River pack answered to. They were also the ones who had been howling at us all morning. I had known them since they had saved my life when I was a smallpup and never knew if they were going to help me or threaten me, but I knew that they would be furious that I had ignored their orders. I didn't want them anywhere near our humans.

I stood, and Ázzuen and Marra rushed to stand beside me. The three of us placed ourselves between the humans and the angry Greatwolves.

"Now what?" Marra asked.

"I don't know," I said.

"Ruuqo and Rissa are at Wood's Edge," Ázzuen said, his

nose lifted high to catch their scents. "We can lead the Great-wolves away from the humans and to the pack. Ruuqo and Rissa will know what to say to the Greatwolves."

I wasn't so sure, but it was as good an idea as any. Great-wolves are faster than we are over long distances, but a young wolf could outpace them over a short run, and I wanted Fran-dra and Jandru as far from the humans as possible. Once we got to Wood's Edge, we could think of some way to explain our actions. I began to trot toward Frandra and Jandru. Áz-zuen and Marra followed. We had gone only forty wolflengths when we heard Tlitoo screech. BreLan, MikLan, and several other humans were trying to follow us. TaLi pushed at them, yelling that they should stay back; she knew better than to be anywhere near angry Greatwolves. All the humans knew that giant wolves roamed the valley, but only a few knew of the Greatwolves' role in humans' lives. And the Greatwolves wanted to keep it that way.

The other humans weren't listening to TaLi, and she wasn't big enough to stop them. Tlitoo beat the humans about their heads with his wings, driving them back. I didn't envy them. A raven's wings are strong and, when spread, can be nearly as wide as a wolf is long. I'd been hit by them often enough to know it wasn't pleasant. He was managing to move them, but not quickly enough. The Greatwolves were getting closer.

"Help him," I said to Ázzuen and Marra. We had all stopped to watch the humans.

Marra dipped her head and set off toward the humans, but Ázzuen paused, clearly not wanting to leave me to the Greatwolves.

"It's *fine*," I said impatiently. Ázzuen had grown annoy-
ingly protective of me in the last few moons. "Go!" I couldn't
wait any longer, the Greatwolves were getting too close. I
started running. Ázzuen followed me for a few steps. "Hurry
up!" I snapped at him. He still hesitated, then looked over his
shoulder. His human, BreLan, was trying to follow him in
spite of Tlitoo's abuse.

"Be careful," Ázzuen ordered, butting my shoulder with
his head. He turned in midstride. "I'll come if you need me,"
he called over his shoulder.

I whuffed at the concern in his voice, then turned and ran
in earnest. When Frandra and Jandru saw that I was coming
to them, they stopped and sat, waiting for me. I lowered my
ears and tail, as if asking their pardon for disobeying them,
and I saw their expressions soften just a little. Then, when I
was a little more than halfway between them and the humans, I turned sharply and bolted toward Wood's Edge. I
didn't look to see if the Greatwolves were following. I knew
they would be as soon as I heard Frandra's angry bellow. Head
down, I stretched my legs as far as they would go, kicking up
dirt behind me.

Now that I was alone, fear tried to rise in me. I concen-
trated on running, knowing that it was up to me to make sure
the Greatwolves didn't go after the humans. To my relief, I
could smell that our pack had indeed arrived at Wood's Edge.
The reassuring scents of my leaderwolves loosened a lump in
my chest I hadn't realized was there.

I didn't slow down when I reached Wood's Edge. I dove
through the wolf-size hole in the low juniper bushes, crashed
into the gathering place in a shower of twigs and dirt, and

tumbled at the feet of the leaderwolves. Gasping, I got to my feet. Ears back and tail low, I quickly greeted Ruuqo and Rissa, the leaderwolves of Swift River pack, and Trevegg, the pack's elderwolf. They all accepted my greetings. Ruuqo looked me over coolly. I could feel every branch and bramble in my fur.

"What did you do to annoy the Greatwolves, this time, Kaala?" he said, his voice mild. "We could hear them yowling all the way at the Alder Grove. We're missing a good hunt in order to be here."

Ruuqo was a large, deep-chested wolf, his fur a medium gray. In spite of his unruffled tone, his lips were tight with anxiety and a scent of concern rose off of him. He held his broad shoulders rigid as if ready for a fight.

I looked up into his dark rimmed eyes. If I lived to be as old as the ancient yew tree atop Wolf Killer Hill, I would never forget that Ruuqo had tried to kill me not long after I was born, that he had killed my littermates and exiled my mother, leaving me to fight alone for my place in the pack. If not for the intervention of the Greatwolves, I would not have lived past my first moon. I would never forget that when he discovered I was spending time with the humans, he had banished me, forcing me to leave the pack—a punishment almost certain to lead to death for a wolf not seven moons old. Not a day went by when I didn't think of my mother, of what my life would be like if she was still with me. Since I had saved Rissa's life three moons before, Ruuqo had accepted me back into the pack, and had even been grateful to me. But I would never forget. Though I owed him obedience and allegiance as my leaderwolf, I would never like him.

"Tlitoo came for us at daybreak," I said, trying to get the

words out before Jandru and Frandra arrived. "He told us that the Greatwolves had changed their minds. I wanted to make sure the humans were warned." *In case the Greatwolves decided to kill them again,* I thought. I saw old Trevegg watching me and stood straighter. He was always telling me that I needed to be more confident in my own strength.

"Changed their minds to what?" Rissa asked, stepping up to stand beside her mate. She was only slightly smaller than Ruuqo, with a bright white pelt unusual in a Wide Valley wolf. While Ruuqo had shunned me throughout my puphood, Rissa had treated me as one of her own pups. I often forgot that Áz-zuen, Marra, and I were not of the same litter. When an elkryn had nearly trampled Rissa three moons before, it had been pure instinct that drove me to leap upon it, taking its nose in my teeth and distracting it so that TaLi and my pack could kill it. Since then, Rissa had almost treated me as an equal. A sister, rather than a youngwolf, and it made me nervous. Once she even called me Neesa, my mother's name. My mother had been Rissa's sister and they had spent their entire lives together until my mother had been exiled.

"I'm not sure," I admitted. "He said there was trouble, and that the Greatwolves were coming and that we should go to the humans as quickly as we could. To warn them."

"And you believed a raven without asking for details?" Rissa asked, amused. "You're old enough to know better than that. And we told Marra that you were to wait for us."

"And how did you expect to warn humans, anyway?" The snide voice came from my right. "You can't even talk to them." I looked at Unnan out of the corner of my eye, wishing with all my heart that Ruuqo and Rissa had left him at the hunt. I hadn't bothered to greet him. He was Ázzuen and Marra's littermate, and my greatest enemy in the pack. His small, weaselly eyes flicked over me. I ignored him and answered Rissa.

"It was Tlitoo. I trust him," I said. "And the ravens don't usually lie much about the Greatwolves."

But Rissa was no longer watching me. She looked over my head, into the trees that surrounded the eastern end of Wood's Edge, the direction the Greatwolves would be coming from. Her nose twitched and her ears shot up. Ruuqo growled, and Trevegg rose and stood rigid-legged behind the leaderwolves. All three raised their back fur. I heard Unnan gasp.

I pricked up my ears to listen for what had startled them all and felt my own tail stiffen. The Greatwolves were coming, as we knew they would. But there were too many of them. Only Jandru and Frandra had followed me from Tall Grass. Now, more than two dozen heavy paws crushed dry leaves and sticks, and the scents of seven Greatwolves blew into the gathering place, assailing our noses with the scents of anger and menace. When I was a smallpup, there had been only a few Greatwolves in the valley and most of them were old. Since the battle at autumn's end, many more had come to the Wide Valley.

My heart pounded and my legs shook as I turned in the direction of the approaching wolves. As I felt the ground rumble with the growls of my packmates, panic closed my throat, so I couldn't have whimpered if I'd wanted to. For the briefest moment, I considered running, but I stood my ground with my packmates, wondering if it would be the last time I would ever do so. Greatwolves came in such numbers for one reason only—to kill packs of wolves that had displeased them.

2

gnoring the trembling in my legs, I walked forward. I wouldn't let my packmates die because I had disobeyed the Greatwolves. Ruuqo, Rissa, and Trevegg all shoved past me to stand between me, Unnan, and the approaching danger. I tried to protest.

"You're still a pup," Ruuqo said gruffly, silencing me. "Swift River protects its pups."

Reluctantly, I stayed where I was. Once Ruuqo made up his mind about something he was immovable. I hoped he wouldn't die for it. If the Greatwolves had indeed come to kill, we wouldn't stand a chance against them, even with all five of us in the fight. I was glad that Yllin, Minn, and Werrna had stayed with the snow deer. They, and perhaps Ázzuen and Marra, might still live if they could flee the valley before the Greatwolves found them.

Trevegg whispered to Ruuqo as the crashing sounds closed in on us, and both of them looked back at me. Then all three adult wolves went completely still as Jandru and Frandra burst into the clearing, glaring at me with such fury that my legs almost gave out beneath me. An instant later, five more Greatwolves stormed into Wood's Edge behind them, trampling the thick juniper bushes that made it such a secure gathering place. These wolves were strangers to me and were breathing hard, as if they had run a long distance very quickly. They looked as big as rock bears. Greatwolves are only half again as large as ordinary wolves, but these seemed so much bigger. They all had their ruffs puffed out and their backfur raised.

"As if they needed to do anything to look intimidating." Ázzuen sidled up beside me, breathing hard. I could've bitten his ears off. He should have been safely away, not here where he could be killed. His appearance made me realize afresh what I had done—endangered those I cared most about by acting so rashly. I glowered at him, trying to push him away from danger with my gaze.

"The humans are safe. Your girl and the raven made them leave," he said, deliberately misinterpreting my expression, "and Marra is watching to make sure they don't come back."

"Get out of here!" I hissed at him. But it was too late. The Greatwolves were advancing on us, growling. Three pulled their lips back over long, sharp teeth. One of them laughed.

Ruuqo rumbled deep in his throat, striding forward to answer the threat, Trevegg and Rissa immediately at his side. Ázzuen, Unnan, and I stood just behind them. I felt my own backfur lift and my throat tighten around a growl. Ruuqo and Trevegg took two more steps forward. Rissa, less able to fight because of her sore ribs, stayed one pace behind them. All three of them lowered their heads and raised their hindquarters. It was the best strategy for a wolf faced with a much larger opponent, to attack from below. There was a time when it would be unthinkable for a smallwolf to attack a Greatwolf. But that was before they had lied to us. That was before they came to our homesite prepared to kill us.

For a long, tense moment, we stood facing them. Then Rissa pushed past Ruuqo and Trevegg, hiding the soreness in her ribs with a stiff-legged gait.

"What is it you wish of us, Lordwolves?" she asked formally. I could see the quivering of her white-furred flanks and the tension in her tail, kept low in deference to the Greatwolves. I could see what a struggle it was for her to keep it from tucking completely between her legs, which was where mine certainly was.

Jandru and Frandra stalked forward to stand just paws-widths from Rissa, Ruuqo, and Trevegg.

"Idiot pup," Jandru snarled, looking past the adult wolves to me.

"We should let them chew a piece out of your hide," Frandra hissed.

I couldn't even swallow. I tried to fill my lungs and found I couldn't. All I could do was stand there, waiting for Frandra and Jandru to lead the attack against us. Instead, after sending one more disgusted look in my direction, they turned to face the other Greatwolves, standing with us against them.

Rissa whuffed in surprise, and Trevegg and Ruuqo stopped growling for an instant before beginning again.

Jandru spoke to a female wolf who stood just in front of the others. "What do you want with a wolf under our protection, Milsindra?" he demanded. "You know that Swift River belongs to us."

The wolf called Milsindra was a tall, lean, light brown Greatwolf with dark flecks in her pale eyes. "If they belong to you," she said, "you should keep better control over them. Your inability to do so threatens every wolf in the valley." Her eyes flicked from us to Frandra and Jandru and back again, measuring our strength. She dipped her head to the male wolf who stood closest to her, and they, along with the three Greatwolves behind them, began to stalk forward, their lips pulled so far back I could see every tooth in their mouths. I felt the wolves around me tense, readying themselves for the attack.

Then Milsindra froze. Her ears twitched and her nose quivered as she looked toward the eastern entrance of Wood's Edge. Greatwolves have a better sense of smell than we do. I followed her gaze.

An eighth huge wolf was making his way to Wood's Edge, more slowly than the others, his steps heavy and deliberate. Every wolf in the clearing, Greatwolf and smallwolf alike, fell silent, watching as an old, gaunt Greatwolf emerged from the junipers just to the right of Milsindra and her followers. Zorindru, the ancientwolf who led the Greatwolves of the Wide Valley, walked calmly into Wood's Edge, as if he had come to our gathering place for a visit. He looked curiously at the moist, soft dirt, the smooth rocks, at the thick junipers and tall pines and, at last, at the five Greatwolves who threatened us. He cocked his head, as if surprised to find them there.

"Milsindra," the ancientwolf said in a voice that sounded like twigs breaking underfoot, "did I not ask you to wait for me?"

Milsindra took two quick steps back. I don't know how Zorindru did it. He was old, older than Trevegg, who had lived nine winters. Zorindru had been old when Trevegg's father led the Swift River pack. Milsindra and her followers were all wolves in their prime. But just a lift of his grizzled lip made the other Greatwolves cower like scolded pups. I could hear my packmates' muscles loosening: Rissa's shoulder blades releasing down her back, Ruuqo's chest relaxing. Next to me, Ázzuen let out a whuff of air that ruffled the fur on my muzzle. My throat slackened, and I sucked in a great gulp of air.

Milsindra shook herself once. Then, as if to make up for cringing away from Zorindru, she growled at him.

"It's our right to be here," she said. "We were promised that we could see for ourselves."

"See what?" a voice croaked from above. Tlitoo peered down at us from a low branch of a pine tree, directly above Milsindra. In one foot he held a good-size stone. In a bend between two branches, he had stacked several others. "Have you not seen wolves before? They are everywhere in the valley."

"To see this pup," Milsindra snapped, keeping a wary eye on Tlitoo. "This arrogant pup who breaks all the rules and is rewarded for it."

"So see her," Zorindru said. His eyes found me just behind Trevegg's rump. "Come forward, youngwolf."

Even as I trembled in fear, I found myself pleased to be addressed as a youngwolf rather than a pup. Ázzuen pressed against me and quickly touched his nose to my face. Ruuqo dipped his head to me and moved slightly to the side, allowing me to step past him.

"That's her?" Milsindra said with unflattering disbelief. She turned her tawny head to Zorindru. "You want us to entrust our future to that scrap of wolf?"

"That scrap of wolf stopped a battle you said couldn't be stopped," Zorindru said. "And the council has agreed to give her a year to find a way for the humans and wolves of the valley to live peacefully together. You know that, Milsindra."

"*I* didn't agree. I would never agree to let an aberrant, mixed-blood wolf take on the task that belongs to the Greatwolves. She'll destroy everything we've worked for!" She lowered her head and pulled back her lips. Three of the four wolves who stood with her growled. I could sense Ruuqo, Rissa, and Trevegg tensing up behind me.

"Enough!" Zorindru said. "You are part of the council, Milsindra, and thus bound by its rules. Unless you wish to challenge me? Here and now?"

Milsindra shifted from paw to paw. For a moment it looked like she might actually attack him. Then the Greatwolf standing next to her, the one who had not growled with the others, shoved Milsindra with his hip, glaring at her out of the corner of his eye. He was as tall as Milsindra and stockier, with fur almost as light as Rissa's.

"We only want what's best for wolfkind," he said, his voice conciliatory, his tail held low. "It's too risky to entrust the humans to smallwolves. Especially to one half grown." He paused. "And especially to one that is known to be unlucky. This pup is dangerous."

A stone fell from above, landing just to the right of the Greatwolf's head. He jumped, then looked up at Tlitoo, who held another stone ready in his foot. Tlitoo raised his wings enough that I could just glimpse the white crescent on the underside of his left wing and quorked at the Greatwolf.

> *"Every raven knows*
> *Gruntwolves talk more than they think*
> *Fine. Their heads are hard."*

Someone behind me laughed. I looked quickly at Zorindru. He was watching the male Greatwolf steadily.

"Thank you, Kivdru," he said to the Greatwolf who had spoken. "I'm glad you're considering the risks of your actions."

Kivdru lowered his eyes.

The Greatwolf Jandru, who had been silent since Zorindru entered the clearing, stepped forward. I held my breath. He and Frandra, as the Greatwolves responsible for the Swift River pack, were accountable for our actions. They had stood with us against the other Greatwolves. But that didn't mean they wouldn't turn against us, as they had at autumn's end.

"You know we have to do something, Kivdru," he said. "I don't like using this pup any more than you do. She's reckless and disrespectful. But the humans no longer listen to our ambassadors, and we *must* find another way to remind them that they are part of the natural world and not creatures apart from all others. "

"As we have discussed all winter!" Zorindru snapped. "It may be the only way to protect the Balance. If Kaala can succeed, we will have made some progress with the humans. If she fails, we are no worse off than before. We have nothing to lose by trying."

"We have everything to lose!" Milsindra snapped back. I

was glad that Zorindru stood between me and her teeth. "You know that it is the Greatwolves who are supposed to watch over the humans! You know that, Zorindru." There was a challenge in her gaze when she stared at the ancient Great-wolf, as if she was daring him to say or do something. This time, it was Zorindru who shifted uncomfortably. When he said nothing, Milsindra gave a small, satisfied grunt. Some-thing had been communicated between the two of them, and I didn't know what. Behind me, Ázzuen whuffed impatiently, as he did when he wanted to ask a question about something and couldn't.

"We are the ones to guard the humans," Milsindra contin-ued. "It is unacceptable to let weak-willed smallwolves take the task. As for this pup, for all we know she is the one come to destroy us all, and we anger the Ancients by letting her live, much less giving her power."

I cringed. From the time of my birth, many wolves be-lieved I might be a wolf of legend, born to either save or de-stroy wolfkind. It was because of my mixed blood. For generations, the Greatwolves had forbidden Wide Valley wolves from mating with wolves from outside the valley. They wanted us to keep our bloodlines pure because they were try-ing to breed smallwolves that were not drawn to the humans. Every few years they would allow a Wide Valley wolf to mate outside the valley so that our bloodlines would remain strong and we would not have deformed pups, but no wolf could do so without their permission. My father was an Outsider wolf, and my mother did not have permission to have pups with him. It was why Ruuqo had killed my littermates and ban-ished my mother. The legends tell us that someday a mixed-blood wolf will be born to be wolfkind's savior or its destroyer, and that the mixed-blood wolf will have the mark of the crescent moon upon it. I have just such a mark, with the bottom of the moon beginning near the top of my forelegs and the top opening up to my face. It's not an unusual mark for a wolf, but all wolves with such a mark are carefully watched. That mark, along with my mixed blood, was why Frandra and Jandru had saved me—and why some Greatwolves still wanted me dead.

Milsindra glared at the ancientwolf and pawed the dirt.

"It's stupid, Zorindru, and much too risky."

I looked at her in amazement. I couldn't believe she had just called her leaderwolf stupid.

"I have heard your concerns, Milsindra, and yours, Kivdru," Zorindru said. "Which is why the council has agreed to your conditions. But the decision stands. You have seen this young-wolf. I've respected your wishes in this. Now return to your territories, or else challenge my leadership and accept the consequences."

Milsindra averted her gaze from Zorindru's and glared at me. "I think you're trouble, youngwolf," she said. "I think we should kill you now and save ourselves the trouble of doing so later and cleaning up the mess you leave behind."

She raised her chin to Zorindru. "She must meet all of the conditions, Zorindru, or you will have your challenge." Her gaze, when it returned to me, was sly. "We will see how things work when you really spend time with your humans."

She shook her head hard, then turned and strode out of the clearing, followed by the four Greatwolves who had stood with her against Zorindru. I was watching Zorindru's face when I heard an angry yelp and turned to see a stone bounce off Milsindra's rump. She snarled up into the trees where Tlitoo stood preening his wings. He cocked his head at Milsindra. She growled, but when Tlitoo picked up another stone, she stalked off into the woods.

▣

It seemed that even the trees breathed a sigh of relief when the angry Greatwolves left the clearing. My legs decided they'd held me up long enough. I sat down hard.

"What was that about?" Rissa asked, staring after the Greatwolves. "Even Milsindra is not usually as bad-tempered as that."

Frandra stretched and stalked over to a pine stump we used as a lookout spot and leapt upon it. "It's about your youngwolf not knowing when to follow orders," the Greatwolf said. "I thought you taught your pups better, Rissa."

Zorindru spoke before Rissa could respond to Frandra's insult. "Milsindra and Kivdru would have caused trouble sooner or later. Still, you should have waited for us, Kaala. Had I not been nearby, Milsindra could have caused your pack real harm. She could have killed your packmates."

"I heard that you'd changed your minds," I said.

Unexpectedly, Zorindru opened his jaws in a huge smile. "Yes," he said, "the ravens will have told you that. You would think that I would have learned by now to look in the trees before I discuss anything I wish to keep secret."

Tlitoo left his perch and glided down to land in front of me. He stood facing Zorindru, his head just below my chin. It was where he stood when he thought I needed defending.

"It is what you said," he quorked.

"Yes, it is," the Greatwolf answered. "You did not, how-ever, wait to hear all that we said. Your flight was too hasty."

Tlitoo croaked an insult. Zorindru shot him the same quelling glance that had so intimidated Milsindra. Tlitoo blinked back at him, unimpressed. The old Greatwolf laughed.

"Very well," he said. "I will tell you what you would have learned if Kaala had come to us this morning as she should have."

Zorindru stretched, and I heard his old joints pop. Ruuqo and Rissa quickly stepped forward to guide him to the best resting spot in our gathering place, a soft mound of earth next to the pine stump Frandra had claimed. Frandra quickly jumped down from the stump so that she would not be stand-ing above her leaderwolf. She sat to one side of Zorindru, and Jandru stood on the other, as if protecting the ancient Great-wolf. Tlitoo took over Frandra's perch on the stump. When the rest of us had settled uneasily around them, Zorindru watched me for a long moment, and then spoke.

"What I did not know at autumn's end, Kaala, was the ef-fect your actions would have on the Greatwolf council. When you stopped the battle at Tall Grass, and when I convinced the council to give you a year to keep the peace, it helped Milsindra win more wolves over to her side."

When he hesitated, Jandru spoke up. I couldn't miss the resentment in his voice.

"Most on the council already believed you smallwolves in-capable of taking on responsibility for the humans. They be-lieve that you are certain to fail, and that when you do, it will be disastrous for wolfkind."

"You promised!" Tlitoo said, interrupting the Greatwolf. "You promised you would give the smallwolves one year. Now you renege. Now you change your minds. It is not fair.

> *"What Gruntwolves say and*
> *What they do are not the same*
> *Always, they tell lies!"*

Jandru and Frandra growled up at the raven. He picked up a twig in his beak and spat it at them.

"The Greatwolf council is twenty wolves strong, plus myself, raven," Zorindru said tiredly. "I do not rule over them completely, and Milsindra and Kivdru have coveted my position as leader since my mate died eight winters past." The sadness that flitted across the oldwolf's face made me lower my eyes. When I looked up again, Zorindru's face was impassive. Jandru and Frandra eyed Tlitoo with contempt.

"Milsindra has spent the winter feeding the council's fear," Zorindru said so calmly I thought I must have imagined his distress. "She has convinced many of them that my mind is weakening, and that I can no longer be trusted with the responsibility for the Wide Valley wolves and their role in the fate of wolfkind."

"I do not find your mind to be weak," Tlitoo said. He hopped down from the stump to stand next to the Greatwolves, hesitated for a moment, then reached up to draw his beak through the fur on Zorindru's chest. I'd never heard a raven apologize to anyone. I thought that this might be the closest I'd ever get.

"Thank you, my friend," Zorindru said gravely. Rissa coughed a laugh. Tlitoo flipped back his wings and leapt back up on the watch-stump. From there, he hissed at Frandra and Jandru and glared around the gathering place.

Zorindru continued. "Milsindra's followers are neither strong enough nor certain enough to challenge me at this time, nor can they force me to deny the promise the council has made."

"But what?" old Trevegg asked, watching the Greatwolf sharply.

"But there is enough opposition to my rule that Milsindra was able to insist upon some conditions, upon a test." The seriousness left his face, and he panted a smile. "Or rather I suggested one and let Milsindra think it was her idea."

"What test?" I said, feeling my stomach clench. Wasn't it enough that I had to find a way to stop wolves and humans from fighting when I was not yet ten moons old? Even with my pack helping, as they had promised to do, it was a daunting task.

"The council says that it is not enough merely to keep peace for a year, that wolves and humans could refrain from fighting for that long merely by keeping away from one another and would fight again soon after."

"I wouldn't do that!" I stood, too restless to stay sitting. "I want to be with the humans." Zorindru's reproving glare silenced me. His eyes rested on me for a moment before he continued.

"The council has decreed that for the course of one year, wolves must live with the humans, as members of the same family, as members of the same pack."

For a moment we all looked at him in shock.

"The two packs must become one," Tlitoo crooned from atop his stump.

"That's what NiaLi told us we should do," I said, remembering the words TaLi's grandmother had spoken. "After the Tall Grass fight she said that the two packs must become one, that it was the only way we could keep peace between wolves and humans."

"You told us later that the council would never agree," Trevegg said. "You said they would never let us be together with the humans, that we would have to find another way. What changed?"

I barely heard the oldwolf as an unexpected surge of anger rose up in me. The humans were mine. I was the one who had brought wolves and humans together in peace. I had risked everything to be with them and had been banished from my pack because of it. I had been called a *drelshik*—a cursed wolf. I had risked my life. And now the Greatwolves were ordering us to live with the humans, when it was what I had wanted to do in the first place.

Then I felt my heart lift. That was it? That was the task? We were to *live* with the humans. It would be me. It would have to be me. I knew the humans best.

"Stop looking so pleased with yourself!" Ruuqo snapped. I realized that my ears had lifted and my tail had begun to wag of its own accord. Quickly I tucked it down between my legs. It rose up again. Ázzuen's tail thumped in the snow. Unnan growled softly.

"Pups," Ruuqo snarled. "We're supposed to entrust this to pups?"

The fury in Ruuqo's voice surprised me. He was always careful to follow the rules of etiquette when speaking to Greatwolves, even when he disagreed with them. I never thought I'd hear him challenge the highest-ranking Greatwolf in the valley.

"Exactly how are we supposed to do this?" he demanded. "We're more likely to grow wings and fly like the ravens than to get the humans to allow us into their homes."

"I have not yet figured that out," Zorindru admitted, "but I wouldn't have agreed to the test if I didn't think it was possible for you to succeed. And if you wish to save your pack, Ruuqo, you must find a way." He looked sharply at the leaderwolf. "You cannot go on as if nothing has changed."

"We have no intention of doing so, Lordwolf," Rissa said. "But Ruuqo is right. The humans will never trust us enough to allow us into their homesites."

Tlitoo quorked into the silence that followed. "I heard more. The Grumpwolves said more."

Zorindru sighed. "What did you hear?"

"They said smallwolves are weak. They said wolves will be the humans' slaves. They said the paradox will make the smallwolves fail and that it would be better to kill all wolves than to let the true nature of wolfkind be compromised. I heard them. They were loud."

The paradox. It was why wolves and humans had never been able to come together peacefully. In order to keep humans from destroying everything around them, our ancestors had promised that wolves would stay close by the humans. Yet every time wolves and humans were together, they fought.

"They said wolves would not be wolves," Tlitoo added. "I did not understand that. What else would wolves be?"

"If wolves are allowed to become too subservient to humans," Jandru said, "as the humans always seem to insist, we will lose something essential to our being, the part of us that is uniquely wolf and part of the Balance. We will be wolf no more. That is why there are two kinds of wolves: Greatwolves to watch over the humans and you smallwolves. One kind of wolf to guard the humans, the other to keep the legacies of wolfkind safe for future generations. Indru himself commanded it be so."

Indru was the leaderwolf of the pack from which all Wide Valley wolves descended, the wolf who had bargained with the Ancients themselves for the survival of wolfkind.

"That," Jandru said, "is why much of the council does not want smallwolves near the humans. They are not the ones meant to be the watchers." He turned his head slightly so he could meet Zorindru's gaze out of the corner of his eye.

Zorindru looked as if he was going to say something. He stopped himself, closing his mouth with a snap.

"So wolves must be with humans for a year," Rissa said when Zorindru remained silent.

"Yes," the oldwolf replied. "You have three moons to get them to accept you into their homes and must stay there for a year after that."

"Will you help us?" I asked.

"I cannot. If I do, the council will claim that it was I, not you, who kept the humans under control. You will not see me again until you have succeeded—or failed—in your task."

My joy at being allowed to be with the humans fled. "What if I can't do it?" I whispered. "What if I fail?"

It was Frandra who answered. "Then the council will do as it wished to do at autumn's end. The experiment of the Wide Valley will be deemed a failure, and the wolves and humans in the valley will be killed. We will try again elsewhere. With smallwolves who actually do what they're told."

"And packs that are able to control their pups," Jandru added.

"Is that true?" I asked Zorindru.

"It is," he said. "If you fail, I will no longer be leader of the council and Milsindra will be able to do as she wishes. If you fail here in the Wide Valley, then we will know that smallwolves cannot be guardians of the humans and that wolves and humans cannot be together. Understand this," the old Greatwolf said, "those on the council who follow Milsindra have agreed to this test because they are certain you will fail. They don't think it's possible to live with humans without fighting them or becoming their slaves. You must find a way to prove them wrong."

Ázzuen began shifting from one paw to another and looking from Ruuqo and Rissa to Zorindru.

"I know," he said. "I know what we can do."

We all looked at him. I thought one of the older wolves might reprimand him for addressing the Greatwolf leader, but they didn't. Ázzuen was already gaining a reputation for being the smartest wolf in the pack. Even wolves from other packs knew he was clever.

"It's something Zorindru said about Milsindra," he continued, shamelessly flattering the old Greatwolf. "We don't ask the humans to let us come into their homesites. We get them to ask us. We make them think it's their idea."

Ruuqo looked at Ázzuen as if all of his fur had fallen off, and Frandra and Jandru and Unnan all laughed out loud. But Zorindru cocked his head.

"I would like to hear this," he said, and sat down once again as Ázzuen began to speak.

3

Ázzuen's plan was simple. In the Wide Valley, a wolf who seeks welcome into a new pack might bring a gift of meat to the pack's leaderwolves. Doing so not only shows that the wolf respects the pack leaders, but also proves she can hunt well, and thus would be a valuable addition to the pack. We would bring such gifts to the humans. The three Great-wolves had listened silently as Ázzuen spoke and agreed to let us try. I was to go to Frandra and Jandru in a quarter moon's time to tell them if it was working. They would tell NiaLi of the plan. The old woman, I hoped, would tell TaLi. I couldn't believe how easy it was to get everyone to agree on the plan.

Agreeing how to go about it proved to be less simple.

Ázzuen, Marra, and I wanted to take our three humans hunting and bring a whole prey to the human homesite. We also assumed that the three of us would be the wolves who went to stay with the humans. Ruuqo and Rissa rejected both plans. They watched silently as Zorindru, Jandru, and Frandra left the gathering place, then huddled together with Trevegg, whispering for several moments. I tried to hear what they were saying, but the wind was blowing the wrong way. Finally they stopped talking and called us over to them.

"Hunting with the young humans is too uncertain," Rissa said, sniffing at the junipers the Greatwolves had crushed. "We have only three moons to gain the humans' trust, and it took you nearly that long just to catch one deer with them. How can we know you'll hunt more successfully now?"

"And how will you convince them you helped with the hunt?" Ruuqo added, joining Rissa at the edge of the gathering place. "Your girl is too submissive in her pack to convince them, and you say they no longer listen to their elder."

That was all true, which didn't make me like it. Unnan smirked. Tlitoo tapped his beak against a rock to get our attention.

"Wolves," he gurgled.

"You three pups can't go anyway," Ruuqo said, ignoring the raven. "You don't know enough to keep from making mistakes. Kaala will go, and we'll send an older wolf with her."

That made me mad. If we'd left it up to the adult wolves, we'd all have been killed by the Greatwolves at autumn's end. I needed my leaderwolves' help, but it infuriated me that they thought they could manage the humans better than we could.

"We've done fine on our own so far." I tried my best to keep my temper from my voice. "Ázzuen, Marra, and I can handle the humans."

"You can handle the youngest of them," Rissa said, stretching in the sun that had begun to seep into the clearing. "The young of any creature are more open to new things. The older humans, the ones who hold the power, may be more difficult." The condescension in her voice made me want to bite something.

"Wolves!" Tlitoo quorked, more loudly.

"We also need the approval of the other packs in the valley," Trevegg added. He had taken over Zorindru's resting spot beside the watch-stump. "Even if their survival depends upon our success, they won't be comfortable with three pups in charge."

"We'll send Trevegg with Kaala," Ruuqo said, ending the discussion. "But the question of how to get the meat to the humans remains. If you just walk into their homesite, even with meat, they will be threatened."

Ázzuen had been silent through all of this, sulking because he was not to be allowed to go to the humans. "There's a way," he said. There was an edge of impatience in his voice, as if he was annoyed that no one else had been quick enough to figure out what he knew. It was the first time I'd ever heard him disrespectful of senior wolves.

"What way?" Ruuqo asked, warning in his voice.

It was Tlitoo who answered. He stalked over to stand between Ruuqo and Rissa. "You do not have to go to the humans, dourwolf. We will bring them to you."

"And why would they follow you?" Ruuqo asked.

Tlitoo picked a bug out of Rissa's fur and swallowed it.

"We take the humans to prey many times," he said. "As we do for you."

Ravens often brought us to prey, living or dead. They could find it much more easily than we could, but they couldn't kill a horse or a deer. And even though their beaks were strong, it was difficult for them to tear through thick hides to get to the meat. When they alerted us to prey, we tore the meat from the carcass, or killed living prey, and shared it with them. I'd always thought it was a unique relationship. So, apparently, did Ruuqo.

"You give prey to the humans?" he demanded. "When there is not always enough for us?"

"We lead humans to prey when it suits us," Tlitoo responded. "They leave behind more meat than you do and are not as fast at catching ravens. Did you think we would allow ourselves to starve every time you are slow chasing prey?"

"You knew of this?" Ruuqo asked Ázzuen.

"I followed them once, when I went to BreLan's *tribe*," Ázzuen said, using the humans' word for their pack. Ázzuen's human, BreLan, and his brother, MikLan, were part of a tribe a half-day's walk from TaLi's home. "I saw them show the humans where an antelope had fallen off a cliff and was dying," Ázzuen continued, his nose in the air. He was risking trouble speaking so rudely to Ruuqo. "I asked Tlitoo about it."

"Do you want the ravens' help or do you not?" Tlitoo asked, raising his wings. "If not, I will find someone who does. Stone Peaks might. Tree Line pack might."

"Yes," Trevegg interrupted before Ruuqo could answer. "We would welcome the help of the ravens. It would be an honor."

Tlitoo considered him for a moment. "Then I will tell my friends. We will bring the humans. Yes, wolf, your humans," he said when I opened my mouth to speak. "I know where they will be. Their minds are nearly as simple as a wolf's." He turned again to Ruuqo. "When you have managed to capture something bigger than a dirt squirrel, I will come for you." With that he took flight, leaving us to plan the hunt.

Two days later, I placed a piece of deer belly on the pile of meat we had set aside for the humans and watched as Yllin and Minn chased scroungers away from what was left of the snow deer carcass. Hyenas, of course. They were always the first to show up when someone else had gone to the trouble of killing something. Minn and Yllin were the pack's young-wolves, one year older than us pups. Yllin had helped me throughout my puphood, encouraging me to persevere when other wolves in the pack thought I would die as a smallpup. She was a strong wolf, and many in the pack assumed she would be a leaderwolf someday. Minn was a bully and I stayed away from him as much as I could. They were faster than the older wolves and still a bit bigger than we were, so discouraging scroungers was their responsibility. They were also the ones who had driven the snow deer from the Alder Grove to the Great Plain, a huge, flat expanse of grass, tall half-moon-shaped rocks, and dirt. One deer had fallen behind the others, and by the time it got to the Great Plain, it was exhausted. We killed it easily. We ate only some of the best parts of the deer—the good organ meat and part of the rich, fatty belly. We would save some for later. The rest would be for the humans.

As Yllin and Minn chased the hyenas off the plain, I trotted over to join Trevegg at the carcass. Werrna—Ruuqo and Rissa's secondwolf—was with him. She was complaining that we shouldn't waste such good meat on the humans.

"They won't appreciate it," she grumbled as she watched Ruuqo set a large, fatty piece of meat aside. Her eyes were restless in her scarred face. Werrna was not born to Swift River. She had joined the pack when she was already three years old. It's unusual for a full-grown female to be accepted into a new pack; she's too much competition for the female leaderwolf. Werrna was extremely strong and always steady, an excellent tracker who never shied away from a fight or challenge, and therefore was a valuable addition to any pack. Still, it said a good deal about Rissa's confidence in her own power that she allowed Werrna to stay. No one had told us pups how Werrna had gotten her scars, and none of us was brave enough to ask. Werrna was easily annoyed.

Trevegg laughed at her. "You're as greedy as a pup. You ate two big pieces of the liver, I saw you, and there's plenty of greslin left."

The greslin was what we called the best meat of a kill, the good organ meat and the rich fat of the belly that Werrna so coveted.

"Still wasted on smoke-brained humans," Werrna muttered.

"We won't get anywhere bringing them gristle and bone," Trevegg said. His eyes lit with mischief. "But I will make you a wager."

"What wager is that, oldwolf?" she said, a reluctant smile beginning to tug at the corners of her muzzle. I'd found out only recently that the adult wolves of our pack liked to place bets on things.

"I will gamble my share of the greslin from our next kill that by the time we have given the humans good meat six times, they will have invited us into their homesite."

Werrna snorted. "I hate to deprive an oldwolf of his

food," she said, "but it will take at least twenty gifts before the humans allow us within farting distance of their fires."

"It is a wager, then!" Trevegg said, his tail wagging. "I look forward to eating well!"

I looked at them in astonishment. How could they be making bets on something so important?

With a grin that made me glad I wasn't prey, Werrna took a huge piece of deer belly in her jaws and dragged it off to the woods. Trevegg watched her go, and for just an instant, the laughter in his face changed to concern. When he saw me watching him, he poked me in the ribs with his nose, dashed past me to the deer carcass, and began to help Ruuqo and Rissa drag it into the woods. I started to follow him, but before I could take a step, the cries of the ravens alerted us to the humans' approach.

Ruuqo barked sharply. Trevegg let go of the carcass and we ran together to the pile of meat intended for the humans, which we had set in a bright patch of sunlight so the humans couldn't help but see it. The carcass was now at the very edge of the plain, thirty wolflengths to the left of the meat pile. We wanted the humans to see the carcass, to see that we had brought down the prey we were offering them. But we also wanted to take what was left of the snow deer with us. There was no reason, Rissa had said, to be overly generous.

Werrna and Unnan darted from the woods and ran to help Rissa guard the carcass. Ruuqo left them there and joined the rest of the pack in the shadow of one of the giant rocks, twenty wolflengths to the right of our meat pile. Rissa said that if the humans saw all of us, they would be too fearful to take our gifts. The sheer face of the rock and the tall grass surrounding it allowed the pack to watch the humans without being seen, ready to protect us if the humans attacked but hidden from weak human eyes. Yllin and Minn were guarding Ázzuen and Marra, who had made it clear that they were unhappy about not being able to go to the humans, but Ruuqo crouched at the very edge of the rock, ready to run to our aid if needed. I swallowed hard. The pack was ready.

Then a gust of wind blew across the plain, and a strong scent of juniper, wolf, and smoke wafted across my nose. At first I thought I was imagining it, so many times had I wished to catch that scent again. I shook my head to clear it, and the aroma only grew stronger. I could not mistake it. The scent seemed to be coming from behind me. Keeping my feet planted where they were, I turned my head as far around as I could.

"Kaala!" Trevegg hissed. "Pay attention! You're not a smallpup to be distracted by a windstorm. Do I have to tell Ruuqo you're not ready to accompany me to the humans?"

It was all I could do not to growl in frustration. I had to follow that scent, but I also had to give the humans their gift of meat. The wind died down and the scent faded. I lowered my ears to Trevegg.

"Sorry," I said.

He was starting to say something else to me when the sound of human footsteps told us they were near. He glared at me instead. He would have plenty to say to me later.

The humans, when they emerged from the woods, were a scant forty wolflengths from where we waited, almost directly in front of where Trevegg and I stood. True to his word, Tlitoo had brought BreLan and TaLi, along with several other humans. He flew above them, calling, then landed just in front of them, so that one of the humans, a large, stocky young male, tripped over him and sprawled on his hands and knees, dropping the two sharpsticks he carried. None of the other humans carried more than one. The male stood, glaring at the raven. A second raven landed next to Tlitoo and immediately began preening.

Some of the humans were young, but some were full-grown and dangerous-looking. I knew that we needed the grown humans to accept us if our plan was to work, but for the first time I was afraid of the humans, afraid of what we were about to do. I met TaLi's eyes and felt myself relax a little in the warmth of her gaze. Still, I was glad to have Trevegg by my side.

One by one, the humans noticed us and their soft conversations stopped. Some of them stepped back. Many raised sharpsticks. I saw a small, trembling boy pick up a rock. BreLan whispered to him, and the little boy lowered his arm, dropped the rock, and smiled. Trevegg and I each picked up a large piece of meat, took a few cautious steps toward the humans, then stopped.

A lean, strong male stepped forward. I remembered him from when we stole food from the humans many moons before. He was the leader of TaLi's tribe, the one she called HuLin. He was not the largest of the humans, or the strongest, but he held himself proudly, and I could tell by the way the other humans watched him that they respected him. He smelled a little bit of fear and a little bit of anger, but mostly of determination. I recognized that scent. It was what Ruuqo and Rissa smelled like when the pack faced a threat or was about to hunt dangerous prey. It was the resolve to care for one's pack at any cost. There are wolves who say that humans have no sense of family, that they are selfish and do not care for one another. When I saw the human leader step forward in spite of his fear, I knew that they were wrong.

HuLin's fear smell had intensified when he moved toward us, but I didn't miss his quick, sharp glance at the meat we carried. It was still winter, and the humans were all thin from its hungry times. The preyskins they wore against the cold hung loosely off their bodies, and some of them looked like the Vole Eater wolves, who had barely made it through the winter alive. I could tell the human leader was trying to decide whether to run, fight, or to wait to see what we did. All leaderwolves have to face fear if they are to feed their packs, and all wolves must learn to balance the fear of danger with the need to eat. I found it fascinating to watch the human leader weighing the risk of allowing us near his followers and the promise of the meat we carried. The humans were so much like wolves it made the fur around my muzzle prickle.

Trevegg whuffed very softly and began to trot toward the humans. I followed him. We held the meat high up to keep it off the ground but kept our ears relaxed and unthreatening. The stocky male Tlitoo had tripped spoke to HuLin, his voice much louder than it needed to be.

"I'll stop them if you want, HuLin," he said, a sharpstick gripped tightly in each of his hands. I could tell by the way he stood, with both feet planted far apart, and by the stiff set of his shoulders that he wanted to impress HuLin. I also heard the fear in his voice and the rapid beating of his heart, and remembered how quickly fear can turn to anger. I paused, and

Trevegg stopped beside me, setting down the rib bone he carried. I let go of the haunch meat I'd been holding. The young male's heartbeat slowed. Trevegg and I both lowered our ears and tails even farther, and tried to make our faces soft and welcoming. Trevegg had told me that was the way that adult wolves greeted frightened pups. I didn't remember that from my own puphood. I had been too busy trying to stay alive.

When none of the humans raised sharpsticks again, we picked up our offerings and started forward once more. This time, we allowed the meat to drag on the ground so we could keep our heads low. When we got within four wolflengths of the humans, we stopped and set down the meat we carried. The smoke and juniper wolfscent blew across my nose again. I shook my head and sneezed it away.

The small boy who had been holding the rock darted forward, running until he was face-to-face with Trevegg. HuLin grabbed at him, trying to pull him back. A look of mischief lit Trevegg's eyes. Before HuLin could pull the boy away, the oldwolf's tongue shot out, and he licked the child from chin to forehead, and then from ear to ear. The boy shrieked with laughter and Trevegg rolled over onto his back, waving his legs in the air and grunting like a forest pig before shaking himself all over and standing again.

"Ridiculous oldwolf," Tlitoo muttered in disgust. "No raven would ever behave that way."

Trevegg didn't dignify Tlitoo's comment with a response. He shook himself once more, pelting the laughing boy with leaves and dirt. HuLin's stiffly held shoulders relaxed.

TaLi stepped forward and placed a hand upon my back. BreLan stepped up beside her.

"You don't have to be afraid," TaLi told the other humans. "They're friends."

I felt a surge of gratitude. We had not had the chance to tell our humans the details of our plan, but TaLi was quick-witted, and I'd hoped she would be able to figure out what we were up to. I could tell that she was a little confused, but she was smart enough to follow our lead.

"Friends?" the young, stocky male said incredulously. "Wolves aren't friends, TaLi. They're dangerous."

"They're not dangerous and they are friends, DavRian," TaLi said, annoyance making her voice sharp. I had to stop myself from growling my concern. I'd never heard her take that tone before.

"TaLi!" HuLin said harshly, making the girl jump. "You're rude to a guest of our tribe."

TaLi lowered her eyes and mumbled an apology. HuLin nodded and spoke again. "Now, what are you talking about? What do you mean, 'friends'?"

At first, I thought TaLi would not be able to speak, she trembled so. I knew how she felt. I found few things as un-nerving as speaking to Ruuqo and Rissa when they were angry with me. She dug her hands into my fur.

"We have hunted with these wolves," she said, stumbling a little over her words, "BreLan, MikLan, and I." BreLan placed his arm over her shoulder. I noticed the stocky male, DavRian, tensed when BreLan touched TaLi. TaLi's voice steadied. "That time we brought home the deer meat that helped ShanLi when she was so sick was from when they hunted with us," she said. "And all those rabbits we caught when it was first getting cold. And now they've brought us meat on their own."

The human leader looked at her as if she had suddenly grown antlers on her head.

"This is nonsense," he said softly.

"No," BreLan said respectfully. "I was there. We hunted with them, and now they bring us gifts." BreLan was a little overbearing sometimes, but right then I wanted to lick him from head to toe. Our humans were finding ways to communicate what we could not. I noticed that BreLan was scanning the plain behind us, clearly searching for Ázzuen. I picked the haunch meat out again, trying to offer it to him. Trevegg picked up his deer rib and held it out to the human leader.

"It's impossible," HuLin said. "Wolves steal from us, compete with us; they don't bring us food."

"Then what is that in their mouths, HuLin? Moss?" a cross voice said. The old woman walked forward, leaning on a branch from an oak tree. It was all I could do to keep from running forward to greet her. She must have been walking behind the other humans, slowed by her aging joints. NiaLi was TaLi's grandmother, and the krianan—the spiritual leader—of the Lin tribe. She had been trained since childhood to speak with and understand wolfkind.

It was through the krianans that wolfkind had kept humans in touch with the natural world. Each moon, the human krianans met with the Greatwolves in ceremonies called Speakings. The krianans would take what they learned from the Greatwolves back to their tribes. NiaLi was the one who had helped me convince the Greatwolves to let us try to keep peace with the humans. She had once commanded great respect among the humans, TaLi had told me, but she had lost much of her influence since HuLin had taken over as the tribe's leader several years before. When I had not been able to find her before, I feared she had died over the winter, as old creatures do, or that HuLin had sent her away for good.

HuLin's face darkened. It didn't take much to realize how much he disliked NiaLi. The old woman held her hand out to me.

"May I have that, Silvermoon?" she asked, using TaLi's name for me.

I walked slowly to her, aware of all of the sharpsticks raised around me. I dropped the haunch meat at NiaLi's feet.

"We want the humans to come hunt with us," I told her. I could only hope that Frandra and Jandru would have told her of the new task.

The old woman dipped her head the slightest bit. I took several steps back. My ears moved back and forth, listening for any potential attack. I had so many questions I wanted to ask her, but they would have to wait.

I heard very soft, slow pawsteps, and out of the corner of my eye, saw Trevegg stepping slowly toward the human leader. He set his meat down and flattened his ears. But something in his manner disturbed HuLin, and the human leader stiffened, raising his sharpstick.

"Move away," Trevegg whispered. "Now." Reluctantly, I obeyed. If we left when HuLin was not comfortable with us, we might not get another chance to win the humans' favor. But if I disobeyed Trevegg, the pack would not trust me with the humans. Slowly, I began to back up.

I had taken no more than three steps when I heard the sounds of a quick scuffle, a yelp, and a frantic scrabbling. Startled, I turned to see Ázzuen pelting across the plain, and a very angry Minn staring after him. Minn started to follow, but Ruuqo spoke softly to him and the youngwolf sat down again. I knew what Ruuqo was thinking. It was bad enough to have one wolf charging across the plain. Two of them running full pelt would certainly upset the humans. I looked for Marra and saw that Yllin was now lying completely on top of her as Marra stared resentfully after Ázzuen.

Ázzuen was going to be in a lot of trouble, but I didn't blame him. If our situations had been reversed, I would have done the same thing. It would have been intolerable to be so close to the humans and not go to them. Still, of all of us pups, Ázzuen was the one who most often followed the rules. Until now.

Ázzuen, barely pausing by the pile of meat, snatched up a good-size hunk of deer belly in his jaws and continued across the plain at a gallop. He had the good sense to slow to a trot and then a walk as he neared us. The humans watched him with varying degrees of interest and fear. By the time he reached us, he had lowered himself all the way to his belly. He crawled pawswidth by pawswidth to HuLin, still clutching the deer meat in his jaws.

When he reached the human leader, he immediately rolled over onto his back, lying perfectly still, and offering his belly and neck as a submissive wolf would do to a leaderwolf. Every muscle in my body tensed. How could he do that? How could he make himself so vulnerable to an unpredictable human? We offered our bellies and necks only when we knew the wolf we so honored was reliable, when we knew that the wolf would not attack us. I couldn't believe Ázzuen would take such a risk. I heard NiaLi's sharp intake of breath and knew that she, at least, knew how open to danger Ázzuen was making himself. HuLin did not. He had no idea what Ázzuen was offering. But he did lower his sharpstick a little and smile cautiously, keeping his eyes on Ázzuen's teeth. Ázzuen began to emit the calming scent that adult wolves use to put pups at ease and let the chunk of deer meat fall from his jaws. HuLin slowly reached for Ázzuen's meat and for the rib bone Trevegg had set down, as if he expected that one of us would snatch them back. He set the meat behind his legs. BreLan stepped away from TaLi's side, knelt down, and stroked Ázzuen's chest. Ázzuen licked the young human's hand.

At a blink from Trevegg, Ázzuen stood, and the three of us began to back away. I wanted to stay longer, to follow them back to their homesite, but Ruuqo and Rissa had insisted that we stay only long enough to allow the humans to accept our offering. We would leave the extra meat in the pile for them to take.

When we had backed several wolflengths away from the humans, we turned and began to run. Out of the corner of my eye I saw that Ruuqo and the others who had been hiding behind the rock were racing to the carcass.

Trevegg hissed angrily at Ázzuen. "What do you think you're doing?" he demanded. He couldn't snarl or growl at Ázzuen without upsetting the humans, but he narrowed his eyes in reproach.

"You know I should be here," Ázzuen said. "You know that Kaala, Marra, and I are the best ones to be with the humans. You know Ruuqo is wrong to leave us out of it."

"I do, as a matter of fact, know that, youngwolf," Trevegg said, winning a surprised glance from Ázzuen. "You are not the only wolf in the pack capable of thought. However, there are ways to do things and there is more at stake here than what happens with this one pack of humans. If you are not bright enough to see that, I will see to it that you are let nowhere near those humans."

Ázzuen started to protest.

"Later!" Trevegg snapped.

We kept running, sprinting past the meat pile and past our packmates, who were dragging what was left of the carcass into the woods. We didn't stop to help them but kept running, as Ruuqo had ordered, until the pine trees concealed us. Once I was well hidden, I did stop, unable to resist looking back at the humans. I watched as they loped across the plain, stopping every ten paces or so to make sure they were safe. I watched as they came upon the pile of good, rich meat. And I watched as HuLin looked from the meat to the woods where we hid, and as he smiled the bared-tooth human smile at the bounty left to him by the wolves of the Swift River pack.

4

The instant we were all safely hidden in the woods, Ruuqo grabbed Ázzuen by his neck fur and slammed him to the ground. Ázzuen's breath left his lungs with a whoosh that made me wince.

"What in the name of the moon were you thinking?" Ruuqo bared his teeth just above Ázzuen's throat and pressed his front paws into Ázzuen's ribs. "How dare you disobey? How dare you risk the safety of your pack? This isn't a game. It's far more important than whether or not you get to play with your humans!"

Ázzuen, lying flat on his back, tucked his tail between his legs, curled all four paws flat against his belly, and licked Ruuqo's muzzle in apology.

"It wasn't working," he gasped, when he regained his breath. "Trevegg and Kaala were trying, but the humans were still afraid. The young male wanted to fight, and the leader was going to refuse Trevegg's meat." He gulped another breath and licked Ruuqo's muzzle again. "I knew we had to find a way to make the humans more comfortable with us. I *know* how important it is. That's why I didn't ask you first, there wasn't time."

"He could have ruined everything," Unnan said. "He knew what he was doing."

I held my breath. Unnan was right. Ázzuen hadn't asked Ruuqo because Ruuqo would've said no. Ruuqo knew that as well as anyone. I had to think of something to say to help Ázzuen. I turned to Marra for help, but she was scowling at Ázzuen.

I looked to Trevegg, but his face was stern; he was still angry. Looking around at the rest of the pack, I caught Yllin's eye. She dipped her head to me and stepped forward to speak to Ruuqo. She was almost as tall as he was, though not as broad through the chest. It was easy to see her lean muscles, even through her winter-thick fur, and she stood with confidence. I felt my chest loosen. If Yllin spoke up for Ázzuen, Ruuqo might listen.

"He acted recklessly, leaderwolf," she said, lowering her ears deferentially, "but the human leader accepted a gift from him and seems to like him. There isn't any way to predict which wolf a human might like. And Ázzuen is smart enough to help us influence the humans." She lowered her head and pressed her ears even farther back, so that there was no way Ruuqo could think she was challenging his authority. "I think we should allow him to go to the humans."

Rissa looked at Yllin, amusement in her gaze. She knew as well as anyone that Yllin was no more submissive than she was. She nudged Ruuqo gently with her nose.

"We need all the help we can get, Lifemate," she said. "It could mean the difference between failure and success. We don't have enough time to ignore anything that gives us an advantage."

"I realize that," Ruuqo snapped. "I'm not a fool." He bit down on Ázzuen's neck, not hard enough to draw blood, but hard enough to make Ázzuen whimper. "You are lucky, youngwolf," he said, still glaring down at Ázzuen, "that it turned out well. I have no choice but to allow you to accompany Kaala and Trevegg to the humans. But you defied me and you threatened the safety of my pack. Do so again, I will leave you to Milsindra and her friends. And you are not in my favor."

Ázzuen flattened his ears and gave a small whine. A leaderwolf's favor is everything in a pack. It means the difference between feeding at a kill and not, between pack acceptance and rejection, and was especially important for a wolf not yet grown. Ázzuen would get less food for a while and perhaps be forced to sleep away from the rest of the pack. But I had been certain Ruuqo would punish him more severely, and certain that he would forbid Ázzuen any contact with the humans. I couldn't believe that Ázzuen's ploy had worked. From the expression on his face, neither did Ázzuen.

With one final growl, Ruuqo stepped off Ázzuen and stalked into the woods, Rissa and Werrna at his side. Unnan stopped for a moment, as if he wanted to stay with us, then grimaced and followed the others. Trevegg started to follow, then stopped, looking over his shoulder.

"We meet at Fallen Tree at darkfall to prepare our next gift to the humans. If I were you, youngwolves, I would find somewhere else to be until then." He shook his head, making his ears flap, then trotted off into the woods.

Minn followed him, but Yllin stayed behind.

Ázzuen lay on the ground for a stunned moment, then leapt to his feet with an excited yip. He almost fell into Marra, who was glowering at him with even more fury than Ruuqo had shown.

He looked at her, concerned, then turned to Yllin.

"Thank you," he said.

"You're welcome," she said. "It's good to see you fighting for what you want. You do need to learn to be a little less obvious about disobeying the leaderwolves, though. Especially with the Greatwolves keeping such close watch on us. I still can't believe Milsindra is letting any of us live with the humans."

"Because she thinks we can't do it," I said.

"Good," Yllin answered. "Then you'll impress the Greatwolves that much more when you prove them wrong!" She touched her nose to my muzzle and bounded after the rest of the pack.

Ázzuen and I were starting to follow her when Marra growled.

"So the two of you get to go to the humans?" she said.

Ázzuen watched her warily. "I'll get you to the humans, too," he said to her. "I promise."

She turned and began to walk away. "I'm going to find MikLan. Are you coming?" she asked, looking over her shoulder at us. MikLan was BreLan's brother, and the two young males lived in a different tribe from TaLi. It was a half-day's walk for a human, but Marra could easily make it there and back by darkfall.

Both Ázzuen and I were silent, not wanting to upset Marra further.

"We don't want the humans to feel threatened," Ázzuen said at last. "Maybe you should wait a little, a day or two."

Marra whirled to face us. "You mean wait until Ruuqo and Rissa finish talking about how the two of you get to go to the humans while I wait with Unnan? Until the pack decides that only a few wolves need to be with the human tribe and the rest of us have to keep our distance. Fine. You go back to Fallen Tree. I'm going to the Lan tribe." She turned her tail to us and stalked off.

Ázzuen met my eyes. I sighed and trotted off after Marra, Ázzuen close on my tail. We caught up with her before she reached the river. We were breathing hard. Marra wasn't.

"Slow down, would you?" I said. "Not all of us are half antelope." We all knew Marra could have easily outpaced us if she wanted to. She must have wanted us to catch up with her. I touched my nose to her cheek. "You know we'll come with you."

Her muzzle softened and the tight set of her mouth relaxed. "I can go to MikLan's tribe, while you're at TaLi's," she said. "Ruuqo and Rissa will never know."

They would know, of course, they would smell it on her. But I didn't want to argue with her about it. We set off for the river at a trot.

"Why do you think Ruuqo decided to let Ázzuen go to the humans?" I asked Marra. "It weakens him to change his mind like that."

"Because he's afraid," Marra said, pausing in the shade of a spruce. "Because he feels like he is losing control." Ázzuen and I stopped, too. Ázzuen was by far the smartest of us, but Marra had the best understanding of pack dynamics. She always seemed to know the reasons behind what every wolf in the pack said and did and how to use the knowledge to her advantage.

"I think he's at a loss about what to do with the humans," she said, beginning to walk more slowly toward the river. "He agreed to help you with the humans because he had to, but I don't think he really knows how. He'd never admit it, but if he thinks Ázzuen can help him succeed and look good in front of the Greatwolves, he'll use him."

"And he's definitely afraid of the humans," Ázzuen said. "I could smell it, even when he was so angry with me."

I grunted. They were both right. Ruuqo had always been uncomfortable even discussing the humans, and he certainly never wanted to be involved with them. If he didn't help me succeed in the task the Greatwolves had set, the Swift River pack would die with every other wolf and human in the valley. Yet consorting with the humans went against everything Ruuqo believed in. For the first time, I felt a little sorry for him.

In the distance we could hear the river, swollen with melting snow, roaring. The humans lived on the other side. The quickest way to get to a good crossing spot was along a flat, open path that both deer and humans liked to use on their way to drink. The adults in the pack didn't like using it because it was so exposed. We had only taken a few steps along it when Marra, who was in the lead, stopped, and cocked her head. A moment later I heard a rustling from above, and a large shape dropped down from a pine tree, knocking Marra off her feet. Before we could react, the human boy rolled off of Marra and grinned.

"I wondered where you were!" His grin widened as Marra licked his face. MikLan was younger than TaLi and exuberant. He was still short and solid, his limbs hadn't lengthened as TaLi's had, and his face was round, even though the rest of him was winter-thin. He reminded me of Ázzuen when we were all still smallpups.

"Hello, wolves!" he said cheerfully.

Marra's gloom deserted her as she leapt upon MikLan and washed tree sap off his face. I was a little jealous. I'd had to be so formal with TaLi when she was with her pack.

Laughing, the boy pushed Marra away.

"I have food!" he announced. All three of us pricked up our ears. He pulled three strips of dried deer meat out of a horse-skin pouch he carried around his waist. It was fire-meat. My mouth began to water. The humans didn't like to eat old meat, and so they had found a way to dry it out and make it last a very long time. That was one of the ways they survived the winter. I had thought they might hibernate, like some of the bears do, but Trevegg said that wasn't it. They did stay in their shelters during the coldest times, and saved food, including firemeat, to sustain them. It was flavorful, every bite tasting like greslin, and one piece gave me as much energy as several mouthfuls of fresh meat.

MikLan gave each of us a thick piece. I tried not to be jealous that he gave the biggest one to Marra. As we chewed the deer meat, trying to savor the delicacy instead of bolting it, he chattered at us.

"TaLi and BreLan wanted to come with me, but they

couldn't," he said, addressing Ázzuen and me. "HuLin wants TaLi to marry DavRian. He was the idiot with the two spears you met on the Vast Plain." *Spears* was the human word for their sharpsticks. "He's from the Rian tribe, and they want an alliance with us. His father, PalRian, is the tribe leader. So TaLi has to stay and be nice to DavRian. So, of course, BreLan is staying around to make sure that TaLi doesn't pay *too* much attention to DavRian. He, BreLan, I mean, wants to ask HuLin to let him stay with the Lin tribe for the whole year so that he can court TaLi. So does DavRian. HuLin hasn't decided whether he'd rather have an alliance with the Lan tribe or Rian, so he will probably let both of them stay." He took a breath. Of all the humans, he spoke most easily with us, as if we were other humans or as if he were another wolf. It never seemed to bother him that he couldn't understand us. It was almost a real conversation. A one-sided conversation.

He buried his face deep in Marra's neck fur. "I have to leave, before they see I'm gone." MikLan threw his arms all the way around Marra's chest. She grunted as he squashed her ribs. He let her go, nuzzled the top of her head, and ran off into the woods, as clumsy as a bear cub.

Marra looked after him, satisfaction on her face.

"Now can we go back?" I asked.

Marra continued to watch the place where MikLan had disappeared, and for a moment I feared she would follow him.

"Yes," she said at last, "we can go back." The contentment on her face was replaced with defiance. "But I'm not staying away from him while the two of you are at TaLi's homesite. I won't do it."

"You can't go if Ruuqo says you shouldn't," Ázzuen argued. "You know that. If he thinks we aren't responsible he might decide none of us pups can go."

Marra lifted her lip at him. I'd had enough.

"Listen," I said, "we will all get to be with our humans. It may take some time, but I'll convince Ruuqo that you have to come, too. You have to trust me."

To my surprise, Marra's fur settled on her back in a way it hadn't when Ázzuen promised her earlier. "Fine," she said. "I'll wait. But I won't wait for long." She licked the last of the firemeat from her muzzle. "I'm hungry. I didn't get much of the deer meat."

"Because Yllin had to sit on you to keep you from going after the humans," Ázzuen said with a grin. "There are squirrels digging up their caches at the scrub meadow. Let's go there. I don't think Ruuqo is going to let me have much to eat right now."

The two of them set off for the meadow. When they saw I wasn't following them, they stopped.

"Aren't you coming?" Marra asked.

"No," I said. "I want to sleep."

"When there's good hunting?" Marra asked, blinking at me in disbelief. Then she grinned. "That leaves more squirrels for me," she said, and bounded off.

Ázzuen looked after her and then to me. Then he shot me an apologetic look and pelted after Marra. I waited until I was certain they were gone and set off in the opposite direction. I hadn't forgotten the pine-acrid scent from the Great Plain. There was only one wolf who smelled like that, and I needed to talk to her.

I returned to the Great Plain and tried to find the scent again, but the air was still, and the scent was gone. I sniffed around the spot where I had last picked up the scent but couldn't find it. I still had several hours before I had to return to the pack, and I wasn't ready to give up. I left the Great Plain and headed west.

If I were looking for an ordinary wolf, I could sniff out her scent in her own territory, or look for her pack, but Lydda was no ordinary wolf. She was a youngwolf who had lived long ago—a wolf who, like me, had hunted with the humans. She had come to me when I was a smallpup and helped me against the Greatwolves, and again after the battle at Tall Grass. That had been three moons ago, and she had not been able to come to me since. Entering the world of the living weakened her. I had looked for her everywhere, in the early mornings and in the shadows of the dusk. I had tried to find the place she had told me about, where the world of life and the world of death came together. But I never found her. Now her scent blew through the valley once again, and if there was ever a time I needed her advice, it was now.

I stopped when I reached a cluster of boulders set in a circle in a patch of dirt and grass. It was where the Greatwolves and human krianans held their Speakings, and the place where Lydda had first told me of her time with the humans. It was as good a place as any to try to look for her.

I waited, hoping she would come to me there. No one came. Then I caught a flicker of movement to my right. I whirled toward it, half expecting to see the spiritwolf there. Instead, I saw a large, scruffy raven perched high on a rock. He screeched at me once, then fell silent.

He was an old raven, his eyes clouded and his legs so thin I didn't see how he could stand on them. His feathers were so ragged I could see patches of skin showing through them, and one of his wings was crooked, as if it had once been broken.

"What do you look at, mewler?" the old raven croaked.

"Nothing," I said. I wasn't going to tell some bird I was looking for a spiritwolf. I lifted my nose in the air, trying to find Lydda's scent again.

"Then you waste time," he said. He dove from his rock straight at my head. I ducked. He pecked my left forepaw, then screeched in my ear and flew away. I leapt upon a low rock and whipped my head from side to side in case the raven returned for another attack. When I heard heavy wings retreating, I relaxed my guard and jumped down from the rock.

I sat in the center of the circle, closed my eyes, and waited. Nothing. No scent, no spiritwolf coming to me as she had done before. I don't know what I had expected. I would have to call to her. Feeling a little foolish, I opened my eyes and spoke.

"Lydda?" I said aloud. "I need your help."

Nothing. Then footsteps in the underbrush, but they were human footsteps, not wolf. TaLi's grandmother, NiaLi, walked slowly into the clearing. Embarrassed to have been caught talking to no one, I lowered my ears.

"You are looking for the youngwolf who used to come from the spirit lands?" the old woman asked. "I sensed her nearby, too, and thought she might come here. Though she told me moons ago she could no longer come into this world."

I could only look at her in surprise. Then I remembered that on the night TaLi and I had spied on the Speaking, Lydda had walked at NiaLi's side. I also remembered that I had not greeted the old woman properly at the Great Plain and did so now, licking her hands to let her know I was glad she had survived the winter.

"She told me that, too," I said. "But I need her."

"You have not been able to find her?" The old woman stroked the fur between my ears.

"No," I said.

NiaLi looked disappointed. "There are stories among the krianans of one who can travel between the worlds of life and death. When I saw you with the young spiritwolf at the Speaking, I thought you might be such a one. Perhaps you are and cannot yet find the way because you are not yet grown." She sounded dubious.

"Why would I be able to do that?" I asked. Lydda had told me of one who could travel between the world of life and the world of death. I'd never thought it might be me.

"Because she came to you. Because no such spirit has come to the world of the living in my memory. Keep trying to find her, Kaala." Although she called me Silvermoon when TaLi was near, she knew my real name and used it when we were alone. "The teachings of the krianans say that the traveler can discover things vital to ensuring that we learn to live as one with the world."

A howl echoed off the boulders in the clearing. Ruuqo was calling us back early.

"I have to go," I said.

"Don't stop trying to find her, Kaala," NiaLi said, taking my muzzle gently in her hand, her voice urgent. "If you are the traveler, we must know."

She released me, turned away, and walked back into the woods. Astonished, I watched her go.

Two days later, we crossed the Swift River to bring food directly to the humans' homesite. Ruuqo wanted to wait longer, to give the humans more time to grow accustomed to the idea of us, but Rissa insisted.

"The sooner the humans get used to seeing us at their homesite, the sooner they will allow wolves to stay with them," she'd said. I thought Ruuqo would argue more, but he took one look at the determination in Rissa's eyes and dipped his head in agreement. He did insist that he and Rissa accompany Trevegg, Ázzuen, and me to the human homesite. The humans lived in the heart of Stone Peak territory.

Five packs of wolves shared the Wide Valley, and the Stone Peak pack had been our rivals for as long as any wolf could remember. Like the humans of TaLi's tribe, they lived across the river from our territory. Wolves don't encroach on one another's lands unless they're looking for a fight. The Greatwolves had decreed that all wolves had safe passage to human homesites so that we could observe them when we needed to, but the Stone Peaks weren't known for following rules. Two half-grown pups and an oldwolf would be no match for them if they decided to fight. Sure enough, when we waded into the river just before dawn, each carrying a piece of snow deer, we saw three Stone Peaks waiting for us on the other side.

Stone Peaks are large wolves; the smallest wolf in their pack was larger than Ruuqo. It was common knowledge that

Stone Peaks only let their strongest pups feed, allowing the smaller, weaker ones to die. They alone among all the wolves in the valley hunted the aurochs—huge, aggressive beasts that roamed the westernmost plains of the valley. Of all the prey in the valley, the aurochs were most likely to kill wolves. The Stone Peaks took great pride in hunting them.

Torell and Ceela, the leaderwolves of the Stone Peak pack, waited on the flat, muddy stretch of riverbank, glaring at Ruuqo and Rissa as we made our way across the river. The third Stone Peak, a younger wolf who held his left rear paw up, as if it hurt him, watched me. I hadn't expected to find him there. The last time I'd seen him, he was lying injured on the Tall Grass plain, abandoned by his packmates after the battle; the Stone Peaks didn't believe in weakness. I surprised myself by being glad he hadn't died from his injuries.

His name was Pell, and he was a tall, sleek wolf who smelled of wind-sage and willow trees. His fur was the color of dry summer grass, and I could see the play of muscles under it as he placed his paw back on the ground and stretched, keeping his gaze on me. I wasn't tall enough to make it across the river without swimming, and I felt stupid and awkward as he watched me paddling with the meat in my jaws.

Ruuqo and Rissa were first across the river. As soon as they emerged, they shook themselves and set down the meat they carried. The rest of us were not far behind. We set down our own pieces of snow deer and stood, ready to confront the Stone Peaks.

As the four leaderwolves glowered at each other, Pell kept trying to meet my eyes. I ignored him. Our packs were enemies. He shouldn't be trying to be friendly to me.

"Hello, Kaala," he said softly when I refused to look at him. I felt my spine go warm and my eyes trying to lift up to meet his. I wouldn't let them, though. Next to me, Ázzuen rumbled a growl.

It was up to Ruuqo and Rissa, as the wolves entering another pack's territory, to greet the Stone Peaks first. They inclined their heads the tiniest bit.

"Hello, Torell. Ceela," Rissa said. "We claim safe passage to the human homesite."

Torell didn't even bother to acknowledge her greeting, as a well-mannered wolf would. He sneered at the five of us like we were hyenas. His face, like Werrna's, was scarred from a battle long ago. But while Werrna's scars covered only one side of her face, Torell's entire face seemed to be one large scar. It made him seem even more intimidating than did his great size.

"Is it true?" he demanded. "Can what I hear be true?"

"I don't know, Torell," Rissa said, shaking more water from her white coat. I realized I'd been too nervous to shake when I climbed from the river. Suddenly, the water in my fur was intolerable, and I shook hard. Water sprayed all over Ceela, who glowered at me.

Rissa stifled a laugh. So did Pell.

"Why don't you tell us what it is you have heard, Ceela?" Rissa suggested.

"I hear you bring meat to the humans," Torell snapped. "I hear you bring it to them as if they are part of your pack." His gaze took in the shinbone Ruuqo had set down on the ground, at the hunks of belly meat that Trevegg, Ázzuen, and I had carried. A look of revulsion crossed his scarred face. "I did not believe it when I heard it. I thought better of you. And

I hear you mean to live with them," he said, as if speaking of some perversion. "Tell me it isn't true, Ruuqo."

"As I have told you more times than I can remember, Torell—what the Swift River pack does and does not do are of no concern to you. Stand aside and let us pass. We don't have time right now to make you do so."

Torell snorted at that. He was a large wolf, even for a Stone Peak, and known for his courage in fighting. It would take a very strong wolf to survive in a pack, much less become its leader, with whatever injuries had left him so scarred.

"You don't deny it?" Ceela was incredulous. "You admit you bring meat to our enemies. Winter is hardly over and the prey still scrawny and you give good meat to the humans? They would kill you as carelessly as you kill a vole. What's wrong with you?"

"Do the Greatwolves know of this?" Torell said slyly. He curled his lip. "You are always such good little wolves, doing everything the Greatwolves tell you. What will they do, I wonder, if we tell them what you're doing?"

It was an empty threat. Torell hated the Greatwolves even more than he hated the humans. Still, I could see Rissa took pleasure in answering him.

"It is the Greatwolves who have asked us to do this," she said.

Asked wasn't exactly the right word, I thought.

"We will be calling a Gathering of all the packs in the valley in a half moon's time," Rissa said. "If you wish to send a representative, do so. We will be at the verge near Wind Lake territory."

"You probably don't want to come yourself, Torell," Trevegg said with a yawn. "Most wolves still blame you for the fight at Tall Grass."

All three Stone Peaks growled at that. It was the Stone Peak pack who had tried to attack the humans three moons ago, and every wolf in the valley would remember that. Torell had taken his pack into hiding throughout the winter. They had emerged only half a moon ago, and no one really knew what their status in the valley was.

A crafty look crossed Torell's face. "Just as many blame your drelshik pup for stopping us from getting rid of the humans," he said. "Perhaps we should discuss *that* at the Gathering." I felt my gut clench. A drelshik was a cursed wolf, a wolf despised by the Ancients who brought disaster wherever she went. It wasn't the first time the accusation had been hurled at me. I wanted to crawl back into the river.

"Perhaps they do," Trevegg agreed, clearly pleased to have gotten a rise out of Torell. "We appreciate your concern and will give it the attention it deserves."

Torell narrowed his eyes at the oldwolf, but Trevegg's tone and expression were too mild to give him reason to take offense.

"We grant you leave to come into our territory," Torell said at last, turning from the oldwolf to speak instead to Ruuqo. "I'm sure you won't mind if we guide you? Just to make sure you don't lose your way."

Ruuqo regarded him for moment, and I thought he might refuse. Then he dipped his head to the Stone Peak leader, picked up the shinbone he had set down when he confronted Torell, and took off at a run, Rissa at his side, and Torell, Ceela, and Trevegg on their tails. Startled by the quick turn of events, I grabbed up my deer meat and ran after them. Ázzuen and Pell ran with me. I made a point of concentrating on where I was going, but after a moment Pell spoke.

"Hello, Kaala," he said again. I had been avoiding looking at him, but it would have been rude to ignore his greeting a second time. I looked up into his eyes, and then away when I saw the warmth in his gaze.

"Hello, Pell," I said, mumbling around the meat I carried. I hadn't spoken to Pell since the first day I met him—the day Ázzuen, Marra, and I had overheard the Stone Peaks plotting to kill the humans. I had only talked to him that one time, but he had made it clear that he liked me, which made me nervous. He didn't know me well enough to like me or not.

"I see you've done well over the winter," he said. "You look healthy and strong."

Many pups did not live through the hungry times of winter. Doing so was evidence of a pup's strength and likelihood of long-term survival. There was no mistaking the admiration in Pell's voice.

"We've all done well," Ázzuen said sharply, sprinting to catch up with us. I was shocked to notice he had left his deer meat behind at the river. "All four of us survived the winter. How many Stone Peak pups did?"

I glared at him. It was rude to ask another pack which pups survived the winter. And I couldn't believe he'd left his deer meat behind. We'd need it to win over the humans.

Pell looked down at him. "Stone Peak had no pups this year."

I thought about that. Did he mean that none had been born or that none had been allowed to live? At nearly three years old,

Pell was the youngest wolf in the Stone Peak pack. If they didn't start having pups soon, Stone Peak would be no more.

"How was your winter?" I mumbled. Then felt like an idiot. It was a stupid question. Pell had been badly wounded at the battle at the Tall Grass plain. He had hurt his left rear leg so severely that he had trouble walking. I was surprised that he was still allowed in the Stone Peak pack.

When Pell didn't answer right away, Ázzuen pressed him.

"How's your leg?" Ázzuen asked.

I almost choked on the deer meat I carried. Calling attention to another wolf's weakness was incredibly offensive. Now I realized why Ázzuen had left his meat behind—so he could harass Pell. The Stone Peak wolf would have been within his rights to challenge Ázzuen to a fight for his rudeness. But Pell only grimaced.

"I cannot yet run the hunt," he said. It must have been hard for him to acknowledge that. A wolf who couldn't hunt wasn't considered a true wolf. I thought it was brave of him to admit it to us.

Without breaking his stride, he bent down to speak softly to me. His sage-willow scent, made stronger by the damp pre-dawn air, seeped into my nose, distracting me. "I am all but useless," he said, and there was real pain in his voice. "If I cannot hunt soon, I will leave the valley."

Startled, I stopped and set down the meat I carried.

"But Torell wouldn't keep you if he thought you were useless!" I protested. "Have you tried hunting?" Suddenly I didn't want him to leave.

"Torell has wanted me as his successor since the day I left the den," Pell said, "but I will not stay to be a burden to my pack. I tried to hunt, but I looked like a fool. I'd rather not do that again."

"Hunt with me sometime," I said impulsively. "I'll help you. Then none of your pack will see you struggling, and you can go back to them when you have regained your strength."

I had no idea why I said it. He was a member of a rival pack, a pack that hated Swift River. I heard an indignant whuff from Ázzuen. Embarrassed, I picked up my deer meat and began running again.

We loped in silence for several minutes, not wanting to get too far behind the other wolves. Even though he was lame, Pell easily kept pace with Ázzuen and me. When we reached the path that led to the humans' homesite, we saw the other wolves waiting for us. Without a word, Ceela and Torell ran off into Stone Peak territory, but Pell bent his head to speak softly to me.

"I will think about your offer," he said. He panted a smile, then noticed Ruuqo and Rissa watching him. "I wish you good luck with the humans," he said to them. He bent his forelegs to bow deeply to the leaderwolves, then followed his packmates into the woods. Ruuqo and Rissa looked after him in surprise. Ázzuen growled.

"What happened to your meat?" Rissa asked him, when she saw Ázzuen's empty jaws.

"I dropped it in the river," Ázzuen lied. "Seeing the Stone Peaks startled me. It won't happen again." He spoke respectfully to the leaderwolves but watched the woods Pell had disappeared into. When he looked again at me, his eyes were filled with resentment and betrayal.

5

ire and meat. Burnt stone and dried mud. Sweat, flesh, and old preyskins infused with sun and smoke. Those were the scents that met us as we neared the human homesite. When the sun rose, we would hear the sounds of rock upon rock as the humans shaped and used the elaborate tools that made them so different from other creatures. We would hear their loud, proud voices, echoing through the woods, as if they were completely unconcerned that every hunter within howling range could hear them. Ravens behaved that way, too, but ravens could fly away from danger.

"It's not as if the humans are trying to hide," Trevegg had said when I'd asked him about it. It was true. The humans of the Wide Valley lived, in many ways, much as wolves did. But unlike wolves, they lived most of the time in their one gathering place. They would leave it for days at a time for hunts or other journeys, and found warmer shelter for the winter moons, but then they returned to their homesite. It was as if they lived always at a den site. They also lived in groups larger than any pack, and each year their homesites grew larger. They called this permanent gathering place a "village," TaLi had told me, and it was only in her grandmother's lifetime that they had begun to live in this strange way.

Ruuqo and Rissa hid in the spiny tartberry bushes on a small hill above the humans' home, while Trevegg, Ázzuen, and I crept as quietly as we could to stand silently at the very edge of the village. We didn't want to frighten the humans, so we had decided that the first time we brought meat to their village, we would simply give it to them and leave immediately. If they accepted our gifts, we would bring them more.

The three of us waited there until the early morning light made it possible for the humans to see us waiting just beyond the glow of their fires. As soon as some of the adults caught sight of us, we set down the meat and slipped away to rejoin our packmates on the hill. We hid for a few moments with Ruuqo and Rissa, watching as the humans took the meat back to their fires. Then we quietly left them and returned to the pack.

We waited two days, keeping far from the humans' paths in case they were angry that we had come to their home. When no human hunting party came after us, we returned with more meat, this time bringing it just a bit farther into the homesite. Once again, the humans watched us from a distance, coming to take the food only after we were gone.

The third time we brought food to the human homesite, it was different. They were waiting for us. We came once again at dawn, since it was one of the times humans were most active and one of the times many of them were gathered together. It was also a time, Rissa had told us, that they would be least frightened of us. The humans could not see well in the dark, and thus were more fearful in the nighttime.

When we crept into their homesite and saw a large group of them standing in a half circle, like the elkryn sometimes did when they challenged us before a hunt, we nearly ran. Ázzuen and Trevegg began to back away, but when I saw TaLi standing, smiling, next to HuLin, I spoke.

"Wait," I whispered, setting down the heavy walking bird I carried. Something had shifted, something had changed.

"Kaala," Trevegg warned, "we can't confront the humans. We'll have to come back another time."

"Trust me," I said. "They aren't afraid, not really. They want us to be here."

He raised his nose to the slight breeze. There were so many scents swirling in the human homesite—excitement, anticipation, curiosity, a little bit of fear—that I knew he wouldn't be able to determine what the humans were feeling solely by scent.

"How do you know for certain?" he asked. Ruuqo and Rissa were leading the rest of the pack on a hunt, so the three of us were alone. Trevegg was responsible for Ázzuen's safety and for mine. "How do you know they won't get frightened and attack?"

It wasn't a smell, or a sound, or even the way the humans had stopped clutching their sharpsticks so tightly and holding their young so closely. It was a change in the air itself. When I had first seen the humans nearly six moons ago, I had felt it—a warmth in my heart, a yearning that could only be eased by moving closer to them, the feeling that something I had lost long ago was within reach. I knew that if I resisted it, the warmth would build to an intolerable burning in the moon-shaped crescent on my chest, and that if I gave in to it and could lay my head on TaLi's chest, the yearning would be replaced by a feeling of rightness and belonging. When the humans had been so fearful of us, the pull had been muted. Now that they wanted us there, it swelled.

"Trust me," I said again, lifting my chin to meet Trevegg's gaze. I would explain everything to him when we had time, but if we were to keep the peace with the humans, if we were to have a chance of succeeding at the Greatwolves' task, the adults in the pack were going to have to rely on my judgment. "You need to trust me," I said.

"Be careful," Trevegg said at last. "At the first scent or sound of trouble, you leave. Understand?"

I dipped my head in agreement, but my chest was already moving forward, drawing the rest of my body with it. Ázzu-en's soft whine told me that he was resisting the temptation to run to the humans. Picking the bird up in my jaws, I walked cautiously forward. Not to TaLi. To HuLin. As I neared the tall human, I began to lose my nerve. I almost set the walking bird down several wolflengths away, but something about the human leader's manner made me keep moving forward until I stood just in front of him, so close that my breath made the fine fur of his deerskin wrap tremble. I waited there, looking up at him, holding the walking bird in my mouth.

And he took it from me. Like it was the most natural thing in the world. For a moment, I stood perfectly still, transfixed by the curiosity in his gaze. A quiet whuff from behind me brought me back to myself and I stepped back, just a few paces. Ázzuen came forward next, giving HuLin a piece of deer shoulder, and Trevegg came last with a rabbit. When the human leader took the rabbit from Trevegg, the oldwolf pressed his head against his hand, and HuLin briefly rested his hand atop Trevegg's head before stepping away from the old-wolf. HuLin handed the rabbit and Ázzuen's shoulder meat off to other humans but he held onto the walking bird, look-ing at it with satisfaction.

There had been an incident with Werrna over that bird. She was the one who had caught it, and in spite of the fact that Rissa and Ruuqo had ordered every wolf in the pack to save food for the humans, she had not wanted to give it up. We came upon her near the river. Walking birds travel with their mates and often one will not leave even if the other has been killed. The feathers and blood sticking to Werrna's muz-zle made it clear that she had already eaten one of the birds. The second one lay, still warm, in the melting snow at her feet. She was digging a hole to bury it in when we came upon her. She looked at us defiantly.

"I will share with my pack," she said, "with elders and with pups. I know my duty. But I will not give any more of my meat to humans."

Ruuqo and Rissa both raised their chins at her. For a mo-ment, I thought Werrna might challenge them. She was strong, and a good fighter; she would be a formidable adver-sary. But after a moment she stepped away from the walking bird, glaring at me.

"We can find something else to take to the humans," I mumbled.

"No," Rissa said, "we cannot."

I wanted to argue. The last thing I needed was for other wolves in the pack to think I was depriving them of meat. Enough of them resented me for making us responsible for the humans anyway. But the look on Rissa's face changed my mind. With an apologetic glance at Werrna, I picked up the soft, warm bird.

Now, watching HuLin admiring it, I was glad Rissa had insisted. Walking birds are rich and fatty, almost as good as greslin meat. HuLin handed the bird to a human female standing behind him. Very carefully, very slowly, he reached out his hand to me. I took two steps forward and sat at his feet.

"TaLi," he said softly, as if he feared a loud noise would startle us, "you say you have hunted with them?" I could tell by the approval in his voice that her status in her tribe was rising.

"Yes," she said, just as quietly. "We've caught small animals together. And some deer."

That was stretching the truth a little. We'd caught one deer. But HuLin seemed fascinated.

"Do you think they would hunt with others of us?"

"Yes," TaLi said, excitement creeping into her voice. "I'm sure of it."

"Bring them," he said. "Bring them next time we hunt. We will see."

For just a moment, the calculating look in HuLin's eyes gave me pause. It was the same look Ázzuen got on his face when he had thought of some way to thwart the leaderwolves' commands without getting in trouble, as if he had just found some new way to get what he wanted. A warning shiver ran down my neck. "Idiot," I whispered to myself. HuLin had just invited us to hunt, and I was worrying about some fleeting expression on a human's face? Once we had shown the humans how useful we were to them, once we had run the hunt with them, it would be only a matter of time before we were welcomed into their homes and proved to the Greatwolves that we could succeed.

Trevegg nipped my flank gently, pulling me from my thoughts, and the three of us backed out of the human homesite.

Even Trevegg bounded like a pup as we ran from the human homesite. None of us could believe how easy it had been.

"He just took it from me!" I said, giddy with excitement. "Like he was a pack member. Like he was a pup!"

"Don't get overconfident," Trevegg warned, "he's no pup. We'll still go carefully." But his ears and tail were high.

"You think you'll win your bet against Werrna," Ázzuen said, grinning at the oldwolf. "If the hunt goes well, it won't be long before they invite us to share their homesite."

"I am concerned only with the well-being of the pack," Trevegg said, his nose high. But his tail wagged even harder. He picked up a fallen pinecone in his mouth and tossed it in the air, trying to catch it on its way back down. When it fell to the ground he pawed at it as he might a mouse.

Suddenly, he froze, then stamped his front paws hard on the earth, the Swift River wolf signal to stop and listen. Ázzuen and I held perfectly still, and all three of us heard a rustling in the bushes as something moved quickly away from us. It could have been anything reasonably large, a hyena hoping we might lead it to prey, a curious bear cub, even a rock lion. Trevegg's eyes narrowed and he lowered his nose to the ground. He followed a scent for a few moments, then whuffled softly. Ázzuen and I crept forward to see what he had found. We all looked at the large paw print embedded in the mud and melted snow. It was the paw of a huge wolf.

"Greatwolf," Ázzuen said.

"Yes," Trevegg agreed. "Can either of you smell which wolf it is?"

"I can't smell Greatwolf at all," Ázzuen said, frustrated, shaking his head hard.

"I can," Trevegg said. "Just a little." He buried his nose in the muddy pawprint, then grunted in annoyance. "Sometimes they can hide their scent. We've never found out how." He sighed. "It stands to reason that they would be observing us." He looked at the two of us, watching him anxiously. "No matter," the oldwolf said. "We will succeed or fail whether or not they watch us. Kaala, can you get your raven to help us bring the humans to a hunt? It would simplify things."

"Yes," I said. I had heard Tlitoo tell the other raven, the female, that he would meet her at a stream not far from Wood's Edge. It was a favorite raven bathing spot.

"I'll talk to Ruuqo and Rissa," Trevegg said. "It's time to get the other packs to allow us to hunt in their territories so we can get enough food for the humans."

"Do you think they will?" Ázzuen said.

"Their own survival depends on it," Trevegg answered. "And Frandra and Jandru will support us on this."

"You go with Kaala," the oldwolf said to Ázzuen. "I don't want either of you alone in the territories right now."

Ázzuen dipped his head in acknowledgment as the three of us began to run again. We crossed the river back into our own territory. Trevegg continued on toward Fallen Tree Gathering Place, where Ruuqo and Rissa would return after the hunt to await word of our encounter at the human homesite. Ázzuen and I each nosed the oldwolf's muzzle, then left him, running at an easy lope along the river until we reached a cluster of elder bushes that marked a spot where a small stream left the river and wandered into the woods.

The ravens' bathing place was another few minutes' walk from that spot, and we found Tlitoo there, with the female raven we had seen at the Great Plain and another female raven I didn't recognize. Sitting next to them in the cool mud was the Stone Peak wolf Pell.

Pell stood when he saw us trot out of the woods to the stream bank, bending his legs a little so that he would not be so much taller than we were. I noticed that he didn't put much weight on his wounded leg.

"I have thought about what you said, Kaala," he said as Ázzuen and I came to a startled stop before him. "If the invitation is still open, I'd like to hunt with you."

I didn't know what to say. I had offered, but now we had to hunt with the humans.

Ázzuen answered before I could.

"We're busy," he said. "We don't have time for practice hunts."

"Of course you're busy," Pell said. "I will not impose on your hunting time. But if you would like to hunt with me sometime, send word with your raven friend."

Tlitoo was busily preening his wing feathers and didn't look at me. I noticed that he had pulled several of his feathers out and dropped them on the riverbank.

I looked at Pell's warm eyes and started to speak, but nothing came out.

He waited a moment, then stretched and stood to his full height. "I'll wait to hear from you," he said. I had the feeling he was trying not to laugh at me. He trotted into the woods, limping slightly.

"Since when do you carry messages for Stone Peak wolves?" Ázzuen snapped, glaring at Tlitoo.

Tlitoo threw a feather at him.

> *"Scruffy, whiny pup.*
> *Ravens are not slaves to wolves.*
> *Maybe I will leave."*

"Don't go," I said to Tlitoo, slamming Ázzuen's hip with my own. "We need your help."

"For what?" Tlitoo pulled another feather from his back. I noticed his plumage was beginning to look patchy, with feathers yanked out unevenly all over his back, chest, and wings.

"Why are you pulling out your feathers?"

"It is too warm to keep them all." He darted forward suddenly to grab a hunk of underfur from Ázzuen's chest. "Winter ends, wolflet. Things change." He threw the tuft of fur into the stream. "And I cannot help you."

"Why not?" I asked, annoyed to hear a whine in my voice. I had counted on the ravens' support. How else would we get the humans to follow us?

One of the female ravens strode over to us. I'd heard Tlitoo call her Jlela.

"He has other things he must do," Jlela said.

"Are you coming, Neja?" said the other female in a voice brash even for a raven.

"That is not my name, Nlitsa!" Tlitoo hissed. "I am Tlitoo, named for Tlitookilakin." His voice rose. "I am the son of Sleekwing and Rainsong, born of the Small Willow Grove of the Wide Valley."

Jlela lifted her wings. "Whatever you wish to call yourself, we must go. Unless you want to have the wolflets give you whining lessons?" She walked away, looked back at Tlitoo, and flew into the woods. Tlitoo watched her for a moment.

"I must go," he said. "I must go to the other ravens." His voice was so troubled I didn't have the heart to argue with him. We would have to find another way to hunt with the humans.

"When will you be back?" I asked.

Tlitoo's eyes found mine, and for the first time since I'd known him, I saw fear in them.

"I do not know, wolflet. I will find you when I can. I will help you if I can. But I do not know." Before I could ask him more, ask him if I could help, he took flight, following the female ravens.

"There's something's going on with that bird," Ázzuen said.

In the woods just across the stream from us, a raven shrieked. The ancient raven I had seen at the Stone Circle soared across the stream, flying so low that Ázzuen and I had to duck to avoid him.

I smelled juniper and smoke, the scent of the spiritwolf, Lydda. The scent seemed to well up from the stream itself. I darted to the water's edge, and the scent rose into the air and wafted across the stream. I saw a flash of a tail disappearing into the woods beyond. The scent disappeared.

"Kaala!" Ázzuen said. "We have to go."

"I know," I said. I wanted to follow the scent but Ruuqo and Rissa would be waiting for us. Slowly, I began to make my way along the stream, back toward the river and Fallen Tree.

Everyone was napping in the late morning sun when we arrived, so I sank down into the pack-smelling earth and slept. I dreamt of the young spiritwolf. I dreamt that she came into the world of life to stay, and that she helped me with the humans. In my dream I was so happy that someone else, someone older and smarter, had taken on the humans. Then the spiritwolf's face turned into my mother's face, looking down at me and smiling. When Ázzuen poked me awake with sharp jabs of his nose, I was furious with him for interrupting a dream of my mother.

"Someone's coming, Kaala," he said, when I awoke growling at him. "A stranger wolf."

I came more fully awake to see that every wolf in the pack was standing, watching the gap between the two large oaks that guarded Fallen Tree. Werrna barked, half in welcome, half in warning. No one was upset or growling; they all watched in anticipation as a wolf I didn't know crept to the edge of Fallen

90

Tree, stopped, and waited. The wolf smelled of Swift River and was giving off a scent of friendliness and entreaty. Rissa's tail began to wag.

The stranger walked into Fallen Tree. He was a dark gray wolf who looked to be the about the same age as Yllin and Minn, and the Swift River scent was strong upon him. Yllin gave a small yip but stood still, waiting for the new wolf to greet Ruuqo and Rissa. The wolf was clearly Swift River, but I didn't know if he had left by choice or if he'd been forced from the pack, if he was a wolf in good standing or an exile. He stopped four wolflengths away from the leaderwolves and lowered himself to his belly. He was sleek and healthy, and he smelled of plants and animals I did not know.

Ruuqo dipped his head the slightest bit, and the young wolf darted forward. Ruuqo's tail began to wave, and Rissa dipped down onto her elbows, her hindquarters raised high in the air. The young wolf bounded toward them, and Ruuqo and Rissa ran to meet him. The three wolves leapt and danced around each other. Trevegg darted forward and knocked the visiting wolf onto his back, stood on his belly, and licked his face.

"Welcome home, Demmen," he said. The youngwolf laughed, licked Trevegg in greeting, and got to his feet.

"He was our littermate," Yllin whispered to me. "He left right before you pups were born to see what was outside the valley. I thought we'd never see him again."

I wanted to greet the youngwolf, too, to ask him of life outside the valley. I crept forward, followed by Ázzuen and Marra. An instant later, Yllin and Minn bolted past us, almost knocking us over, and leapt upon Demmen. The three young-wolves wrestled for several moments, then stood, shaking mud from their fur. Yllin reared up and placed her paws on Demmen's back. She was a dominant wolf and wanted to prove it. Demmen whoofed good-naturedly and slipped out from under her, pawing at her chest. They rolled each other over a few times and then stopped, panting, neither of them having won the dominance match.

"I thought you would be as fat as a swamp pig in summer, Demmen, now that you can keep all the greslin for yourself."

"The prey run faster outside the valley, Yllin," Demmen said.

Yllin ducked her head uncertainly, as if unsure if Demmen was making fun of her or not. For the first time since I'd known her, Yllin seemed a little flustered, as if overawed by this youngwolf who had seen the outside of the Wide Valley.

We pups came forward shyly. After looking to Ruuqo and Rissa for permission, Yllin introduced us.

"This is Demmen," she said, "the biggest prey hog in the valley. Don't let him near your greslin. Demmen, these are Swift River's surviving pups: Kaala, Ázzuen, Marra, and Unnan." I was surprised that she had mentioned Ázzuen second. Wolves were introduced in order of dominance, and Ázzuen had so recently been the weakest wolf in the pack.

We pelted Demmen with questions. What was it like outside the valley? Where had he been? Why did the Greatwolves allow him back? Was he staying? He patiently answered most of our questions and deliberately ignored others.

"Four strong pups who survived the winter," he said when we'd all paused to catch our breath. "My compliments, Rissa. I know of no other pack that kept more than three alive this year," he said formally. She grinned at him.

"We have been fortunate," she said.

"How many in the litter?" he asked. "When I left you had not yet pupped. And where are Neesa and her young?"

My whole body went cold and heavy. I found myself wanting to shake hard, as I did when my fur was drenched with water and mud. All around me there was silence. Neesa was my mother. Demmen should have been able to smell that.

"I'm so sorry," Demmen said, his ears low. "I've asked something I should not have asked."

"It is not something you could have known of," Rissa said. "Marra, Ázzuen, and Unnan are three of the six pups I bore. Kaala is Neesa's daughter, and the only one of her litter to survive." She paused. "Neesa has left the pack."

She did not say that my mother had been driven from the pack, or that Ruuqo had killed my three sisters and my brother. I kept my eyes lowered. There were times when I would go weeks at a time without thinking of my mother or my lost littermates. I had been so busy with the humans, I had not been battered down by despair for nearly a moon. I had done my best *not* to think about them because whenever I did, a cloud of sorrow and bitterness would descend upon me, making everything seem heavy and dark. It might find me as I was hunting smallprey, or as Ázzuen, Marra, and I were running the territory. A scent of damp earth and pine roots would remind me of my mother's den, or an expression on Ázzuen's face would make me think of my lost brother, Triell, and I would suddenly find it hard to move, so weighed down would I be by misery. Sometimes it wasn't a heaviness, but rather an emptiness in my chest or a shadow darkening my vision. I always pushed it away. It was worst when I thought of my mother, so I had done my best to stop thinking about her. When Demmen mentioned her name, I felt as if all the sadness I had been trying to avoid slammed into me. I closed my eyes for a moment, forcing it away, and made myself pay attention to the pack.

Something about the youngwolf's demeanor made me think he was not surprised by what Rissa had told him. His smell was all wrong. Tension in a pack is upsetting, and his scent should have reflected remorse or anxiety at the distress his remarks had caused. It didn't. He was calm, almost calculating. His eyes rested on me for just a moment too long before he licked Rissa's muzzle in sympathy.

"I am sorry for your loss," he said.

He took in Ruuqo's rigid stance and Rissa's sadness and the discomfort of the entire pack. He shook himself and opened his mouth in a smile.

"I scent that the snow deer have not yet left the valley for winter's end. Do you hunt them tonight?"

"We do," Ruuqo said. "You will join us for the hunt." It was a statement rather than a question.

"I would be honored," he said. "Perhaps in the meantime, your pups can reacquaint me with Swift River territory. I understand you have reclaimed Gale Hill from the Stone Peaks since I left."

Ruuqo nodded his permission, and Demmen trotted from the gathering place, looking over his shoulder at us pups.

Ázzuen, Marra, and Unnan pelted after him. I did not. I wanted nothing more to do with this wolf who so casually reminded me of my lost mother and littermates. I was sneaking away to be alone with my thoughts when Tlitoo landed in front of me with a thump. He smelled of warm rocks and of other ravens. Even more of his feathers were coming out, sticking out at odd angles from his wings and back.

"Aren't you supposed to be somewhere else?" I snarled at him. "I thought you couldn't be bothered with helping us."

"Go with them, wolflet," he said. "There is a raven watching the humans for you. An old raven that none of the others will miss. I have made sure it is so. But you must go with the strangerwolf, now. It is important." He darted forward, as if to pull out a tuft of my underfur, then stopped just short of my chest. "Unless you would rather stand here and whine."

I looked around Fallen Tree to see Ruuqo, Rissa, and Trevegg watching me with looks of pity on their faces. Yllin and Minn wrestled with each other, excited by Demmen's visit, and totally oblivious to my feelings. Werrna watched me coldly, probably still thinking about her moon-cursed bird. I certainly didn't want to be with any of them. I would have gone off to be by myself, but I knew Tlitoo would just harass me if I tried. He was pacing in front of me, pecking at the dirt, even though there were no insects or worms to be seen.

Pushing away the sorrow that was still trying to overwhelm me, I found the scent trail left by Demmen and the others and followed it. Tlitoo quorked with what sounded like relief and followed me, flying just low enough to avoid the branches of the spruce trees.

I found them at the birch grove, watching a family of lizards scurrying for cover. Marra was gulping down one that hadn't scurried quite fast enough. Unnan was standing in front of Demmen, his tail waving.

"This is where I caught a hare two moons ago," Unnan said. "Ruuqo told me I had the best reactions of any pup in the pack." Demmen bent his head to listen to Unnan, giving off an approving scent. Unnan's chest swelled with pride. Marra and Ázzuen watched with disgust. Demmen looked up from Unnan when I walked into the grove.

"You're Kaala," he said. "You're the one who's not of Rissa's litter."

"She's one of us," Ázzuen snapped as Unnan smirked.

"She was barely allowed to stay in the pack." The smugness in Unnan's voice made me want to bite him, but I didn't think Demmen would let me get away with it. He clearly liked Unnan. It made me sorry I'd come. "There are wolves in the valley who think she shouldn't have been allowed to live," Unnan continued. "They say she's unlucky."

My lips pulled back as Demmen looked at me. Tlitoo gave a krawk of warning. I expected him to fly at Unnan, but it was me he was watching.

"I see," Demmen said, taking in the tension between Unnan and the rest of us. "So, tell me, what are the best places to hunt smallprey in Swift River territory this season?"

"I'll show you," Unnan said. "These three spend so much time being curl-tails to the humans that they barely know what it is to be a wolf, much less what the best parts of their own lands are." Unnan took off at a trot with Demmen beside him.

I stayed where I was. Ázzuen and Marra stayed, too.

"Aren't you going with him?" I asked. "You don't have to wait here just because I do."

Marra stretched her long, lean body. "I don't like the company he keeps. Let's go see if there are any voles to catch at Dry Knoll."

A soft rustling of leaves alerted us a moment before Demmen returned. Without Unnan.

"That one reminds me of Minn when we were pups," he said, shaking leaves from his fur. "Yllin and I used to dunk him in the river when he behaved that way. I have left him searching for walking bird tracks, which should keep him busy."

I looked at Demmen in astonishment. The overly formal, condescending behavior that had so annoyed me had been replaced by a sharp focus and straightforward manner. I had never known a wolf who could so quickly change his demeanor. I couldn't help but wonder which attitude was real.

He looked the three of us over and cocked his head, his expression thoughtful.

"You can say what you have to say now," Tlitoo croaked at him.

"My message is for one set of ears, raven, not four," Demmen said, annoyed. Tlitoo had that effect on a wolf. Demmen glowered at him, but Tlitoo just crouched in the dirt and began picking bugs out of his wing feathers.

"He'll just listen from the trees, anyway," Marra said when Tlitoo had made it clear he wasn't leaving.

"And anything you tell one of us, we'll tell the others," Ázzuen added.

Demmen sighed. "Very well," he said, less than graciously. He sat, and the three of us sat, too. He was silent for a long moment, then looked straight at me.

"Kaala," he said.

I stood in surprise. He had all but ignored me after Unnan had told him I was unlucky.

"I have a message for you," Demmen said, "from your mother."

My breath caught in my chest. "My mother," I said in a soft voice that didn't sound like me.

Ázzuen pressed himself against me. Demmen, who had been so aloof, was now looking at me with such kindness and sympathy, I couldn't stop myself from saying the first thing that came into my head.

"They sent her away," I said. "She didn't leave. They exiled her. They killed my littermates." The injustice of it, of what Ruuqo had done, which I had to ignore most of the time if I was to be part of the pack, overwhelmed me.

"I know they did, youngwolf," Demmen said.

"How do you know?" I asked, and then understood. Of course. "You've seen her. You've seen my mother."

"Three moons past," he answered. "She was desperate with worry about whether you had lived or died. She heard from the ravens that you were well but was not sure whether or not to believe them."

Tlitoo clacked his beak and grumbled something I couldn't hear.

"Where is she?"

"I don't know," he said gently. "She was going into hiding, and for her own safety and mine would not tell me where."

Panic tightened my chest. She was in danger. "What did she say? What is she hiding from? Was my father with her? Frandra and Jandru said they knew where she was at autumn's end!"

"Slow down, youngwolf, and do not attract attention. In spite of what I told Ruuqo about joining tonight's hunt, I don't wish my presence in the valley to be widely known. The Greatwolves would not be pleased to find me here. For now, your mother is safe, though she is pursued by Greatwolves outside the valley who are determined that the two of you should not be reunited. No other wolf was with her when I saw her. She is not where your Greatwolves last saw her. She has asked that you come to her. She said it's important not only to her but also to the greater good of wolfkind. You are to leave the valley by the Eastern Mountains. Once you cross the mountains you will see a vast plain to the south of you. In the distance is a rock as large as a small hill and a grove of birches. A messenger will find you there."

My head felt like it was full of leaves, my lungs packed with dirt. After all this time, my mother had called to me. And I couldn't go to her. I couldn't leave the humans.

"How are we supposed to find her with so little information?" Ázzuen demanded. At the moment, that was the least of my worries, but Ázzuen was always practical.

"I didn't know you were invited." Demmen looked down his muzzle at Ázzuen. Ázzuen was not extraordinary to look at. He was tall, lanky but not heavy. He did not have the bearing of a leaderwolf or even a secondwolf. Demmen was sleek, and his muscles made it clear he was a strong wolf. Ázzuen would be submissive to him in any pack. Demmen looked surprised when Ázzuen didn't lower his tail and ears to him. Marra stepped up beside Ázzuen. The tightness in my chest loosened just a little.

"We're pack," I said. "We run together."

"You know best," Demmen said after a moment. "There will be messengers who will find you along the way once you leave the valley. They are looking for a wolf with the mark of the crescent moon on her chest. I will let them know that she may be accompanied by other wolves." Tlitoo croaked. Demmen sighed. "And a raven. You must get to the hill rock by the night the Denning Moon is halfway through its cycle."

It was impossible. The Denning Moon would be halfway through its cycle two moons from now. We couldn't possibly leave the valley by then.

"We can't go," I said. "We have to keep peace in the valley between wolves and humans."

"How do we know you're telling the truth?" Ázzuen interrupted me. "I don't trust him, Kaala," he said to me.

I was shocked that he would say so with Demmen standing right there, but I could understand why he said it. There was something about Demmen that wasn't entirely trustworthy.

"Why not?" I asked him, aware of Demmen's eyes upon us.

"Why does he come now? Why does he come with the news right after the Greatwolves have allowed you to be with the humans?" He narrowed his eyes at Demmen, who glared right back at him.

"What's this about the humans?" Demmen demanded, turning away from Ázzuen.

I told him.

"I had heard of the events that occurred at autumn's end, but not of this. It may change things," he said, "but it may not. As for whether or not I speak the truth, I can tell you what your mother told me, Kaala," Demmen said. "Your sisters' names were Onna, Tannla, and Suuna, after the flowers that grew near your den site, and your brother was Triell. You and he were especially close, and you challenged Ruuqo over his death. When your mother left the valley she told you to gain acceptance into your pack before you came to seek her. Now she says you must come with or without it."

It was all true. He had, at the very least, spoken to my mother. Yet there was still something about Demmen that bothered me, and I trusted Ázzuen's instincts. I couldn't just accept what Demmen said. But I couldn't disbelieve him either. If my mother had called me, I had to go to her. And I couldn't go. I couldn't leave TaLi and I couldn't break my promise. I had to stay in the Wide Valley.

"We can't go," I said again.

"It may be that the promise you made to your mother overrides this one you have made about your humans. Neesa said the fate of wolfkind may depend upon it."

A commanding howl interrupted him: Ruuqo calling us to the hunt. Approaching pawsteps and a familiar scent alerted us that Yllin was nearing us.

"It would be best," Demmen said, "if you didn't share what I have told you with others in your pack."

A moment later, Yllin burst into the birch grove. She listened with us as Ruuqo howled again.

"It's the human hunt," Yllin said. "Kaala, you and Ázzuen are to meet Trevegg at Oldwoods Plain. An old raven told us that's where the humans are going to hunt a herd of horses. Marra, you, too. Ruuqo says your speed will be helpful but you are not to go near the humans after the hunt." Marra yipped in excitement. "And none of you is to hunt until Trev-egg gets there. The rest of us are to follow Ruuqo to hunt the snow deer. Where's Unnan?" She paused for breath and took in the tension in the grove. "What's going on?"

"Nothing," Demmen said. "The youngwolves were just telling me of the interesting pact you have made with the Greatwolves, and I was telling them of things outside the valley."

Yllin was instantly suspicious. "What have you been telling them, Demmen?"

"Something for their ears only, Yllin."

"Something for the Swift River pups and not for the rest of the pack? Spit it out, Demmen. You didn't used to speak in riddles."

"There are things out there you know nothing of, Yllin, safe here in your valley," he said, a nasty edge to his voice. He saw Yllin's hurt expression, and our startled ones, and his face softened. "Come with me to the snow deer hunt, Yllin. I will tell you the things I told these youngwolves of life outside the valley."

I was once again struck at how quickly he changed his manner. One moment he was angry and bad-tempered, the next kind and gentle. It made me uneasy.

Yllin narrowed her eyes at him. Demmen averted his gaze, and Yllin smiled slightly. He had just given way to her, granting her dominance. He kept his muzzle tightly closed, refusing to tell her what he had told us. But I wasn't going to keep secrets from Yllin. I told her about my mother and Demmen's news of her. Demmen glared at me as I did so. I ignored him. Yllin was pack.

Yllin listened carefully to me, her eyes widening.

"Demmen's right," she said. "Ruuqo and Rissa don't need to know about this. I'll help you if I can, Kaala, but don't do anything stupid in the meantime. There's always a way to work things out."

Ruuqo howled again.

"Are you coming to the hunt?" Demmen demanded irritably.

"Yes," she said. She bolted from the clearing, and Demmen, caught by surprise, followed her disappearing tail. Unnan stumbled into the grove, his fur covered in brambles, just in time to glare at us, and to follow Yllin and Demmen to the snow deer hunt.

Ázzuen and Marra watched them go, then began to trot toward Oldwoods Plain. They stopped when they saw I wasn't following them.

"I don't know what to do," I said.

Tlitoo hopped forward twice, stopping just to my left.

"Wolflet?" he quorked.

I turned on him.

"You could find out if you wanted to! You could fly outside the valley and find out if Demmen is telling the truth about my mother." I placed a paw on either side of him, trapping him. "You have to go."

"I cannot," he said, ducking under my chin and stepping away.

"Why not?" I demanded. "It's nothing to you to fly outside the valley!"

"It is *not* nothing, blatherwolf!" he hissed. "You do not know anything." He opened his beak, as if to say more, then clacked it shut.

"I must go meet with the other ravens. In a place for ravens, not wolves!"

He stalked away from me, raised his wings, and took flight. Stunned, I watched him go. I took a few steps after him, then stopped, uncertain of what to do next.

"We have to go to the humans, Kaala," Ázzuen said. "We may not get this chance again."

I just stood there.

"Kaala," Marra said impatiently. "We don't even know if Demmen is telling the truth. If we lose our chance to be with the humans, nothing else matters." I knew she wanted us to get to the humans as soon as possible so she could try to find MikLan. She and Ázzuen both looked at me, clearly irritated that I was slowing them down.

Suddenly I was so angry my vision blurred and my ears stretched so far back along my head they made my eyes ache. My nose wrinkled and my lips pulled back to expose my teeth to the cool air.

"You have your mother," I snarled. "You have no idea what it's like not to!"

"It's been eight moons since she left, Kaala," Marra said, perplexed. "I thought you'd be over her leaving by now."

"What do you know about it?" Despair began to enfold me, and a sudden hollowness made my chest feel as if it might cave in on itself. I'd had to ignore my sorrow for so long just to survive. Now it was demanding its due. I didn't want it. I growled at Ázzuen and Marra. They both stepped back.

"You never mentioned anything," Ázzuen said.

"No, I never mentioned anything. What was I supposed to say? That I'm so miserable about her being gone that sometimes I think of letting the river carry me away when we cross it? That sometimes I couldn't care less if I ever hunted prey again? That sometimes I'm afraid to go to sleep because I dream of her being dead?" I stopped, panting, trying to get air back into my lungs.

Ázzuen and Marra looked at each other. They were no help to me. I'd never felt so alone in my life. I thought of just leaving, of leaving them and their ignorance and obliviousness behind and going on my own to find my mother. Ruuqo howled again. I swallowed hard and took several deep breaths to calm myself. Whatever else I did, I couldn't abandon TaLi. I had to go to the hunt.

"Kaala," Ázzuen began.

"Never mind," I snapped. I stalked out of the grove and toward the hunt, walking at first, then breaking into a run, staying only pawswidths ahead of the misery that threatened to engulf me.

7

The sun was just beginning its descent by the time we reached Oldwoods Plain, but it was warm and the snow had completely melted from Oldwoods' hard-packed dirt. Neither Trevegg nor the humans had arrived. The horses were there, though, lazily chomping the grass, almost begging us to hunt them.

Oldwoods Plain had once been forestland. When Trevegg was a youngwolf, a fire had swept through the area, leaving nothing but burnt stumps and bare ground. The trees had begun to grow back but were sparse and as small as bushes, and the faint scent of burnt wood still haunted the air. Someday, the forest would take over again, and Oldwoods would be no good for hunting grazers, but for years it had been one of our best hunting grounds.

The horses looked up at us when we loped into the meadow, then went back to eating, all but ignoring us. We prefer to hunt in the cooler parts of the day and night, and most prey know this. Any prey that runs every time it sees a hunter will tire quickly, making itself easier to catch, so they learn when they're young how to determine whether we are hunting or just watching. And horses are strong, arrogant prey. They know they can sprint just a little faster than we can and can use their hooves to crush us. When we were only pups, a herd of horses had killed Reel, one of Ázzuen and Marra's littermates. Since I had dared the other pups to chase the horses, many in the pack blamed me for Reel's death.

One of the mares swept over us with her eyes, blew a great gust of haughty air from her nose, then went back to grazing.

My anger, which I had managed to suppress a little on the run to Oldwoods, surged again. The horses of the Wide Valley owed me a hunt. "Start running them," I ordered Ázzuen and Marra. "We can see which ones are prey."

Ázzuen and Marra, who had been keeping at least three wolflengths behind me during the short run to Oldwoods, stopped and exchanged a glance, then looked at me. I met their eyes, daring them to challenge me. I gave them the look Ruuqo gave the pack when he wanted them to obey him, the look a dominant wolf gives a more submissive pack member. Marra snorted, turned her tail, and walked a few paces away. Ázzuen sat down and began licking a front paw.

"We're supposed to wait to hunt with the humans," he said.

"We can't disrupt the herd," Marra added, her back still to me.

I growled in frustration. "We're just testing them," I said. One of the ways to find out if a prey is weak and ready to be killed is to chase it for a little while. "So we know which are the best to hunt."

Neither Marra nor Ázzuen answered me. "I'm starting the hunt," I said. "You can join me if you want to." I wasn't going to apologize to them.

I turned away from them and stalked toward the horses. I heard a sigh and a grumble, then reluctant pawsteps behind me.

Most of the horses were thin from winter's scarce food, but they were also the ones who were strong enough and smart enough to survive. We walked slowly among them, not wanting to startle them before we were ready for the chase. After just a few minutes, I found a mare that smelled different from the others. She was reasonably plump, and I almost overlooked her, but she smelled of the breathing disease, and her left haunch twitched in nervousness when I walked by her. She was excellent prey. Her plumpness meant she had been healthy throughout the winter and had only recently weakened from her sickness. It was rare to find prey that was both well fleshed and vulnerable. I whuffed to Ázzuen and Marra and stared at the horse I had selected. Ázzuen dipped his head, and Marra barked softly. The sickly horse was trying to hide in a group of her healthier sisters, so we would have to separate her from them.

I took a breath of air thick with horse sweat, and before any of the horses could tell what I was going to do, I began to run. The horses bolted. First, a young quick one dashed away, so fast her legs seemed to blur. Then two older, slower ones split off. I considered following them but decided to stay with my first choice. The hunt thrill overtook me, and I realized the three of us could make a kill right there and then. All of my anger, all of my hurt, transformed into the desire to bite into the flesh of prey. I wanted that horse. I whuffed an order to Marra, and she ran through the center of the group of horses. It was a dangerous move, because a horse could easily kick her, but Marra was agile as well as quick and easily dodged in and out among the horse hooves. All on her own she managed to split off a smaller group that included the sick horse, and to turn it toward me and Ázzuen. The healthy horses abandoned their weaker companion, leaving her to us. I caught Ázzuen's eye as he sprinted up to the horse's right flank, and I prepared to bring her down. Then a furious howl startled us. I stumbled, and Ázzuen fell back a few paces. Taking advantage of our distraction, the horse escaped. Trevegg rushed across the meadow toward us.

He ignored our attempts to greet him. "Why did you hunt?" he demanded. "Why didn't you wait?"

Ázzuen and Marra were silent.

"We were testing the prey," I answered.

"It didn't look like you were testing them. It looked like you were hunting. You've made the horses anxious and aware of our intent to hunt them. If you can't behave yourselves I'll send you home."

"You can't send me home," I snapped. "You need me here. And the fat mare with scabs on her left leg is ready to be hunted." I stomped away and flopped down in the sun, placing my face in my paws.

Trevegg stalked toward me, his face tight with fury. I didn't care. I was tired of being told what to do. An instant later, my chest grew warm and I heard loud footsteps. The humans were coming. I stood. Trevegg, still several wolflengths away, halted, watching as the humans crested the gentle slope that led to the plain.

As soon as the humans caught sight of us, TaLi bounded over. She squatted down and wrapped a strong, skinny arm around me. I felt the warmth of her, smelled her scent of fire and herbs, and felt safe and whole as I did only with her. Being with TaLi was the only thing that eased the ache that came whenever I thought of my mother's exile. I knew that I could never seek my mother if it meant abandoning TaLi.

"HuLin pretends to lead the hunt, but it's really KiLi who does so," she whispered into my ear. I saw Trevegg's ears twitch to listen.

I licked TaLi's arm to let her know that I understood. It was the same with wolves. Sometimes when a less dominant wolf is good at something, like tracking or hunting, she will let the leaderwolf take credit for her skill so that the leaderwolf doesn't feel threatened. At autumn's end, Marra had told me that the humans didn't want their females to hunt anymore. The hard winter must have changed their minds.

"He'll watch to see which horse KiLi chooses, then he'll tell us which one it is. Once we start hunting we'll wait for you to help." TaLi stood, stroked my head, and galloped off back to her pack.

The humans spread out across the plain, and Ázzuen, Marra, Trevegg, and I slipped in among the prey, who had returned to their grass chomping in spite of Trevegg's concern that they would run off. We pressed ourselves down into the low, scrubby grass, so it would be harder for the horses to see what we were doing. I noticed that some of the humans had the sturdy spears they used to kill animals at short range while others had the lighter sharpsticks that were thrown using another stick that they rested upon their shoulders. This time, I resisted the urge to fall completely into the hunt thrall and did not run among the horses. We wolves had decided to let the humans lead the hunt, and so I stayed where I was, allowing my senses to do as much as they could from where I lay. It didn't take me long to find the plump, sickly female, only ten or twelve wolflengths from where I waited. I crept over to her on my belly, then stood up. I tried to catch a human's eye to let them know, as I would with a packmate, that I had found easy prey, but none of them paid any attention to me. They just spoke softly to one another, pointing out different horses and talking some more. Sighing, I sat back to watch them. Ázzuen slunk over to join me.

It seemed that they hunted much as we did. The younger, fleet humans ran after clusters of horses, testing to see which ones were weak and which were strong. I felt a little sorry for the humans. They couldn't smell sore joints or hear fragile bones, so they had to rely only on the horses' behavior, which meant that a clever prey could fool them by pretending to be fit when it was really weak.

Still, within only a few moments the female who must have been KiLi chose a horse, and HuLin gave the order to chase it. It was a spindly one, hungry after surviving the winter. Decent prey, though not the best. As soon as the humans began to run, driving the mare toward where Ázzuen and I sat waiting, I leapt to my feet. Ázzuen, too, jumped up, and we ran to the horse, heading her off so that she could not escape the humans.

Scrawny as she was, the horse moved well. She swerved just as the humans raised their sharpsticks, but she swerved right into Ázzuen and me. When she saw two wolves running toward her, she panicked, rearing up on her back legs. She wasn't accustomed to humans and wolves working together. I ran faster, preparing to jump, knowing that we would have her, certain that the hunt would be successful.

Then I heard TaLi's shriek.

I looked up and saw a human's face, suffused with fury. It was DavRian. He held a sharpstick, a *spear*, poised to throw, but not at the horse—at me. He thought I was stealing his prey. Just as he tried to let loose the spear, TaLi knocked his arm aside. I was already dodging, diving under the belly of the horse, ducking hooves and rolling in the dirt. When I stood, dizzy and coughing from the dust and from my fear, Ázzuen was beside me. Frantically I looked for Trevegg and Marra. They were standing atop a flat rock, out of the way of the frenzied horses and unpredictable humans. Trevegg saw me watching him and, as the horses calmed, leapt from his rock and loped over to me.

"That is enough of that," he said when he reached me. "We will have to find another way to gain their trust."

If they wouldn't behave like reasonable creatures, there was no other way. I looked back at the humans. TaLi had seized DavRian's weapon. She threw it down to the ground and stomped on it. Quick as a hawk's strike, DavRian's hand flew from his side and struck TaLi, hard enough to make her stagger.

I didn't think. Before DavRian had pulled back his hand, my legs were moving, and before TaLi had regained her balance I was standing in front of her, snarling. The air before me blurred and my ears filled with wind. I could feel my lips pulling all the way up past my teeth. All the fury and frustration I felt, all the loss and helplessness, came together in a powerful desire to knock DavRian from his feet and bite deep into his flesh. I was only dimly aware of the deep menacing growl throbbing in my throat. I didn't hear or see the horses, my packmates, or the tribe of humans. I saw only DavRian's surprised face and his thin, furless neck. And only very dimly, his sharpstick rising above his head.

"Kaala! Stop! Now!"

At first, I didn't recognize the voice. I had never, never heard Trevegg shout. There was such command in his voice, the command of a leaderwolf, that I immediately stopped growling. I was aware that my fur was standing straight up along my back and my tail was so taut it was hurting my lower back. It took everything I had to force my fur back down and to make myself sit. I stopped snarling and hid my teeth, but I still glared at DavRian. He needed to know it was not acceptable for him to hurt TaLi. HuLin stepped up beside DavRian, his expression both angry and bewildered.

"I told you they were dangerous!" DavRian hissed.

It was then that I realized what I had done. The whole reason we were bringing the humans meat was to gain their trust. The reason we had joined them in the hunt was to convince them we were worthy companions. I had just destroyed our chance of making that happen. I couldn't face Trevegg, Ázzuen, or Marra. I couldn't return to my pack. TaLi gripped my fur, but I pulled away from her. Ignoring Trevegg's command to return to him and TaLi's hand groping for me, I ran, wanting to put as much distance as I could between myself and those I had failed.

I had gone no more than five hundred wolflengths when I ran smack into what felt like a huge boulder of fur and muscle. I bounced off of it and landed hard on my side. I lay there for a moment, stunned, then sat up and shook my head to clear it. I blinked dirt out of my eyes, trying to get a sense of what I might have hit. I was in a thick copse of spruce trees and juniper bushes, and at first, all I saw were the trees, bushes, dirt, and rocks. Then the sky above me darkened, and I looked up to see a huge head lowering to meet mine. I choked back a squeak of fear as I found myself nose to nose with the Greatwolf Milsindra.

I tried to stand, but my legs wouldn't let me. The last time I'd seen Milsindra, she'd made no secret of her desire to kill me. She looked at me now the way I might look at a rabbit trapped in the thick branches of a dream-sage bush, or at a deer with a broken leg—something I knew I could catch without trouble, something so vulnerable that I could savor the moment before the kill without worrying that my prey might escape me. I saw the satisfaction in her face, as if she knew that I wouldn't run from her. She was right. I was already dazed by my failure with the humans and by the news of my mother waiting for me outside the valley. And, to make things worse, the desolation I had been trying to push away by hunting the horses returned. This time, I couldn't make it go away. That had never happened before. I'd always been able to ignore it, to pretend it wasn't there. This time, it stayed, and I could no more run from Milsindra than I could fly to the top of the nearest pine tree. I sat there, waiting for whatever she might do.

"Kaala, of Swift River," she rumbled, "I am so glad to have found you."

My senses sharpened at her courteous tone, and my head cleared. She was trying to sound friendly, but there was a nasty, condescending edge to her voice that made my backfur bristle.

There was a small bird in the Wide Valley that we called the grub-finder, because it could locate the succulent white beetle larvae that lived in the bark of only a few trees in the valley. The ravens loved these grubs and would do almost anything to get them, and would often try to wheedle the grub-finders into showing them where the tasty larvae hid. The grub-finders were both simple-minded and easily upset, and one harshly spoken word would send them skittering away to hide deep inside the hollow of a tree, sometimes hiding so long that they starved to death. So the ravens spoke gently to the stupid birds. But they couldn't keep the contempt from their voices, for ravens have no respect for the slow-witted. I'd heard Tlitoo talking to one once and couldn't believe the grub-finder wasn't insulted at Tlitoo's condescending tone, but the stupid bird only heard the feigned kindness and showed Tlitoo where a cluster of grubs hid. Milsindra's voice sounded just like a raven speaking to a grub-finder.

I managed to get my paws under me and stood, trying to keep my spine from sagging. I knew I should greet Milsindra, should say something, but anger at myself for growling at

DavRian and fear of Milsindra thickened in my throat, and when I tried to speak, nothing came out but a whuff of air.

Milsindra smiled a narrow smile, just the tips of her sharp teeth showing. "I was following the trail of a grouse, and caught your scent," she said. "How are things with your humans? I heard you gave a walking bird to the human leader and that he was pleased."

At the mention of scent I realized that Milsindra did not smell like Greatwolf. She smelled like pine and dirt and forest. I remembered what Trevegg had said about Greatwolves being able to hide their scent. Some wolves said it was the power of the Ancients that allowed them to do so. I'd never believed it. Yet there Milsindra was, smelling nothing like wolf. She watched me, awaiting an answer.

I thought about lying, telling her that everything with the humans was fine, but she could almost certainly smell my distress. I remembered the paw print we had seen by the human homesite, the rustling bushes. Had she been following us? Did she have spies in the valley? How much could she have seen and heard if she was creeping around smelling of the woods, and what would she do to me if she knew I was lying? Thoughts darted through my mind like mice running for cover in tall grass. I couldn't possibly follow them all.

Milsindra watched, waiting for a lie. Through the aroma of forest that disguised her wolfscent, I caught a whiff of something. An eagerness. The smell of a wolf before the hunt. I took a step back.

"You weren't so quiet the last time I saw you," she said, licking a paw. "Are you not brought up well enough to answer a krianan wolf when she addresses you?"

That made me whuff in surprise. I'd never before heard a Greatwolf refer to herself as a krianan—it was the term the humans used for their spiritual leaders and for the wolves that met with them.

"I must speak to Rissa about the way she raises her pups," Milsindra said.

I at last managed to find my voice.

"It's only been a quarter moon since we started bringing meat to the humans," I said, pleased that I was able to speak calmly and respectfully. "We have more than two moons left to complete our task." *And only two moons to get outside the valley if I'm going to find my mother,* I thought. The thought of my mother waiting for me while I was stuck in the valley stole my words away once again, and I blinked stupidly at Milsindra. She waited. For me to lie, for me to admit failure. I didn't know what to say. Then I remembered how Marra could answer a question without really answering it, saying just enough to be respectful without actually giving up any information.

"It isn't easy," I said, averting my gaze. "There are challenges, but we still have time to figure it out."

"Challenges?" Milsindra scoffed, dropping her polite demeanor. "You can barely keep from killing one another. One hunt. One hunt and you almost bit one of them and they almost skewered you like firemeat." She laughed, then seemed to remember that she was trying to be nice to me. "It is not your fault, Kaala. You cannot help what you are." She lowered her head to meet my eyes. "Do you know why I permitted that decrepit oldwolf to convince the council to grant you the challenge of living with the humans?"

"Because you had to," I blurted. "You don't have enough support on the council to stop it. Zorindru made you."

Milsindra laughed.

"Zorindru can make me do nothing. *I* allowed it because I know that you are too much a wolf to allow the humans to bully you, to treat you like a curl-tail. Not like your mother and Ruuqo's brother." My ears rose at the mention of my mother. Milsindra's arrogant gaze stopped me from interrupting her. "Hiiln and Neesa were the humans' *strecks*." I winced at the insult. A streck was the lowliest form of prey. "They rolled over and offered their bellies to the humans, and they lost what made them wolf. They put us all at risk of becoming no more than curl-tails to the humans. But I knew you would not do so." Her ears flattened in amusement. "I am always right."

"What do you mean about my mother?" I finally managed to say. I knew that Hiiln, Ruuqo's brother, had been exiled from the valley for consorting with the humans long before I was born, but no one had told me my mother had done so, too. My heart quickened. Milsindra had to know where my mother was, what she wanted from me. "What does my mother have to do with the humans?"

Milsindra ignored my question. "I allowed the test to go forth because I knew you would fail. And the sooner you fail, the sooner I prove that I am right and that you are an affront to the Ancients, that Frandra and Jandru should never have saved your life. The sooner you and your humans are dead, the safer we all will be."

A fanatical gleam came into her eyes, and I stepped back. She followed me. I realized that fleeing would be a bad idea.

Like any wolf, she would chase the prey that ran. I gripped the earth with my paws, forcing myself to stay where I was. Milsindra regarded me.

"You have courage, youngwolf. You have spirit. You are a wolf that others follow. But you are not the savior of wolf-kind. Only a Greatwolf can be that. Any wolf who truly follows the Ancients knows that Indru chose the Greatwolves to lead wolfkind because we are closest to the Ancients in the Balance. We are the ones chosen to control the humans. We are the ones with the strength to do what must be done."

Hearing the fervor in her voice shocked me. I found that I was panting hard, trying to get enough air into my lungs. I had thought Milsindra only wanted power, but it was more than that. Ruuqo and Rissa followed the Ancients, as we all did, but I'd never heard any wolf speak as Milsindra spoke, as if the Ancients were her leaderwolves, as if they told her what to do as one wolf would tell another. I wondered if it could be true, if the Ancients themselves thought I was unlucky. Milsindra certainly believed it.

I heard Ázzuen howl that he was coming. The knowledge steadied me. "Zorindru doesn't think it's the will of the Ancients that I should fail." My voice was quiet, but Milsindra heard me.

"And that is why I must take the council from him." The amusement left her face. "The Ancients entrusted us with the task of controlling the humans, and when Zorindru allowed you to consort with them he put us all in jeopardy. Those on the council who support him are as dangerous as he is, and the Ancients will punish them. Those who do not know whom to follow are weak and will be easily swayed when you fail."

"And if I don't fail?" I said, still not meeting Milsindra's eyes.

"You will," she said, carelessly chewing at the fur of her shoulder. "And if you don't, I will find a way to make your success a failure. Even if you do get to your humans"—she laughed—"which you won't, not after you growled at them. Even if you do manage it, I will find another way to make the council doubt you. It's not difficult, you know. All I have to do is tell my followers it was luck that you succeeded, and that we need more proof. That we need to see humans living with you, too. Or that we need to see that when you live with humans your own hunts improve. That we need a wolf to lead a human pack. It doesn't matter what. Fear is a powerful force. All I need to do is make enough of the council and enough packs in the valley afraid of you and what you represent and I will win."

I said nothing. I felt slow and stupid and couldn't think of anything that would contradict Milsindra.

She took two more steps toward me. There was nowhere left for me to back up.

"Where is your raven friend?" she asked, almost nonchalantly, lowering her head until her nose pressed against the top of my muzzle. I again caught the pungent scent, the smell of a wolf waiting to attack.

"I don't know," I said. "I haven't seen him."

"Don't lie to me," Milsindra said, allowing a threat to enter her voice. She took my muzzle between her teeth, then released it. "I can smell a lie as well as I can smell your fear. What did he say to you when you met with him at the river? What did he say to you today? Has he asked you to go on a journey with him?"

I watched her, trying to figure out how much she knew—why she was interested in Tlitoo.

"He just said he was busy," I lied. "That's all."

"You know, Kaala," Milsindra said, almost gently, "that I would kill you now if I could. But Zorindru still holds too much power. I will take word of what happened with the humans today to the council. It may be enough. But if not, when you fail, and fail you will, I will have all the proof I need that I am right and Zorindru, Jandru, and Frandra are wrong. I will stop you from destroying wolfkind and will lead the krianan wolves to new strengths. Once we rid the valley of these humans and you streck wolves, we will succeed. We will fulfill Indru's promise."

The promise you lied about, I thought. *The promise you almost killed us over.*

All at once, fury rushed through me. Ever since Zorindru had told us of the task the Greatwolves had invented for us, other wolves had been telling me what I must and must not do. I had all of the responsibility for keeping humans and wolves from fighting but no power to do so, and now Milsindra was telling me that she would thwart me even if, in spite of this, I succeeded.

It was all I could do not to growl at the Greatwolf. There was no way I could challenge her, no way I could stop her. I stared at the ground beneath my paws, keeping myself from looking into Milsindra's eyes, trying to hide my emotions from her.

She whuffed a small laugh and took a few steps back. Then cocked her head. "You are not the only Swift River wolf who is troublesome, are you?" she said.

A moment later I caught Yllin's scent and heard her steady pawsteps. She walked calmly into the copse and greeted Milsindra. Then she walked over and stood by my side.

"Lordwolf," she said to Milsindra, her ears and tail lowered and her voice the very model of respect. "Our pack would like Kaala to join our snow deer hunt, if you don't need her anymore."

Yllin was standing with ease. Although her ears and tail were lowered and her legs slightly bent to show respect to Milsindra, her bearing was confident. If she had actually said so, it could not have been clearer that although she honored the Greatwolf's dominance, she was a strong wolf in her own right. I watched her in admiration and envy. I would never be that confident.

Milsindra looked Yllin over, her gaze considering. She could certainly kill both of us, but it wouldn't be an easy fight. Just then Ázzuen's bark sounded through the trees.

Milsindra planted her huge paws in the dirt and stretched, her lean muscles rippling under her fur. "Of course, if she is needed for a hunt, she must go." She kept her gaze on Yllin, then smiled her narrow smile once more. She turned her tail to us and bounded from the copse, as light of heart as any pup.

A moment later, Ázzuen dashed into the spruce and juniper grove, just as I released my anger and frustration in a low, fierce growl. Ázzuen stopped, startled. He greeted Yllin and then touched my face with his nose. My fury abated, just a little.

"Ruuqo wants us to come to the snow deer hunt?" I asked Yllin.

"No"—she grinned—"but when you left for Oldwoods, I

thought you might need some help, so I've been following you. The humans are sensitive, aren't they?" She slammed her head into my shoulder, knocking me to the side.

I laughed in spite of my concerns, and felt warmth and gratitude wash over me. Nothing bothered Yllin. She always seemed to be able to find a way to rise above anything that happened.

"How did you do that? With Milsindra?"

"She wasn't going to hurt either one of us," she said. "I could tell. And even Greatwolves respect a wolf who seems assertive; it's instinctive." She thought for a moment. "There are ways to get around those in power without actually challenging them. You have to follow the rules so you don't get in trouble, but still get what you want. You just have to find new ways of doing things."

"I'll never be as strong as you are," I said to her.

"Why? Because you couldn't stand up to a Greatwolf when you're not even a year old?" she said. "You'll be fine, Kaala. You're strong and smart and have packmates who stand with you. Just don't get stuck thinking about what you can't do." She licked my muzzle. "I have to get back to the snow deer hunt. I told Ruuqo I was following a forest deer trail." She poked Ázzuen in the ribs, picked up a pinecone in her jaws, and ran from the copse.

I took a breath, controlling the anger and frustration that still roiled in me, allowing them to feed me rather than overwhelm me, trying to be as calm and confident as Yllin was.

"Trevegg sent you to bring me back?" I asked Ázzuen.

"Yes," he answered, his gaze intent upon my face. "He said that he thinks we can still get HuLin to trust us. HuLin laughed at DavRian after you left. But we have to get back to Oldwoods before the humans leave."

"We'll go back," I said, "but not quite yet." An idea was forming at the edges of my mind, a way to thwart Milsindra in her attempts to undermine me. Her own words had given me the idea. And Yllin's encouragement made me think it was possible. If Yllin could stand fearlessly, face-to-face with a Greatwolf, I could try something different. First, however, I needed to know about my mother—if she had really called to me. And I knew who could tell me.

I raised my nose to the light breeze, trying to catch any nearby raven-scent. Tlitoo had told me that he would be gathering with other ravens. My guess was that they would be at Rock Crest, a steep, rugged hill not far from Fallen Tree Gathering Place. It was a favorite meeting place for the ravens, since its sharp rocks and craggy cliffs provided plenty of hiding places and perches. Sure enough, I could smell raven not far to the south of us. Rock Crest was in that direction. Keeping my nose lifted to the breeze, I began to track the scent.

"Where are you going?" Ázzuen demanded, scrabbling to follow me.

"To find Tlitoo. I'm going to make him go outside the valley to find out if Demmen was telling the truth."

"You're going to *make* him?"

Ignoring his dubious tone, I set off for Rock Crest. Ázzuen, huffing in protest, followed. As we ran, I told him what Milsindra had said. About the council, about me, about Tlitoo. Ázzuen listened, his ears twitching. He asked me several questions as we ran, most of which seemed pointless to me. I was just getting annoyed enough to tell him to shut up when raven-scents grew strong all around us. We were nearing Rock Crest, and soon we heard belligerent raven voices. Suddenly uneasy, I stopped. This was not the normal strident raven conversation. The birds were angry; they sounded like they did when they attacked something.

Ázzuen and I crept cautiously up the hill until we could peer down into a round rocky depression where the ravens had gathered. They were indeed surrounding something, attacking it with sharp jabs of their beaks. I had an impression of black feathers and furious, clacking beaks. I had seen the ravens attack a weasel that way once. Ravens despise weasels, who steal and eat raven eggs. They kill any weasels they find and attack anything that gets between them and their quarry.

I began to back away.

Then I heard a familiar krawk, distorted by fear and pain. I met Ázzuen's wide eyes, and we began to run down the hill as we realized at the same moment: it wasn't a weasel the ravens were attacking. It was Tlitoo.

8

We ran full pelt down the craggy hill, hurtling the last wolflengths to land hard amid the horde of angry ravens. A beak struck my shoulder as wings smacked my head. A sharp talon caught the skin behind my eye, another the soft folds of my neck. My fur, still winter-thick, protected my neck, but the claw digging into the skin near my eye made me yelp. I swung my head from side to side, knocking ravens aside. I saw Ázzuen bat several other ravens away with his paws. I didn't want to bite any of them. I'd recognized Sleekwing and Rainsong, Tlitoo's parents. They were the ravens who most often led our pack to prey. They would be angry enough at us for intervening, and I didn't want to risk making permanent enemies of them—or any raven, for that matter. Tlitoo darted behind me, and I lowered my head and closed my eyes, preparing for the onslaught of raven beaks and claws. The ravens abruptly ceased their assault. A low muttering and a clacking of beaks rose up around us.

I opened my eyes. Beside me, Ázzuen crouched down, his vulnerable nose buried in his paws. When he realized he was no longer being clouted by raven wings, he raised his head, then stood.

I looked at the beady eyes regarding us. I counted nine ravens, all of them glaring at us, some of them with wings half-raised. I waited for them to say something, but it was Tlitoo who spoke, his voice ragged.

"Why are you here, wolflet? This is a raven place," he rasped. I bent my head between my front legs and lifted my tail to look at him. His head and chest were speckled with blood, and more feathers were pulled out than could be attributed to molting. The skin on one of his legs was torn to shreds. He held his head hunched down below his wings.

"They were hurting you," I said. I looked up and found Sleekwing among the ravens. "Why were you hurting him?"

"Because, wolf, he flies from his duty as you scuttle from yours," Sleekwing hissed. "Wolves may accept such cowardice. Ravens do not.

> *"Wolves may run and hide*
> *When tasks grow hard or daunting.*
> *Ravens never whine."*

I whuffed in annoyance. I had already been nearly gored by DavRian, threatened by a Greatwolf, and had all but ruined our chances to succeed with the humans. On top of that, somewhere outside the valley my mother needed me and I could not go to her. I didn't need to hear criticism from Sleekwing, some stupid bird who was not even part of the challenges I faced.

"What does it matter to you?" I snapped, glowering at Sleekwing as I had seen Rissa do. *Sometimes you have to remind the ravens that you are the larger hunter,* she had said once, *so that they do not get above themselves.* "You get food either way," I said, "whether it's from us, or the humans, or the Stone Peaks. What do you care what I do with the humans?"

"Wolflet, hush," Tlitoo quorked from behind me.

Sleekwing darted forward so quickly I saw only a dark blur before something stabbed me hard on the head. I yelped. Sleekwing pecked me twice more as I backed up against a rock, almost tripping over Tlitoo, who rolled to get out of my way, then rolled again to crouch between me and the rock I had backed into. Ázzuen stood by my side, growling softly. Sleekwing settled back to glare at us. His mate, Rainsong, strode forward to stand beside him.

"Stupid, whiny, arrogant little wolves," she spat, the feathered ruff around her neck puffed out so far I was surprised she could see anything. "Do you really think the Gripe-wolves' challenge involves only mewlers like you? Do you think we spend our time with you because we cannot find food of our own? We have bound our destiny to that of wolf-kind and thus must put up with your stupidity. We do not, dimwolves, have to put up with your insolence. Neja has a duty, and he will fly from it no longer."

"That is *not* my name!" Tlitoo said, peering out from behind my rump. "I am Tlitoo, named for Tlitookilakin, the raven king." He hunched his head down between his wings again, as if expecting another attack. "I am Tlitoo," he whispered.

My head ached from my ears to my teeth from Sleekwing's attack. When the raven sprang forward again, I winced but held my ground.

"Two wolf pups and a raven barely fledged," he said in disgust. "Together you understand as much as a half-eaten worm."

When he spoke again, his voice was gentler.

"It is the same thing, Nejakilakin," he said to Tlitoo. "It is your task to speak for ravenkind as did Tlitookilakin."

"Tlitookilakin was the raven king, wasn't he?" Ázzuen said to Sleekwing. "Ruuqo and Rissa told us about him when we were smallpups. He argued with the Ancients in the time of Indru. He was the one who convinced the Ancients to let the wolves try to watch over the humans."

Tlitoo had told me that, and I'd forgotten. Wolves and ravens had been partners ever since, which was why Tlitoo had befriended me in the first place.

"You're part of the challenge the Greatwolves set us, aren't you?" Ázzuen said, his eyes agleam and his words tumbling over themselves as they tried to keep pace with his quick mind. "You're part of the promise! That's why you care about the humans."

A deep thrumming arose from the throats of the ravens standing all around us. A few of them clacked their beaks.

Startled, Ázzuen took a few steps back.

"Be quiet, babblewolf," Tlitoo hissed from behind me.

Four ravens strode forward, still humming. I braced myself for an attack. Then Sleekwing screeched something at the advancing ravens. I didn't understand what he said, but it made the ravens stop and swivel their heads to look at him. Then they turned away, as if they did not much care what we did, and flew to perch on nearby rocks.

"Ha!" Sleekwing quorked at Ázzuen. "You are the one who is not as moss-brained as other wolves." He stalked forward to stand in front of Ázzuen. Sleekwing was a large raven, his raised beak almost level with Ázzuen's nose. I could see Ázzuen tense up, trying not to flinch away. Sleekwing cocked his head to one side, examining Ázzuen, then spread his wings, slapping Ázzuen in the muzzle as he did so, and flew up to a rock a few paces in front of us. Rainsong flew to join him.

"The Gripewolves are not the only ones who talk of saviors and destroyers," Sleekwing said, looking at me, "and wolves are not the only ones whose future depends on what the humans do and do not do. It is time for Neja to fulfill his role in the destiny of ravenkind. We will not allow him to avoid it any longer."

"And you, wolf," Rainsong said to me, "must now help him, as he has helped you in your puphood." I was surprised at the kindness and sympathy in her voice. Ravens didn't usually evince much of either. She blinked at me several times. "It is time you stopped being afraid to take on that which belongs to you, wolf. It is time that you stop acting on what you fear and start acting on what you know to be right.

> *"Time to make a choice*
> *To no longer follow those*
> *You should be leading."*

Sleekwing krawked. "If you are done coddling the mewler, we will leave." He glared at Tlitoo. "Remember your duty, Neja. Next time, our reminder will not be so gentle." He fixed his beady gaze on me once more. "As for you, ask Nejakilakin what he did not tell you when he woke you the morning of Ice Moon's wane."

With that, he hopped upon a higher rock and then upon another and took flight, krawking something I didn't understand to the other ravens, who rose as one to follow him, leaving us alone with Tlitoo on the rocky hillside.

Tlitoo limped out from behind me and hopped unsteadily onto the rock that Sleekwing and Rainsong had occupied. Carefully, he began to preen, pulling out some feathers and smoothing others. "Thank you, wolves," he said.

I wanted to find some way to comfort him. Had he been wolf, I would have licked his muzzle, or bumped my hip against his. I took a few steps toward him, but he leapt away from me. He looked so uncomfortable, I decided to stay where I was.

"So, what was that all about?" I asked him. I looked up at the sun, now more than halfway down the sky. I had to get back to Oldwoods before the humans called off the hunt for the night, but I also had to know what Sleekwing and Rainsong meant.

"I cannot tell you, yet," Tlitoo said. "I will tell you soon."

Ázzuen opened his mouth to protest, then looked up, startled. I followed his gaze to see two raven-shapes soaring toward us.

I readied myself for another attack, but Tlitoo warbled in welcome as the new ravens spiraled down to us. I recognized Jlela and Nlitsa, the two females I had seen with Tlitoo at the river. They landed beside Tlitoo on his rock and immediately began preening his feathers and crooning to him.

"I am sorry," Jlela said to Tlitoo. "We were too far away to get here before now." She glared at me. "Why did you let this happen?"

"I didn't let anything happen," I protested.

"You did not fulfill your task and brought to the attention of the raven leaders the fact that Neja had not yet fulfilled his. We needed more time. If you were not such a bumblewolf we would have had that time. "

"*What* are you talking about?" I asked, snarling a little. Ravens could be indirect and evasive in the best of circumstances, and I needed to know what was going on.

Jlela did not answer me. She and Nlitsa turned their heads right and left, as if something on the hillside held their attention. Tlitoo started to speak and then, after a darting glance at Jlela, closed his beak.

Ázzuen woofed impatiently. "It's obvious, Kaala. It's important to the ravens that you succeed in the Greatwolves' challenge. And it's obvious that Tlitoo's task is linked to yours. Otherwise, Sleekwing and Rainsong wouldn't care about what you did today, and Milsindra wouldn't have asked about Tlitoo. What I haven't figured out," he said to Tlitoo, "is exactly what it is *you* need to do, and if we don't know that, we can't help you."

"The Gripewolf spoke of me?" Tlitoo asked.

"Yes," I said. "She wanted to know where you were and if we had journeyed together, whatever that means."

"What did you say to her?" Jlela clacked.

"I didn't say anything to her. Why would I?"

Jlela quorked at Tlitoo. "Do you wish me to tell them, Neja?"

"No," Tlitoo said, blinking his eyes hard. "I will. Another

time. Not now." He hunched his head below his shoulders, as he had when attacked by the other ravens.

Jlela ran her beak through Tlitoo's back feathers, regarded me for several moments, then dipped her head in a very wolf-like gesture.

"Nlitsa will fly from the valley," she said to me, "and find out if the new wolf has been truthful about your mother. She will find out if she does indeed wait for you. Will you then be able to give attention to your task?"

"How do you know about that?" I demanded, feeling exposed.

She and Nlitsa exchanged glances and gave loud, krawking laughs that echoed off the rocks of the hillside. "You wolves are supposed to have such good noses and ears," Jlela said. "But you never think to look around you." She laughed again. "Or above you."

"Why would you do that for her?" Ázzuen asked Nlitsa. He was mistrustful of raven motives.

"We would like her to focus on what she must do," Jlela said, stabbing at the dirt with her beak.

"I would like that," I said before Ázzuen could say anything else. "Thank you."

"Good," she replied with a decisive clack of her beak. She hopped up next to Tlitoo again and murmured something to him. Then Jlela ran her beak twice through his head feathers and, without another word to me, took flight. A moment later Nlitsa followed.

"Jlela and Nlitsa flew alone from the time they were barely fledged," Tlitoo said, watching them go. "Their father and mother and all of their nestmates were killed by a long-fang while Nlitsa and Jlela were berry hunting. They know what it is like to miss a mother and a father. That is why they wish to help you."

"Thank them for me," I said. "Why can't you tell me what's happening?"

"You must trust me for a little while longer, wolflet," he said. "Will you do that?"

"Yes," I said.

Tlitoo looked from me to Ázzuen. "I promise I will tell you when I can."

He looked so dejected and alone that I had to go to him. Without thinking, I trotted over to his rock and licked his feathery back. His feathers tasted different from the walking bird's, smokier, with a touch of tree bark and prey-meat. Walking birds ate only plants and berries, and their feathers bore a lighter taste. Curious, I licked Tlitoo again.

Suddenly the rocky hillside disappeared as did the scents of the cooling day, replaced by a jolt of freezing air, then darkness and a complete absence of scent. I couldn't see or smell anything. Then the darkness blurred, and I saw feathers, and beaks, raven heads as large as my own bearing down on me, attacking me. Wings beating me, talons tearing at me, my heart pounding in fear and pain. Then two large, furred shapes bearing down pushing away the ravens. I yelped, and the image disappeared as suddenly as it had come. I leapt back to find myself once again at Rock Crest, and to find Tlitoo standing several wolflengths away from me, his wings fully extended.

"What happened?" I gasped.

"Do not do that again, wolflet." Tlitoo's eyes were

haunted. "You must not touch me. Do not ask me why. Do not ask me anything. I will come to you when I can."

With a stumbling leap, he took flight, flying south, toward the river.

We watched him in silence. I had no idea what had happened when I had come in contact with Tlitoo, but it had shaken me. I watched him go, uncertain of what to do next. After several moments Ázzuen spoke. "We have to go back to the humans, now, Kaala. You know they don't like hunting in the dark."

"I know," I said, looking after Tlitoo. The humans' weak eyes were no good for night hunting. I shook away the strangeness of what I had seen when I had touched the raven. "But I'm going after my mother, too."

"I know you will," he said. "I would, too. Trevegg and I talked about it after you left the Oldwoods. I figured out what we can do." He spoke rapidly, as if he thought I would interrupt him. "The Greatwolves said that wolves have to live with humans, but they didn't say which wolves. So we get the humans to accept wolves as packmates, and then Trevegg will take over the promise. There are other wolves in the valley who like the humans and want an excuse to be near them. Yllin does, and several youngwolves from Vole Eater and Tree Line. Once we know that Trevegg is succeeding, we take our humans and leave the valley. We start our own pack. We just have to get the humans to accept us in two moons instead of three, so we can leave the valley and look for your mother."

He looked expectantly at me.

"You told Trevegg about Demmen and my mother?" I asked, my mind reeling a little.

"Yes," Ázzuen said, half apologetic, half defiant, "he needed to know."

My mind worked fast to try to keep up with Ázzuen and to try to work what he had told me into what I had already decided. My tail began to wag even before my mind caught up with the fact that Ázzuen had just given me the solution I needed.

When Milsindra had threatened me, I knew that I would have to do more than just get the humans to accept us as pack, and I knew I would have to do it quickly enough to find my mother. I also realized that Milsindra had shown her own weakness. If there were, as she had said, those on the Greatwolf council who saw me as a curse and would see my failure as evidence of that, there were also those who saw me as a savior and would see success as proof of that. The greater the success, the more likely Zorindru and his followers would win out over Milsindra. She said she would make things more difficult, set more challenges if I succeeded with the humans. So I would meet those challenges before she set them. The only thing I hadn't figured out was how I could keep wolves and humans together for a year and still be able to leave the valley to look for my mother. If there was any chance that Demmen was speaking the truth, I was going to find her. Now, thanks to Ázzuen's clever, clever mind, there was a chance I could.

"It will change everything," I said, mostly to myself.

"Yes," Ázzuen agreed, "but things are changing no matter what. We can't be afraid of it."

I wasn't afraid. For the first time since Demmen had given me his message, I felt invigorated. Change was what I wanted. I licked Ázzuen's muzzle. His eyes widened.

"Yes," I said, licking him on the cheek as well, "it's a perfect idea."

"But what?" he asked suspiciously.

I gave him a smile that I realized was every bit as narrow and sharp-toothed as Milsindra's had been.

"We don't get the humans to accept us in two moons, Ázzuen. We get them to accept us today. Now. And we do more than become part of the human pack. We show the council that we can succeed even better than they thought, that wolves and humans are meant to be as one." With each word I spoke, I felt myself growing stronger, becoming less a wolf blown about by the whims of others and more a wolf in charge of herself and her own choices.

"That you're the savior, not the destroyer," Ázzuen said.

"If that's what they want to think." I didn't care if they thought I was Sky's own daughter, as long as I could keep my humans and my pack alive and have the chance to find my mother. I began to trot in the direction of Oldwoods and the humans. Ázzuen followed.

"Kaala," he said, still suspicious, "exactly how do you plan to do more than getting the humans to accept us as pack?"

"I have some ideas," I said, bumping his shoulder hard with my own, "and you can help me figure out the rest." I took off for Oldwoods at a run, with Ázzuen at my side.

We reached Oldwoods to find the humans standing together, glowering at the horses, all of whom were still alive. Everything in the humans' bodies said they had been hunting hard. Their shoulders slumped, and some of them leaned on their sharpsticks. Others sat, their backs against trees or rocks. I could smell their exertion and sweat. TaLi had told me that they had trouble hunting this kind of horse because they were not only fast but had also learned how to dodge sharpsticks.

"They haven't caught anything yet," Ázzuen whispered in relief.

I dipped my head. That would make my task much easier. I ran past Trevegg and Marra, who were crouched, watching both the humans and the horses. I nosed Trevegg's cheek in greeting and apology but did not stop when he called my name. I continued at a trot to the humans as Ázzuen spoke hurriedly to Trevegg and Marra, explaining what we had planned.

I saw HuLin notice my approach and slowed to a walk, my ears and tail low. When he did not raise his sharpstick, I continued. TaLi, BreLan, and DavRian hurried to HuLin's side. DavRian's whisper was loud enough for a half-deaf wolf to hear.

"You have to stop it," he hissed to HuLin. "It's a danger to all of us."

I stopped, awaiting HuLin's reaction.

"Not all of us," the human leader said with a laugh. "Just you. And not without reason. If the wolf had not rebuked you for hitting TaLi, I would have done so myself." He turned his gaze to me. "Get over here, wolf," he commanded.

I'd thought I would have to find a way to convince HuLin to let me be near his pack again, but he held out a hand to me in a gesture of one accustomed to being obeyed. I felt the fur on my back trying to rise in protest of his tone—no one but a leaderwolf had the right to speak to me that way—but I forced it back down. Slowly, I crept forward and licked HuLin's outstretched hand.

He reached down to rest his hand upon the moon-shape on my chest. Then he gripped the skin underneath it hard, digging his fingers deep into my flesh and twisting. I yelped. TaLi caught her breath in a sharp gasp.

"So, wolf, you will fight to defend those you see as under your protection? I can understand that. You will not, however, growl at me. Do you understand that?"

I wanted so much to bite down on that arm, to show HuLin that I was not a wolf to be bullied. But I had a more important task to think about. I forced my fur to stay flat, my lips to remain relaxed over my teeth. It took everything I had, but I forced myself to remain small and unthreatening, to resist the temptation to growl at HuLin and bite down on the hand that held me. Instead, I tucked my tail between my legs and licked the human leader's wrist.

He smiled and nodded, as if something had been confirmed, then released me. I whimpered at the pain in my chest but licked HuLin's hand once more. His grin widened. "You see, DavRian," he said, "you just have to know how to speak to them. Now," he continued, "we have two hours of light left to hunt. We'll see if they are as useful as TaLi claims they are."

HuLin raised his arm, and he, TaLi, BreLan, and several other humans walked out among the horses. I shook myself, caught Ázzuen's eye, and followed. When HuLin paused, studying the horses, I bumped my hip gently against his legs. He looked down at me and I walked to the plump, sickly mare I had found earlier that day. She whinnied and shied away from me. I looked over my shoulder at HuLin. This time, he caught my meaning and gestured to his followers.

Ázzuen and Marra dashed over from Trevegg's side to join me. The three of us began to chase the mare. She bolted, and two other horses ran with her. All three moved well enough to make catching them difficult.

"Block them!" I barked to HuLin. I know he couldn't understand my words but hoped he would understand my meaning. He did. He looked from me to the fleeing horses, and called to the other humans. The humans darted out in all directions and formed a half moon around the horses so that in running away from us, the prey had no choice but to run into humans. My heart raced as I smelled the horses' shock and confusion. In a moment of clarity I will never forget, I drove the fat mare directly to HuLin, and just as if he had been a member of my pack, he herded her back to me. She reared up, and her stout haunches almost fell into my jaws. I ripped into her tough hide, trying to drag her down. Ázzuen woofed a frantic warning and I dodged out of the way just as her hoof kicked out at me. In that moment, BreLan jabbed at her with his sharpstick. She landed on her side, staggered to her feet, and kicked out at the young human. Two of the lighter throwing spears hit the horse. One bounced off, but the other entered deep into the horse's hide. I spared a quick moment to hope that the humans had good enough aim to hit neither us nor their tribemates. Then Ázzuen grabbed at the mare's belly, tearing into her flesh. The horse stumbled, and I forgot everything but the hunt. Four humans, led by HuLin, converged on her, stabbing her with their sharpsticks. That was all it took. The mare screamed and fell. I heard a human shriek of triumph and saw that Trevegg, Marra, and three humans had taken down one of the other horses. We didn't have to show the humans what to do again.

As the sun fell below the trees, we hunted the no-longer-complacent horses. We caught four of them. Four. More than any hunt I'd ever heard of. When the sky darkened and the remainder of the horses fled Oldwoods, wolves and humans alike celebrated a successful hunt. Ázzuen and Marra chased each other around the cooling horse carcasses, growling at any foxes that dared to venture near, as several young humans wrestled in the stubby grass. One of the humans, a muscular male I didn't know, came up behind me, rolled me onto the ground, and thumped me so hard on my ribs that he made me cough. He was smiling and laughing, so I took it as a sign of camaraderie.

When I stood, wheezing, I saw that Trevegg, Ázzuen, and Marra had already torn into one of the dead horses. The steam rising from the beast and the rich aroma of the meat made my teeth ache. I pushed myself away from the brawny human and bolted across the plain, running so fast that I actually stumbled over the horse when I got to it. I landed half on top of Marra, who growled at me.

Trevegg had ripped into the horse's belly and had most of his head inside of it. Ázzuen and Marra were right beside him, trying to eat as much as they could as quickly as they could. I pushed in next to Ázzuen and took a huge piece of succulent horse belly in my jaws. I had barely swallowed that first bite when Trevegg barked an order to us. I took another bite, swallowed it quickly, then took one more, and backed away from the horse.

HuLin and three other humans strode across the plain toward us. Trevegg flopped down flat on the grass half a wolf-length from the prey, and Ázzuen, Marra, and I lay down next to him. My mouth watered and my nose tried to pull me back to the horse, and I could feel Marra trembling with meat-hunger beside me, but we all stayed where we were. We had to, if the next part of our plan was going to work.

In any pack, the leaderwolves decide when and how much other wolves feed at a kill. This both ensures that the best meat is given to the wolves that the leaderwolves favor and also reinforces the leaderwolf's position. Every wolf learns as a pup how to surrender prey to a leaderwolf, even if we don't want to. When I told Ázzuen of my plans to get the humans to welcome us as quickly as possible, he'd come up with the idea of seeing if we could make HuLin feel like a leader-wolf by relinquishing freshly killed prey to him.

It was almost impossible to just lie there as the humans approached the still-steaming horse, but we did. We waited, and it was worth it. When HuLin saw that we gave up the prey to him, he grinned the biggest grin I'd yet to see from a human. His chest swelled, and I could smell that our acquies-cence made him feel proud.

He held out an arm, blocking the three humans who accompanied him. "The wolves helped us with the hunt," he said. "They should get some meat."

"Helped them?" Marra muttered. "They'd be eating dirt tonight if not for us."

"Be quiet," I said, watching the humans' every move.

HuLin sat back on his haunches as the other humans moved to the prey. We scooted out of their way. It took them forever to cut through the rest of the horse's hide. Some of the humans had sharpened stones, which I had seen many times before. One of them had what smelled like the bone of an elkryn, sharpened as well, which was attached to the end of a thick piece of wood. Out of the corner of my eye, I saw Ázzuen creeping forward to sniff at the humans' tools and Trevegg placing a restraining paw on his back. With a sigh, Ázzuen settled back to watch. We could have torn off meat much faster on our own, especially since the humans saw so poorly in the half-dark, but after what seemed like forever, the humans managed to do so. They didn't give us any of the greslin, but the meat they gave us was adequate: most of a haunch and some shoulder meat. We devoured a third of it before Trevegg made us stop and drag the remainder into the woods for the rest of the pack. We found a stream to rinse our muzzles, since I remembered that a blood-covered muzzle disturbed TaLi. When we returned to the plain, I saw her standing at HuLin's side. I took a breath and walked over to them. When I reached them, HuLin placed one large hand upon my back and squatted down to be at my level.

"It was a good hunt with the wolves helping us, HuLin," TaLi said, squatting down beside him. Her voice was shy, her tone tentative.

"One of the best," he agreed, ruffling his other hand through her headfur. He reminded me of Ruuqo praising one of us after a successful hunt. "I am glad you brought them to us."

He paused for a moment, his hand above TaLi's head, then reached over and gently ran his hand through my own headfur. Then he pushed us both gently away, stood, loped over to the other humans, and began to help them cut up the horses. TaLi threw an arm around my neck, pressed her face to mine, and then followed HuLin.

The humans did not return to their homesite that night but instead built their fires at Oldwoods, setting up guards around the dead horses to keep scroungers away. Two young humans, one male and one female, took thick sticks as long as their arms and stuck them in one of the fires so that the flames leapt from the fire to the end of the sticks. Then they took off at a run in the direction of the human homesite, holding the sticks high to light their way. Trevegg sent a reluctant Marra back to the pack to let them know of the successful hunt.

The humans cooked much of the meat then and there. When the young humans who had run off returned with more of their tribemates, the work began to go more quickly. The humans tied some of the horse flesh into bundles they could lift onto their backs; the rest they piled onto what looked to me like two small trees linked together by many small branches and preyskins. TaLi called it a *sled* and said that the humans carried large loads upon it. Ázzuen couldn't stop sniffing at it.

"They can't see at night and have no fur," he marveled, "and so they find ways to make the night warmer and brighter with their fires and firesticks. They can't hold much meat in their bellies, and so they make things like sleds, to carry it back to their homesite."

Ázzuen kept snuffling at the sled and licking the small pile of sticks the humans used to light their way. I left him to it and watched HuLin, wondering if we'd done enough, if we would be able to get them to invite us into their homesite after such a short time. It seemed almost as if the humans had forgotten us already as they gathered their meat and celebrated with one another. I heard two of them bragging about the hunt, as if they had done everything themselves. Every once in a while, though, I caught HuLin watching us.

Then, an hour before dawn, the hyenas struck. Four of them skulked onto the plain, trying to steal meat directly from a pile of horse that the humans were preparing to place in a fire. I saw them first and barked a warning. Several sharpstick-wielding humans leapt to their feet, but before they could get anywhere near the hyenas, Ázzuen, Trevegg, and I pelted after the scroungers. The hyenas must have seen and smelled only the humans, for when they saw three wolves running at them, they fled without a fight. Two of them even dropped the meat they carried. The third got away, but the fourth, their leader, stopped to snarl over her shoulder at me. I lunged forward and got my teeth into her rump, pulling out a chunk of her fur. She snarled and snapped at me, her teeth just missing my muzzle, then disappeared after her sisters.

Pleased with myself, I trotted back to Oldwoods. HuLin was waiting for me. He saw the hyena fur in my mouth, took it from me, and pounded me on the ribs in the way the human males seemed to think was affectionate.

"Good work, wolf," he said. I stifled a grunt of satisfaction. The humans were as easy to influence as smallpups.

It was well past midday when the humans began the journey back to their homesite, moving slowly with their heavy loads. We followed them, keeping in their sight as they tramped through the woods and struggled across the river. Twice more, scroungers tried to attack, and each time they did, HuLin called to us to help keep them off. When the humans finally reached their village, we stopped and waited, prepared to run if they were not pleased to have us there. But HuLin caught sight of me and held out his hand. My chest grew warm and I felt my mouth soften into a smile as Ázzuen, Trevegg, and I walked to him. It should have been harder. We should have had to convince the humans to allow strangers into their home. But HuLin sat down at one of the fires and pulled me to him on one side and Ázzuen on the other. Trevegg sat in front of him. I heard some of the humans growl and saw several of them flinch, but HuLin was their leader and they would do what he told them to do. HuLin gave each of us a piece of fire-cooked horse meat and allowed us to stay there, resting by the warmth of the humans' fire.

9

I awoke in the night to the sound of voices murmuring. At first I thought it was Rissa and Ruuqo, planning the hunt, for it was dark by then and Rissa's favorite hunting time. Then I smelled fire and meat and the unmistakable smoke-and-flesh aroma of the humans, and remembered where I was. I lifted my head, my heart beating fast. I couldn't believe I had let myself sleep so deeply, surrounded by such unpredictable creatures as the humans.

HuLin was gone, his scent trail leading to one of the stone-mud structures. Ázzuen still snored by the fire, but Trevegg was awake, his head on his paws, his eyes and ears following the quiet activity of the human homesite. Most of the humans had disappeared into the stone-mud structures they used for dens, though some slept or worked quietly by the fires while still others guarded the edges of the homesite. I felt guilty for having fallen asleep, leaving Trevegg to guard us. When he saw that I was awake, he grunted, sighed, and settled down to sleep.

I stood and stretched, working the sleep kinks out of my spine. Then I heard the soft voices again and understood what had woken me. One of the voices was TaLi's.

She and BreLan crouched over a small fire as BreLan handed TaLi a small bundle that smelled of snow deer. At first I thought he was giving her a gift of meat, which would make sense if he wanted her as a mate, but we had hunted horses, not deer, and the bundle didn't have the smell of prey freshly killed. It smelled like the skins the humans used to cover themselves against the cold, yet it seemed too small to cover much of even a human as small as TaLi. Curious, I padded over to the two humans. TaLi placed a hand upon my neck as I sniffed at the preyskin, which was folded in upon itself so that it was no bigger than her forearm. BreLan snatched it away, holding it high over my head.

"Careful, wolf," he said. "It's not for you."

I knew that. I stared at BreLan until he blinked, ran his hand through his headfur, and handed the bundle back to TaLi. She smiled and held the deerskin out for me to smell. I still couldn't figure out what it was. Only when TaLi took off the ragged skins she wore around her feet and unfolded the oddly shaped gift did I realize that BreLan had brought her foot-coverings. The ones TaLi had been wearing were lined with bear fur against the cold, but they were almost worn through in several spots and flapped open when she walked. BreLan's gift would be perfect to protect her feet in the warmer end-of-winter days. He would be a good mate for her. Forgiving him for his earlier rudeness, I licked his face in thanks. He looked at me, startled, then grimaced and wiped his hand across his mouth.

I heard footsteps and turned to see a female human approaching us from behind. The woman was not tall, but was solidly built, and carried herself with authority. She was older than TaLi, but younger than NiaLi, and smelled so much like them both that she had to be a close relative.

"What's this, then?" she demanded. "What do you have, TaLi?" She held out her hand.

BreLan scrambled to his feet. I had noticed that humans stood when a more dominant tribemate came near. It made no sense to me, since wolves make every effort to make ourselves small when we know ourselves to be less powerful than another. The humans' insistence on standing baffled me, but TaLi stood, too, then reluctantly gave the older woman the foot-coverings.

"BreLan has given me boots, Aunt," she said. *Boots*, then, was what the humans called the foot-coverings.

The woman grimaced. After a moment, she handed the foot-coverings back to TaLi and looked up at BreLan, her hands on her hips.

"Do you court her, then?" she demanded. "You have not discussed it with me."

For a moment, BreLan seemed unable to speak. Then he straightened himself and said, "Yes, RinaLi, I do. I will ask Hu-Lin's permission tomorrow."

TaLi smiled.

The woman, RinaLi, narrowed her eyes. "You know that TaLi is to be the Lin tribe's healer? We will need to know you can provide well for her."

Even with what little time I'd spent with the humans, I could tell that this was a demand for more gifts. BreLan's shoulders sagged a little in relief, for it was also an admission that the tribe would accept his courtship of TaLi.

But TaLi's whole body tightened with rage.

"I've told you, Aunt, that I am not going to be a healer. I'm promised as krianan and will take over for Grandmother when she is too old to continue her duties. KanLin agreed three years ago."

RinaLi grabbed TaLi's arm and hissed at her. I took several steps forward. RinaLi pushed me aside with her hip, but it was BreLan's warning hand upon my back that reminded me to keep my temper.

"That is not to be," the woman said. "KanLin is long dead and HuLin leads the tribe now, and you will accept the role given to you. Do not let me hear any more of this krianan nonsense, or I'll see to it you never see that old woman again." She took a breath, and if she'd been a wolf she would have been settling the fur along her back. "And we will not discuss this with outsiders." She looked up again at BreLan, who was trying to catch TaLi's eye.

"Thank you, BreLan of Lan tribe," RinaLi said formally, drawing his attention. "We accept this gift. You may ask HuLin tomorrow if you may stay here with us."

It was an obvious dismissal. BreLan dipped his head to her, then pulled TaLi close. "We'll be together, TaLi, I promise," he said to her in a voice too soft for the other human to hear. "Don't cause trouble. Let them think you will do as they say." He looked at me. "Don't let Silvermoon cause trouble either." I lowered my ears to let him know that I understood. BreLan gently pushed TaLi away, and only when she gave him a brief nod did he step away and smile at RinaLi.

"I thank you," he said. "I will return tomorrow to speak to HuLin." He stroked TaLi's headfur, then strode into the woods. RinaLi gave TaLi a warning look, then stomped across the homesite into one of the stone-mud structures. TaLi stood still for a moment, breathing hard, then sat down at the fire and pulled me to her.

"Stay here with me, Silvermoon," she said. She clutched the foot-coverings to her chest and curled up by the fire. For long moments, she lay shaking until at last her breathing evened out and I knew she slept. I extricated myself from her grasp, trotted over to HuLin's fire, and pawed Ázzuen's face to awaken him.

When he blinked up at me, I quickly told him what had happened with TaLi and BreLan, and that BreLan had left the Lin tribe for the night.

"BreLan told me that DavRian wants to be TaLi's mate and that HuLin likes DavRian better." Ázzuen looked off into the woods. "I'm going after BreLan in the morning if he's not back." Ázzuen's steady gaze dared me to argue with him.

"Fine," I said, "but keep watch for now. I'm going to stay by TaLi."

I padded back across the clearing and lay down next to the girl. I meant to stay awake to make sure I was there if TaLi needed me, but I was more tired than I thought, and before I knew it, TaLi's warmth and her soft, even breathing lulled me back to sleep.

The next time I awoke, it was to shouts and the sound of stone hitting wood. I leapt to my feet and looked around the village. I found TaLi across the homesite, her back pressed against the wall of the herb-smelling structure where I'd first met her. Facing her were HuLin, DavRian, and RinaLi, the woman TaLi had called Aunt.

In the early light of the dawn, TaLi stood, her arms crossed over her chest, her lips pressed together, the scents of anger and distress rising off her like steam from a pond on a cold day. DavRian, shifting uneasily from foot to foot, held out to her a large piece of elk hide. His arms were only half-extended, as if he thought TaLi might bite him. HuLin's face was dark with fury, as was RinaLi's. She stood between the two males, one hand upon each one's shoulder.

Ázzuen crouched several wolflengths away from the humans, watching them, motionless except for the twitching tip of his tail. Trevegg still slept by the fire. Moving as quickly as I could without attracting attention, I slunk across the clearing to lie beside Ázzuen.

"They're angry because TaLi won't accept the *cloak* DavRian wishes to give her," Ázzuen said, tasting the human word. I didn't know what it meant. From where I lay, the cloak looked like one of the skins the humans used to cover themselves when they slept. I knew the humans valued such skins, since they were so large. The hide of an elk might make several of the tunics or leg-coverings the humans wore, but only one or two of the larger covers.

"RinaLi insisted that TaLi take it, and TaLi threw a rock against a tree. She threw it hard enough to kill prey," he said with admiration.

"Why doesn't she want the *cloak*?" I asked. It looked warm, and TaLi was so skinny she would need the warmth.

Ázzuen ignored me and began to creep closer to the humans. I followed. "Thank you, DavRian," TaLi was saying, her voice flat with suppressed emotion. I could tell from the trembling of her legs that it was a struggle for her to keep her voice calm and polite. "I am grateful, but I cannot accept your gift."

"Why not?" DavRian asked, sounding like a pup denied a scrap of meat.

TaLi didn't answer. DavRian lowered his eyes. When he saw the foot-coverings—the boots—that BreLan had given her on her feet, his hurt turned to fury. "You accept a gift from the Lan tribe but not from me?"

"Yes," TaLi snapped, giving in to her temper. "I accept a gift from BreLan and not from you. I have chosen him, as is the right of a krianan, and he has chosen me." She stepped forward, shoving her chin out toward DavRian. "Why don't you just leave? I don't want you." Her voice was loud. Out of the corner of my eye, I saw two humans look up from fires where they were preparing food. Several more emerged from shelters.

DavRian stepped back, clutching the cloak to his chest. HuLin looked as if he was going to strike TaLi. I began to move forward. I wouldn't bite the human leader, but I could put myself between him and TaLi.

RinaLi beat me to it. She placed both hands upon HuLin's chest and spoke to DavRian.

"TaLi is young and doesn't yet understand all of her duties," RinaLi said, soothing the young man. "We welcome your gift, and we welcome you to stay here with us for a little while."

"To court her," Ázzuen said in a low growl, "along with BreLan."

"It's not unexpected," Trevegg said, padding up to join us. "The humans often mate to form alliances with other tribes. Your girl should be quiet and then do what she wants."

TaLi opened her mouth to protest RinaLi's invitation to DavRian, but the older woman looked at her with such fury that the girl lowered her eyes. I expected to see tears or fear in them, but what I saw was ferocious anger. I pawed her thigh then pressed my nose into her boots, trying to remind her of BreLan's words, his warning to make her leaders think she would obey them.

DavRian looked from TaLi to RinaLi and HuLin, still clutching the cloak to his chest. Then he thrust it into TaLi's arms, knocking her back almost to the wall of the herb den.

"Thank you, RinaLi," DavRian said at last. "I know she's young, and I accept your offer."

TaLi's aunt smiled at him. She took the cloak from TaLi and placed it over the girl's shoulders. It fell to her knees. A rabbit fur–lined head-covering was attached the rest of the cloak. RinaLi pulled it up over TaLi's head. It completely hid her face.

"It's beautiful," RinaLi said, stroking the fur lining. "Thank you."

DavRian smiled back. "I'll tell my father I'll be spending time here," he said. He turned as if to go, then stopped and rubbed his hands against his thighs, and turned back to the Lin leader. "You know, HuLin," he said, his voice quiet and re-spectful, "that the Rian tribe no longer follows the old way of doing things. We do not follow the old krianans."

"I had heard that," HuLin said. "My son, TonLin, told me before he left us. It's one of the reasons I have considered you for TaLi." Anger had returned to the Lin leader's voice, and he glowered at TaLi when he mentioned TonLin.

"He and I were friends," DavRian said. "It's for him that I tell you what I haven't told anyone except my father." He lowered his eyes as if embarrassed, but looking up at him, I could see an eager smile on his face. "The Ancients have spoken to me directly, as TonLin told me they spoke to him. They have told me, as they told him, that it is the destiny of humankind to command the world around us. The krianans that came before have misunderstood, and the Rian tribe is no longer bound by the whims of those who go into the woods and speak to the trees. We take what's rightfully ours. The Balance the old krianans speak of is a myth, a way for them to keep power. Trying to maintain it weakens us, makes us no better than these wolves." He swept his arm down to us. His hand was temptingly near my teeth.

"You're a fool," TaLi said, pushing the head-covering off. It had mussed her dark hair, which now fell into her face. "If we don't keep the Balance, there will be nothing left for us to 'command.' You don't know what you're talking about."

DavRian flushed but didn't answer her. He lifted his head to meet HuLin's eyes.

"What other creature makes spears and knives? What other creature makes shelters and clothing and rules the power of fire? The old ways no longer serve us, HuLin!" He had raised his voice, and several humans began to make their way over to us. I recognized KiLi, the woman who had helped lead the hunt at Oldwoods.

I could see that HuLin liked what the young man was saying. So could DavRian.

"I'm sorry if I spoke too passionately," DavRian said. "I tell you this so you will know that if you choose me for TaLi, she will have the status of the krianan as my mate. She will lose nothing."

TaLi took a deep breath, clearly planning to insult DavRian again. HuLin clutched her arm, hard. I could see the red marks his fingers made, and it was all I could do to keep from leaping at him. Ázzuen and Trevegg both pressed against me.

"Thank you, DavRian," HuLin said. "I will consider what you've said."

DavRian dipped his head to HuLin, then tried to catch TaLi's eyes. She kept her head down, her face hidden by her hair. DavRian reached out, as if to touch her, grimaced, then turned and loped into the woods.

TaLi pulled her arm from HuLin's grasp. He let her do it.

"He's lying," TaLi said, looking up at HuLin. "He goes off into the woods and smokes the dream-sage leaves. I'm not surprised he thinks he's hearing the Ancients. That's not how true krianans learn of the needs of the Balance."

"Then how do you?" HuLin demanded. "Neither you nor the old woman will tell me."

TaLi pushed the hair from her eyes and looked at her feet. She certainly couldn't tell HuLin that the krianans spoke to the Greatwolves. "You know we have to preserve the Balance," she said at last.

"She's right, HuLin," KiLi said. The female had been hanging back, watching HuLin and DavRian. Now she stepped forward. The male at her side came forward with her. He was tall and strong-looking, and he and the female looked formidable together. Four other humans stood in a loose half-moon shape around them, offering silent support. "We can't give up our old ways on a whim. And you can't force us to do so. Your son tried that."

"And you and your friends humiliated him so much that he left us," HuLin said through clenched teeth.

KiLi kept her voice calm. "We all want what's best for the Lin tribe. But we won't be rushed. We respect you as our leader, but we can't let you toss aside everything we've known. We have no objections to you choosing TaLi's mate as you will—it's your right to do so—but we must decide as a tribe what is best for us. You know that." She placed a hand on his shoulder, and she and the male walked away. The other humans followed.

Once, when I was a smallpup, Ruuqo was furious with me and wanted to send me away. But too many other wolves in the pack considered me a valuable pack member, and he had to accept their will. A leaderwolf only leads if others follow. Clearly it was the same with the humans.

HuLin watched his tribemates go, then turned on TaLi.

"You will not drive the Rian boy away as you drove my son away," he snarled. "If I choose him as your mate, you will go to him. And I *will* get the tribe to renounce the nonsense that old woman has fed them."

He stalked off to one of the shelters, threw aside the pelt at its entrance, and ducked inside. As soon as he was gone, TaLi shrugged off the cloak so that it fell into the dirt.

RinaLi hissed at her. "Are you a fool? It is the most valuable gift any woman of Lin has received. And if DavRian is the Rian tribe's krianan you will have all the status you could want. Though if he still wants you after your behavior today, we'll be lucky."

TaLi's face went pale, then darkened, and she opened her mouth to answer back. Then she took several deep breaths and pressed her lips shut. She grabbed a handful of my fur, and I leaned against her. RinaLi regarded us both for a moment, then nodded. She picked up the cloak, stroking the soft, thick hide.

"He's a more suitable match than BreLan, but having them both here will make DavRian value you more." Satisfaction filled her voice. "We'll give the two of them until the Spring Gathering, then you will take DavRian as your mate."

TaLi kept her lips pressed tightly together, saying nothing. Her grasp on my fur tightened enough to hurt, but I stayed at her side. After a moment, RinaLi shook her head once, and stalked off, taking the cloak with her.

TaLi released her grip on my fur, reached down for one of the stones at her feet, and hurled it against a nearby tree, sending bark flying from it. I remembered the sound that had woken me and saw several stones around the tree trunk. She stood there next to me, shaking for a moment, then rubbed one of her foot-coverings against the other.

"Come on, Silvermoon," she said. "I'm not supposed to marry a swamp snake, I am supposed to be this tribe's krianan." She pulled herself up to her full scrawny height, then stomped off into the woods toward NiaLi's shelter. I didn't try to stop her. I needed to talk to the old krianan, too. I'd hoped to hunt several more times with the humans, to gain their trust more completely before moving on to the next part of our plan, but if TaLi was going to be sent away, we would have to act more quickly.

Ázzuen agreed to stay at the human homesite while Trevegg and I followed TaLi to her grandmother's shelter. NiaLi lived across the river from the other humans, in our own territory. She had lived with the other humans of TaLi's tribe, until HuLin had grown tired of her telling him what he could and could not hunt. He hadn't been able to stop her from being the tribe's krianan, but he had sent her to live away from the rest of the tribe.

Trevegg and I easily swam the river, then waited for TaLi to pick her way across, stepping from rock to rock in a disturbingly precarious manner. I kept a nervous eye on her, ready to jump back into the water if she fell. The first time I found her was when she had toppled into the river trying to make just such a crossing.

"You need to teach her to swim," Trevegg said to me, watching TaLi's unsteady progress. "I can't believe she doesn't fall in more often."

TaLi leapt the last wolflength of the river, landing in a squat on the muddy riverbank. She saw the two of us watching her and made a face.

"I know what I'm doing," she said.

Trevegg snorted and trotted off into the woods. I followed with TaLi. She moved swiftly for a human, and I expected to get to NiaLi's home quickly. But when we reached the deer path that led to the old woman's shelter, TaLi stepped off the path and into the woods, walking in the wrong direction.

"This way, Silvermoon," she said.

I whined at her and took several steps in the direction we

were supposed to be going. When she didn't follow, I walked back to her, pawed at her thigh, and whined again, looking down the path to NiaLi's.

"She doesn't live there anymore, Silvermoon," TaLi said. "Not since TonLin left the tribe." She crouched down so that her face was level with mine. I noticed river mud on her ear and licked it off. Trevegg, who had realized we were no longer behind him, padded over to sit beside us.

"After the big snowstorm, HuLin tried to make his son kri-anan without consulting anyone. Those in the tribe who believe in honoring the Balance wouldn't let him. Then, when I told TonLin I wouldn't be his mate, he left, and HuLin blamed my grandmother. So did a lot of other people who want to abandon the old ways. They threatened her and tried to burn her shelter. So she had to find a new place to live, a secret place. BreLan, MikLan, and I built her a new shelter. It's this way."

She walked quickly through the woods, avoiding the paths the humans usually liked to use. When she reached a narrow, rocky pathway, she broke into a run. Trevegg and I followed at an easy lope.

We had run only a few minutes when we smelled Great-wolf. We slowed and then stopped when Frandra and Jandru, the Greatwolves who watched over the Swift River pack, stepped out in front of us.

My relief that it was the two of them rather than Milsin-dra and my surprise that they were not disguising their scents as she had done were quickly replaced with trepidation as I remembered I had promised to meet them at the quarter moon to tell them of our progress with the humans. That quarter moon had come and gone and I had been so involved with the humans that I'd completely forgotten to seek out the Greatwolves.

I lowered my tail and ears as I slunk forward to greet Frandra and Jandru, my mind racing as I tried to think of what I could say to excuse myself. Ázzuen and Marra were both better at thinking up excuses than I was.

As I opened my mouth, hoping that something reasonable would come out, Trevegg whuffed in warning and Jandru's head snaked out toward me so quickly I saw only a blur of fur and a flash of teeth. The Greatwolf seized my neck fur in his jaws, flipped me over onto my back, and began dragging me through the woods. I was nearly grown, but Jandru pulled me through the dirt as easily as if I were a newpup. I was uncomfortably reminded of the way I had once hauled a shrub-hare around before snapping its neck and eating it.

I twisted around and scrabbled to get my feet under me, but only succeeded in kicking up dirt and leaves into my own face. I tried to dig a paw into Jandru's chest, but he just shook me hard once and flipped me back over onto my side. Frandra, running beside him, jabbed me hard in the ribs with her muzzle. I decided it would be best to stop struggling. I hung limp, looking at Jandru's mud-dampened chest fur as he pulled me along.

He and Frandra moved quickly, and I heard Trevegg's scrabbling pawsteps as he raced to keep up and TaLi's running feet not far behind him. The humans could move fairly quickly when they wanted to, and Trevegg was fleet for a wolf of his age, but the Greatwolves were faster; they quickly left

TaLi and Trevegg behind. They didn't bother finding a clear, quiet path through the woods. They just pushed through whatever bushes might be in their way. After several jolting minutes, Jandru crashed through a thicket of prickly tartberry bushes and dumped me on my rump in a puddle of muddy snowmelt.

I sat there for a moment, dizzy and disoriented. I smelled Greatwolf fur, mint, spruce trees, berry bushes, and smoke. The most powerful scent, however, was the aroma of human. I also heard the sound of preyskins flapping against stone. I shook my head, confused, and when my dizziness subsided and my vision cleared I saw to my surprise that I was sitting in front of a human shelter. I smelled herbs, and a familiar human scent. It had to be the old woman's new shelter.

Like her old dwelling, NiaLi's home was not separate from the woods surrounding it like other human shelters, but rather grew up from the ground, as a tree might. Its stone and mud base made it as sturdy as any of the other human shelters, but NiaLi had cleared only a small space around it, so that it felt as comfortable as any of our gathering places. Or at least it did when there weren't two angry Greatwolves hovering over me.

I stood and shook puddle water from my fur. Jandru immediately seized me in his jaws again, dragged me to NiaLi's shelter, and pushed his way through the antelope skins that hung in a narrow opening to the structure. Then he tossed me onto the hard-packed dirt and dried grasses inside.

"I think she would have come on her own four paws, Jandru." The old voice, filled with amusement, calmed me.

"She needs to remember who's in charge in this valley,"

Frandra snarled, stalking into the old woman's home. "You were supposed to come to us five nights ago, pup."

Shakily I got to my feet and greeted NiaLi, then faced the Greatwolves.

"I was coming," I said. "I was trying to get the humans to accept us in their homesite first. Then we could tell the council we were succeeding."

Frandra glared at me.

"You really do think we're fools, don't you? Do you think I don't know that you care more about your humans and your friends than about the Greatwolf council? You do whatever you like and then make excuses for it afterward. You think you know everything, but you don't know enough about what happens in this valley to make decisions without consulting us. You had better learn that, pup." She took a breath to calm herself. I watched her, surprised. I wasn't used to seeing Greatwolves overcome by emotion. When she spoke again, her voice was strained. "Things have changed since Ice Moon's wane." She shook her shaggy head, as if to clear it. "The council may no longer be satisfied with our bargain."

"I know that," I said before I could stop myself, then wished I hadn't. I didn't mean to tell the Greatwolves about my encounter with Milsindra.

"How do you know?" Frandra demanded.

Just then, Trevegg pushed his way into the old woman's shelter. He greeted NiaLi first, accepted the bit of firemeat she slipped to him, then acknowledged the two Greatwolves. They did not return his greeting.

"If we wanted you to be here, oldwolf, we would have asked you to join us," Frandra snarled. "Leave."

Trevegg sat next to the old woman's fire and wrapped his tail around his legs. Jandru raised his hackles and bared his teeth, I scooted back against the wall of the shelter, but Trevegg glared right back at the Greatwolf.

"Oh, quit marking your territory, Jandru," the oldwolf snapped, his own hackles lifting in annoyance. "I've lived nine winters and hunted a valley's worth of prey. Do you think I fear anything you can do to me?" Trevegg glared at the two Greatwolves. "Now, what is this about?"

Jandru closed his lips over his teeth, and Frandra gave a soft growl. I watched the two Greatwolves, doing my best to avoid staring at them in a way they might consider disrespectful.

The old woman's new shelter was small and the fire in the center took up some of the space. Four wolves and one human crowded it. I pressed myself against the stone-mud walls as both Greatwolves growled.

"Come now, my friends," NiaLi said at last, breaking the tension. "Frandra, Jandru, you did not bring us together to keep your secrets." Both Greatwolves looked at the old woman, and Jandru lowered his ears to her. I couldn't have been more surprised if he'd lowered his ears to a forest deer. I'd never have thought a Greatwolf would treat any human as an equal.

"We didn't bring *all* of us together at all," Frandra said, glaring at Trevegg.

"Ask the pup," Jandru grumbled, "since she seems to know so much that she doesn't have to consult us when she's supposed to."

Four pairs of eyes turned to me. I considered whether or

not to tell the Greatwolves what I knew. Jandru and Frandra were two of our only allies among the Greatwolves, but I didn't trust them the way I trusted Zorindru, the Greatwolf leader. They had been willing to let my pack and my humans die and to use me the way the humans used their tools. I looked down at my paws.

"Come over here, Kaala," NiaLi said. She sat near the fire, on a pile of furs and preyskins, wrapped in still more skins. I walked over to her and sat at her feet, pressing gently against her. She smelled of the skins and of herbs dried in the sun.

"Will you tell me?" she asked. "I would like to know."

I would do anything for NiaLi. Still, I hesitated, torn between my need for allies in the Greatwolf council and my fear of betrayal. I looked up into the old krianan's wrinkled face. She was thinner than she had been, as many of the humans were after winter's hardships, but there was something else, too. She smelled of weakness, of a fading of life, and in spite of that she also smelled of strength and confidence, of a certainty of what was right. I took a breath. She had known Jandru and Frandra longer than I could imagine. I might not trust them, but I trusted her. And Trevegg. I caught the old-wolf's eye and saw that his hackles had lowered.

"I think it's all right, Kaala," he said.

I told them about Milsindra, how she had threatened me after the failed hunt at Oldwoods, though I revealed nothing of my mother or of my plans to outwit Milsindra and leave the valley to find her. I did tell them of Milsindra's belief that the Ancients wanted me to fail, and how fanatical she was about it. I told them that she had said she would do everything she could to make sure that I did fail, even if I was able to get the humans to accept us.

"And you didn't think to tell us this?" Frandra snapped. "It is not fanatical and Milsindra is not the only one who thinks it may be so. She has told the council that you have hunted with the humans and that it is unnatural that a wolf should do so. She said no true wolf would hunt with the humans and fail to let the council know. She's convinced half the council that this proves that you are an aberrant wolf and a risk to wolfkind."

When her words came to an abrupt halt, I raised my eyes and was shocked to see her shaking, unable to continue speaking. NiaLi reached out to Frandra, pulling the huge wolf down beside her.

"Why would they believe that?" I asked. "Are they stupid? It doesn't make any sense." Trevegg shoved his hip against mine in warning.

"Doesn't it?" Jandru hissed, his eyes glittering in the light of NiaLi's fire. "Well, perhaps this will. Milsindra has told the council that by hunting with the humans, you have angered the Ancients and that we will soon see the consequence of their wrath. If we do not stop behaving in ways unfit for wolves, they will send disaster down upon us. That we have had one warning already."

"What warning is that, Jandru?" NiaLi interrupted, her voice gentle. "I have not heard of these warnings. Is it something you have neglected to tell me?" She was stroking Frandra's chest, calming the trembling Greatwolf.

Jandru's furious gaze left my face and softened when it settled upon NiaLi. He addressed her respectfully, as he would a wolf of equal status.

"If the Ancients grow displeased with a wolf or wolves, Nia, they will give three warnings—and if these warnings are not heeded, the Ancients will send death down upon us. The warnings can be a winter that lasts too long, or prey leaving the valley and causing starvation and war, or an illness that wipes out entire packs. Or"—he paused and looked at me hard—"wolves begin to disappear with no explanation and with no mark left behind."

Trevegg rumbled loudly, deep in his chest. I went cold. A wolf *had* disappeared. Because of me. When I had long ago dared the other Swift River pups to chase the horse herd and Reel had been trampled, his death was not the only thing the pack blamed me for. Borlla was another of Rissa's pups and my greatest enemy in the pack. She, Reel, and Unnan had terrorized me when I was the smallest and weakest Swift River pup. After Reel died, Borlla had stopped eating. Then she disappeared. With no explanation. With no mark left behind.

"Borlla," I said. "This is because of Borlla?"

"We never found her, Jandru," Trevegg said, "but she could have wandered away on her own. She was grieving. It can't be enough to mean anything."

A flicker of movement from above caught my eye. I looked up as a feather floated down to land on my muzzle. I sneezed, then twisted my head to peer up at the top of the old woman's shelter. Hanging upside down, in the hole that allowed the fire-smoke to escape the dwelling, was a dark bird-shape. Tlitoo saw me watching him, quorked once, and pulled himself back out of the shelter.

Jandru's gaze was still upon me. "Two nights ago," he said, "a Wind Lake wolf went missing, a youngwolf not yet a year old. They have not found him, nor any trace of him. They looked everywhere to see if he'd gone exploring and they howled for him. There was no answer and he left no scent trail. No wolf has disappeared from the valley in my life-time. Now two have vanished in less than half a year, and both of them after Kaala pulled the human child from the river."

"How can it be my fault if a Wind Lake wolf disappeared?" I protested. I was tired of the Greatwolves changing the rules and then blaming me if I didn't follow them. "I've done what you told me to do. I'm getting the humans to accept us more quickly than you thought I could. You should stop letting the council change the rules!" Trevegg bumped my hip again, hard enough this time to make me stagger.

NiaLi looked disappointed in me, but it was Jandru she addressed. "You know what I think of those stories, Jandru," she said. "You know I do not believe that Sun, Moon, Earth, and Sky act in such a way."

Jandru dropped his gaze from hers. After a moment NiaLi reached out her hand to him, and he shuffled to her and sat pressed against her, so that she was almost hidden between the two Greatwolves.

"And I know that you do not agree with me," the old woman said, reaching up to stroke his great muzzle. "It doesn't matter. What matters is what we do now." She stroked him once more, then frowned at me. "What they are not telling you, Silvermoon, is how great a risk they are taking for you. They stood up against the council when they saved you as a pup, and again when you were allowed to live after you and your friends stopped the fight at the beginning of winter. If you fail, they will lose more than their status in the Greatwolf pack. They will be killed, and not gently."

I looked at Frandra and Jandru, seeing them for the first time not as all-powerful creatures, but as wolves who could be harmed, just as I could be. I had been so afraid of them for so long, and so angry at them for lying to me, that it never occurred to me that they could be frightened. Now that I had met the other Greatwolves, I could see that they were young for their kind. And now that I was looking for it, I could see that they were afraid.

The words left my mouth before I realized I had decided to speak them. "We have a plan," I said, "a way to convince the council our way is right."

I was sure the Greatwolves would laugh at me, as they had so many times before, but Jandru's gaze was sober, and Frandra looked at me as if she thought I might have an answer to their problem. I swallowed once.

"What plan?" Trevegg demanded. Ázzuen and I had been working it out since we'd spoken to Tlitoo at Rock Crest and had not yet told the oldwolf.

Two more feathers fell upon my head as Tlitoo swung himself back through NiaLi's smoke hole. He dropped rather than flew into the dwelling, landing with a thump at my feet.

"The wolves will not just live with the humans!" Tlitoo said. "The humans will also live with the wolves. Whole packs and whole tribes will hunt together. It is a *good* idea." He looked up at me. "It might work, wolflet," he whispered. His eyes were bright and less troubled than I'd seen them since he'd awoken us at Ice Moon's wane. I wanted to find out what had changed since the other ravens had attacked him, but all three wolves were staring at me.

"This is true?" Jandru asked.

"Yes," I replied. "Milsindra said she'll find ways to make the council challenge our success even if the humans allow us to live with them. So we'll succeed in a way that can't be questioned." I felt myself grow more certain with each word I spoke. "We'll have humans live in wolf homesites, as well as wolves at human homesites, to show that we don't have to be subservient to the humans, that they will follow our ways, too. We'll be so successful hunting together that no wolf in the valley will question the value of joining with the humans, not even the council. We have other ideas, too." Or at least we would once Ázzuen came up with them.

"You will show that wolves and humans together are stronger than they are apart," NiaLi said, a slow smile spreading across her face.

"Yes," I said. I looked down at Tlitoo's feathered back, preparing to defend myself from the Greatwolves' derisive laughter and scornful remarks. When none came I looked up to see a glint in Frandra's eye.

"The raven is right," she said. "It could work." She stood, turned in a circle, sat, then stood again. "It might not be enough, but it could be. There are many on the council, Kaala, who wish to believe that you are the wolf come to save wolfkind. They are willing to be convinced."

The eagerness in her voice made me nervous. I didn't want to be the savior of wolfkind. NiaLi must have sensed my uneasiness. I often thought it was she, not the Greatwolves, who could read minds.

"It doesn't matter what they think you are, Kaala," she said. "It is a good idea, even if you are only a youngwolf doing the best she can."

"If we thought that's all she was," Jandru grumbled, "we would have dropped her off a cliff moons ago."

NiaLi smiled. "Either way, it is a worthwhile plan. Just two of us, to begin with, I think, Kaala? So your packmates will not be threatened? I will bring TaLi to your pack."

As if NiaLi's voice had summoned her, TaLi burst into the shelter, huffing and puffing. Her legs, chest, and face were covered in dirt, and her knees and hands were scraped, as if she had fallen in her haste to catch up with us. She held a rock in her left hand. I wanted to lick the dirt from her face, the blood from her knees, but I didn't know what she was going to do with the rock. If she was planning to hurl it at one of the Greatwolves to defend me from them, I would have to stop her. She looked around the crowded dwelling, her nostrils flaring, as if even her weak human nose could smell the tension in the air. She raised the rock.

"You should watch who you threaten, human pup," Jandru grumbled. But I could see he was trying not to laugh at how small and weak TaLi looked with her rock. If he'd seen how TaLi threw stones, I thought, he might not be so amused.

"It is safe, child," NiaLi said. She reached out to the girl. TaLi stayed where she was, but she did lower the hand holding the rock.

"There is some trouble in the human homesite," Trevegg said. TaLi, of course, could not understand him, but NiaLi looked sharply at the girl. I had almost forgotten why we had come to speak to the old woman in the first place.

"What is happening at the Lin village, TaLi?" NiaLi demanded.

TaLi spilled out her story. She was shaking when she told NiaLi that HuLin was going to insist that she not become krianan, and that he favored DavRian. I crossed the dwelling to press myself against her. She dropped her rock and clutched my fur.

"She must come to the wolves, Nia," Jandru said to the old woman. "If she doesn't, it will be one more reason for the council to mistrust the humans. It will allow Milsindra to say that Kaala has failed."

"She will come," the old woman said. "There have been those who wish to ignore the krianans' teachings since I was a child. Lin tribe has been divided for at least that long."

"It's gotten worse," Jandru said. "You know it has."

"Yes," NiaLi said, "I do. So we will find a new way. If the Lin tribe sees that the wolves do as TaLi asks them, and thus bring the tribe to more successful hunts, it will help. We will find a way to keep the krianans' promise."

She spoke with confidence, but with weariness, too. Tlitoo flew from beneath my chest to stand in front of the old woman and ran his beak through the furs she nested in. Frandra leaned over to nuzzle NiaLi's cheek. I whuffed in surprise. I never thought I'd see a Greatwolf show affection for a human. Frandra saw me watching her.

"You will get your pack to accept the humans today," she ordered.

"Today?" I choked. That would give us only a few hours to convince the pack to allow the humans in our gathering place.

"It should be today," NiaLi agreed. "If HuLin is angry

enough, he can keep TaLi from going off on her own, and she will not be able to come to me."

"Then it will be today," Trevegg said with a confidence I envied. "We will prepare the pack for your arrival, NiaLi." The oldwolf used the krianan's name shyly. "It may take some time. Where will you wait for us?"

"At the poplar grove where TaLi leaves food for me," the old woman said. "Silvermoon knows where it is."

"Good," Frandra said with a sharp dip of her head. "We will await word of your success or failure at the Stone Circle, and then decide what is next. You *will* come to us and involve us in the decisions, Kaala. If we have to come find you again, I'll help Jandru throw you off that cliff."

Tlitoo hissed at her. Frandra ignored him. She nosed NiaLi gently once more, then she and Jandru stomped out of the shelter.

When Trevegg pressed gently against me, I realized I was trembling.

"Don't worry about Frandra," Trevegg said. "She won't do anything to you if she thinks you're valuable to her."

But it wasn't Frandra's harsh words that made my legs weak. Her anger was almost a relief. When I'd told the Greatwolves of our plan, they had spoken to me as if I were a wolf worthy of respect, as if my ideas might be worthwhile. I had wanted to be taken seriously, to have the Greatwolves support me. Their confidence should have made me feel strong. Instead, it made me feel like I was stepping off a cliff with nothing but my own fur to keep me from falling to the ground below.

10

I followed Trevegg out of NiaLi's home and into the sun, stumbling behind him until he stopped to drink at a stream not far from the shelter. Too queasy to drink any myself, I just watched as the oldwolf lapped at the water. Tlitoo landed beside the oldwolf and began bathing in the stream. When Trevegg finished drinking, he sat back and looked at me.

"Shouldn't we howl to assemble the pack?" I asked.

"We should," he said.

I waited for him to do so. He just sat there, watching me.

"It's your gathering, Kaala," he said at last. "It's your howl."

A thrill of excitement lifted the fur along my spine. I'd never howled to assemble the pack. Pups were not permitted to do so unless they needed help or were warning the pack of some danger. Howling to call together the pack was a privilege allowed only to adults and to youngwolves favored by the leaderwolves. My throat went as dry as if I had been running for miles in the hot summer sun. I gulped a huge mouthful of water from the stream, getting as much up my nose as down my throat, and had to sneeze several times before I could take a breath. Then I sat on the damp ground and closed my eyes. I took a deep breath. Then released it. Then opened my eyes. Trevegg and Tlitoo were still staring at me.

"Just howl, wolf," Tlitoo grumbled. "You don't have any trouble making noise other times."

I took another breath and thought about what I wanted to share with my pack. I had to communicate that the gathering was urgent, without sounding disrespectful to my leaderwolves and without letting the other packs in the valley—or the Greatwolf council—know what we were doing.

I thought of TaLi and NiaLi and of my pack. I thought of wolves and humans coming together, of peace in the valley, and of the threats Milsindra had made. I closed my eyes and held the scents of my pack and of my humans in my mind and took one more breath. I bent back my head, opened my throat, and howled.

I was surprised at the resonance in my own voice. When I howled with the pack, my voice mixed with the voices of the Swift River wolves; I had not realized how resounding my own howl could be. After a few moments, Trevegg added his voice to mine, reinforcing my request to come together. Ruuqo answered almost immediately that the pack was at Fallen Tree and would wait for us there. Yllin howled to hurry up because she had something to tell us, and Ázzuen answered that he was on his way. Just like that I had called my first pack gathering.

When I opened my eyes and stood, I found I was no longer shaking and my stomach no longer roiled with tension. I met Trevegg's eyes.

"Nicely done," was all the oldwolf said, then set off in the direction of Fallen Tree.

"Finally," Tlitoo quorked. He jabbed the ground in front of my feet. "I am going now," he said.

"Wait," I said. I wanted to know what had happened since I'd last seen him, why he was no longer so afraid.

"No," he said, and took flight, leaving me to follow Trevegg back to Fallen Tree.

Yllin awaited us in a spruce grove not far from Fallen Tree. She greeted us both.

"I'm glad you're here, elderwolf, Kaala," she said. Her ears were pricked, her tail high. She gave off a scent of excitement mixed with apprehension.

"You're leaving?" Trevegg asked.

"I'm leaving," she said, with barely suppressed eagerness. "Demmen goes from the valley tonight and said he'd take me with him."

"What? Where are you going?" I asked. I depended on Yllin, even more than I depended on Trevegg. I had counted on her to help me with the humans and the Greatwolves. She always said she wanted to be Swift River's leaderwolf someday. I couldn't believe she'd just leave.

"It's nearly the Brightening Moon, furbrain," she said good-naturedly, as if that should explain it. When she saw my baffled expression, she laughed. "Spring is coming, littlewolf, and Ruuqo and Rissa will be mating soon."

"So?" I said. I knew that there would be new Swift River pups in a few more moons. It seemed to me that a strong youngwolf like Yllin would be invaluable to the pack when they arrived.

"So Yllin is too old to be here when Ruuqo and Rissa are mating," Trevegg said. "She's a strong female in her own right, and Rissa won't want her here."

"Even though she's her daughter?" I asked.

"Yes," Trevegg said. "It's time. Male youngwolves leave as well. I wouldn't be surprised if Minn left soon, too."

That I didn't mind. Minn was a bully. "What about Werrna?" I asked. "She stayed." Too much was changing already. I didn't want Yllin to leave.

"Werrna has chosen not to have pups and has agreed never to challenge Rissa's leadership," Trevegg answered. "That's a promise Yllin can't make. She's too dominant, and if she stayed she would try to start a pack nearby and cause trouble. It's wise of you to leave before Rissa has to send you away," he said to Yllin. "She would hate that."

"I do want my own pack," Yllin said, "and the Greatwolves told me I could try to find an acceptable mate outside the valley. They said they want me to have pups and that they might allow me a mixed-blood litter." Her voice was filled with pride. Wide Valley wolves were usually not allowed to mate outside the valley, because the Greatwolves wanted us to keep our bloodlines pure. But if we never mixed our blood with other wolves, our bloodlines weakened and we bore sickly pups. The Greatwolves chose only a few wolves to mate outside the valley. It didn't surprise me they'd chosen Yllin. She was strong and would be a good leaderwolf.

"Will you come back?" I asked.

She drooped a little.

"That's up to the Greatwolves. If they approve of the wolf I choose to have pups with they might let me return. I won't know until then." She shook herself. "But I'm not staying here doing nothing for the rest of my life, and there's no wolf in the valley I want for my Lifemate. The only interesting one likes you, anyway, Kaala."

"Oh, really?" Trevegg said, his ears pricking in interest.

"Pell of Stone Peak," Yllin replied. "I don't want Torell's bloodline for my pups, so don't worry, Kaala, I won't compete with you for him."

"I don't want him," I said, embarrassed. I didn't know how I felt about Pell, but I certainly didn't want to discuss it in front of old Trevegg.

Yllin gave me a skeptical look. "Anyway," she said, "Demmen will show me the way and help me once we're outside the valley. He says there is plenty of open territory and prey enough to support a new pack." She couldn't keep the excitement from her voice as she looked toward the mountains. Then she returned her gaze to us.

"I'd like to talk to Kaala for a moment, elderwolf, if it's all right with you."

"It is," Trevegg said. Then he bent his grizzled muzzle to touch Yllin's face. "I won't see you again, Yllin, whether or not you return to the valley."

Yllin blinked at him a few times and started to contradict him.

"It's true, youngwolf," Trevegg said softly. "It is the way of things."

Yllin lowered herself all the way to the ground and lay at the oldwolf's feet, looking up at him.

"You are Swift River wolf," the oldwolf said, "and always will be. Carry with you into the world the values of Swift River."

"I will," she said, her voice barely a whisper. Trevegg licked her face and took her muzzle in his mouth. Then he trotted off toward Fallen Tree. Yllin watched his retreating form, stood, shook herself once, then spoke.

"I'll try to find out about your mother for you, Kaala. If the Greatwolves let me back in the valley, I'll come to you here. If not, I'll look for you outside the valley."

"I'll be at the hill-rock Demmen told me about," I said. "Ask him about it. He'll know what I mean. I'll get there by halfway through the Denning Moon." I told her of our plan to succeed in spite of Milsindra's determination that we fail.

"I knew you'd think of something," she said with a smile, but her gaze returned to the distant mountains. "Either way, Kaala, I'll try to find you. Of all of this year's pups, I hope our trails cross again."

"Thank you," I said, feeling it was insufficient. She had given me confidence and strength when I was weak, she had stood up for me, time and time again. *I don't think I would have made it through my first moons without you*, I wanted to say. But Marra and Ázzuen were the ones who were good with words. "I always wanted to be like you," I managed.

She ducked her head. "You'll find your own way," she said. "You've already shown that. Your instincts are good, and other wolves follow you. Marra and Ázzuen are good allies, so don't try to do everything alone." She hesitated. "And don't trust the Greatwolves, Kaala, even Jandru and Frandra, even

Zorindru." She looked over her shoulder and bent down to whisper to me. "Even Ruuqo and Rissa. They want what they think is best for Swift River, and that may not be best for you, or your humans. They're your leaderwolves and you'll want to believe in them. But be careful. Even if you don't get romma. Even if you are an outcast, do what is best for you and those who follow you."

Shocked, I just stared at her for several breaths. There are two kinds of wolves in the world. Those who have been granted romma, and those who have not. Romma is a scent mark given to a pup or youngwolf by her leaderwolves to prove that she has been accepted by her pack and granted full status as a grown wolf. A wolf who has been granted romma, even if she is a curl-tail, will get at least some food and protection from her pack. More than that, she gets a sense of belonging to a pack, of being part of a family. Even a wolf who runs without a pack is better off if she has been given romma. It's a sign that her birthpack has found her acceptable, that she is a true wolf. A wolf without romma is an outcast, forever apart, forever alone. I had almost lost my chance to gain romma once; I wouldn't risk it again.

Yllin saw my hesitation.

"Rissa and Ruuqo are the best pack leaders in the Wide Valley," she said, "but they obey authority, as most wolves do. It's a reason I may never be able to be a leaderwolf in the Wide Valley; I question too much, as do you. Ruuqo and Rissa will follow what the Greatwolves say, even when it's wrong. If the Greatwolves tell them the Ancients think you are unlucky they'll believe them. So you'll be careful?"

"Yes," I said, my voice tight. Then, impulsively, I blurted

to her, "Don't trust Demmen, either, Yllin. There's something about him that isn't right."

"Thank you, Kaala," she said. "I can take care of myself around Demmen. He's still not fast enough to catch me when I don't want him to! And I know when he's being sneaky."

A cool breeze rippled her fur. She raised her muzzle to it, taking in the scents of the valley. "Tell Ázzuen I'm sorry I didn't say good-bye to him." She took my muzzle in her mouth and placed her paws upon my back. Then she shook herself and dashed into the woods.

I stopped at the edge of Fallen Tree, Swift River's largest gathering place. It was the first place we had come as pups when we left the den site and began our lives as pack members. It was a wide clearing, shaded by spruce and pine trees and split down the middle by a large spruce that had fallen in a storm when Ruuqo was a pup. The earth was soft enough to be comfortable but firm enough to keep from washing away in the rains. The scents of juniper, spruce, and oak mingled with the scents of my pack, reminding me of a time when I felt safe and protected. I stood between the two oaks that guarded one of the entrances to the clearing, and took in the sounds and scents of home.

I expected to find Trevegg telling Rissa and Ruuqo about our plan, but the oldwolf stood off to the side, watching with a bemused expression as Ruuqo and Rissa chased each other around the hillock we used as a lookout spot. Ruuqo and Rissa had been anxious and watchful since the Greatwolves had set our task. Now they were acting like pups in the snow. Rissa bounded over to me and touched her nose to my cheek. Leaderwolves usually wait for lower-ranking wolves to come to them. I returned her greeting, gently licking her white muzzle.

"You spoke to Yllin?" she asked.

"Yes," I answered.

"I'm sorry to see her go," she said, sadness tingeing her voice, "but it's time. It won't be long before some of you pups leave, as well." I startled, wondering if she knew what we had planned. Then I remembered that many youngwolves left their birthpacks once new pups arrived. Yllin and Minn were only two of five pups Rissa bore the year before I was born, and Demmen had been only eleven moons old when he left Swift River. Relieved, I licked Rissa's muzzle once again, then trotted across the gathering place to greet the rest of the pack: Ruuqo, who was almost as friendly as Rissa; Werrna, who, to my relief, was as irritable as usual; Minn, who seemed preoccupied, probably by Yllin's departure; and Marra, who nipped me hard on the ear.

"What happened when you left Oldwoods?" she demanded. "Ruuqo talked to the other packs and they'll let us hunt in their territories for now. What's it like in the Lin tribe's homesite?" Her breath in my face was hot and impatient. "Why are you back? You'd better tell me everything."

"I will in a minute," I said, licking her muzzle.

Last of all, I greeted Unnan, giving him just the slightest touch of my nose to his face. I had to acknowledge him, since he was pack, and I had called the gathering, but I didn't have to pretend to like him. Usually, he ignored me as much as he could, but this time, he bumped up against me and whispered in my ear.

"I know things about you," he said. "Things you don't want the pack to know." Unnan was always listening behind trees and bushes, biding his time until he could do the most damage with what he knew. Annoyed, I placed both paws on his back and pinned him to the ground.

"I don't care," I said. "You're a curl-tail and always will be. No one cares what you know."

He struggled under me. When he couldn't push me aside, he lay still, looking at me with hatred.

"Youngwolf!" Ruuqo shouted, sounding more like his usual self. "Get over here." I pressed my paws into Unnan's chest to make sure he knew he had lost the fight, then let him up and walked over to Ruuqo. He had gathered the rest of the pack around him at the lookout hillock.

"What is it you have to tell us?" he asked me.

"Do you have more food from the humans?" Rissa said, her eyes sparkling. "I would be happy to have it. I'm getting too old to run after everything in the valley." She caught Ruuqo's eye as she said this and stretched her long, lean back, causing the strong muscles under her snow-white fur to ripple, making it clear that she was anything but old. Her sore ribs were certainly not troubling her today. Ruuqo watched in appreciation.

He shook himself, avoiding Rissa's merry gaze, a smile stretching the corners of his mouth. "Yes," he said, "we oldsters mustn't waste all our energy running after prey." Marra and I exchanged embarrassed glances.

"You'd think they'd have other things on their minds right now," Marra muttered.

Rissa gave Ruuqo one more look out of the corner of her eye. I watched them, too embarrassed to interrupt. Ruuqo caught me staring at them and looked down his muzzle at me. "You had a reason for bringing us together?"

The rest of the pack looked at me expectantly. Ázzuen dashed into the clearing, his fur still wet from the river. He looked around the gathering place, greeted the pack, then flopped down on the ground, his ears twitching in curiosity.

I thought carefully about what to say. If our plan were to work, we would need Ruuqo and Rissa's support and the support of the entire Swift River pack. Getting them to allow humans into the gathering place was only the beginning. The entire pack would need to hunt with the humans and share even more food with them than we already had. We would have to get other packs to join us. We would need to trust them as we would another wolf. I took a deep breath.

"She wants to bring the humans here, to our homesite," Unnan said. "She thinks it's a good idea to show them where we rest so they can kill us in our sleep. Next, she'll show them our den sites."

"Is this true?" Ruuqo demanded, his good mood gone. "You want to bring the humans here?"

"Just two of them. TaLi and her grandmother, NiaLi."

Quickly I explained about Milsindra and the council, and why I thought we needed to do more than just live with the humans. Minn and Unnan laughed outright, as I had expected the Greatwolves would, but Ruuqo and Rissa did not.

"You think this is a good idea, elderwolf?" Ruuqo asked Trevegg.

"I think it's a necessity," Trevegg said. "The Greatwolves truly believe that Kaala might be the wolf of legend. Whether she is or is not doesn't matter. We have to make the council believe that her actions are for the good of wolfkind."

My fur prickled along my back. It was one thing to talk

about being the savior or destroyer with NiaLi or the Great-wolves. With my pack it just seemed silly. I tried to make myself as small as I could.

"Werrna?" Ruuqo asked his secondwolf. Werrna had been a warrior before joining Swift River, and Ruuqo and Rissa depended on her to plan strategies for battles and for evaluating any new undertakings. She was cautious and hesitant to try anything new. I was certain she would say no.

She shifted her weight from one leg to the other, a grimace on her scarred face. "It's risky," she said. "If we allow the humans here, they could come to kill us in our sleep. They could bring more of their kind and take Fallen Tree from us with their sharpsticks and their tools." She said the human words as if they were distasteful. "But it is a risk I am willing to take. Doing nothing is just as dangerous."

"I agree," Ruuqo said. "We will allow them to come this one time, and then decide if it's safe to bring them again."

I blinked in amazement. I couldn't believe how quickly Ruuqo had accepted our plan. Uncertainty began to gnaw at my confidence. What if I was wrong and was leading my pack to disaster? I caught Ázzuen's eye. He was the smartest wolf I knew. If he thought it was a good idea, it couldn't be all that foolish.

A disbelieving growl came from the direction of the fallen spruce.

Unnan was staring at the leaderwolves, his face contorted with disgust. "It's wrong," he spluttered. "It's unnatural. We may as well tell them where our dens are, so they can kill our pups when they come. Or show them all our caches, so we'll starve. They've done it before. Killed whole packs. Pirra of Wind Lake told me."

I wasn't the only one staring at Unnan in shock. He was the lowest-ranking wolf in the pack. It was unthinkable for him to speak to Ruuqo and Rissa in such a way.

"That is enough, youngwolf," Rissa chided. "Some risks must be taken."

"We're to be the humans' strecks then?" he demanded. "It's repulsive."

"Enough, Unnan." Ruuqo's voice sank into a growl. "You are a member of the Swift River and you will follow the will of the pack. If you do not wish to do so, you can leave now."

Unnan looked as if he would say more but stopped himself.

"Kaala," Rissa said, "when will you bring your humans?"

I dragged my gaze away from Unnan. "They're waiting for us now," I said. "Not far away. I can bring them when we're ready."

Her eyes widened in surprise. "Now?" she said. "You're not wasting any time, youngwolf." She cocked her head, considering. "Very well," she said. "We will meet these humans of yours."

The pack was silent as I led TaLi and NiaLi into Fallen Tree. NiaLi stood at my left flank, TaLi at my right as we walked slowly through the wide gap between the oak trees. The two humans stopped, then waited politely for the leaderwolves to invite them into the gathering place.

Ruuqo and Rissa stood, but the rest of the pack sat or lay flat so as not to intimidate the humans. I realized belatedly that I hadn't told the humans how to greet the leaderwolves. I needn't have worried. NiaLi was as gracious as any visiting wolf. Clutching her walking stick in one hand and my fur in the other, she lowered herself to her haunches. TaLi, following her example, flopped down on my other side, making a cloud of dust rise up around her.

Ruuqo and Rissa started forward, then stopped, staring at me. I looked back, not understanding what they wanted me to do. A look of annoyance flashed across Ruuqo's face, but Rissa laughed.

"You can stand aside, Kaala," she said. "We won't hurt them." I realized I had taken up a guard stance in front of the two humans. Abashed, I stepped away. I was lucky that Rissa was amused. It could have been seen as disloyal to the pack to stand with humans against them. I licked Rissa's muzzle in apology, then, ignoring Unnan's outraged growl, walked over to the flat sunning rock. Marra and Ázzuen were waiting there for me. We had agreed that we would let the other wolves of the pack examine the humans.

It was Rissa who greeted the humans first. She walked calmly to where NiaLi crouched and stopped half a wolf-length away. "Welcome to Swift River pack," she said formally. "You are welcome here and will be safe." She took a few steps forward and sniffed NiaLi.

"Thank you," NiaLi said, just as formally. "I am grateful for your welcome and will treat your home with respect."

Rissa's ears shot up in surprise. I had told her that NiaLi could understand our language and would reply to us in her own, but it must have been a shock to hear the old human answer.

Ruuqo came forward then, sniffing NiaLi first and then TaLi.

TaLi smiled. "Hello, wolf," she said, her natural friendliness winning out over her fear. She held out her hand to him. Startled, Ruuqo stepped back, then jutted his head forward. To my surprise, he licked TaLi's outstretched hand, then her face. TaLi laughed. I felt my mouth drop open. Ruuqo hated the humans.

Rissa whuffed softly, and stepped aside. It was the signal for the rest of the pack to greet the humans. Marra and Ázzuen shot from my side like rabbits running for the shelter of a warren. Werrna and Minn started forward more slowly, then trotted to the humans with an impatience that surprised me. They had both so often spoken of the humans with contempt, but now there was no mistaking the eagerness in their gaits. Soon the humans were surrounded by wolves. Only Unnan hung back, watching in disgust from a depression by the fallen spruce. My packmates were careful with NiaLi, understanding that she was an elder and frail, gently mouthing her hair and the skins she wore for warmth. They were not as careful with TaLi. Marra and Ázzuen were always exuberant around her, but Minn and Werrna were fascinated. Werrna kept sniffing and sniffing at the girl and poking her nose at TaLi's face while Minn pawed at the girl's long skinny legs. TaLi did her best to stay sitting upright, but when Minn placed his paws on her shoulders just as Werrna poked at her with her muzzle, the girl toppled over onto her back.

"Enough!" Rissa laughed. "Stop behaving like unruly ravens. Treat her as you would a pup."

Minn placed a paw on the girl's chest. Werrna licked her once more, as if tasting her. Then they both stepped aside.

"She's a big pup," Werrna muttered.

As the wolves moved away from the two humans, NiaLi nodded to TaLi. The girl scrambled to her feet and darted into the woods. She returned, holding one of the humans' large preyskin sacks. She handed it to NiaLi. The old woman reached into it, pulling out several large pieces of firemeat. She set them down in front of her. Then, leaning on her walking stick and on TaLi, she stood.

"I thank you all for inviting us into your home. I hope you will allow us to return again." She looked around Fallen Tree and smiled. Then she took TaLi by the hand, and the two humans walked back into the woods.

The firemeat was gone before the human footsteps had faded. Ruuqo, Rissa, Werrna, and Trevegg bolted it down before any of the rest of us could get near it.

"They're more courteous than I would have expected," Ruuqo said, licking his chops.

I forgot the firemeat. I could tell my packmates liked the humans. Ruuqo caught me watching him. "It's too early to tell if we can trust them," he said, "but it is not out of the question. They are welcome to return."

"Never thought I'd hear Ruuqo say that," Marra whispered to me.

My tail lifted and began to wave. The humans had come to my pack and my pack had liked them. Even Ruuqo and Werrna had liked them. Two moons ago I wouldn't have believed it possible. I could get my humans and my pack to join together. I knew it as well as I knew my own paws.

Trevegg, Ázzuen, and I followed the humans' trail out of the gathering place to find them waiting for us in the poplar grove. NiaLi sat on the ground, but TaLi stood, balancing one-legged on a log. BreLan sat on the log, looking up at her. Ázzuen hurled himself at his human, standing on his back legs to lick the boy's face over and over again. TaLi whooped and leapt upon me, wrapping her arms around my ribs and pulling me to the ground.

"We did it, Silvermoon!" she bellowed. I rolled away from her, butted her with my head, then pounced on her. We wrestled in the dirt. Trevegg circled us, barking excitedly. I allowed TaLi to pin me so she wouldn't get discouraged, then threw her off me and stood over her. When she started to get up, I tripped her, and she rolled head over feet to land on her rump. As NiaLi and BreLan laughed at her, TaLi brushed dirt and leaves from her clothing. BreLan pushed Ázzuen away and rolled to his feet. He loped to TaLi and helped her up. Ázzuen and I took one look at each other and ran at their legs, tripping them up again.

"Enough, now, all of you," NiaLi said, still laughing. "There is something we must do. TaLi, come here."

The girl scrambled up from the ground and went to her. I followed, pressing up against TaLi's leg.

"You cannot truly be krianan until you have completed your training and initiation and been accepted by at least five elders," NiaLi said. "But you have completed your first step on your journey—you have found your wolf companion," she smiled at me, "and have begun to work with her to preserve the Balance. It's time for you to commit yourself to the role of krianan. Are you ready to do so?"

BreLan got to his feet and came to stand on the other side of TaLi, not quite touching her. Ázzuen ran to join him, clearly not wanting to let his human get too far away from him. TaLi blinked at the old woman and swallowed several times.

"Yes," she said at last, "I'm ready."

"It would be better to wait until the next Speaking to do this," NiaLi murmured to herself, "but there is no way to tell if there will be another Speaking, and we cannot wait."

From beneath the many layers of skins she wore for warmth, NiaLi pulled the long, sharp tooth of a long-fang lion embedded in a small piece of alder wood. It hung around her neck from a woven strap of reeds. I remembered that she had used it to call together the Greatwolves and humans at the Speaking many moons before. It was the sign of her status as krianan. She took it from around her neck and placed it over TaLi's head. It hung down past the girl's chest. Trevegg walked over to sniff at it, then sat beside NiaLi.

"TaLi of the Lin tribe," the old woman said, "I pass to you the responsibilities and privileges of a krianan of Lin. It is your task to ensure that those you serve honor the Balance, that they do not kill too much prey, nor strip bare the forests or the plains. As krianan it will be your responsibility to ensure that those under your protection do not forget that they are creatures of the world of nature, and that their pride does not overcome this knowledge. It is your duty to keep forever the promise the krianans have made to cherish and protect the world that gives us nourishment, shelter, and life itself. If you accept this task, you will not be able to change your mind. It becomes more important than your life, more important than any man you take as mate or children you may bear. You will defend the Balance until your death. If the Lin tribe ceases to exist, you do not cease to be krianan. Wherever you go it is your sacred task. Do you accept?"

TaLi straightened, every muscle in her body taut with determination. "I do accept it."

The old woman smiled. "Good," she said. She took TaLi's face in both of her hands and pressed her lips to TaLi's forehead then looked in the girl's face for a long time. "Once all of this is over, we will go outside the valley to the other elder krianans, and you can begin your initiation."

I almost yelped aloud. As soon as NiaLi had said TaLi was taking over as krianan, I had begun to worry. If she was the Lin tribe's krianan, it would mean staying in the valley, and I meant to take her with me when I left. I don't know what expression was on my face, but NiaLi looked at me in concern.

"I will not take her from you for long, Silvermoon. It is less than a moon's journey. Or you may come with us, if the krianan wolves allow it."

"I want to come with you!" I blurted out. I told her what I had not been able to tell her with the Greatwolves around— about my mother and how I meant to find her.

"I didn't know Neesa," NiaLi said, "but I will be glad to meet her."

I felt as if a huge weight had been lifted from me. I had wondered how to get TaLi from the valley. BreLan and MikLan would follow where the girl went. I looked around BreLan and TaLi to catch Ázzuen's eye. He opened his mouth in a grin.

But NiaLi wasn't finished. "As for now, the krianans outside the valley will need to know what we are trying here, and neither TaLi nor I can go to them. BreLan, you will take them news of how things have changed, and prepare them for our arrival. If we succeed here, we will follow at the rise of the Warming Moon."

"Warming Moon" was the human's name for the Denning Moon.

Next to me, TaLi stiffened.

"I can't go," BreLan protested. "Not when TaLi needs me. HuLin and RinaLi are going to try to give her to the Rian tribe. TaLi says they've already invited DavRian to stay with them. They haven't invited me." There was no mistaking the anxiety in his voice. "I serve you, NiaLi," he said respectfully, "but TaLi is mine to protect."

"You serve the krianans, BreLan, not any one person," NiaLi said. "I have just told TaLi of her responsibilities. Have you forgotten yours?"

BreLan looked down at his feet.

"It's all right, BreLan," TaLi said. "It won't be for long, and I can handle HuLin."

"That's what I'm worried about," he said, but he smiled. "You have to promise me not to be reckless, TaLi. You have to promise me not to make him angry. Wait until I get back to do anything that challenges him."

"I will," she said.

BreLan crouched down and looked me in the eyes.

"And you have to take care of her while I'm gone, Silvermoon. You have to."

"I promise," I said, touching my nose to the palm of his hand. He couldn't understand my words, but he knew enough about us to know what I meant.

He stood and pulled TaLi to him, burying his face in her headfur.

"Listen for a moment, TaLi," NiaLi said, "then I will leave you to say your good-byes."

The girl turned in BreLan's arms to look at NiaLi.

"You will have to prove yourself," the old woman said.

"We do not have witnesses to your new status, and the false krianans will do everything they can to hinder you. But you are a krianan nonetheless." The old woman looked down at the three of us. "And you must help her, my friends," she said. "If she can convince the tribe that you hunt at her will, they will value her more."

"We will," I said.

"I know you will," she said. Leaning on her stick, she got to her feet and walked slowly to the edge of the poplar grove. She looked at the two young humans and at us, then walked into the woods toward her shelter. Taking the hint, Ázzuen, Trevegg, and I left as well.

We were planning to return to the human homesite, but we had barely left the poplar grove when I heard scuffling pawsteps and smelled Unnan. I didn't think he'd be stupid enough to try to attack me with Ázzuen and Trevegg there, so I wasn't too concerned. He stopped when he reached us.

"I'm leaving," Unnan said. "I won't be part of a packful of human lovers. I've been invited to join Wind Lake, and Ruuqo and Rissa have given me permission to do so."

"That is not an easy decision to revoke, youngwolf," Trevegg said.

Unnan's tail drooped just a little.

"But perhaps it's for the best," the oldwolf said, looking at me and at Ázzuen. "I know you have not often felt welcome here, and every youngwolf must find his own path. If yours is not with Swift River, so be it."

I didn't say anything. I wasn't going to pretend I was sorry to see Unnan go.

Trevegg touched his nose to Unnan's face.

"Go in health, and honor the Swift River pack."

Unnan touched Trevegg lightly on the nose, then turned his tail to Ázzuen and to me, and walked away.

"The gathering places will smell better from now on," Ázzuen said after a moment.

"And the prey won't hear us coming from forty wolf-lengths away." I laughed.

"That is more than enough," Trevegg said. "If you wish to be a leaderwolf someday, Kaala, you had better learn how to get along with wolves you don't like. Unnan is an adequate hunter and would have helped us feed new pups. You never know which wolves will serve you well. I know for a fact that Werrna dislikes you, but she will stand up for your ideas when she believes in them."

I lowered my tail to show him respect, but I couldn't disguise my glee at Unnan's departure. I was tired of his spying and his nastiness.

Trevegg watched me for a moment and rumbled a quiet growl.

"Frandra and Jandru will be waiting to hear what has happened," he said. "I will meet you back at the human homesite. Think about what I've said, Kaala."

As soon as the oldwolf was out of hearing range, Ázzuen slammed into me. "The pack is better off without Unnan, Kaala," he said. "Now we don't have to worry about him all the time."

I was about to answer when Ázzuen nudged my shoulder.

"Look," he said. I followed his gaze. There, in a soft patch of mud, was a large paw print like the one we had seen after we gave the humans the walking bird. We found two more nearby. They smelled of Milsindra and of Kivdru. This time, they hadn't bothered to hide their scents.

"They're still watching us," Ázzuen said.

"Good," I said. "They can see how well things are going. We'll bring the whole pack with us to the next hunt, and they can watch all they like." I started to walk away, then stopped. I returned to the paw prints. I squatted over one of them and left a pile of dung atop it. Ázzuen's eyes were wide in his face.

"Let them watch that," I said, and stalked off to the human homesite.

For nearly a quarter moon, Trevegg, Ázzuen, and I stayed with the humans, hunting with them and sleeping by their fires. We had two more successful hunts, though neither was as spectacular as the hunt at Oldwoods. TaLi and NiaLi came once more to Fallen Tree, this time bringing MikLan with them. The boy's infectious good humor made even Werrna laugh. DavRian came to the Lin tribe almost every day, but returned each night to his own tribe, and TaLi seemed less and less worried about him. The humans grew used to seeing us in their homesite and gave us meat as if we were their packmates.

Then, five days after NiaLi and TaLi first came to Fallen Tree, a wrongness in the air awoke me—a feeling of dread that yanked me from my dreams and drew a whimper from my throat. It was not quite the middle of the day, the best sleeping time, and I had no idea what had woken me, had pulled such panic from deep within me, but I knew that something was terribly amiss.

My whimper had awoken both Ázzuen and Trevegg.

"Something's wrong," I whispered when Trevegg cracked open an eye.

The graying of his muzzle had reached the fur around his eyes, and he looked more like an oldwolf than ever. I felt guilty about waking him. He blinked sleepily at me for a moment and yawned. Then his eyes widened and he sniffed the air. He stood and sniffed again, turning in a tight circle three times to catch the complexities of the scents around us. Then he whined. I'd never heard Trevegg whine. Without even stopping to stretch the sleep stiffness from his joints, he ran from one end of the human homesite to the other, nose high in the air, then snuffling close to the ground. Then he dashed into the surrounding woods.

"What's he doing?" Ázzuen asked, still half asleep.

Trevegg bolted back into the homesite, moving more quickly than I'd ever seen him move.

"We have to go," he said. "We have to warn the pack. We have to find Jandru and Frandra." Trevegg was the calmest wolf I knew, but I couldn't miss the urgency in his voice. He turned once, and then again, his nose held high.

"Why?" I said. "We can't just leave. The humans are just starting to trust us. We have to stay with them if we're going to keep the peace."

"There will be no peace. If it is as bad as I think it is, it will not be a question of if we go to war with the humans, but of when."

"Why? What's going on? Trevegg, you have to tell us."

Trevegg stopped his anxious circling. "It's the prey, Kaala. The prey is leaving the valley."

11

There are scents you never notice until they're no longer there: the aroma of fresh horse dung carried on the wind, the smell of tree bark mixed with the sweat of an aging elk, a draft of wind that tells you the deer are running three miles away. Only when the scents are gone do you realize how much they were a part of your life.

It was the absence of scent that had awoken me. As soon as Trevegg identified it, it seemed obvious. Once before, some prey had left—when the humans had killed too many of them. This was different. Too much of the prey was leaving, and if the prey left, there would be death in the valley. There would be hunger and there would be war. All the hunters in the valley—humans, wolves, rock lions, long-fangs—would do anything necessary to feed themselves and their young and would fight to the death for whatever prey was left. The peace between wolves and humans would be shattered.

For once, I didn't worry about disturbing the humans. I lifted my head and howled for Tlitoo. He would be able to find out where the prey was going, and one way or another, I would make him do so. Ravens couldn't always understand the complexities of our howls, so I just howled as loudly as I could for him to come, while Trevegg and Ázzuen stood by. One of the humans, annoyed at the noise, threw a stone at me. I ducked it and ran into the woods with Trevegg and Ázzuen.

The three of us stopped a few paces outside the humans' homesite, and I prepared to howl again. Before I had finished taking a good, deep breath, Tlitoo dropped down from the trees. Three feathers fell from his back and wings as he landed in front of me.

"There is no need to yell, wolflet," he gurgled. "I have been waiting for you to open your furry eyes and come to me. I know already about the prey." Tlitoo was calm, even more so than he had been at NiaLi's home.

"Why didn't you wake us?" I asked, exasperation rising up in me. Why did he choose now to be so composed?

"Because it would have done no good. You wish to know where the prey has gone. I do not know. I looked. I found nothing. Jlela looks still. The aurochs remain. And the elkryn. Others, too. Voles. Rabbits. The smallest of the prey. And the largest."

"Why have you stopped looking? You can't have searched the whole valley, even with Jlela helping."

"Because there is something I must tell you, wolf. It is time now for me to do so."

"Now?" Ázzuen said. "Why now, when you've been avoiding us for most of a moon?" I thought Tlitoo would peck at Ázzuen or at least screech an insult at him, but he just raised his wings a little, and then lowered them again.

"It was not time then," he said. "It is time now."

"Whatever it is you wish to tell them will have to wait, raven," Trevegg said. The oldwolf pawed at the ground. "You two need to find Frandra and Jandru," he said, jabbing his muzzle in our direction. "Now. They will know more than we do and will know how the Greatwolf council is reacting to the prey flight. I will speak to the pack. Go." He turned in a tight circle once more, then ran into the woods.

"Wolves," Tlitoo began.

"Later," I snapped. I knew that he had his own troubles, but I wasn't going to be guided by the whims of a raven.

He cocked his head, then clacked his beak twice.

"I know where the Grumpwolves are, wolflet," he said to me. "Once you have talked to them will you see what I have to show you?"

"Yes," I said. "Where are they?"

"At the circle of rocks, talking about you. They told me you are to meet them there at late-sun. They will speak to you then and you are not to be late."

We couldn't wait until late-sun. Ázzuen and I took off at a run. Tlitoo krawked loudly but didn't follow us. Curiosity about what he had to tell me prickled at the back of my mind, but it would have to wait. It felt good to run. When we traveled with the humans, we had to move at their pace. I stretched my legs and let the smells of the forest stream past my nose, the scents blending as they did only when we ran.

The shortest path to the Stone Circle took us through the center of Stone Peak territory. We usually crossed the river at the Flat Bank Crossing, which was in the lands that the Great-wolves had set aside for safe passage to and from the human homesite, but if we wanted to get to the Stone Circle quickly we would need to cross farther upstream. Without needing to discuss it, Ázzuen and I pelted toward a place at which a huge alder had fallen across the river, making for a quick crossing not far from the Stone Circle.

We reached the well-trodden path that led to the crossing. That was when we heard the crashing in the bushes behind us and smelled the unmistakable willow scent of the Stone Peak wolves. We were only three minutes from the river. We might, I thought, still have time to get to our own territory before the Stone Peaks caught up with us.

"We won't make it," Ázzuen said. "The path widens up ahead. They'll catch us there."

"We'll go around it, back into the woods." I gasped, leaping over a fallen branch. Since the Stone Peaks are bigger and heavier than we, we could best outrun them in thick under-growth and dense woods. In open spaces, their long legs gave them the advantage.

"They'll circle around and catch us," Ázzuen responded. "We have to fight them. It's only Torell and Ceela. We can knock them off balance and then run."

It was better than waiting to be caught. It had been gener-ations since a fight between Stone Peak and Swift River had resulted in the death of a wolf, but the animosity between the two packs had grown in the past years. Every year we fought over the contested territories to the north, and Torell hated that Swift River was strong enough to do so. More than that, Torell despised the humans. He considered them worse than hyenas and said that they were the reason there was not enough land for every pack in the valley to have all the territory it wanted. When he had led his pack, along with the Tree Line wolves, to try to kill the humans at autumn's end, it was the culmination of a long campaign against them. He knew Ázzuen and I helped stop him that day, and that we were the ones who brought humans and wolves together in the first place. I didn't think he would kill us if he did catch us. He wouldn't want to risk Ruuqo and Rissa taking revenge. But he could injure us, and he would certainly delay us. If we couldn't escape, we would have to fight.

I let Ázzuen take the lead. He was better than I at finding strategic hiding spots.

"Here!" he said. We had reached the widening of the path.

A willow stump stood on one side of it, at a bend in the path. I scrambled up onto the stump while Ázzuen crouched in the bushes across from it. I had time to take two quick breaths before Torell and Ceela, the Stone Peak leaderwolves, came barreling down the path.

The instant I saw Ázzuen bolt from his hiding place, I leapt. Torell whuffed in surprise as I landed atop him, but even so, he barely moved. I didn't expect that I'd be able to knock him over, but at least I thought he'd stagger. Instead, he just bent his legs a little, shifted his weight, and let me slide off his back. I landed on my side and rolled over to see Ázzuen entwined in Ceela's legs. He had been smarter than I, going for the legs. At least he had a chance to topple her that way. Ceela jumped, disentangling herself from Ázzuen, and landing just beside him. I didn't have time to see what Ázzuen did next. I lunged for Torell again, this time going for the soft part of his belly. I tried to bite at it, but he moved just the slightest bit so that my teeth came together in the air and my nose jabbed into his hard ribs. I didn't see him angle his hip until it was hitting me in the face, knocking me back to the ground. I leapt up, thinking fast. I'd won every fight I'd had with Unnan and most of the challenge fights I'd had with Ázzuen and Marra, but nothing I did to Torell seemed to work. I lunged, trying to bite at his flank, but then his flank wasn't there. Finally, in desperation, I dove for one of his rear legs and grabbed it in my teeth.

He grunted. "Oh, for the love of Indru," he growled. He twisted around and grabbed the back of my neck in his jaws, biting down with his teeth until I yelped and released his leg. Then he slammed me down onto my back and stood over me. Out of the corner of my eye, I saw Ceela pin Ázzuen on his side, pressing her forelegs into his ribs.

I looked up into Torell's scarred face, felt his warm, panting breath on my muzzle. "I am trying to avoid hurting you, pup," he said, glaring down at me. He lifted the leg I had bitten, shook it a little, and then set it back down. "Do you want to find out what is happening to the prey or not?"

I tried to keep my face from showing my confusion. I pressed my paws into Torell's chest, trying to free myself. He growled, then took my neck in his teeth again.

"Why don't you let her up, Torell?" Pell's voice was mild, but there was a challenge in it. I hadn't heard the youngwolf come upon us.

"I will gladly do so, Pell," Torell answered, "if she will promise to stop nipping at my ankles." He lowered his head so that we were muzzle to muzzle. "Are you two done showing us how poorly Ruuqo and Rissa have trained you to fight?"

I tried to think of something clever to say, some way to show him I wasn't intimidated. He waited.

"Yes," I said at last. He stepped off me and nodded to Ceela, who growled at Ázzuen once more, then released him.

Ázzuen coughed, then stood and shook himself. Pell stepped between me and Torell, glaring at his leaderwolf. He licked my neck where Torell had bitten it, then sniffed at my back where Torell had slammed it against the hard-packed dirt. Then he turned to face Torell, standing between me and the Stone Peak leaderwolf. Wolves communicate as much with body language as with words. Pell was making it clear to Torell that he would protect me.

Flustered, I stepped away from Pell. I couldn't say I minded either his touch or his defense of me, but I wasn't going to let him think I needed his help to face Torell. Still, I was disconcerted enough by his behavior to find it difficult to get my thoughts together.

Ázzuen had no such trouble.

"How do you know where the prey is?" he demanded of Torell. "How do we know this isn't a trap and that you won't take us farther into your territory, and then claim we trespassed on your lands?"

It was a good question. If we were deeper in Stone Peak territory, instead of at its border, they would be within their rights to kill us.

"Because we could have already killed you if we wanted to," Ceela muttered.

Pell growled at her, but it was Torell's lifted lip that made her lower her eyes.

"You don't have to believe us," Torell said. "Just follow us for a little while. We will walk through the thicker part of the forest so that you can escape us if you wish."

"What did you mean about the prey?" I asked, finding my voice.

"You won't believe me if I tell you," he said, looking pointedly at Ázzuen. "So I will show you. You have my word that you will be in no danger."

"I won't let anything happen to either of you," Pell said.

I thought about it. If the Stone Peaks wanted to hurt us they could. They didn't need to take us somewhere else to do it, and I wanted to see what Torell had to show us. I also didn't want them following us when we went to look for Jandru and Frandra. I looked at Ázzuen. He dipped his head slightly.

"All right," I said. "We'll go with you." I glared at Torell and kept my ears high, to show him that, although we agreed to go with him, we were not under his command.

A small smile tightened his scarred muzzle. He turned back down the path, the way he had come, and began to run, away from the river, and deep into the heart of Stone Peak territory. In spite of my anxiety over the prey leaving and my concern about being with the Stone Peaks, I took in every scent and sound that I could. Our territory was made up mostly of pine, spruce, and oaks, with some alders and poplars. The Stone Peak lands had the same dream-sage, berry bushes, and spruce as ours did, but were also thick with willow, birch, and poplar, which had lost their leaves for the winter. It made the forest brighter as the sun filtered in through the bare branches. We passed a patch of wind-sage bushes. It was the scent I most associated with Pell.

Torell set a fast, long-legged pace, and I had to sprint to

keep up with him. We didn't run one by one, as wolves often do to disguise our numbers. I figured Torell was showing off again, making it clear that he didn't care who knew where he was. He and Ceela were in the lead, and Pell, Ázzuen, and I ran after them. As we moved farther away from familiar lands and from the safety offered by our pack, I grew more uneasy. Pell noticed.

"Torell won't hurt you, Kaala," he said. "He likes you. That's why he came for you. He has no use for most of the other wolves in the valley."

Ázzuen whuffed skeptically, and I didn't know what to say, so I asked Pell something that I'd been wondering about for a long time.

"Why are there only four Stone Peak wolves?" I asked him. "How can your pack survive?"

We'd reached the bottom of a steep hill. Torell and Ceela bounded up it easily in spite of their bulk, and took off along a narrow pathway that ran along the edge of the hillside. Pell followed just as agilely but waited at the top for me and then Ázzuen to scramble after him. I noticed Ázzuen staring at Pell's injured leg and glowered at him. He ignored me and followed Pell as the youngwolf bounded along the path. Now we did have to run one behind another along the narrow ledge, which at some places dropped off into steep, dangerous cliffs and in others sloped gently down. Torell and Ceela loped ahead of us, but Pell hung back to answer me.

"There are more," he said, looking over his shoulder and paying no attention to the steep drop to his right. "We brought four more to the battle at Tall Grass. Don't you remember?" I didn't. There had been so many wolves on the plain I couldn't keep track of them. "It's supposed to be a secret," Pell said. "No one outside Stone Peak is supposed to know about them."

"Where are they?"

"In hiding," he said. "In case something happens to us."

That seemed excessively cautious to me. The Stone Peaks were strange wolves. "Why did you tell me?" I asked him.

"I didn't want to keep any secrets from you." He stopped and touched his cool, moist nose to my muzzle.

My breath, already short from our run, caught in my chest. Ázzuen stopped just behind us and growled. Pell looked down at him, pulled his lips back just a little, and trotted off.

"We were just talking," I said to Ázzuen.

"I heard," he said, looking at me as if I had just given good prey to a rival pack. "Are you going to just stand there?"

Pell had run ahead of us and had nearly caught up with Torell and Ceela. I didn't answer Ázzuen but took off at a run after the Stone Peaks. I had gone about twenty paces when I realized Ázzuen was not behind me. I turned back to see him peering over the edge of the path.

"Kaala, come look at this," he said.

Exasperated, I ran back to him. The Stone Peaks were getting ahead of us and he was staring at something that was probably completely unimportant.

"What is it?" I said. He was leaning precariously over the ledge. I stood next to him and looked down. All I saw was a gentle slope covered with dry bushes, rocks, and stunted trees.

"What?" I demanded. "I don't see anything."

I heard the shifting of paws on soft dirt, and then Ázzuen shoved me hard from behind. I tumbled down the hill with a great crashing of bushes. The slope was gentle and I landed unhurt in a clump of half-dead berry bushes.

Ázzuen yelped a cry for help, even though he could see perfectly well I was fine.

"Kaala?" Pell, running ahead with his leaderwolves, could still hear Ázzuen's call. I couldn't miss the panic in the Stone Peak wolf's voice. I was still trapped in the prickly branches of the berry bush but could see Pell race around a bend in the path. He leapt over a large boulder, and ran fast, almost as fast as Marra did, then pelted down the hill to me. By the time he had reached me, I had managed to disentangle myself.

"Are you all right?" he asked.

"I'm fine," I said. *Except for the fact that Ázzuen just pushed me down a hill . . .*

I allowed Pell to lead me back up to the path.

Ázzuen was waiting for us, a smug expression on his face. "Your leg doesn't seem to bother you much," he said to Pell. "I guess you won't need help hunting after all."

Pell narrowed his eyes at Ázzuen. "No," he said, "I don't suppose I will." He looked like he was going to say more but just whuffed in annoyance and ran after his leaderwolves. Astounded, I stared at Ázzuen. He had pushed me down a hill just to show that Pell wasn't as injured as he pretended to be.

"Are you coming?" he said to me. He clambered over a low boulder and ran after the Stone Peak wolves.

There was nothing for me to do but follow. And to think about the fact that Pell had been using his injury to gain our sympathy. *My* sympathy.

We ran far to the east, toward the tall mountains that sheltered our valley. I had never been so close to them, and when we reached the top of a small hill, I stopped to look at them. Yllin would be outside the valley by now with Demmen. My mother was out there somewhere, too, waiting for me. *I could just run. I could run until I reached the mountains and beyond.*

"We're almost there," Torell said. "It would be best not to stop."

I shook off my thoughts and realized I had been standing still for several moments. Torell was watching me, impatience clear on his face and Ceela's. Ázzuen was looking at me with concern. I couldn't read the expression on Pell's face.

"Sorry," I said.

"Let's go," Ceela said, annoyed. She took the lead, loping down the hill.

We ran for another five minutes until we reached the border of Stone Peak lands, where their realm gave way to Tree Line territory. We crested a cypress-covered hill and hid ourselves among the trees. Our hill was taller than the ones around it, and we could see all the way to the mountains.

"There," Torell said, pointing with his muzzle.

In the distance, wolves chased a herd of horses. Something about the hunt looked wrong. The horses seemed much smaller than they should. Then I realized that it wasn't the horses who were small, but rather the wolves who were large. It was a Greatwolf hunt. I held my breath, waiting for the Greatwolves to notice us, but they were several hundreds of wolflengths away and upwind. I saw that none of the Stone Peaks seemed concerned, and made myself relax.

I pressed forward to the very edge of the trees. I'd never seen the Greatwolves hunt, for they always did so in secret.

There were stories that they sat in the grass and waited until prey came by, then killed at once, with one leap, but it wasn't true. They were hunting like ordinary wolves. They had killed five horses already, and these were being guarded by a lone Greatwolf. One horse for each wolf, I thought in amazement. The Greatwolves did not stop to eat but continued to run the prey. Four Greatwolves chased a large herd made up of close to a hundred horses. I expected them to separate out some of the horses the way we would, but they didn't. They kept chasing the entire herd.

"They can't kill them all," Ázzuen whispered. "What are they doing?"

I was watching the hunt, but I knew that Ázzuen's ears would be twitching in curiosity. The Greatwolves continued to pursue the herd. When some horses broke off, the wolves did not try to separate out the weakest of them and bring it down, as any sensible wolf would. Instead, they herded the stray horses back to the others. When the entire herd tried to bolt toward a downslope that led to a marsh, the Greatwolves wouldn't let them, even though if the horses had entered the mire they would have been easier prey. Every time the horses deviated from the path they were on, the Greatwolves brought them back, chasing them toward a cleft in the low hills that led to the mountains.

"They're driving them away," I said, turning to Torell. "They're chasing them out of the valley!"

Torell bared his teeth in what could have been either a snarl or a grim smile. His face was so ravaged by scars that part of his mouth was permanently pulled back, giving him the look of a grimace even when he had none.

"The horses, the small elk, the snow deer, the forest deer, the swamp pigs," he said. "All of the smaller of the large prey. Yet the aurochs and the elkryn remain in the valley. What do you think those prey that remain have in common?"

"They're all big," I said. "So what?"

"The Greatwolves hunt them," Ázzuen answered, looking at Torell.

"Yes," the Stone Peak leader said. "They are the preferred prey of Greatwolves, and difficult and dangerous for ordinary wolves, for long-fangs and rock lions, and even for your humans, to catch."

"They're making our prey leave on purpose?" I asked, stunned by the implications of what Torell was saying.

"So we'll fail," Ázzuen said with certainty. "So that humans and wolves will fight."

"I know of the task the Greatwolves have set you," Torell said. "They do not, it appears, have any intention of letting you succeed."

Without another word, he and Ceela turned around and trotted down the hill back toward their own territory. Pell, Ázzuen, and I stayed for a moment on the hillside.

"Milsindra and Kivdru," I said. "It has to be them."

"We have seen up to ten Greatwolves chasing away prey," Pell said.

I blinked at that. It was half the council.

"Torell has more to tell you, if you'll come," Pell said.

It occurred to me then that we could run away, now that Torell and Ceela were gone. I needed to talk to Frandra and Jandru, and to tell the pack what was happening, and just because Torell had shown us the prey drive didn't mean we could trust him. The hatred between Swift River and Stone Peak went too far back to be so lightly dismissed.

"You can rely on Torell's word, Kaala," Pell said, reading my expression. "He takes his honor seriously. He wouldn't hurt you after promising not to. It would be worse to him than killing a packmate."

Ázzuen was trying to catch my eye. Pell noticed.

"The two of you can discuss it," he said. "We have a small gathering place behind the alder grove to your left. We'll be there for another ten minutes." He bent his head to touch my cheek lightly with his muzzle, then limped down the hill after his packmates. Halfway to the alder grove he seemed to remember that Ázzuen had just shown how little his leg hindered him, and he sprinted the rest of the way to the trees.

"We need all the information we can get," I said to Ázzuen.

"I know," he said. "Just don't be so quick to trust Pell. He pretended to be more injured than he is so you'd feel sorry for him. Because he likes you."

I had no answer for *that*. And I did find myself wanting to like the Stone Peak youngwolf. But Ázzuen didn't need to know that. "We need Marra," I said. "She would know what Torell was really up to."

"We can't howl for her," Ázzuen said. "It'll tell every wolf in the valley where we are."

I looked up, hoping to find Tlitoo nearby. Of course, when I wanted him, he was nowhere to be found. "We'll find out what Torell has to say," I said.

"All right," Ázzuen said, agreeing much more quickly than I had expected. I should have known, though. Anytime there was something new to learn or a mystery to solve he would want to be there. With the feeling I was diving once again into a river I could not swim, I ran down the hillside, following the paw prints made by Pell's uneven gait.

If someone had told me that I would walk willingly into a Stone Peak gathering place, I would have thought they had been sitting too long near a burning dream-sage bush. I don't know what I expected—that it would be guarded by twenty wolves, or that it would be barren and thus more suitable for fighting—but it was just an ordinary, fairly small gathering place smelling of alder, sage, and mint. The Stone Peaks couldn't have been there more than a few minutes, but already they were relaxed, lying on the moist earth as if readying themselves for a midday sleep. Ázzuen and I stopped at the edge of the gathering place, waiting for Torell or Ceela to invite us in. Torell and Pell both rose, though Ceela did not, and Torell dipped his head to us, granting us permission to enter.

"You are welcome here," Torell said formally as Ceela inclined her head the slightest bit. "I am glad you decided to join us."

"As am I," Pell said.

Ázzuen and I quickly greeted all three wolves, then stepped back to the edge of the gathering place. Before Pell or Torell could say anything else, I spoke.

"Why are you helping us?" I asked. "You hate the humans. I would think you want us to fail."

Torell regarded me. "Ordinarily, youngwolf, I would, and I

would do everything in my power to ensure that you did fail, even if it meant my own death at the Greatwolves' teeth. I have no love of the humans, nor of any wolf who consorts with them. I do not really think you are drelshik; that is nonsense. I do think that the way you treat the humans as if they are packmates is repulsive. But I am not inflexible, and I will do what I must to protect my pack. And I would like your help." He laughed at the startled expression on my face, then sobered. "I have been watching you since you were a small-pup, as has every wolf in the valley."

I shifted uncomfortably. It did seem that every wolf in the valley knew things about me.

Torell ignored my unease. "Ruuqo has not allowed you to see the power that you have, Kaala. You and your friends."

I couldn't help but snort at that.

Torell twitched an ear.

"Why do you think the Greatwolves fight over you, of all the wolves in the valley?" he asked.

"Because of my mixed blood and the mark on my chest," I said. "The Greatwolves think I'm the wolf of legend, and that what I do can either save wolfkind or anger the Ancients so much that they'll destroy us."

"The Ancients." Ceela sneered. "The Ancients are no more than tales made up to fool gullible wolves who can't think for themselves. You may as well say an alder tree will get angry and push you into the river."

Shocked, I stared at Ceela, wondering if she could be serious.

"Never mind," Torell said. "It doesn't matter what you or I think of the Ancients. What does matter is that the Greatwolves are hiding something, and we need your help to find out what it is. They watch me too closely, and they trust you. They talk to you. They might let you near enough to find their secret cache and find what they hide there."

I was still too bewildered to answer.

"And why should we help you?" Ázzuen said when I remained silent. "We would have found out about the Greatwolves and the prey eventually; the ravens would have told us. What good does it do us to help you?"

Ceela barked a laugh, just barely raising her head from her paws. "Well, for one thing, we can teach you how to fight. I don't know what Ruuqo and Rissa were thinking, letting you run alone with no fighting skills."

I glared at her and began to back out of their gathering place. I didn't need to be insulted, and I didn't need any information the Stone Peaks might see fit to share with me. I felt Ázzuen at my side.

Pell darted forward. "It's important, Kaala," he said, glowering at Ceela. "Whatever the Greatwolves are hiding affects you and your task. We can help you find out what you need to do to succeed. Even if the prey leaves." He rested his head on my neck, leaving it there longer than was really necessary to apologize for Ceela's rudeness. "We'll help you find ways to hunt with the humans even with so much of the prey gone."

"Thanks," Ázzuen said, "but we'll find out what we need to know on our own. And we don't need your help with the humans."

I wavered. I could feel Torell's gaze upon me. Against my better judgment, I met his eyes.

"What will you do if you do succeed, Kaala," he asked, "if you get your humans to accept you for a year?"

I was going to leave the valley to find my mother, but there was no way I was going to tell Torell that. I didn't answer. He tried again.

"Is it true that the only way you've managed to get the humans to accept you so far is to abase yourself, to make yourself submissive to them?"

"So?" I said. "It worked."

"What is the reason that wolves and humans must be together?" he asked. "Do you know?"

"Of course I know. Wolves have to be with humans so that the humans don't lose touch with nature."

"If the humans don't understand that they are part of the natural world," Ázzuen added, "they'll just destroy it. It's the promise of the Wide Valley wolves."

"And if you are curl-tails to the humans, how will you do that?" Torell asked. "You will become part of their unnatural world; they will not be part of ours."

I said nothing. This was the heart of the paradox. We had to be with the humans, and yet whenever wolves and humans were together, the humans tried to enslave the wolves, and the wolves fought back. It was why Milsindra was so certain we would fail. I hadn't let myself think of it. I would gain the humans' trust and then worry about it.

Torell waited for me to answer. When I didn't, he spoke again. "Tell me, then, why do you abide by the will of the Greatwolves?"

I laughed at that. "Because they'll kill us if we don't."

"I can kill you, yet you defy me," Torell said. "There are

twenty-one Greatwolves in the valley. If every wolf rose up against them, they would rule over us no longer."

Ázzuen exhaled a long breath as the three Stone Peaks watched us.

"You accept their rule," Torell said, "because you fear them, because they are bigger and stronger and have always ruled over you." He held my gaze. "And you believe that the Greatwolves are the emissaries of the Ancients. I, however, believe none of that. I believe that the sun and the moon are just great fires in the sky and that the sky is nothing but the air that wolves and other creatures breathe. I believe that if the wolves of the Wide Valley were to come together, we could overpower the Greatwolves—rule the valley, our lives, and ourselves. And I believe that to do that, we must find out what it is the Greatwolves are hiding. I can tell that Ruuqo and Rissa have told you none of this, though I have discussed it with them. Once they almost joined me in defying Great-wolf rule, but in the end they did not. They are interested only in protecting their pack for one more season—one more generation. I think that protecting oneself at the cost of one's freedom is a fool's choice."

I could hardly breathe. I had never heard a wolf speak in such a way. I'd always thought that Torell fought for the sake of fighting, that he made trouble because he enjoyed hurting others. Ruuqo always said it was because Torell wanted attention and power, and I had always assumed it to be true. Now I didn't know what to think. I turned to Ázzuen, expecting to see the usual skepticism on his face, but he was watching Torell with an intensity that made me look away.

Pell was watching me, his eyes alight. "There are places,

Kaala, where the lives of wolves are their own to live, where wolves are not governed by the whims of a few erratic Greatwolves. Places where you can choose to have pups when you like and can move freely across the land."

The way he looked at me when he mentioned having pups made the fur around my ears twitch.

"That won't do us any good if we starve to death," Ázzuen said practically. "If the prey is gone, everyone will be too busy surviving to fight the Greatwolves, and we'll be too busy trying to keep the humans from fighting us to do anything else."

"You have to stop thinking like a curl-tail!" Pell said impatiently. "If you find out what the Greatwolves are hiding, you can find their weakness. If we know their weakness, we have a chance to defeat them, with or without the other packs."

That was assuming a lot. The Stone Peaks were strong, but the Greatwolves were so much stronger.

"And why should you starve," Torell asked, "with the aurochs and elkryn still plentiful?"

The elkryn were cousins of ordinary elk, but they were huge—well more than twice as tall as a wolf—and extremely strong. They also had giant antlers that they could use to crush any hunter who challenged them. And ever since we had fought them at the battle of Tall Grass, they had hated the Swift River wolves.

"The elkryn are difficult prey," I said, "and we don't hunt the aurochs."

"We do," Ceela said. "We always have."

I yawned. Every wolf said the Stone Peaks were crazy for hunting aurochs. The great beasts killed wolves easily and were much harder to bring down than the elkryn.

"I can teach you," Torell said. "I can teach you to hunt the aurochs, and to hunt the elkryn more successfully," he said. "I can show you how to hunt them with your humans."

"The leaving of the prey does not have to be a bad thing, Kaala," Pell said. "Your humans will be the best-fed humans in the valley. Because of you."

It was what I needed most, to have the humans value us so much that I could let other wolves take my place and leave the valley with TaLi. It was too much for me to take in. I couldn't dismiss Torell's words, or Pell's—I found myself wanting to trust Pell in particular—but I couldn't just reject everything I'd ever known about the Stone Peaks.

"What do you want us to do?" I asked. "How are we supposed to discover this cache?"

Torell seemed to accept my return to the practical. I tried to ignore Ázzuen, who was quivering with curiosity beside me.

"We have been studying the Greatwolves for many years," Torell said. "We believe we know their hiding place, but we can't go to it ourselves. The Greatwolves know we don't easily accept their rule, and they watch us closely. That's why we need you. The Greatwolves believe you'll do as they say, and they expect you to cross territories as you try to complete your task. You might be able to find out what they hide."

"So tell us where it is," Ázzuen said, still suspicious in spite of his fascination with Torell's words.

The Stone Peak leader grimaced. "I trust you no more than you trust me, youngwolf. If you were to tell your Greatwolf friends what I've told you today, I would be dead in a quarter moon's time, as would my pack. You could tell them what I have already told you, I know that, and I have trusted you not to do so. But before I tell you more, I need to know that you're not just a curl-tail who will tell everything you know the first time you are pressed. I need to know you can stand up for yourself."

It seemed everyone had a test for us. I wanted to be annoyed, but I was excited. More than ever, I wanted to thwart Milsindra. If I could hunt aurochs and elkryn with the humans, I would prove that humans and wolves made good packmates. I would teach other wolves how to hunt the large prey. If we could show that even with most of the prey leaving the valley we still succeeded with our humans, and if the council knew that we did so in spite of the fact that Milsindra had driven away the prey, she would lose and Zorindru would win. It was worth a risk.

I sighed. "We have to find Frandra and Jandru before latesun," I said, "or they'll come looking for us."

"There's no reason you should not be able to prove your courage to me and still return to your territory by then," he said. "And you may tell them of the prey drive. As you said, you would have found that out for yourselves."

Torell was being suspiciously accommodating. Stone Peak had been our rivals too long for me to trust him. I thought about what Marra would do, how she would figure out if he was trustworthy.

"If we succeed in your challenge, do we have to join you?" Ázzuen demanded before I could think of anything to say. "If we decide we don't want to help you find what the Greatwolves are hiding, will you let us leave unharmed?"

Torell and Pell just blinked at him, but Ceela laughed. "Smart little wolf," she said. "No, until you accept our help hunting the giant prey, you owe us nothing except your word that you will not reveal our plan to overthrow the Greatwolves."

"As for joining us," Torell said, "if you would like to do so, you would be welcome as Stone Peak wolves, as would your fleet-footed littermate and the oldwolf who counsels you."

I whuffed in surprise. He had certainly been watching us carefully if he knew enough to know we would want to bring Marra and Trevegg with us.

"You may as well come out," he said to one of the sage bushes that surrounded the gathering place.

Marra emerged from the bush. I had caught her scent as soon as she arrived, a few minutes before, but had hoped the Stone Peaks would not. She greeted the Stone Peak wolves, then sat calmly, her front paws together, her tail wrapped around her rump. I was glad to have her there.

I should have been afraid. I should have been worried about making it back to Jandru and Frandra by late-sun and at making any sort of pact with the Stone Peaks. Instead, I was exhilarated. Milsindra expected me to be afraid, to hide and to wait to see what she would do. Torell was offering me another way. I looked at Ázzuen out of the corner of my eye. He dipped his head. I caught Marra's eyes, and saw them alight with excitement at the challenge.

"All right," I said. "What do you want us to do?"

Torell smiled. "Come with me," he said.

12

I lay in the dirt, looking up at Torell's broad chest.

"Why do you hurl yourself at me like a berry-drunk badger?" he demanded. He stood over me, his paws planted on my chest. I had leapt at him, as I had on the path to the river, trying to knock him over. It was like trying to topple an oak tree.

Torell had decided to test us by teaching us how to fight. He'd led us deep into the woods to a small clearing hidden by thick pines and dense juniper bushes. He said that he wanted to make sure no passing Greatwolf would find us.

As soon as we arrived, he, Ceela, and Pell had huddled, whispering together. I quickly grew impatient. It was already past midday. We would have to leave soon to find the Great-wolves, and so far we had learned nothing of value. When Pell walked over to tell us that Torell wanted us to prove we could learn to fight well, I had grunted in annoyance. It seemed silly to me that a leaderwolf would want to challenge half-grown youngwolves in such a way. It seemed to verify everything Ruuqo and Rissa had said about Torell and his need to always prove his strength. I said as much to Pell.

"It may seem that way, Kaala, but it isn't," he had said. "He needs to know that you're strong enough and skilled enough to hunt aurochs without injuring yourselves or those who hunt with you. But it's more than that. Most wolves grow up learning to follow orders. If you're to challenge the Greatwolves, he needs to know you're willing to take risks. That you won't back down if it gets hard."

"I've done plenty of risky things," I said, thinking of pulling TaLi from the river, of refusing to follow Jandru and Frandra outside the valley. "It seems stupid to me. Why don't we just try hunting the aurochs with your pack?"

Pell was silent for a few moments. "Do you know how Torell got those scars on his face?"

"In some fight?"

"Stealing someone else's territory?" Ázzuen said.

"No," Pell had said, looking down his snout at Ázzuen. "He wouldn't have been so injured by an ordinary wolf."

I wanted to laugh at his arrogance, but the intensity of his gaze stopped me.

"He got them three years ago. He didn't lower his ears quickly enough to a Greatwolf, and the Greatwolf took offense. The next day, three Greatwolves came to kill Torell's pups—his first litter. Torell fought them off. Your secondwolf, Werrna, was part of Stone Peak then, and she helped him. Werrna's mate, Lann, was killed in the fighting, and she swore never to take another. The three of them stood against the Greatwolves until Zorindru came and stopped the fight. Torell vowed that he would someday live free of the rule of the Greatwolves. That's why he's so careful. The vow means everything to him. More than his own life, more even than the life of his pack. He's trusting you with that."

Now, as I lay pinned under Torell's paws and looked up at his ravaged face, I imagined what it must have been like. I'd been helpless before Milsindra, and she was only one wolf. What would it have been like to fight three Greatwolves at once? I had always assumed Torell's scars proved he was too aggressive and foolhardy to be trusted. But he was a hero.

He frowned and stepped off me, allowing me to get up.

"I weigh much more than you do," he said. "You will not overpower me. You're not strong enough."

"I'll get stronger," I said, panting as I scrabbled to my feet. My pride was hurt. A weak wolf was a useless wolf.

Tlitoo quorked from a nearby rock, watching. He had found us shortly after we arrived at the clearing, but had refused to help us fight the Stone Peaks. "I know already how to fight, wolflet," he had said.

"You'll never be stronger than an auroch," Torell said to me. I started to argue. He butted his head against me. "But that doesn't have to be a disadvantage. What does a hill dancer do when it fights?" he asked.

A hill dancer, a small, light-boned deer that came down from the mountain in the deepest of winter, was almost impossible to catch. The marrow in their bones was particularly succulent, tasting of the sweet mountain flowers they fed upon, but we almost never caught them. In addition to being quick, they're smart prey, wily and unpredictable.

"They twist around and kick you before you can get

away," Ázzuen answered, warily eyeing Pell. The Stone Peak youngwolf seemed to be enjoying throwing Ázzuen into a pile of branches and twigs over and over again.

"And what," Torell asked, keeping an eye on his young-wolf, "does a weasel do when fighting a wolf?"

"Comes up from underneath you and bites," Marra said with feeling from where she lay pinned beneath Ceela's paws.

"You've been bitten?" Pell asked her, his voice full of sympathy. I felt an unexpected growl rise in my throat and swallowed it down. Why should I care if Pell was nice to Marra?

"Yes," she said, "two moons ago. It had caught a rabbit I wanted. I tried to pin the weasel under my paws to take the rabbit from it, and it twisted around and bit my leg."

"Exactly," Torell said. "They do not try to overpower hunters much stronger than they are. They use their own strengths to win their fights. With killer prey you must do the same thing. You must think like prey and act like hunters."

I looked at Torell's thick chest and strong legs and thought about how I could be a hill dancer. It was no use. I was no prey. I looked over at Ázzuen and Marra to share my disgust, but Ázzuen's eyes were narrowed in concentration, and Marra was getting to her feet, watching Ceela carefully.

"You're fast," Ceela said to her. "Faster than any wolf I know and certainly faster than any auroch. Use it." Ceela took a stick from the twig pile and placed it between her paws. She raised her hindquarters high in the air and lowered her face to the stick. "Take this from me," she said.

Before the words left her mouth, Marra had darted forward. She ran in a circle around Ceela twice, then darted under Ceela's chest to grab the stick. Ceela tried to pounce on

Marra but succeeded only in swiping Marra's forehead with her paw.

"Like that?" Marra said, grinning around the stick and blinking a trickle of blood out of her eye.

Ázzuen walked over to her, as if to examine the stick. Then he veered suddenly to the left, catching Pell's tail in his teeth. Pell whipped around as Ázzuen leapt atop the branch pile. Torell looked expectantly at me. I saw that he had placed a stick just behind him. I thought hard. I could dive under his legs and attack on my way through. Or leap over him, though I thought he might be ready for that. Instead, I ran straight toward him. Then, at the last moment, I dodged to the right, trying to get past him. He easily knocked me aside, flipped me onto my back, and bit down gently on my neck.

"Don't commit yourself to an attack until the last instant," he said, releasing me. "You'd already decided to go to the right, so when I moved, you had no other options. You could have changed directions, backed up, or bitten my paw. You have to keep thinking as you move. Leave your options open. Try again."

An hour later, Ázzuen, Marra, and I stood, panting but triumphant in front of the Stone Peak wolves. We had all successfully gotten past each of the three Stone Peaks. Tlitoo, bored with our practice, searched for insects in the pile of branches.

"Good," Torell said. "I think that we can help each other." I was breathing too hard to answer, which was probably for the best. It seemed idiotic to me that Torell believed that being able to fight made a wolf trustworthy. Pirra, the Wind

Lake leaderwolf, was one of the Wide Valley's best fighters, and she was no more trustworthy than a hyena.

"We think that the Greatwolf cache is somewhere beyond the Western Plains, not far from where we'll take you to hunt aurochs if you would like to go," Pell said. "At the very edge of the plain there's a ridge of low hills. The land beyond the ridge is flat, and you should be able to see far beyond it. We've seen groups of Greatwolves going together over that ridge. That's where you should look."

"It is in territories the Greatwolves have claimed as their own." Ceela grinned. "Which is another reason auroch-hunting is dangerous."

"You will want some time to decide whether or not you wish to accept our offer," Torell said. "Do not take too much time. The Greatwolves are more wary of us than usual. Go meet Frandra and Jandru as you said you would, so that they will not be suspicious."

"Doing what the Greatwolves tell her to do is what would *make* them suspicious of her," Tlitoo said from his branch pile.

Something that sounded like a chuckle came from Pell's direction. When I looked at him, his eyes were half-closed, as if he were concentrating on something, but his muzzle was tight with the effort not to smile. Ázzuen and Marra laughed aloud. I glared at all of them.

"Go to your Greatwolves and your pack," Torell said to me, a slight smile on his muzzle. "Meet us at our gathering place by the prey drive in two nights' time if you decide to hunt with us and to help us find what the Greatwolves hide."

I dipped my head to him, finding myself compelled to

treat him as I would one of my own leaderwolves. "Thank you," I said. Gingerly, I held my muzzle out to him. He took it gently in his mouth, then did the same to Ázzuen and Marra. I felt myself relax at his gentle treatment of us. Marra licked me and then Ázzuen on the cheek, then set off for the Lan tribe's lands. With one last look around, I began to back out of the clearing, then stopped. Something Torell had said earlier was still bothering me.

"Ruuqo and Rissa wouldn't betray a promise. They wouldn't sacrifice their honor for their safety. They told Zorindru they would help us, and they won't go back on their word."

Torell started to say something, then stopped himself. "I hope you are right, youngwolf. In any case, if you wish to help us and, I think, yourselves and your humans, come to us two moonrises from now."

Once again, I began to back out of the clearing. I stopped, startled, when a wolf emerged from the bushes beside me. It was Arrun, Torell and Ceela's secondwolf. He was a brawny, dark-coated wolf. I had met him before and found him slow-witted and obstinate.

Torell narrowed his eyes. "Aren't you supposed to be at Hidden Grove by now?" he asked his secondwolf.

"There is something you need to see, Torell," Arrun said. "The Swift River youngwolves should see it, too."

"What is it?" Ceela demanded.

Arrun met her eyes. I had no idea what he communicated to her but she dipped her head sharply, and when the secondwolf left the clearing, she and Torell went with him.

"Will you come?" Pell asked.

Ázzuen's tail twitched eagerly. It wasn't late-sun yet. We

still might make it back in time to meet the Greatwolves. Or we might not.

"Yes," I said, and allowed him to precede us out of the clearing.

Arrun led us to the north, along the boundary of Stone Peak and Wind Lake territory. It was rocky, dusty land, with little for prey to eat. I remembered Torell once telling Ruuqo that we Swift River wolves had much of the valley's best hunting grounds. I had dismissed it as a ploy to gain more land, but I began to wonder if he had spoken the truth.

Arrun ran at a slow lope through Stone Peak lands. Although I was tired from our long run to the prey drive and Torell's fighting lessons, the muscles in my legs twitched with the longing to run faster. I still had to find Jandru and Frandra to tell them about the prey. I began to doubt the wisdom of staying so long with the Stone Peaks. Arrun kept looking over his shoulder as he ran, looking at me and at Ázzuen, as if he wished to say something to us. I'd had nothing but bad experiences with Arrun and made a point of avoiding his gaze.

Arrun stopped at a shallow pond to drink. Gratefully I lapped at the still, stale water. I much preferred the running water of the river, but I was thirsty enough to drink anything.

When we finished drinking, Arrun began to walk, his slow, almost hesitant pace making me want to growl my impatience. One look at Torell and Ceela stopped me from doing so.

"Where are you taking us, Arrun?" Pell asked, noticing my annoyance. I shot him a grateful look.

"Aspen Glen," Arrun replied, and would say nothing more. He stopped a few minutes later, at the very edge of the slender trees. He lowered his head to Ceela and Torell, and stepped aside so they could take the lead. I saw a flicker of black just above me, and looked up to see Tlitoo peering at me from one of the aspens. The two leaderwolves pushed past us and began to walk across a flat, grassy plain. Arrun and Pell followed them, and Ázzuen and I came last. Ceela's sharp intake of breath and Pell's quick, anxious look in my direction didn't prepare me for what was there.

At first, as I walked behind the Stone Peak wolves onto the plain, I didn't understand what it was I scented. I smelled Swift River wolf, but no Swift River wolf would be so far into Stone Peak territory. I took a few steps, then stopped, perplexed. Ázzuen shifted his weight uneasily from one paw to the other. Then I gave a yip of excitement as I finally realized what it was that I smelled through the confusion of grass and aspens and Stone Peak wolf. It was Yllin; she was still in the valley!

Unable to restrain myself, I squeezed past the Stone Peaks and began to run in the direction of the scent.

It took a moment to realize just what the grayish lump in the grass was. I didn't truly understand until I stood almost directly over the limp pile of fur and flesh.

Yllin had not been dead long. Her flesh was cool, but not yet stiff; the blood at her belly and chest was sticky and fresh-smelling. I stared at her. She was not the first dead wolf I had seen. Ázzuen's littermate, Reel, had looked and smelled much the same after he had been trampled to death by the horses, but I still wasn't prepared for the strangeness of the scent, the smell of Yllin but not quite Yllin. Of wolf but not wolf.

Ázzuen whimpered softly. I hadn't heard him come up behind me.

I drew closer to Yllin and saw that her belly had been torn open—a huge gaping tear that could only have been made by very large teeth. A rock lion's teeth could have made such a wound, or a bear's. But the other scent mixed with Yllin's fear and blood was the scent of the Greatwolf Milsindra.

My body seemed to understand what my brain did not and my chest grew heavy and my legs weak. It took all my strength to turn to face the Stone Peaks. They had stepped back respectfully, leaving us alone by Yllin's body.

"The Greatwolves killed her," I said. The rasp of a voice that came from my throat sounded like some other wolf. I remembered how Yllin had stood up to Milsindra at the spruce grove. Surely that couldn't be enough reason for Milsindra to kill her.

"I was on my way to the Hidden Grove Gathering Place," Arrun said, his usually surly face gentle. "She was still alive when I found her. She said that she and another wolf were leaving the valley five nights ago when they were intercepted by the Greatwolves. The Greatwolves told them it was forbidden to leave the valley, that no Wide Valley wolf would be allowed to leave for any reason. Then the Greatwolves attacked. Yllin and the other youngwolf fled. They got separated, she said, and she hid in a cave until today, when she grew too thirsty to stay hidden any longer. She was making her way back to Swift River territory when Milsindra found her and attacked. I stayed with her until she died," he said gruffly, "so she would not have to die alone."

A violent rustling shook the trees behind us. Tlitoo's shriek pierced my ears as he flew to us. He circled Yllin's body once, screeched again, and returned to his aspen, hissing.

"They told her she could go," I said in that strange, strangled voice that seemed to be the only thing that could come from my throat. "They told her she could mate outside the valley!"

"Evidently, they changed their minds," Torell said, his scarred face grim.

"But she was going back," Ázzuen said. "Why did they kill her if she was obeying them and going back home?" His voice cracked on the last word.

"To make an example of her," Ceela said. "To show other wolves in the valley what will happen if they try to leave."

I shook my head, trying to clear the mud from my thoughts. I could see Yllin running, faster than even Marra, leaping over a stream the rest of us had to wade. She wasn't even two years old. She should have led a pack someday.

I opened my throat to howl for her.

"Kaala, wait," Pell said urgently. "The Greatwolves will hear you."

"So what?" I said. I didn't care what they heard.

"*Think*, Kaala." The harshness in his voice forced his words through the thickness of my thoughts. "What do most packs do when the prey leaves?"

"Follow the prey," I said automatically. "Where the prey goes, so goes the pack." It was what every pup learned.

Then I realized what Pell was trying to tell me. The Great-wolves had forbidden any wolf from leaving the valley, then drove the prey away.

"They've trapped us." At first I didn't recognize Ázzuen's voice. I had never heard such anger and bitterness in it. "They sent the prey away and will not let any wolves leave. So we'll have to fight each other and the humans."

None of the Stone Peaks answered. If we howled for Yllin, the Greatwolves would know we had found her and it would give them the advantage.

"I will tell the others, wolf," Tlitoo said. He circled Yllin one more time and then took flight back toward Swift River territory.

"They should be the ones to sing for her anyway, Kaala," Ázzuen said.

I sat, staring at Yllin's body. Ázzuen sat at my side, not quite touching me. I couldn't make myself decide what to do next. I looked at Ázzuen, but he was still watching Yllin, as if she might suddenly get to her feet and talk to us.

"Take them back to Swift River land," Torell said at last, addressing Pell. "Keep them safe in their passage through our lands."

"I will do so, leaderwolf," Pell said formally.

"Find your Greatwolves and your pack, youngwolves," Torell said to me. "We will await your decision about what you wish to do."

Ázzuen and I each touched Yllin's cool flesh one more time, inhaling her scent so that it would always be part of who we were, and so that she would always be part of Swift River. Then we left her to the earth. Pell led us silently through Stone Peak territories. I was grateful to him for not trying to talk to me and not trying to get me to talk to him. As soon as we could hear the river that divided our lands, he touched his nose to my face, dipped his head to Ázzuen, and left us.

13

We didn't have to search for Frandra and Jandru. They were waiting for us at the riverbank. I stopped a few wolflengths from them, not knowing where to begin, what to tell them first, but as soon as they saw us emerge from the woods, Jandru spoke.

"We know about the prey, youngwolf," he said. "And the raven has told us about your packmate."

Tlitoo balanced on a very small rock in the middle of the river, watching the water intently. The ancient raven stood on a larger rock next to him. I was glad I wouldn't have to say aloud that Yllin was dead; it made it too real.

"What are you going to tell the council?" I asked. Amid my grief I felt the smallest measure of relief. The council would have to act against Milsindra now. She was tampering with the very Balance.

Frandra shook river water from her shaggy coat. They

must have swum across to the Stone Peak side of the river just before we arrived at the riverbank.

"The council won't punish Milsindra for disciplining a wolf trying to leave the valley when forbidden to do so," she said. "As for the prey, the council, for now, is choosing to do nothing. We will, when the time is right, try to change their minds." She lowered her muzzle just a little. "I am sorry for the loss of your packmate."

She didn't sound sorry. She sounded like Yllin was just one more part of the Greatwolves' power struggle.

"Why aren't they doing anything?"

"That isn't your concern," Frandra snapped. "You will go back to your humans and let us deal with the council."

I didn't think. I just launched myself at her, slamming into her hard, muscular chest. I fell back on the muddy riverbank and leapt again, forgetting everything Torell had taught me about fighting. Frandra snapped her teeth together, seizing my neck fur. She shook me once, then dropped me on the ground. When I got dizzily to my feet, Ázzuen was standing between me and the Greatwolves and Tlitoo was soaring across the river. He didn't touch the Greatwolves, but he hovered above them for a moment, talons extended. The ancient raven screeched at him, and Tlitoo settled next to Ázzuen and began jabbing at nonexistent bugs in the river mud.

"I will allow you that, youngwolf," Frandra said, her voice flat with anger. "I understand you are grieving. But do not try my patience."

I was shaking. With fear. With anger and sorrow. With

frustration at my inability to get the Greatwolves to avenge Yllin's death, or even to admit it was wrong. I was more grateful than I could express when Ázzuen spoke.

"Why can't you get the council to do anything about the prey?" he asked. His voice was even, controlled. "Every wolf in the valley will suffer, and the council is supposed to take care of us."

If I hadn't been watching her so closely, I wouldn't have seen Frandra's shoulders sag. She immediately straightened.

"Milsindra is winning more wolves over to her side. We will try to reason with the council, but they may not listen."

"Pell said ten Greatwolves were chasing the prey, Kaala," Ázzuen said over his shoulder. "Remember? Half the council."

"Exactly half," Jandru said, shuffling forward to stand beside his mate. He didn't ask us how we knew; he would assume the ravens had told us. "Any wolf with sense can see that Milsindra should not drive away the prey. But when wolves wish to believe in something, the truth won't stop them from doing so. Milsindra's followers believe that the Ancients wish them to rule wolfkind and control the humans. She has convinced them that if they wish the Ancients' favor, they will help her prove that you and your humans are a threat to wolfkind."

Ázzuen spoke into the silence that followed, his indignation clear. "So, first the council said that if we couldn't live with the humans for a year without fighting, it would show that the Ancients don't approve of humans and wolves being together. Now, they're saying that it's acceptable for Milsindra to *make* us fail because that's what the Ancients would really want?"

Jandru blinked a few times, trying to catch up with Ázzuen. I knew how he felt.

"Yes," he said, slowly. "I had not thought of it that way, but it appears to be so."

"So you're just giving up?" I said, finding my voice at last. I didn't understand how they could be so weak. Torell's words sounded in my head. He spoke of fighting and taking chances. Frandra and Jandru sat on the riverside as if the fight were already over. I couldn't keep the contempt from my tone. "You are giving up."

"Why don't you fight them?" Ázzuen challenged. "We can get the other packs in the valley to help us," he said, carefully not mentioning Torell.

"We are not giving up!" Jandru's growl made the ground beneath my feet shake. "We have been fighting for longer than you have been alive to give us trouble. And the other packs will do nothing for you."

"How do you know?" I demanded.

Jandru shook his head hard. "Idiot. Why do you think your packmate was killed? Do you even know?"

"To trap us."

"They made the prey leave and now no wolf can leave to follow it," Ázzuen added. Tlitoo quorked softly, still pretending to be intent on his search for food. The old raven had joined him on the riverbank.

"That is only part of it," Jandru said. "You're supposed to be smart," he growled at Ázzuen. "Think about it. What other message does it send?"

I didn't know. That they had power over us? That they could kill us whenever they wanted? We already knew that. Neither Ázzuen nor I answered.

"By siding with us," Frandra said, "Ruuqo and Rissa have

made enemies of Milsindra and her followers. Milsindra is letting other packs in the valley know what will happen if they
take our side against hers. Ruuqo and Rissa did so, and Milsindra killed one of their most promising youngwolves."

I nearly vomited up the stagnant pond water I had lapped.
Frandra didn't need to say the rest. Ruuqo and Rissa had
helped me, and Yllin had died.

"It's not Kaala's fault!" Ázzuen said. For once I wished he
couldn't read me so easily. Tlitoo looked up from his investi-
gation of the riverbank and clacked his beak sharply. "It was
Zorindru's idea," Ázzuen said. "We didn't have any choice."

"Of course it's not her fault," Frandra said, surprised. "We
never said it was. But it's why you must leave the council and
its affairs to us."

Zorindru. The ancient Greatwolf leader had said he
couldn't help me, but surely if he knew what Milsindra had
done he would come out of hiding.

"We have to let Zorindru know what the other Greatwolves are doing," I said, forcing my eyes up from the ground.

"He won't interfere," Jandru said.

"He will if he knows what Milsindra is doing," I said stub-
bornly. "We have to find him."

Both Jandru and Frandra smiled at that.

"If that oldwolf doesn't want to be found, you won't find
him," Frandra said. "He could be standing two wolflengths
from us and we wouldn't see him. If he wants to come to us,
he will, but I wouldn't wait for him to do so."

She shook what was left of the water from her fur and
turned back to the river, then growled. Three wolves stood at
the far bank, in Swift River territory, watching us. When they

saw us notice them, they lowered their ears, waded into the river, and swam across to us. The whole time they swam, their lips were pulled back slightly in smiles of submissiveness. I wondered how they could swim that way without swallowing water, but they were doing everything they could to show that they were no threat and that they were being as respectful as possible. As well they might, with two Greatwolves awaiting them.

At first I thought the river was unusually deep, since the wolves had to swim almost all of its width, but when they emerged, tails tucked between their legs and ears flat against their heads, I realized that they were particularly small wolves, the size Ázzuen and I had been when we were five moons old. I didn't recognize any of them, and their scent was unfamiliar to me. To my surprise, after the three wolves greeted Frandra and Jandru and after Frandra gave them permission to stay with a slight inclination of her head, the three wolves greeted me with almost as much deference as they had shown the Greatwolves.

"What brings Vole Eater pups here?" Frandra asked.

That was why they were so small. Vole Eater wolves were the smallest in the valley, and if Fandra was calling them pups, they had been born at the same time Ázzuen and I had. One of the Vole Eaters lowered his head to acknowledge Frandra, but it was me he addressed. He kept his eyes lowered.

"You're Kaala, aren't you? I'm Prannan of Vole Eater and this is Amma and this is Briall," he said, nodding to the two other wolves. "We want to help you."

"Help me what?" I asked, mystified.

"Help you with the promise," he said, surprised. "Help

you with the humans. We will watch them for you when you go to find your mother."

"What? What is this about Neesa?" Jandru demanded.

I winced. Frandra and Jandru knew nothing about my plans to leave the valley and find my mother.

"A raven told us," Amma said apologetically.

I considered lying to Frandra and Jandru, but I no longer had the energy to keep secrets. I told them of my plan to leave the valley, find my mother, and then return. Jandru shook his head so hard water from his ears hit me in the face.

"When will you learn not to keep things from us?" he demanded. "We cannot work together if you keep secrets from us."

"I don't trust you," I said simply, too tired to care if I made him angry. "And you keep secrets from us. I know there is something you aren't telling us, so why should we tell you everything?"

I thought the Greatwolves would be furious, but Jandru just gave a soft, weary growl. "It's important, Kaala," Frandra said. "Your mother is important. I want you to find her. As for our secrets, we cannot share them with you. It is not our decision to make. We have taken a sacred oath not to reveal the secrets of our kind." She pressed her head against Jandru's and whispered something to him. I strained my ears to hear what it was but couldn't. The three Vole Eater youngwolves weren't even paying attention to the Greatwolves. They were looking at me with awed expressions on their faces. My skin grew uncomfortably warm under my fur, and I returned my gaze to the Greatwolves.

"We will allow this," Frandra said to me, then addressed

Prannan. "Do you have an adult wolf to help you with this?" she demanded.

"Our leaderwolves will help," Prannan answered.

"And Trevegg will, too," Ázzuen said. "He was planning to, anyway."

"Good," Frandra said. "If we win against Milsindra we will allow other wolves to take over for you while you find your mother."

I was stunned. I'd never expected them to help me find my mother. For the first time since finding Yllin's body, I began to feel some hope.

"And if you lose?" Ázzuen asked.

Frandra barked a laugh. "Then you'll be on your own, since we'll be dead. But don't worry, so will you."

She lowered her head to touch Prannan's cheek with her nose. "Go back to your pack. We'll send for you if you're needed."

All of the Vole Eaters bent their forelegs to bow to the Greatwolves and then, to my embarrassment, to me.

"We will keep the promise," Prannan said. He dipped his head to his companions, and the three of them waded into the river and swam back across. The ancient raven took flight and soared across the river to follow the Vole Eaters. When they had disappeared into the thick woods, Frandra turned back to me. "I won't bother to order you to tell me everything you know, Kaala." She laughed a little. "There's not much point. You'll do what's best for yourself and your friends. I know that. But if we are going to continue to risk ourselves, you must tell me: Will your pack continue to support us? Will Ruuqo and Rissa lose their nerve? There's still time for us to build a truce with Milsindra if not. It's our last chance to stop all-out war between the Greatwolves."

"They'll keep their word," I said. Torell was wrong about them. "I know they will."

"Then we will do what we can about Milsindra. You must stay out of trouble until then. The two of you must return to your humans. Do not confront Milsindra or Kivdru. Don't do anything that will draw more attention to yourselves."

The three youngwolves had distracted me from my grief and anger. Now both returned with even more intensity than before. I growled in protest.

Frandra looked at me sharply. "Do *nothing* to make the other Greatwolves look for you. I know you're angry. I know you want revenge. But you have a responsibility to the wolves of your pack, who have risked everything for you, and to us. Tell us when the humans have realized the prey has left and take no action that will disrupt things further."

I opened my mouth to object.

"Go!" Jandru ordered, apparently at the end of his patience. I was surprised he had let me say as much as I had. He placed both muddy paws on my back and forced me down to the ground. "Stay with the humans and keep them from trouble until we tell you otherwise." He stepped off me, and both Greatwolves stalked down the riverbank and into the water. They swam easily across and disappeared into the woods.

When I stood, my legs barely held me. I was exhausted, drained by my sorrow and my rage. It didn't matter to the Greatwolves that Yllin was dead. It wouldn't matter to them if every wolf in my pack was dead. I met Ázzuen's eyes.

He looked back bleakly.

Tlitoo picked his way through the mud to stand next to us. "Now will you see what I have to show you, wolves?" he asked. "It is important."

What could be so important? I looked wearily at him. I just wanted to swim the river and lie down with my pack.

"I have told your pack of the youngwolf's death," he said. "They will sing her deathsong when they can. They will send the fleetwolf for you when it is time for the pack to come together. What I have to show you is near the human homesite, so you need not go out of your way. Will you come?"

When Ázzuen and I just sat there, staring at him, he turned his back on us and strode back to the river, where he began to splash water over his wings and back. His feathers had finally stopped falling out, and he looked sleek and strong under his lighter spring plumage. His legs were scabbed over from the attack of the other ravens, but he didn't seem bothered by them. He looked up from his bath, his manner casual, but his eyes keen. "I think it will help wolves. Help find what the Grimwolves hide. Help find out what it is we are to do."

"Can't you just tell us?" I asked.

"No, you must see for yourself," he said. He flew from the river and landed in front of me. He leaned forward, as if to run his beak through my chest fur, then stopped himself and cocked his head to look up at me. "I cannot make you come. You must choose." He was watching me, but I had the feeling he was talking mostly to himself. Then a sly look came into his eyes. "If you would rather stay here and mope, instead of taking action to make things right, then I will go alone."

He took flight, soaring a few wolflengths to land on a

branch at the edge of the woods. He turned away to pick at a scab on one of his legs.

"That wasn't very subtle," Ázzuen said, humor creeping into his voice.

"No, it wasn't." Sometimes Tlitoo acted as if Ázzuen and I were still smallpups. I watched the raven as he pretended not to watch me. For all he feigned indifference, he clearly wanted us with him. I didn't have any better idea of what to do. I needed to regain my composure before returning to the humans, and needed some time to figure out whom I could trust—or whom I distrusted the least. Following Tlitoo was as good a thing to do in the meantime as anything else.

Catching Ázzuen's eye, I walked slowly toward the raven. Tlitoo gave a triumphant shriek and led us into the woods.

I could barely feel the earth beneath the pads of my feet as we ran. My whole body was numb, my thoughts sluggish as Ázzuen and I ran to keep up with Tlitoo. I couldn't get the sight of Yllin's body out of my head or the smell of her blood from my nose. There was part of me that couldn't believe she was really dead. I had seen her body for just a few moments, but she had been part of my life, vibrant and alive, from my earliest memories. A world she wasn't in didn't seem possible. The thought of it made me so weary I could barely keep up with Tlitoo. Ázzuen's steady tread just behind me kept me going, but I was ready to tell Tlitoo I had to stop to rest when he banked sharply to the right.

"This way," he said.

The breeze shifted, and I smelled TaLi. I stumbled after the raven and found her, curled up with BreLan on the soft dirt between the roots of a large ancient oak. I understood from the faint scent of smoke that we were near the human home-site. That was the last thought to stumble through my mind before I staggered to TaLi and threw myself down beside her. Ázzuen scrambled over us, scratching me with his claws, to lie half on top of BreLan. TaLi murmured in her sleep and threw a skinny arm around me. This was what I was fighting for, I told myself. For just a little while I could forget about the Great-wolves' power games and who was in charge of the valley.

I pressed up against TaLi's warm skin and inhaled her smoke-and-herb scent, allowing myself to be comforted by the soothing sense of being one with another creature, the knowledge that, at least for this one moment, I was not alone. I rested there, regaining my sense of who I was and what was most important to me. Then, grateful to Tlitoo for bringing us to our humans, I took one more breath of TaLi-scented air and started to get back to my paws, feeling more able to face the other humans and my pack.

"No, wolflet, wait there," Tlitoo said to me from one of the roots of the great oak. "We will go to the human home soon. This is more important."

He hopped onto my back, walked over TaLi and BreLan, then pecked Ázzuen's shoulder. Ázzuen yipped.

"*You* stay where you are. You must not touch me or Moon-wolf." I raised my head in surprise. He had never called me that. Only NiaLi had called me that, and that had been when I had first met her. Tlitoo didn't notice my surprise. He was still staring at Ázzuen. "Do you promise, wolf?"

"Yes," Ázzuen said sleepily, "but why?"

Tlitoo didn't answer him. He stalked back over the two humans, hopped down, and stood in front of me, peering into my eyes. He took two steps toward me, bending his head close to me. The last time I had touched him had been at Rock's Crest, and contact with him had been terrifying. I pulled away.

"You must not be afraid, wolflet," Tlitoo said. "You must trust me. This is what I am. This is what I can do." He took two more steps toward me. I forced myself to remain still as he leaned his head against my chest. And then it came. The darkness and the absence of scent, the cold and the feeling of falling. I heard the sound of a thousand wings flapping. Scent came back to me and air filled my lungs. It was still dark, though. My eyes were closed, I realized.

I opened them and was immediately dizzy. Everything looked different, blurry and indistinct. Yet the colors around me were brighter than any I had ever seen before, richer than I thought colors could be. I was looking at the mud-rock base of a human shelter, but it was vibrant with bright colors I couldn't name. The dizziness overtook me, nausea making me weak. I pulled sharply away and found myself back in the clearing, rolling away from TaLi and onto Tlitoo, who scrambled to get out of my way. Ázzuen, BreLan, and TaLi still slept.

"What did you do to me?" I gasped as he preened his ruffled feathers. He jutted his head forward so that we were beak to nose. I winced, anticipating a peck to the nose, but he just peered into my eyes.

"It is all right, wolflet," he quorked. "It is what I do. What we do. Moonwolf and Neja raven together. You see what she sees, know what she knows. It is all right. I was afraid before, but I am not now."

My mind tried to catch up with his words. "I'm seeing what TaLi sees?" I couldn't believe it.

"Not all," he answered. "What she is remembering, what she is thinking of, dreaming of, now. I am not sure. I am very new at this." He raised his wings protectively over his ears. "It is what I am supposed to do. I am not afraid."

I just stared at him. I had never heard of such a thing. The dizzy, sick feeling scared me.

"I'm seeing things that TaLi is remembering?" I repeated. I had no idea that Tlitoo could make that happen. I hadn't known it was possible.

"Please, wolflet, will you try?"

Fascination and fear rolled over me. Fascination won out; I'd always wanted to know what was going on in TaLi's head. I lay down next to the girl, leaning against her. Tlitoo pressed his back to my chest. This time, I was prepared for the shock of the lack of smell and the cold, the sensation of dropping off a cliff. When I opened my eyes to a bright, blurry world, I understood that I was seeing things the way a human might, and I wasn't used to seeing things through human eyes. I would have to adjust. Experimentally, I pulled away just a little from TaLi's mind, then a little more. I realized that, if I wanted to, I could pull away and return to myself in the clearing. Knowing I could do so took away my fear, and when I felt myself losing touch with TaLi, I drew closer again, until I felt as if I was watching TaLi's memories as I might watch my packmates hunt in the distance. What I saw, I realized, was her dream. She was dreaming of a time before I knew her, and I eagerly settled in to watch TaLi when she was little more than a pup.

⊡

TaLi was five when she told her older cousin she could speak to the animals. Her cousin laughed at her and called her a baby. So TaLi told her aunt, RinaLi, who had taken care of her since her mother had died. RinaLi did not laugh. She grabbed TaLi by the wrist so hard that the girl began to cry. RinaLi pulled TaLi close to her and whispered harshly, "You do not understand the animals. Never say that again. Never!" She gave TaLi's arm one more twist and shoved her away, looking anxiously around. Sobbing, TaLi ran to the edge of the homesite, behind the herb house, and flung herself down in the warm dirt.

"I can so hear the animals," TaLi said. "I can. I spoke to a raven, and he told me I smell bad, and the dhole said I was smart. I couldn't talk to the rabbits, though," she said thoughtfully. "They didn't want to say anything."

Her grandmother found her there and asked her why she wept. TaLi told her, then gulped back her tears, afraid her harsh-tongued grandmother would yell at her as her aunt had done. But the old woman squatted down beside TaLi.

"Of course you can't hear the rabbits," the old woman said. "They never have anything much to say. And don't believe everything a raven tells you. They are terrible liars."

TaLi looked at her grandmother in wonder, and when the old woman stood and held out her hand, TaLi swallowed one last sob and got to her feet. The old woman, walking slowly, led the stumbling girl away from the homesite and into the woods. When they reached a quiet copse of trees by a brook, she sat again, and the girl sat beside her.

"Your mother spoke to the animals," the old woman said. "It is

a gift. When your mother died, her older sister, your aunt RinaLi, believed that it was because of her conversations with animals. Nonsense, of course, but people will believe what they will believe, and my older daughter has always been fearful. This is why she will not let you speak of the animals."

The old woman talked to TaLi like an adult, not a stupid child, and TaLi felt her chest rise in pride.

"You're too young, yet, to do much, and I don't know if you will be able to speak to them when you're grown," the old woman said, as much to herself as to TaLi, "but if the ravens have found you, we'd best not wait any longer." She stood and dusted the dry winter dirt off her deerskin tunic. "I will come for you tonight. Sleep apart from your cousin and your aunt. It is time that you met some friends of mine."

⊡

TaLi was dreaming of rabbits when something shook her awake. She would have cried out if a gnarled hand had not covered her mouth. In the glow of the fire she made out the face of her grandmother.

"Come with me," the old woman said. "Make no noise." And although she was frightened, TaLi obeyed. It would not have occurred to her to disobey the old woman, who was the tribe's krianan, their spiritual guide.

TaLi followed the krianan silently until they reached the river. Then she let out a cry of fear. She had crossed the river only once before, when the entire tribe had gone on a hunt, and she had clung to her aunt's back rigid in terror. Her grip had loosened only the slightest bit and she had felt the river pulling at her like a hungry beast intent on swallowing her. Her aunt had taken her by the wrist and pulled her along to safety, leaving dark bruises on TaLi's arm.

She had been smaller then, and her aunt was stronger than her grandmother. She could not imagine crossing the fast-moving water on her own.

"Quiet," the old woman ordered. She tied together several strips of soft, strong antelope hide, fastening one end around TaLi's waist and then to her own. The other end she tied to a long strand of skins that stretched all the way across the river. TaLi could just make out through the moonlight that far across the river, the skins were tied to a stout trunk of a willow.

The old woman set out across the river, stepping agilely from one half-sunken stone to the next, using her walking stick to steady herself and the antelope skins as a guide. TaLi, tethered to the old woman, was forced to follow. Her legs were too short to manage the stones, so she clung to the skins with desperate determination. At first, where the river was shallow, she managed to stay upright, stumbling in the mud. But when the river deepened, she could only flop in the water and crawl from stone to stone.

When she reached the halfway point across the river, she saw a boy, a few years older than she, standing next to the willow and holding tight to the skins. Each time she fell, he pulled against the skins, ensuring that neither she nor her grandmother was pulled under. After what seemed like an entire night, TaLi stumbled the last few feet across the river.

"You're going to need to learn to swim," the old krianan said, "but you are not without courage. That, at least, is a start."

TaLi swallowed her fear. If the old woman thought she was brave she would be so. Without another word, the old woman strode into the woods. With a curious look at the young boy, TaLi followed.

Ten minutes later, TaLi crouched in the old woman's shelter, still shivering in spite of the warm, overly large bearskin clothes the old woman had given her. She drank tea from a thick gourd cup and immediately felt revived. She wondered what her grandmother had put in it.

"Good," the old woman said when TaLi had finished her drink. "Come on, now."

□

They walked for almost an hour to a flat clearing encircled by stones. There were people there, people TaLi didn't recognize. They greeted her grandmother.

"This is the girl, Nia?" asked a woman, frowning. "She's much too young."

"She'll get older," TaLi's grandmother said.

"And then she'll forget how to understand the animals. As has every other child we've brought the wolves since KaraLi died."

TaLi stood up straighter. KaraLi had been her mother's name.

"Perhaps," the old woman said, unruffled. "We won't know until she's grown."

"Can she understand the guardian wolves?"

"That is one of the things we're here to find out."

The other woman opened her mouth, then cocked her head, just like the raven who had made fun of TaLi. TaLi laughed.

"They're coming," the frowning raven woman said, and TaLi was surprised at the mix of excitement and fear in the woman's voice. "Too late to do anything about her now. You'd better hope they aren't hungry." The woman grinned at TaLi. "Do you taste good, little girl?" The woman cackled, and TaLi's grandmother placed her hand upon TaLi's head.

"She'll be fine," the old woman said. "Do you really think I *can't recognize one who has the gift? I even found you, InaLa, and your talent was hidden behind pride and silliness."*

Whatever the younger woman was going to say was stopped when eight giant wolves strode into the clearing. TaLi stifled a gasp and pressed close to her grandmother.

The huge wolves—they seemed almost twice as large as any she had ever seen—stared at TaLi. Two of them strode forward, sniffing at the girl. TaLi resisted the temptation to scream, to run, to push the wolves away. She held perfectly still and allowed the beasts to smell her all over.

One of them gave what TaLi swore was a laugh. NiaLi listened intently then spoke to TaLi.

"Jandru says he likes you," she told the girl. "He says he considers you worthy."

The wolves and humans spoke for hours, or at least that's what TaLi assumed they did, since to her the wolves merely made noises and moved their faces. When weariness overtook her fear and curiosity, TaLi fell asleep.

She awoke surrounded by the soft fur of a wolf. The wolf smelled of forest and of flesh, and TaLi felt warm, protected. At first all she could see was the fur and a bit of pink flesh showing through it. When she turned her head she saw her grandmother's face looking pleased.

"What do you think, Jandru?" TaLi heard the old woman say to the mountain of fur that surrounded her. The rumbling in the wolf's chest sounded like a laugh. TaLi felt the last of her fear depart as NiaLi pulled her from the wolf's embrace. TaLi was so tired that she nearly fell flat on her face, but she told her legs to move and, stumbling, her mind full of questions, she followed her grandmother into the wolf-scented night.

I felt a jolt, then heard the flapping of wings. Then I was lying next to TaLi, listening to her heartbeat, inhaling her scent. Tlitoo stood a few steps away, watching me.

"You saw it, wolf? You saw?"

Thoughts raced through my mind. When I'd first seen the spiritwolf, Lydda, when I was four moons old, I had worried I might be crazy. Now I was seeing the thoughts of another creature. But I wasn't alone. Tlitoo was there, and he had seen it, too.

"How come you can do that?" I demanded. "Does it only work with humans?"

"No," he said. "I do not think so." He hopped over to where Ázzuen slept and looked a dare at me.

"I am Nejakilakin," he quorked, "the winged traveler, the first born in the memory of any living raven. I bring together the worlds. It is what I was born for."

"Winged traveler?" I said. Both Lydda and NiaLi had told me to seek answers from the one who traveled. When I was a pup and Tlitoo a fledgling, he said he had been sent to me.

He peered at me and quorked again.

> "The winged traveler flies
> Between worlds and betwixt thoughts
> Lest the Balance fail."

I just stared at him. I had known Tlitoo most of my life and he had just been an ordinary raven.

"Do you want to see if it works with others than your girl, or not, wolf?" he asked, sounding more like himself. "I do!"

Watching TaLi's memories had made me as tired as if I had run three hunts, and I felt my eyelids trying to close. Besides, it seemed wrong to go into Ázzuen's mind without asking him. I wouldn't want someone doing it to me. But of course I wanted to see.

Tlitoo had said that what he could do was important to our task. Ázzuen was my closest friend. Maybe he wouldn't mind. I got to my feet and walked as quietly as I could over to where Ázzuen slept beside BreLan. He had rolled a little bit away from the boy. Tentatively, I lay down beside Ázzuen and pressed up against him. Tlitoo immediately leapt upon my back. Scent disappeared and flapping wings lifted me, then dropped me. This time, I was prepared for the feeling of falling, and because I was seeing things through the normal senses of a wolf, I felt neither sick nor dizzy. I felt Ázzuen's breath match mine, his heart beating evenly. I rolled over with him, and he shifted in his sleep and fell more deeply into the world of dreams.

⊡

Ázzuen remembered the day he first opened his eyes. Before that day, everything had been about the taste of a sweet nourishing substance on his tongue, the softness of a warm form next to him, the feel of a heavy, steady beat, and the scent of moist earth. There were also other squirming forms that sometimes shoved him away from the place where the warmth and nourishment came from. The first thing he saw, when he opened his eyes, was soft fur and the rise and fall of his mother's belly. Later, the other pups told him that they couldn't remember opening their eyes. They couldn't even remember the first time they heard a sound. It was as if their brains were deadened in some way. Marra said she could just barely re-member the first day she was out of the den, though to Ázzuen it was like a thousand sensations dashing across his nose, a tumble of thoughts pounding in his brain.

Ázzuen remembered hearing Ruuqo and Rissa talking about him that first day outside the den. One of the squirming bodies had stopped moving, and Rissa had shoved it aside. Somehow, though he did not know how, Ázzuen knew the pup was dead. The pup who had told him that every time she woke up she wanted to howl in joy for the day. She loved the milk that came from Rissa's body, but she had trouble drinking it. After she was dead, Ázzuen real-ized it was because she was drinking the wrong way, but it was too late by then to save her.

He knew he was smart. He knew that he understood things other pups didn't, but he didn't see how that would help him.

"This one won't make it either," he heard Ruuqo say to Rissa. "You should save your milk for the others."

"He still suckles," Rissa had answered. "He still lives. If he is willing to fight for his life, I will let him."

"I've seen weaklings before," Ruuqo said. "Weaklings hurt the pack. I know this one will not live. You know it, too, Rissa. It's cruel to let it suffer."

"I know he will most likely die," Rissa had said. "But I will give him the chance to live."

Ázzuen thought he would be able to live. He knew where the milk came from, how to stay warm, even once he had left the den. What he hadn't planned on was the other pups, who wanted him to die. They kept him from the milk, from the warmth of the den, from being part of the pack. He grew angry and then despondent. One day, when the other pups had gone in *to feed, he decided not to bother anymore, that it would be easier to die.*

But she *wouldn't let him. The pup, smaller even than he was. She was not of his litter. She, too, was supposed to die since her mother had broken pack rules by having pups without the leader-wolves' permission. But she had not given in. When Ruuqo tried to kill her, as he had the other pups from the forbidden litter, she had fought back. She bore the pale mark of the moon on her chest and she smelled, even as a tiny pup, of a wolf of strength. She made him live, not just that day but yet again, when they crossed over a vast plain to their first gathering place. Her scent was the scent of home, the sound of her voice the sound of his future. The pups they would have and the life they would live together was the reason for each breath he took and for each and every beat of his heart.*

This time I was the one who pulled away, jerking myself guilt-ily from Ázzuen's thoughts with a sense that I had seen what I should not have seen. I offered a silent, shamed apology to Ázzuen. Fatigue overwhelmed me even as I did so. I couldn't remember if I had ever felt so tired. All I could think about was lying down and sleeping. Before I knew what was hap-pening, I was back in the dark, scentless place, more than ready to return to the sun-warmed clearing.

"Wait, Moonwolf." Tlitoo's voice was faint, but clear, and much deeper than I remembered it being. There was a blur-ring of the darkness and the same sense of disorientation I had felt when I had entered into TaLi's thoughts.

"Look," Tlitoo said.

I slowly opened my eyes, expecting to find myself back in

the warm clearing with TaLi, BreLan, and Ázzuen. Instead, I was standing with Tlitoo in the middle of the Stone Circle where the human and Greatwolf krianans met once a moon.

"How did we get here?" I asked. The Stone Circle was across the river and a fifteen-minute run through thick woods from the clearing where the young humans slept.

"I am not sure, wolf," Tlitoo said. "I do not know what this place is. It is not what it seems."

I sniffed the dirt at my feet. The Stone Circle smelled of pine and rock, Greatwolf and human. This place smelled of nothing.

We both caught the slight movement at the same time and turned to see the form of a wolf emerging from the woods. I could not smell her juniper and fire scent in this place of no smells, but I knew her just the same. Walking toward us, as if it were a perfectly natural thing to do, was the spiritwolf, Lydda.

14

When I had last seen the spiritwolf, she'd been frail and hungry-looking, a result, she had said, of coming too often into the world of the living. Now she looked as if she had fed well after a long famine—her fur was still thin and dull, but her weight was returning to her, and her eyes were bright. I breathed in the still air around me, hoping to catch her smoke-and-juniper aroma even in this scentless place.

That was when I realized that something was wrong with my nose. It was so cold it ached. Unlike many creatures, wolves are almost never bothered by the cold. Our fur grows thick in winter, even between the pads of our feet, so that we can run the hunt even on the coldest of nights. Only our noses, furless to allow scents to flow freely to us, are sometimes at risk. When we sleep in the cold, we make sure to cover them with our tails. My nose had never been as cold as it was as I watched Lydda walk to me. I wondered if it was possible for it to fall off.

Lydda reached me and looked me over carefully, then opened her mouth in a smile.

"I thought you would find your way here," she said, touching her own nose to my frozen one. I imagined I could feel the heat of her breath on my face, but it did nothing to warm me. I returned her greeting as best I could.

"Where are we?" I asked, looking around at what appeared to be the familiar rocks and dirt of the Stone Circle. "Is this the world of the spirits?" My heart skipped as I thought I might see Yllin, to be able to say good-bye to her, to thank her for the many times she stood up for me and told me I was strong. Then a gust of terror overwhelmed me as I wondered if I might have died trying to return from Ázzuen's mind.

"It is not," Lydda reassured me. "It is a place between the realm of life and the realm of death. I found my way here when it became imprudent for me to venture into the living world."

Her voice was kind as she looked down at me. She reminded me so much of Yllin I wanted to howl. I couldn't have done so even if I hadn't stopped myself. My muzzle was nearly as cold as my nose.

"Tell me!" Tlitoo darted to Lydda. "What is this in-between place? What am I supposed to do here? I do not know and no one can tell me." He leaned forward to whisper to Lydda. "There has not been a Nejakilakin for many years, and no raven remembers much." He seemed unbothered by the cold, which was now making my entire face ache.

"I cannot tell you much," Lydda said, touching her nose to Tlitoo's chest. "I asked a wolf who is sympathetic to me what this place is, and how creatures of life could come here.

He told me that it is *Inejalun*, a place of not-life and not-death. He told me that the Nejakilakin, the traveler, is a creature who can pass between life and death and can see into the memories of others. He is born when there is need, and to use his gift fully he must find a companion to travel with him."

"Nejakilakin and the Moonwolf," Tlitoo agreed. I felt like they both understood something I didn't. I tried to open my mouth to ask what they meant. Ice held it shut. "I can come here alone," Tlitoo continued, "but must have the Moonwolf to see memories and dreams."

"Yes," Lydda said. "There's not much more I can tell you about this place. Sometimes I can find it, sometimes I cannot, and neither I nor Kaala can safely stay here long. My friend would not tell me more."

I at last managed to force my jaws apart. "Why did you tell me I had to find the traveler?"

Lydda looked at me sharply, taking in my shivering, my stumbling words.

"You're cold," she said. "You really can't stay here long, Kaala. The barrier between the worlds of life and death were thinned when the Nejakilakin was born, which is why I could come to you before, but doing so was not safe for me. And it's not safe for you to stay here. No living creature other than the Nejakilakin can stay here without losing hold on the world of life. We must speak quickly." She darted a quick glance over her shoulder, as if she expected someone to be looking for her. She lowered her voice to a whisper. "I see some of the things of your world but not all. I know of the task Zorindru has given you and your success with it, but something has changed. I could feel your distress in my sleep. Tell me, sister-wolf, what has happened?"

The kindness in her voice warmed me for a moment, and the tension I had been carrying in my chest melted. I spilled it all out. Yllin's death. How Milsindra had said she would do everything she could to thwart me, how she was driving away the prey to trap us and to warn us against defying her, my fear that no matter what I did, the Greatwolves would make me fail.

Lydda listened carefully, then lay down, her paws tucked neatly under her chest. She had a moon-shape of pale fur on her chest, just as I did. Her relaxed posture calmed me. She lay there, thinking for long moments as the cold crept through my chest to my ribs.

"I am not surprised to hear of what Milsindra is doing," she said at last. "Your success is a threat to her as mine was to the krianan wolves in my time. But you have advantages I did not. You know you cannot trust those who call themselves Greatwolves. I did what they told me to do because I believed it was my duty to do so, and I missed my chance to make things right with the humans."

The remorse in her voice would've made me howl if my throat had not been frozen. The thought that I might fail TaLi brought on an ache so deep I whimpered. Lydda watched me closely.

"You have the chance to make it right, Kaala. You have something else I didn't have: the gift your raven friend brings you to see into the memories of others. It is why it was so important for you to find the traveler. This gift will help you discover that which the Greatwolves have kept hidden, that which no wolf has been able to find from the time I walked the earth."

"Torell said they were hiding something," I was startled into saying. "He said it was important." I didn't think Torell's prohibition against telling others included wolves of the spirit realm.

"It's not a thing they are hiding, Kaala," Lydda said softly. "It's a truth. One they have been guarding from long before I was born. That is what you must find."

"How?" I said, desperation overtaking me as my belly grew cold. I could no longer even shiver. "All we can do is see memories or dreams."

"There's more," Lydda said. "There has to be more. I wish I knew what it was. All I know is that the Nejakilakin holds the power to find what is hidden."

"I do not yet know everything I can do, wolf," Tlitoo said. "It is all very new. We might find a way." He didn't sound very certain.

"You must," Lydda said, rising, the kindness in her voice replaced by a desperate intensity. "For the secret of the krianan wolves holds the solution to the paradox itself. And if you do not discover it, you will not be able to help your pack or the humans of TaLi's tribe. You will fail as I failed." I was gratified that she remembered TaLi's name. But of course she would. She had once loved a human.

She looked at me in concern.

"You have to leave, Kaala. I have heard that the Great-wolves' secret is hidden beneath a giant yew tree, but I don't know if it's true. Find what the krianan wolves hide. Find it and do what is right with what you find."

"When can I talk to you again?" I asked. There was too much more I needed to know. I needed her help. I couldn't take on the Greatwolves without it.

"I don't know if you can. When I last came to this place I had to sleep for days to recover. It was a weariness close to death. This is not a natural place, and I think neither the living nor the dead can survive here long. Nor can I always find the way here. I will try to find a way to do so."

I felt the cold creeping down my backbone to my tail.

"Go, or you will not be safe. I promise to find a way for us both to return here." I somehow managed to shiver. "Take her. Now," she said fiercely to a startled Tlitoo. He quorked and leaned up against me. Through frozen ears I could barely hear the flapping of wings, and the sensation of falling was welcome after the cold. I opened my eyes to find myself lying against Ázzuen, pressing myself to the warmth of his living flesh.

A weariness close to death, Lydda had said. And so it was. I couldn't stay awake long enough to speak to Tlitoo or to rouse Ázzuen. I had enough time to realize that I was terribly hungry and thirsty before my head dropped onto my paws and I fell into a sleep so deep I couldn't help but wonder if Tlitoo had not taken me away soon enough. I couldn't worry about it. If it was death and not sleep I fell into, then there was nothing I could do. I lay my head upon my paws and let my weariness overtake me.

When I awoke it was dark, Tlitoo and the young humans were gone, and my body felt as if a hundred horses had trampled it. My eyes were sticky and the tips of my ears hurt as if burned. I raised my heavy head to find Ázzuen and Marra watching me. Ázzuen darted to me and began to lick my face. He poked his nose into my jaw. Startled, I took his muzzle in my mouth, then released it. He tasted of worry.

"Where's Tlitoo?" I said over a thickened tongue. The encounter with Lydda had left me with more questions than I'd had before. My stomach ached with hunger, as if it had been three weeks since I'd last eaten, but my body felt wonderfully warm.

"You slept for two *days*," Marra said, her voice a mix of awe and concern. "We couldn't wake you up. Trevegg came, and Rissa, too. The raven said you'd be all right, and NiaLi said you just needed sleep—and food and water when you woke up."

My nose still wasn't working quite right, and I hadn't noticed that the old woman was there. I turned my head to find her sitting on a tree root, leaning on the thick oak stick she used to help herself walk. She held out a gourd to me. It had been dried and cut open, and was filled with fresh-smelling water. I hauled myself to my feet and stumbled to her. I licked her hand in greeting, then gulped the water in the gourd.

"Your friends have told me that the prey has gone, and TaLi has told the tribe," the old woman said, placing her hand upon my back. She grinned, her eyes disappearing in her wrinkled face. "They didn't believe her, but since they've found nothing bigger than a marmot to hunt for the past two days, HuLin has sent runners to look throughout the valley. When they return, he'll know TaLi is right. She told them she learned of it when in the krianan's trance."

"They'll find the aurochs and elkryn," Ázzuen pointed out.

"They will," the old woman agreed. "But it still doesn't leave enough prey for everyone in the valley. Besides, it can take days to hunt an auroch, and they feed far from the Lin village."

"Then they'll accept her as krianan, won't they? When they learn she's right about the prey?" Marra asked.

NiaLi's expression grew serious. "They may, or they may not. I want you to watch out for TaLi when they do find out, Kaala. She treads dangerous ground in asserting her role as krianan, and I worry for her." She shifted on her tree root. "I'm no longer permitted entrance to the Lin village."

"Why not?" I asked her, then licked out the last drops of water from the gourd.

She lifted her shoulders and let them drop again. "I told HuLin he was a fool for forcing TaLi into a marriage she didn't want and by ignoring her power as krianan, and that he would regret it. He told me the krianans are no longer needed. I told him he had the brain of a rock and the manners of a weasel. I probably should not have said that. And TaLi will soon take on the krianan's role. She will be the one to tell them they have to hunt less, and I want you there to protect her when that happens."

"I will," I promised.

Marra brought over a hunk of old horse meat. It smelled of Rissa, who must have brought it for me from one of our caches. I swallowed it down, relishing the taste of Swift River food. Feeling a little better, I tried to gather my thoughts.

"I slept for two days?" I said. A fresh wave of sorrow

washed over me as I remembered what had happened. "Yllin died," I said.

"The pack sings for her tonight," Marra said.

I looked at her more closely than I had before. Her shoulders drooped and her fur was a little ragged and damp in patches; she always chewed her fur when she was upset.

"The pack knows?" I said. Marra had said so, had said that they were to sing of Yllin's death, but my mind was still moving sluggishly.

"They know she was killed by Milsindra for trying to leave the valley," Ázzuen answered, "and that the Greatwolves chased away the prey. They don't know the rest."

The rest meaning our conversation with Torell and his plans for rebellion. I wondered if Tlitoo had told Ázzuen and Marra anything of our strange journey together. I hoped not. I wasn't ready to explain it to myself, much less to anyone else. I looked closely at Ázzuen and Marra. If Tlitoo had told them, they would be asking me about it.

"Sonnen and Pirra have called a Gathering of the packs," Marra said. "In an hour's time at the Wind Lake verge." Sonnen was the leader of the Tree Line pack, and Pirra led Wind Lake. A verge was the neutral land between wolves' territories. Any wolf could cross into a verge without fear of attack, so that's where the Gatherings were always held. We had planned to call a Gathering to discuss the Greatwolves' test, but Ruuqo had decided to speak to the other packs less formally. Now someone else had called a Gathering and would set its rules and tone.

"They specifically asked that the three of us come," Marra continued. "If you hadn't woken up, we were going to have to go without you."

I licked the last of the horse meat from my muzzle. Pack Gatherings were called when something that affected all the wolves in the valley necessitated cooperation or a decision. Any leaderwolf could call one, but if the other packs deemed the Gathering unnecessary, they could punish the wolf who had brought them together, so they were rare. There had never been a pack Gathering in my lifetime, and I had never heard of one that included youngwolves like us. Usually, only leaderwolves attended.

"Because of the prey?" I asked.

"And because of Yllin," Marra said. "There's something happening, Kaala. I can't tell what it is, but the Tree Line youngwolf who came to tell us about the Gathering was hiding something. And why are we supposed to be there?"

I didn't know. All I wanted to do was sleep for another two days, but the pack Gathering could give us the opportunity to see if the other packs knew any more than we did about what the Greatwolves were planning. I turned my head from side to side, trying to work out the soreness in my neck. If the Gathering began in an hour in Wind Lake lands, we would need to leave soon. I planted my paws on an oak root and stretched the aches from the rest of my body. Then I rested my head against Ázzuen's back, gaining strength from him, then buried my nose deep in Marra's fur, reminding myself that in spite of Yllin's death, we were pack. I sniffed her fur, then sniffed again.

"You smell like MikLan!" I accused. "You'd better disguise his scent," I said, "or every wolf at the Gathering will know you've been with him."

"I don't care if they know," she said defiantly. But she

rolled in some fox dung anyway. It wouldn't really disguise the human-scent, but it would do enough so that Ruuqo and Rissa could ignore it if they wanted to. The other wolves were not familiar enough with either Marra's or MikLan's scent to be able to tell for sure where the scent came from. They would assume she was coming with us to the humans.

The food and water were beginning to revive me. I wouldn't want to have to run down prey, but I could make it to Wind Lake territory. I trotted to NiaLi.

"There may be a way for us to help the tribe hunt, even with most of the prey gone." I didn't know whether or not I was going to accept Torell's offer, so I didn't want to promise NiaLi that we would, but I told her about the possibility anyway. "If we can learn how to hunt the aurochs, we'll come to you so you can tell TaLi. And I'll take care of her. I promise." I placed a paw on the old woman's knee.

"I know you will," she said, covering my paw with a gnarled hand. "It is what lets me know it is all right that the time of my death nears." I didn't want to think about her dying. I knew she was old, older for a human than Trevegg was for a wolf, but I wasn't ready for more death. I touched her soft hand with my nose, then led Marra and Ázzuen to the Gathering of the packs.

⊡

I recognized Sonnen, the leaderwolf of Tree Line, and his mate, Krynna. I liked Sonnen, even though he had almost joined the Stone Peak wolves in attacking the humans at Tall Grass. He was a straightforward wolf, comfortable enough in his power that he never bullied even the most submissive wolf in his pack. The brawny, dark-coated wolf next to him was his secondwolf, Frallin, recognizable by his torn left ear, a wound he received protecting the pack's pups from a rock bear two summers ago. The tall thin wolves that smelled of birch and algae had to be Pirra and Velln, the leaderwolves of Wind Lake. I had never met them, but Rissa's muzzle always tightened when she mentioned Pirra. The third Wind Lake wolf was all too familiar, even with his back to me.

"Here comes the savior or destroyer of all wolfkind," Unnan said, looking over his shoulder at me. Pirra laughed. I winced. It was awkward enough being a youngwolf among so many leaderwolves without Unnan calling attention to me. I couldn't imagine why Pirra and Velln had brought him. Each pack was allowed to bring three wolves into the verge itself. All other wolves, including Ázzuen and Marra, would have to wait in the woods surrounding it. I was allowed to enter the verge as a fourth Swift River wolf because I was what they were talking about, but Wind Lake could have brought any wolf in the pack. They didn't need to bring a youngwolf who had been part of Wind Lake less than half a moon.

Ruuqo, Rissa, and Trevegg strode into the verge while the rest of the pack halted at the edge of the woods. I could see that the other packs had brought reinforcements, too. The night air was saturated with the scents of Tree Line and Wind Lake wolves. I could make out dark shapes at the edges of each territory, at least twelve wolves in addition to those of us taking part in the Gathering. As far as I knew there had never been a fight at a Gathering, but no one was taking any chances. Aware of every nose attuned to me, I followed my packmates into the verge.

"This is the one?" Pirra asked, looking me over. Not waiting for an answer, she sidled past Ruuqo and Rissa so that she was standing atop a slight slope. Several wolves growled their displeasure. The reason we met at a verge was that it was neutral territory and no wolf or pack would have dominance over the others. Pirra's action could easily have been taken as a threat, but Rissa's voice was mild when she spoke.

"Yes, this is our youngwolf Kaala. Are Maccon and Milla coming?"

"The Vole Eater leaderwolves declined our invitation," Sonnen said. "They're concerned about gathering enough food, now that we all must hunt the smallprey." Vole Eater wolves subsisted primarily on smaller prey. With all the other packs in the valley competing for it, they would struggle. In times of hunger, not all wolves respected the rules of territory, and the Vole Eaters were not strong. "If you have no objection," Sonnen continued, "we'll begin." He looked up startled, then, at the sound of hurried pawsteps.

"Maccon is coming after all?" his mate, Krynna, said as the scent of male wolf wafted onto the verge. Vole Eater's territory abutted ours. They would need to come through Swift River lands to reach the verge. All wolves were allowed safe passage through the territories when a Gathering was called. But it wasn't a Vole Eater wolf. I recognized the arriving wolf's gait, and then his scent. So did Pirra.

"It's not Maccon," she said, snarling a little. The light breeze picked up the scent of Stone Peak wolf. Several wolves growled. When Pell loped onto the Verge, their growls deepened. Many in the valley still blamed the Stone Peak wolves for the battle at Tall Grass.

"Stone Peak was not invited, Pell," Pirra said.

"And we forgive the oversight. We understand this Gathering was called quickly and know that you would not break the rules of the Gathering by excluding us." Pell spoke formally, with the authority of a leaderwolf. Pirra must have thought so, too.

"Why didn't Torell come?" she asked. "He has little respect for the Gathering if he sends us only his lamed second."

Pell ignored the insult. The fact that he had come alone, among more than twenty wolves not of his pack, spoke of his courage.

"Torell is occupied elsewhere," he said simply. "I am now his second and will lead Stone Peak when he no longer can. And Stone Peak has as much to say here as any other pack. The dead wolf was found in our territory, and we will suffer from the lack of prey as much as you will."

Which wasn't entirely true, I thought, if they were going to hunt the aurochs and the elkryn.

"All packs are welcome to a Gathering, Pirra, you know that," Trevegg said. He was the oldest wolf at the Gathering and would be respected because of it.

Pirra growled something under her breath. The other wolves watched her. Her mate and her second would support her if she wanted to fight Pell. I wasn't sure what the others would do. A Gathering was always tense—too many dominant wolves too close to one another's territories—and the prey leaving the valley had left everyone on edge. A fight would be disastrous. Pirra looked Pell up and down, measuring his strength and resolve, daring him to challenge her. I wanted to speak up, to tell him that if he did so, he would ruin Stone Peak's chance of participating in any Gathering.

He didn't need my help. He bent his forelegs and raised his hindquarters high in the air. He grinned at the Wind Lake leaderwolf. "Come, Pirra," he said. "Surely our minds are stronger together. You, of any wolf, know how important strength is."

It was obviously flattery. Pirra never tired of telling everyone how she had triumphed over three wolves, all bigger than she, to win the role of Wind Lake leader. But it worked. Pirra wrinkled her nose in a smile. "Fine," she said, "we will see if a Stone Peak wolf can have manners."

All around me, wolves relaxed. I caught a satisfied smile tugging at Pell's muzzle before he saw me looking at him and smoothed out his face.

Sonnen stepped forward to speak.

"I won't waste your time," the Tree Line leader said. "We've received an offer from the Greatwolves." He twitched an ear. "From Milsindra and Kivdru."

I bent my head to chew at the fur of my shoulder, trying to look relaxed as my heart began to pound. Any deal with Milsindra and Kivdru could only be bad for us.

Sonnen continued. "You all know that the prey is leaving the valley and that we cannot follow it. I asked Milsindra why we are not permitted to leave to follow the prey. She told me it would upset the Balance, and that we must remain in the Wide Valley. There is a way, however, that we can feed our packs until the prey returns."

"What way is that, Sonnen?" The sharpness in Rissa's voice made me bite the skin of my shoulder harder than I'd intended. I tasted blood.

"You know that there is a struggle for power in the Great-wolf council," Sonnen said, meeting Rissa's gaze, "between the leaderwolf Zorindru and Milsindra, who wishes to replace him. If we support Milsindra and her followers in this struggle, they will ensure that we have enough to eat until the prey returns. Enough to bring forth and feed our pups."

"But Milsindra is the one making the prey leave!" I said. I was one of the youngest, least dominant wolves there, but I had to speak up.

"So you say," Pirra responded. "But how are we to know that you speak the truth? I've heard that you don't always do so."

I blinked. I had been accused of being stupid and reckless, of being prideful and too quick to act, but no one had ever accused me of being dishonest. I saw Unnan standing next to Pirra, a self-satisfied expression on his weasel-face. Then he pressed up against his new leaderwolf and shot me a look of such hatred I could only stare at him. I don't think I realized until that moment how deep his loathing for me was.

"I have also seen the Greatwolves driving away the prey," Pell said. "All of Stone Peak has. As have the ravens."

Pirra laughed. "I trust the Stone Peaks no more than I trust ravens. Neither has the interest of most wolves at heart."

Ruuqo spoke. "You know that it's the Greatwolves themselves who have set this challenge, Sonnen, who have bid us stay with the humans. And every wolf in the valley dies if we don't succeed."

Sonnen looked levelly at Ruuqo and Rissa. His mate stepped to his side. Her voice was surprisingly soft for a leaderwolf's.

"That is no longer so," Krynna said. "Milsindra and Kivdru have told us that if we support them in their struggle, things will be as they were before. We will not be allowed near the humans nor permitted to kill them. The Greatwolves will take over the task of guarding the humans once again, and we will live in peace. Things will be the way they were before."

"The offer is open to your pack, too, Ruuqo," Sonnen said. "I made sure of that."

"And you believed the Greatwolves?" Trevegg said. "When they lied to us and were willing to kill us all not four moons ago?" He stood beside Ruuqo and Rissa, who had both gone silent. I couldn't tell what they were thinking. Milsindra had said she would do whatever she needed to do to win, but it had never occurred to me that she would ask smallwolves for help. Trevegg looked at Ruuqo and Rissa, waiting for them to speak. When they didn't, he stepped forward to stand nose to nose with the Tree Line leaderwolf.

"There is more going on here, Sonnen, than a power struggle among the Greatwolves," he said, speaking as a leaderwolf would to an inferior. "You must look beyond this season's prey."

"I realize that, elderwolf," Sonnen said. "Do you think so little of Tree Line that you believe we would sacrifice our honor and the well-being of wolfkind just to fill our bellies?" He lowered his head and stepped back and away from the oldwolf.

Yes, I thought, dread creeping up on me, *you would*.

"What Milsindra and Kivdru spoke of only confirms what has long troubled us," Krynna said, "that the only way wolves can live with humans, as your youngwolf is trying to do, is to give up that which makes us wolf, as has happened every time wolves and humans have come together."

It was the paradox again. But they had known of it before, when they agreed to help us. Every wolf knew of it.

"They say that if your pup is allowed to continue on her path," Sonnen said, "wolfkind will be weakened and the humans will wish to enslave us once again. That is unacceptable to us. It's too great a risk to the safety of our packs. Have you been submissive to them?" he asked me.

"Only a little," I said, startled to be addressed. "So they wouldn't fear us."

"More than a little," Unnan said, interrupting me. "I saw it. She let their leader grab her and shake her as if she were prey. And she did nothing to him. She licked his hand."

I hadn't seen or smelled Unnan anywhere near Oldwoods that day. He must have been hiding, sneaking around as he always did. I was beginning to understand why Pirra had brought him along.

Ruuqo grunted. I turned to see that he and Rissa were watching me. We hadn't told them about that part of the hunt at Oldwoods.

"And she is drelshik," Pirra said, not even trying for Sonnen's polite tone.

"So Milsindra says?" Trevegg challenged, fury deepening his voice to a low rumble. Ruuqo and Rissa remained silent. "That wolf will say anything to get what she wants. Swift River lost one of our most promising youngwolves not three days ago. And you tell us about risk?"

"You are not the only ones to lose a wolf!" Pirra darted forward, and for a moment, I thought she might break verge neutrality and attack Trevegg. Her mate slammed his shoulder into her hip, and Pirra stopped just in front of the oldwolf, who hadn't moved a pawswidth.

"Nine nights ago, Ivvan, the strongest pup of my last litter, disappeared. Right after your youngwolf hunted with the humans. Vanished as no wolf should. Just as your pup vanished five moons ago." She swung her head to Ruuqo and Rissa. "Why did you allow the mixed-blood drelshik to stay in your pack when your pup disappeared? Now the prey is gone, and my pup has gone missing." She began to stalk toward Ruuqo and Rissa. Ruuqo stepped forward to meet her.

"We have never thought her a true threat, Pirra," he said. "You overstep yourself." The cold anger in his voice made her stop and raise her hackles.

"Was Kaala responsible for your pup's disappearance, Ruuqo?" Sonnen asked.

Ruuqo was silent.

"She was," Unnan said. "There were three of us she didn't like. She made the horses stampede and kill Reel. Then Borlla disappeared. That's why I left Swift River. She would have done something to me next. She's drelshik."

"She's unlucky, Ruuqo, and that's the truth," Sonnen said, almost kindly. "No one blames you for keeping her. No leaderwolf wants to send away a pack member, especially a pup. But we all must do what is best—for our packs and for the valley. The Denning Moon nears, and we must prepare for our pups. We will support Milsindra. As will Vole Eater and Wind Lake. As should you."

"What does supporting involve, Sonnen?" Trevegg asked.

"If you hurt Kaala, or stop her from going to the humans, you will have Frandra and Jandru to contend with, and I promise you, they won't be gentle."

"We would not harm the youngwolf," Sonnen said. "We have promised Milsindra and Kivdru that we will stand by them if there is a fight. As for stopping her from going to the humans, that's not up to us."

"What does that mean?" Ruuqo asked.

It was Pirra who answered.

"The prey is gone, and we are all hungry. If you're busy helping your youngwolf grovel to the humans, you will not be able to defend your territory well. And, as of tonight, you are no longer welcome to hunt in our lands to feed your humans."

"They want your pup to fail, Ruuqo," Sonnen said. He lowered his eyes. "If you lost much of your territory you would struggle to support your pack, and you wouldn't be able to help this wolf in her task. I suggest you accept the offer Milsindra has made. Your pack and your pups will live, and things will be as they were before."

I was furious. They were all just doing what was easiest for them, for all they said it was for the good of wolfkind. And they were being stupid. The Greatwolves' way of watching over the humans was failing long before I had pulled TaLi from the river, long before the battle at Tall Grass. Milsindra had lied before and would lie again. But the other wolves didn't want to hear it. Trevegg was still arguing with them, telling them that Milsindra and Kivdru were not reliable, but Pirra just smirked and Sonnen and Krynna wouldn't even meet his gaze. Ruuqo and Rissa were looking at each other, still silent, obviously tempted by Sonnen's offer.

Youngwolves weren't supposed to interrupt leaderwolves,

but I didn't care. "I can prove Milsindra's wrong," I said. Pirra, who was telling Trevegg that the mark on my chest was another sign that I was a drelshik wolf, stopped talking to glare at me.

"It's too late for that," Pirra responded, dismissing me.

Before I could respond, Pell spoke.

"You should know that Stone Peak will not accept Milsindra's offer. And we will stand by Swift River if they choose to fight against you. We will help them defend their territory and will help the youngwolf Kaala find food for her humans and her pack."

He bowed to Ruuqo and Rissa, gave me a sharp look, then turned his tail on the other wolves and trotted from the verge.

The Wind Lake and Tree Line wolves shifted uncomfortably, and I smelled uncertainty rising from them. Stone Peak and Swift River had been rivals for so long, it had probably never occurred to any of them that we might fight together. It would make it much harder for them to take our territory or our prey. It was Sonnen who broke the silence.

"I respect you, Ruuqo. I always have. You speak your mind and do what you think is right. I can stall Milsindra for a quarter moon's time, tell her I have to find a denning site for this year's pups. I owe you that much for what happened at Tall Grass. In the meantime, I advise you to think about the offer Milsindra has made. I do not wish to have you as an enemy."

He dipped his head to his mate and his secondwolf, and led them from the verge. Pirra and Velln did not make eye contact with any of us as they returned to their packmates and set off for Wind Lake lands.

None of us spoke until we were well into our own territory. Ruuqo and Rissa led us to the top of a breezy hillock. Any wolf could see us standing there in the moonlight, but the small hill also gave us the advantage of seeing any attack that might come. The leaderwolves must have been nervous if they were that fearful of attack. I was concerned at how quiet Ruuqo and Rissa had been at the Gathering. So, apparently, was Trevegg.

"Don't do it," Trevegg said to the leaderwolves as soon as they stopped. "I don't care what Milsindra and Kivdru say they'll do, you can't trust them." Ruuqo looked across the plain, Rissa back toward the heart of Swift River lands. Trevegg looked from one leaderwolf to the other. "You can't be considering it."

"We have to consider it!" Ruuqo said. "We can barely survive as it is. If other packs are challenging us we'll have to put all of our energies toward protecting our lands. We won't be able to feed ourselves."

"Much less the humans," Werrna added. I remembered how much she hated giving up the walking bird for the humans. "My advice is to accept Milsindra's offer. We will eat well and won't have to deal with the humans anymore."

Like that worked so well before, I thought.

"I can bring us enough food," I said. "The humans will help feed us." I told them of Torell's offer, of his belief that Milsindra and her followers were hiding something and that if we could find it, it would weaken her. I did not tell them of his plan for rebellion. I had promised Torell I wouldn't. Ruuqo considered me.

"The question of whether or not you are drelshik remains, Kaala," he said. "You know I have never been certain that Jandru and Frandra were right to spare your life. If I have protected a drelshik wolf, I will have to answer for that. If keeping you caused Borlla's disappearance and the Wind Lake pup's disappearance, I must answer for that. If Jandru and Frandra are wrong, it is more than our pack that is at risk."

"Borlla left on her own," I said, annoyed that he was bringing her up. She was long gone.

"You should not so easily dismiss your responsibility," Rissa rebuked. "If you want to be a leaderwolf someday it's your responsibility to care about wolves you influence. And I don't like making agreements with the Stone Peaks."

She seemed ready enough to consider an agreement with Milsindra. And I didn't see why Borlla's choices were my responsibility. I opened my mouth to object. Trevegg bumped my hip with his own.

"What if Sonnen and Pirra are wrong and Milsindra doesn't defeat Zorindru?" he said.

"It's a risk," Rissa admitted. "But Zorindru won't kill us if he succeeds. Milsindra might."

"So because Milsindra is more ruthless, she wins?" Marra asked, incredulous. "You follow her because she doesn't honor her word and Zorindru does?"

"Quiet, youngwolf," Ruuqo snapped. "You cannot possibly understand the complexities of what we're dealing with."

"I understand it," Marra said. "I understand that you'll follow a wolf who scares you rather than one who does what's right."

We all stared at her. Marra had strong opinions, and she was clever enough to know when to express them. I could tell by the trembling of her flanks that she was furious.

"Leave," Ruuqo commanded. "You can come back when you obey the rules of the pack." Marra looked from Ruuqo to Rissa, then stared hard at me. She stalked down the hill.

I was tempted to follow her. To take Ázzuen, Marra, and our humans and take our chances getting out of the valley. But the pack was in trouble because of me, and I had promised Zorindru, Jandru, and Frandra that I would stay. I remembered the three youngwolves who had come to me at the river. Sonnen didn't know as much about the Vole Eaters as he thought he did.

And Rissa was right. It wasn't just about what I wanted anymore. But it wasn't just about what Swift River wanted, either.

"I'll get us more food," I repeated. "And I'll prove that Zorindru is right and Milsindra is wrong."

Ruuqo came to a decision. "I want to talk to Sonnen again, and with Vole Eater, and I want to hear what Frandra and Jandru have to say. We will make use of the quarter moon that Sonnen has given us. If you can bring us good food, Kaala, it will bear on our decision."

Without another word, he set off down the hill. Rissa and Werrna followed him. Trevegg did not.

"I'll talk to him," Trevegg said to me and Ázzuen, "but be prepared for the worst."

I pushed away my worry. Ruuqo and Rissa just needed to know the pack could be fed and safe. I would show them we could easily do so. They had responsibility for the entire pack, and I would prove to them it was in the pack's best interest to stick with the promise.

"Go speak to Torell," the oldwolf said. "Hunt with your

humans. Then find me at NiaLi's. I will tell you if I've made progress with Ruuqo."

"Why NiaLi's?" Ázzuen asked.

"I'm worried about her," Trevegg said. "While you were asleep, Kaala, she told me of her troubles, and I fear for her. She told me perhaps more than she told you. I think she fears for her life. She is not afraid to die but said she doesn't want to do so before TaLi is established as krianan. Send the ravens if you need me." He took my muzzle and then Ázzuen's in his jaws, and trotted down the hill after the pack.

Ázzuen and I followed Marra's scent to the bottom of the hill. She stood when we came near.

"That took long enough."

"Let's go find Torell," I said.

15

T he trick to hunting aurochs," Torell said, "is to make them so angry that they lose what good sense they have. If you hunt them the way you hunt elkryn or other prey, you might succeed in the hunt, but you will likely lose a pack-mate."

I believed him. I had never seen an auroch up close be-fore. They were nearly as tall as the elkryn and broader bodied with thick, shaggy fur that kept them warm even in the cold-est days of winter. Their shoulders were huge, and hard mus-cles bunched up underneath their dark fur. Their eyes moved restlessly in their faces. Torell had not exaggerated the length and sharpness of their horns, which curved out from their heads and gleamed in the sunlight. The aurochs looked formi-dable even as they grazed. I had hunted elkryn, snow deer, and horses, but I shivered at the thought of being gored by those sharp auroch horns. Torell had insisted that I sleep for several hours before we began the long run to the auroch feeding grounds, even though that meant we would have to hunt them in the daylight. So I was rested. But I was still nervous about my ability to hunt the great beasts.

"So how do you make them angry without getting killed?" Ázzuen asked. He was trying to sound nonchalant, but his ribs were heaving and his breath came in quick pants.

"You're about to find out," Torell answered. "You don't learn to hunt aurochs by watching."

I jerked my head up to stare at him. Ruuqo and Rissa always made us watch them hunt new prey before allowing us to take part in the hunt. Torell ignored my surprise.

"You're the fastest," he said to Marra. "You go with Pell. The two of you will be the ones to anger the auroch." Marra blinked at him a few times, then dipped her head.

"You two will be with me," Torell said to me and to Ázzuen. "Ceela and Arrun will wait and come to our aid if needed."

He trotted out onto the plain as calmly as if he were hunting rabbits and voles. Ázzuen, Marra, and Pell followed. I looked at Tlitoo, who was busily stripping bark from a twig.

"Are you coming?" I asked him.

"I am not stupid, wolflet," he said. He flipped his wings at me and flew to the low branch of a pine. I saw Jlela there waiting for him. Jlela ran her beak through Tlitoo's back feathers, and then both ravens flew to the higher branches of the tree. I peered up into the branches, trying to see them but could not. I followed Torell and the others onto the plain. They were all waiting for me, standing in a small group and watching the aurochs.

"In auroch hunting," Torell said when I reached him,

"you don't necessarily find the weakest beast, as you do with other prey. You seek the ones that react most strongly to your presence."

They all seemed to react to us. Their eyes followed us suspiciously as we moved among them. A beast standing right next to me shook its head sharply. I leapt nearly a full wolflength off the ground and scrambled away from it. All four wolves just looked at me.

"It's just getting rid of flies," Pell said kindly. I felt like an idiot.

"What do we do once we select one?" I asked Torell, trying to make up for my cowardice.

He didn't answer. His head was lowered, and he was staring an auroch full in the face, his jaws open to reveal all of his sharp teeth. The beast met his gaze and scraped its hoof in the dirt. I hadn't noticed before, but even their hooves were sharp and dangerous. I wondered if it would speak to us as the elkryn did, but it just blew a great gust of air from its nose.

"This one," Torell said, his voice a whispered growl. His eyes flicked quickly over to Pell, who butted Marra's shoulder and trotted to the other side of the beast's head.

"When it gets angry, it forgets to look from side to side," Torell whispered to me. "Remember that." His bared teeth opened in a wide grin, and the scent of excitement rose from him. He was enjoying himself.

"Now!" he barked.

Pell and Marra darted in at the auroch, stopping just short of its face and snapping at it. Then they dodged out of its way. They ran back in, snapping their teeth together even closer to its face, causing the beast to shake its head back and forth.

Then it whipped its head to stare at Torell, Ázzuen, and me. I noticed that it turned its whole body to look behind itself. As soon as it turned away from them, Pell and Marra darted in, biting at its flank.

My fear did not abate, but the thrill of the hunt began to rise in me. The scent of the beast filled me, and suddenly it was no longer just an auroch: it was prey. A moment before it had seemed invulnerable. Now, as it whipped its head back and forth and turned its bulk from Marra and Pell to us and back again, I knew it was ours.

The next time they darted in at the auroch, Marra nipped at its ear and Pell actually took its jowls in his mouth. Pell certainly didn't need anyone's help hunting. His gait was uneven as he dodged in and out of the way of the auroch's horns, but he was as quick and agile as Marra. The auroch shook them off, then stood perfectly still staring at them, his breath shallow. Then his head began to swing back and forth. Pell barked softly to Marra, and the two of them leapt at the same time, slamming into the auroch's head, then leaping away and running. The auroch bellowed in rage and took off after them, its deadly horns aimed at their soft bodies.

The instant it began to run, the three of us were upon it. My fear became irrelevant as the beast tried to kill my packmates. For in the hunt, Pell had become my packmate every bit as much as Marra and Ázzuen were. I didn't need to watch for Torell's signal. He, Ázzuen, and I leapt almost simultaneously upon the auroch's rump. I bit down hard through its thick hide. The taste of its flesh flooded the back of my throat, and a growl of hunger and greed rose up in me.

Infuriated, the auroch turned on us, kicking up its back

legs and throwing all three of us off its back. We sprinted away in three different directions. Confused, it stood and scraped its hoof over and over again in the dirt. Pell growled, and it turned to look at him. I darted forward, diving under its belly, just as I had when Torell was teaching us how to fight. The Stone Peak leader woofed encouragement to me as the auroch tried to turn its large body around quickly enough to catch me. As it did so, Ázzuen followed me under its belly as Pell and Marra leapt upon its rump. They bit into the beast. Hard.

I had never seen a creature so enraged. It kicked and bucked and screamed and tried to attack. But it didn't do so intelligently. It was so angry it just swung its head side to side and jumped full in the air, trying to gore whichever wolf was closest.

"Together!" Torell shouted. It was the agreed-upon command for all of us to jump at once at the beast. I was near its neck and balanced on my hind legs to lean upon it and sink my teeth into the soft underpart of its throat. I was overconfident. Pell woofed a warning as the auroch swung its head around. It seemed as if it barely turned its head, but when the side of one of its horns caught me, the force of the blow slammed me to the ground. Stunned, gasping for breath, I found myself lying on the ground, looking up at its head and the sharp horn bearing down on me. There was nowhere to run. Just as the furious beast lowered its head to gore me, two wolves slammed into its head, Ázzuen and Pell leaping at the same time, slamming into each other as they collided with the auroch. I heard a scream of agony. Terrified, I leapt up, wondering which wolf had been gored. But it was the auroch screaming, screaming as Torell and Marra bit into its belly.

Arrun and Ceela, unable to sit on the side any longer, pelted across the field, jumping on the auroch's hindquarters and tearing into it. I leapt at the upper part of one of its legs, which was still kicking and threatening to hurt a packmate. Then the hunt frenzy overtook me. Blood, warm flesh, a thrashing prey giving up its life to us. We tore at it until its legs stopped kicking and it gave a deep groan. Pell yowled in triumph and tackled me, rolling me in the dirt in celebration. Then he licked the top of my head and let me up. Gasping, my heart pounding, I got to my paws and looked at the auroch, dead now, its horns no longer a threat, transformed in an instant from a dangerous beast into good meat. We had done that. We had killed an auroch.

Ázzuen figured out how to make the auroch hunt work with the humans.

"They use their two kinds of sharpsticks differently," he explained as we made our way to NiaLi's shelter. Now that we had accepted Torell's offer and knew how to hunt aurochs, we had to tell NiaLi so she could tell TaLi. It would be up to the girl to get the humans to come to the auroch grazing grounds.

"The humans use the thicker sharpsticks, the spears, when they are closer to prey. The lighter sharpsticks are used with the throwers. They have different kinds of blades, too."

The blades were sharpened rocks, antlers or bones that the humans attached to the ends of the sticks to make them sharp and deadly.

"And different humans are better with different ones," Marra added. "MikLan told me that he's still not quite strong enough to use the spears, but he can use the throwing sticks. The Lan tribe doesn't let their young use the spears against large prey until they are full grown." Marra had obviously been spending a lot more time with the Lan tribe than she admitted. I had noticed the difference between the two kinds of sharpsticks but hadn't paid much attention. Now that Ázzuen and Marra mentioned it, though, I remembered that TaLi had used the throwing stick against the elkryn she had helped kill at the Tall Grass battle and one of the spears to kill a rabbit.

"So some of the humans can throw sharpsticks at it from a distance and others can help us up close to the prey," Ázzuen concluded. "We just have to watch which humans are best with each kind of sharpstick and drive the prey to them based on that."

I was glad Ázzuen had figured it out. Now we just had to get the humans to follow us to the aurochs. We reached NiaLi's shelter, and Trevegg came out to greet us. "She's waiting for you," he said, and led us inside.

⊡

"I *told* you the prey was gone," TaLi said, her arms folded over her chest. It was almost a full day since I'd awoken from my journey to the Inejalun and three days since we'd seen the Greatwolves chasing the prey. Half of HuLin's runners had returned from their search to tell of missing horses, elk, and deer.

"You'd better not take that tone with HuLin," RinaLi said. She and TaLi were standing next to the herb structure, glaring at each other. Ázzuen and I sat beside TaLi while Marra hid in the bushes surrounding the village. RinaLi had her hands on her hips as she glowered at the girl.

"I'm not stupid," TaLi said to her aunt. "But the sooner he accepts me as krianan, the less time we'll waste."

"Don't even think of telling him that," RinaLi snapped. She stopped speaking abruptly as HuLin, two other males, and KiLi strode over to them.

"How did you know about the prey, TaLi?" HuLin demanded. "How could you possibly know?"

"It's my task to know," she responded, her voice respectful. I was impressed that she could change her manner so quickly. One instant she was angry and forceful, and the next she was diffident and respectful. She would have made a good wolf. "It's the krianan's role to listen to the messages the world around us shares."

HuLin grunted rudely at that. "We found some giant elk east of the Dry Hills," he said. "Giant elk" was the humans' name for the elkryn. "Aln tribe is hunting them. We may have to fight for them. The aurochs are feeding in the Western Plains, but we're less likely to be able to hunt them. It's too close to their mating time, and they'll be aggressive."

It was the opening TaLi had been waiting for.

"We can hunt the aurochs with the wolves." She placed her hand on my head, and I stood.

"Have you done so before?" KiLi asked, concerned. I walked over and licked her hand; she was a friend to TaLi and I wanted her to know that meant she was my friend as well. Startled, she hesitantly stroked my neck. I licked her hand again and returned to TaLi.

"I know that we can hunt them," TaLi said, deliberately

not answering KiLi's question. We hadn't hunted aurochs to-gether yet, a fact that concerned me more than I would admit even to Ázzuen. "And I can take you to the ones that will most easily fall to our spears."

The other humans were silent, considering her words.

"She was right about the prey being gone, HuLin," KiLi said.

"It's almost a half-day's journey to the Western Plains," one of the males complained, "and it's almost dark. The giant elk are closer. And less dangerous."

"And being hunted by Aln," KiLi retorted. "The other tribes may or may not know that the prey is gone, and thanks to TaLi's warning, we do. We can get to the aurochs first."

TaLi spoke again. "If we have the wolves hunting with us, the aurochs are no more dangerous than giant elk." She sounded like an adult, like a true krianan, not a child, and I was proud of her.

"We may as well hunt the aurochs," one of the males said. "It's no more dangerous than fighting Aln for the giant elk. And it would bring us honor."

"Why would it bring them honor?" Ázzuen asked me.

"I don't know," I answered.

The other male, the one who had protested the distance to the aurochs, grunted in agreement. "I'm not afraid of a good hunt," he said. "And if game is scarce, I'd like other tribes to know we are auroch-hunters. They'll think twice be-fore fighting us for other prey."

HuLin threw an arm around each of the males. "Then we'll hunt the aurochs and show the other tribes in the valley what Lin can do. TaLi, you will bring the wolves," he said, as if it was his idea to do so.

"Yes, HuLin," TaLi said.

HuLin smiled and ruffled her hair, then strode off with the other males. KiLi gave TaLi a concerned look and followed them.

RinaLi watched the four of them leave, then glared again at TaLi. "I hope you're right about your wolves," she said, and stalked away after the other humans.

TaLi waited until she was out of hearing range and then crouched down to bury her face in my neck fur. "So am I," she whispered.

All four of my legs ached and I had bruises along the entire right side of my body. Marra had a cut over her left eye, received when she tried to scoot under Ceela's chest, and Ázzuen kept licking his right forepaw, which had somehow ended up between Pell's hip and a sharp rock. Torell had insisted on giving us one more fighting lesson before we hunted aurochs with the humans. He said that we needed to hone our reflexes and learn to pay attention to that which we couldn't see. He and his packmates had thrown us into the hard dirt again and again until they were satisfied that we were ready.

For some reason, TaLi had chosen the auroch feeding grounds that were most distant from the human village, and told us to meet her there. We were so far to the west that in the distance I could see the hills that bordered the western edge of the valley. I could also see, just to the south, the low ridge of hills that Pell had spoken of. One of the hills had a line of poplars and low bushes across the top that might hide us. It would be a simple thing to get there and look for the Greatwolf hiding place. The hunting ground was also more than half a day's walk from the human village, and the humans waited half the night before leaving so that they could arrive at daybreak. Which had given Torell plenty of time to toss us around. As a result, all three of us stumbled rather than walked from Stone Peak territory back to the humans.

It was worth it. An auroch lay dead on the ground, and the humans celebrated.

I looked in satisfaction at the auroch and the humans. Torell had done us more of a favor than he realized by helping us hunt the aurochs. The humans prized them above all other prey not just for their meat, which was nourishing and rich, but also for their hides, tough enough to last many seasons. Killing an auroch was seen as an act of great prowess and bravery among the humans. That's what the human male had meant about the honor of killing one. HuLin was so pleased that he had given us twice as much meat as he had at the horse hunt. I watched as TaLi was honored by her tribe. If she continued to bring them to prey and we continued to help them hunt, they would value us, and her as well.

I looked down the plain to the edge of the forest closest to the ridge of hills. Frandra and Jandru were there, lying on their bellies and watching. Only their muzzles and paws were easily visible, so the humans, unless they were looking carefully, wouldn't see them. NiaLi had told the two Greatwolves of our plans, and they had wanted to see us hunt the aurochs for themselves. Frandra saw me watching them and dipped her head to me. Then the two Greatwolves slipped back into the woods.

Tlitoo pulled my ear. "The meat does no one any good sitting on the ground, wolf," Tlitoo said. "Your pack will not care how well the humans hunt if they do not get their meat."

His beak was bloody and his belly distended. The instant the humans had cut into the auroch, Tlitoo and Jlela had zoomed in, diving for the entrails that spilled from the beast's belly. The humans swatted them away, HuLin nearly succeeding in hitting Tlitoo with the blunt end of his sharpstick, but not before the ravens had stolen good greslin. The birds had returned twice more, taking care to steal meat as far from HuLin as they could. "If you do not want the meat for your pack," Tlitoo quorked, "we will take it."

"I'm surprised you can still fly," Marra said, eyeing the bird's swollen belly. "But he's right, Kaala. The sooner we take meat back to the pack the sooner we show them we can still succeed with the humans."

I stood, groaning at the pain in my ribs. I had just picked up a piece of greslin in my jaws when TaLi saw me and called to me.

"Silvermoon!" she shouted, and held out her hand.

HuLin stepped up beside her. "Wolf," he said. "Silvermoon, come over here."

He had never called me by name before. Curious, I set down the meat I held and trotted over to them. I heard Ázzuen's and Marra's pawsteps behind me. I reached the humans and pressed myself against TaLi.

"I thought you'd already gone," she said, "and I'm going to need you."

Both she and HuLin were looking across the plain. I followed their gaze and saw a cluster of strange humans emerging from the woods. They strode onto the Western Plains and stopped eight wolflengths from the Lin tribe. Their alder scent was familiar, but it took me a moment to place it.

"DavRian's tribe," Marra said.

"Your girl brought us to their territory to hunt," Tlitoo said smugly.

"Why would she do that?" I asked. Did she want to anger DavRian's family so that they wouldn't want her in their tribe?

Sure enough, DavRian was there, along with nine other humans who smelled like him. He still hadn't come to live with Lin, in spite of RinaLi's invitation. Probably because TaLi always snarled at him. But as soon as he saw TaLi, he started forward. Another male, tall and rangy with hair the color of Rissa's fur, stopped him and whispered to him. All of the Rian humans held either their spears or the sticks and throwers used for hunting.

TaLi crouched down to whisper in my ear. "I'm getting rid of DavRian," she said.

"What do you mean?" I asked, dread rising up in me. TaLi could be reckless—as reckless as Marra—and didn't always show good sense. I had no idea what she had in mind, but the determined gleam in her eye made me nervous.

"She wants a challenge," Marra said, admiration in her voice. "MikLan told me of them. The humans bet, just like we do. It's risky, but if it works, she'll be rid of DavRian."

"BreLan would never let her do it," Ázzuen said. But BreLan wasn't there.

The humans of the Rian tribe hadn't moved. The white-furred male spoke. "These are our hunting grounds, HuLin," he said. "You should have asked our permission before killing here."

The fur along my spine rose. Among wolves, trespassing on another pack's hunting grounds was reason for a fight. Just two moons ago Wind Lake and Tree Line had fought over hunting grounds, and two wolves had been injured. But the white-furred human's tone was mild in spite of the challenge of his words. I had the sense he was trying hard not to be angry and trying not to anger HuLin.

"As if they could kill an auroch," TaLi muttered loudly enough that even a human could hear. I was too far away to see DavRian's face clearly, but I saw his body tighten. HuLin glared at TaLi, but she ignored him. She folded her arms. "They couldn't hunt an auroch if it lay down in front of them and fell asleep." I leaned up against her, hard, so that she stumbled up against HuLin. Tlitoo pecked at her feet. "It's true," she said, whispering now. "I'm not joining their tribe. I'd rather live in a tree."

The white-furred male watched her for a moment, then turned his gaze to HuLin.

"They are contested lands, PalRian," HuLin said. "I know you and my father argued about them, but he never agreed to cede them to you." I remembered MikLan mentioning that name. PalRian was DavRian's father and the Rian tribe's leader.

"Your father and I had an agreement, even then," PalRian said. "We would discuss hunting here before doing so, and share what we killed. I know you are new to leading the Lin tribe, but I would expect you to honor your father's promises."

"We would be happy to share some meat with you,"

HuLin said, opening his arms toward the auroch carcass. "There is plenty more to be had." I wondered if the Rian tribe knew the prey was leaving the valley. Humans were rarely able to smell lies.

PalRian smiled and gestured to his followers, who lowered their sharpsticks and walked forward until they were within touching distance of the Lin tribe. As he came closer, I saw that PalRian was considerably older than HuLin. His joints did not move as smoothly, and his skin was looser on his bones. But he was healthy and assured in his leadership of Rian.

"You know I have no wish to fight with you, HuLin," the older male said. "You know I want an alliance with your tribe." He looked TaLi up and down. A female standing next to him smiled and reached out to the girl, stroking her strong arms. TaLi did not flinch back as I expected her to but met the female's eyes. If she were a wolf, the fur on her back would be raised.

"I wish it very much," PalRian said. "Still, this is Rian territory, and I would appreciate it if you would not take what isn't yours. You need to ask us before hunting here. Your father and I had a way of doing things that worked well for us."

"Then I will make you a wager," HuLin said pleasantly. "Whichever tribe can more quickly bring down another auroch will have hunting rights here for two years' time."

PalRian smiled a little.

"Why should I wager for what's already mine?" he asked.

TaLi took a deep breath and looked to HuLin for permission. He dipped his head to her.

"To prove yourselves worthy of an alliance with Lin," she said.

DavRian drew in a sharp breath. Every member of Rian was now staring at the girl.

"Your son wishes to marry our healer," HuLin said. "If you win, she is his—along with these hunting grounds. If we win, this land is ours and we gain the Moss Forest for two years as well." TaLi had told him that in spite of the flight of most of the valley's prey, the Moss Forest was replete with walking birds, forest pigs, and smallprey. It was because it smelled of damp moss, a scent the Greatwolves hated.

PalRian could not hide his excitement. His heartbeat quickened, and he looked TaLi over, as if she were smallprey and he a lion. I had no idea why she was so valuable to him, but he clearly wanted her.

This was what TaLi had meant about getting rid of DavRian. I felt sick. She was putting a lot of confidence in our ability to hunt the aurochs. I pawed at her leg.

"No risk no gain, Silvermoon," she whispered. "I have to do this, or there's no chance for me."

"We accept your wager," PalRian said eagerly, reminding me of Werrna accepting Torell's bet. "It will be a pleasure to show you how the Rian tribe hunts." It was obvious he thought HuLin was arrogant and inexperienced.

"Wait, Father," DavRian protested, "they'll use the wolves. The wolves help them hunt."

PalRian barked a laugh, and several of DavRian's tribe-mates laughed, too.

"You said the wolves were a hindrance, DavRian," TaLi said. "You said they were dangerous."

"If you're afraid of the wolves," HuLin said smoothly, "we will use fewer hunters. I will hunt with TaLi and just one of my other hunters. You may use as many as you like."

"Agreed!" PalRian said quickly, clearly thinking he was getting the better deal. DavRian tried to protest, but when his tribemates laughed at him again and began howling and growling, as if they were wolves, his face darkened and he stopped arguing. He glared at me fiercely. I turned away from him and lifted my tail to show him my backside. Ázzuen and Marra did the same. Then we began the hunt.

We won, of course. The Rian tribe hunted well, but they didn't know what we knew and did not have the combined skills of wolf and human. They were still testing the aurochs, looking for ones weak enough to kill without getting injured in the process, when we found an especially aggressive one, angered it, and killed it. That was enough for the auroch herd. They thundered away, leaving us alone with the Rian tribe.

PalRian took his loss with good grace, though I could tell he was unhappy.

"I assume my son can still bargain for the girl," he said.

"Of course," HuLin said, and TaLi gasped. "We would welcome it. And we would be happy to share this kill with you."

PalRian clasped HuLin's shoulder. "It's yours, honorably won," he said. "I look forward to wagering with you again." He looked TaLi over. "And to other discussions."

He nodded to his tribemates, and they began to drift from the plain. DavRian stayed, sulking where he stood until his father took him by the arm and led him away. As soon as they were gone from the field, HuLin gave a great whoop, lifted TaLi in the air, and spun her around. He set her down and gestured to the rest of the Lin tribe. They began cutting into the new auroch.

"He wasn't supposed to do that," TaLi whispered. "He was supposed to send DavRian away for good." She stood still for a moment. "I won't do it, Silvermoon. No matter what, I won't."

HuLin called to her then. She held my fur tightly and then went to him. I watched her go, wanting to go after her.

"The meat, wolflet," Tlitoo said. "You must bring it to your pack."

"I know," I said, still watching TaLi. "Where are they now?" I asked Tlitoo.

"Swamp Wallow Gathering Place," he answered. There was no such gathering place. Tlitoo had made up the name after the pack had followed us to the very edge of Swift River territory to a marshy, fly-infested patch of ground sheltered by sparse cypress trees and patchy juniper. Tlitoo had taken one look at it and dubbed it Swamp Wallow. The pack had chosen it because it was as close as they could get to the auroch grounds and remain in Swift River lands. After discovering the biting flies and marshy ground, the pack had considered moving farther back into our territory. Evidently, they had not.

"Let's go, then," Ázzuen said, licking his sore paw, reminding me of the pain in my ribs and legs. Only Marra seemed unaffected by our exertions. She bounded a few paces toward Swamp Wallow and looked back over her shoulder at me. I knew she was so impatient because she wanted to get back to MikLan.

"We're going," I said. I loped back to the meat HuLin had

given us, picked up a good piece of auroch belly, and led Áz-zuen and Marra toward Swamp Wallow. In spite of my concern for TaLi and my aching muscles, I felt good. We had succeeded with the humans and were bringing good greslin to the pack. We would bring our pack food, and then seek the Greatwolf cache. We were on our way to succeeding.

It was just past midday by the time we reached Swamp Wallow, and the pack slept soundly. Rissa lay curled up, her nose tucked into her forepaws, snoring hard. Ruuqo was stretched full length in the sun. Minn, who always got warm when he slept, rested in the scant shade of the cypresses. When the three of us squelched into the copse carrying the meat, Werrna opened one eye, then came fully awake. She stood, stretched, and walked over to us.

"Leave it there," she said before we'd even had a chance to set down the meat. She looked it over. "Is that all you brought?"

"There's more," I said, annoyed at her tone. How much did she think three wolves could carry? She didn't even thank us for bringing meat to the pack. "What did Ruuqo and Rissa find out?" I asked. The two leaderwolves smelled of Pirra and Sonnen. They must have been speaking to the Wind Lake and Tree Line packs.

Werrna didn't answer me. She just pushed the meat we'd brought around with her nose, looking for something wrong with it. But it was all good greslin. She picked up the belly meat I had brought and stalked to Minn. She set down the meat and poked him awake.

"Get up," she said. "We're taking this to New Cache."

Minn groaned but rose and stretched. Werrna returned to us. "Go get the rest of the meat," she said. "Then meet us back at Fallen Tree by darkfall for a pack meeting."

"Fallen Tree? That's an hour's run," I protested. "We still have to find what the Greatwolves are hiding, and we aren't done with the humans."

"Why can't we talk to Ruuqo and Rissa now?" Ázzuen demanded.

"Because they haven't slept more than two hours at a time since the Gathering!" Werrna said, glaring at me as if it was my fault. "Give them their rest or you'll answer to me for it."

She picked up the meat that both Ázzuen and Marra had carried, managing to get all of it in her powerful jaws, and stalked across the copse.

Marra blocked her path.

"Did Pirra and Sonnen agree to stand with us?" Marra demanded. "Something's happened. I can tell." She sniffed the mud in front of her paws as if she could smell the change in the dynamics of the pack. Ázzuen and I stared at her in shock. A wolf not yet a year old didn't challenge a secondwolf in that way. Werrna didn't even change her direction. She just shoved Marra aside. I thought she would keep going, but she set down the meat and glared at Marra.

"It is not for me to speak for the leaderwolves," she growled. "And it's not for you to demand it of me." But her scarred face was tight, and she shifted uneasily. Werrna was a straightforward wolf, and keeping secrets was not her way. "Go look for what the Greatwolves are hiding, then get back to the auroch kill and bring the rest of the greslin," she said.

She picked up the meat again and squelched from the clearing. Minn dashed after her, kicking up mud behind him. Marra and Ázzuen waded across the copse. I began to follow, then stopped as Tlitoo flew into the copse, hovered above Ruuqo, and landed on the sleeping wolf's back.

"Are you coming?" Ázzuen asked when he saw I had stopped.

"We have to look for the Greatwolf hiding place before the humans notice we're gone," Marra said.

"I'll follow you in a minute," I said. "You can wait for me at the bottom of the poplar hill."

Mara started to protest, but I glared at her. Grumbling, she and Ázzuen left.

"Hurry up, wolf," Tlitoo said as soon as they were out of earshot.

He had refused to come to Swamp Wallow, claiming it stank too much. Now he perched atop Ruuqo, looking at me expectantly.

"I thought you wouldn't come here," I said, snapping at the flies that tried to land on my muzzle. "Why aren't you up a tree with Jlela?" I could hear my voice was a little nasty.

He launched himself at me. I flinched back, but he only landed at my feet and glared at me.

"She is watching your humans for me, Moonwolf," he said. His use of that name made me uneasy. "We may not have another chance to do this."

"We don't have time," I said.

"We must have time," he quorked. "There are still things to know. And I must practice. The motherwolf said it was important." That was his name for Lydda. He hopped back onto Ruuqo's back.

Tempted, I took a few steps toward him. I'd felt guilty seeing Ázzuen's memories of me, but I had been fascinated. And if I knew what Ruuqo was thinking, I might better be able to convince the pack—and Sonnen and Pirra—to follow us. And we did need the practice. Maybe if we practiced we could find a way to see Lydda again.

"Quickly," I said.

He quorked in approval and hopped down next to Ruuqo. Cautiously, so as not to wake him, I lay down next to the leaderwolf, and Tlitoo pressed gently between us.

I thought I was ready for the cold and the falling sensation, for the absence of scent, but it still shocked me. My heart raced and it took all my will to keep from pulling away, but I forced myself to tolerate it. The darkness shifted into the bright light of midday and the no-scent was carried away by the aroma of cool autumn grass. Ruuqo was not thinking of Pirra or Sonnen or of the pact with the humans, nor of the covenant of the Wide Valley. He was dreaming of a young wolf whose white fur shone like snow in the sun and the agony of yearning for what he could never have.

⊞

"Wake up, Scrounger," Hiiln said. He pounced on Ruuqo, waking him from a midday nap.

Ruuqo had always hated his brother's nickname for him, earned when he was a pup and afraid to hunt. He stood and stretched, looking in irritation at Hiiln, who was nearly half a head taller than he. Ruuqo was a large wolf, but now that they were nearing two years old, he knew he would never be as large as his brother.

Hiiln, noticing Ruuqo's annoyance but misinterpreting the cause, poked him hard in the ribs. "Stop whining," he said. "You'll be glad I woke you up. Come on." He bolted from Fallen Tree, muscles taut, fur rippling in the breeze.

Ruuqo scrambled after him. "What's so important?" he panted, running as always a full wolflength behind his brother.

"Females," Hiiln said. "Two of them. From the Warm Hill pack. The rest of their pack joined Wind Lake when their leaderwolf died, but they stayed."

Hiiln slowed when they reached a small hill at the edge of Swift River territory and lowered himself to his belly. Ruuqo flopped down beside him. From where they lay, they could see two young females across the verge. Warm Hill territory had not yet been taken over by another pack, though soon it would be. The two youngwolves would not be able to defend it. One was an ordinary-looking wolf, a little on the thin side. She smelled of a submissive wolf. The other wolf was glorious, with a pure white coat like that of no wolf Ruuqo had ever seen. He watched, entranced as the two youngwolves played together, wrestling in the warm sun. The white wolf was so strong and graceful Ruuqo couldn't take his eyes from her.

Hiiln stood, showing himself to the youngwolves. They didn't run, nor did they challenge the strange wolves. They wagged their tails in welcome.

Ruuqo and Hiiln crossed the verge and introduced themselves, allowing the Warm Hill females to sniff them from tail to head. When Ruuqo, in turn, inhaled the aroma of the white wolf, he could barely catch his breath. He knew that, more than anything in the world, he wanted her.

But of course, Hiiln was there first. Of course she had eyes only for him, his commanding presence making it clear he would someday be a leaderwolf.

"I'm Rissa," the white wolf said. "This is my sister, Neesa."

Neesa looked shyly at Ruuqo. He acknowledged her with the briefest glance before returning his gaze to Rissa. It was already too late. She smelled of attraction to Hiiln and of readiness to find a mate.

Within a quarter moon, the four wolves were inseparable. Ruuqo ignored Neesa until he realized that Rissa was trying to push the two of them together. The he began to woo her and was rewarded by the approval in Rissa's gaze.

When Rissa and Neesa took the Swift River wolves to watch the humans, Ruuqo was disgusted, but Hiiln was fascinated. Ruuqo pretended to be, too. Rissa and Neesa were satisfied to watch the humans, but Hiiln was not. He insisted on going to the humans again and again and soon began to return to the gathering place smelling of human sweat. Traan, their father and the leader of Swift River, noticed and ordered him to stop. Hiiln would not, said he could not.

Two moons later, Hiiln left the valley. Or rather was chased from the valley. By Greatwolves and his own father. Ruuqo was certain that Rissa would go with Hiiln, but Hiiln made her promise to stay. Before he left Hiiln spoke urgently to Ruuqo, extracting a promise Ruuqo was reluctant to make. But he made it. Hiiln was his brother and he might never see him again, and so Ruuqo promised that he would lead Swift River and keep the pack safe. Ruuqo watched him go with a mingling of sadness and gratitude. When Rissa howled her sorrow, Ruuqo howled with her.

⊡

Six moons later, Ruuqo stood bereft over the body of a wolf who seemed too strong to die. Traan had led Swift River for over five years, and his death meant a time of trial for the pack. Ruuqo stood over the body of his father and then looked up into the eyes of his packmates. Trevegg, now too old to lead Swift River, the young-wolves, Annan and Senn. Neesa. And Rissa. Rissa, who met his gaze with a trust and confidence that dared him to be a coward and walk away. Rissa, who had given up her love to do what she thought was right, who now carried his pups. Traan had known he was dying and had insisted that Ruuqo and Rissa mate so that Swift River would have pups in the year to come. Now, looking at Rissa's bright gaze, knowing that the future of Swift River grew in her belly, he was terrified. He was not the one meant to lead Swift River. That was Hiiln, and Hiiln was gone forever. He was not ready. He was not strong enough. He did not want to do it. But Rissa expected it of him, and for her, he would move the very world.

⊡

Something sharp hit my head over and over again, and my ear was on fire. I opened my eyes to find Tlitoo and Jlela pecking and pulling at me.

"Wake up, wolflet!" Tlitoo said. "Your packmates return and it grows late. You have too much to do before darkfall to lie here doing nothing."

I growled at him as I staggered to my feet. It had been his idea to enter Ruuqo's mind. I took a few steps away from Ruuqo and groaned. I wasn't as exhausted as I had been when

I had gone into the Inejalun, but I was tired. And shaken. I'd never thought that Ruuqo could love someone so deeply. He'd always seemed so cold and serious.

I heard Werrna's heavy tread coming toward Swamp Wallow. It was time to go. I planted my front paws in the mud and raised my hindquarters, trying to stretch the fatigue from my bones. Jlela clacked her beak and looked at my forepaws speculatively, as if deciding which one to peck.

"I'm going," I said, coming out of my stretch. I looked at Ruuqo, deep in his dreams of Rissa. Ignoring the ravens' impatient squawks, I touched his cheek gently with my nose before leaving Swamp Wallow to find what it was the Greatwolves hid.

16

"here were you?" Marra demanded. She and Ázzuen crouched at the bottom of the poplar hill, waiting for me.

"I wanted to find something out."

"What?" Ázzuen demanded.

I wasn't ready to tell them about Tlitoo and what we could do together. Ázzuen and Marra never treated me like I was some wolf of legend, and I wanted to keep it that way.

"It doesn't matter," I said. "I didn't find anything. Come on."

I took off up the gentle slope before they could ask me anything else, and they followed me. The hill was covered with dry grass and short, scrubby bushes, and the poplars atop it were sparse. I stopped halfway up the hill and looked back down. I could see the humans behind us on the auroch plain. They were cutting up the carcasses and packing up the meat to take back to their village. If we wanted to get more meat for the pack, we would have to be quick. I wouldn't put it past the humans to take our meat if we weren't guarding it.

"Hurry up!" I said, and dashed the rest of the way up the hill. Ázzuen and Marra darted after me, and the three of us ran full pelt up the hill. Pell had said that the land beyond the poplar hill was mostly flat. I was hoping that I'd be able to see the ancient yew tree that Lydda had spoken of from atop the hill, and that it wouldn't be hidden among other trees.

What we saw when we reached the top was at least seven Greatwolves not three hundred wolflengths from us. They were milling around a small hill—really just a rise on the plain—near something that looked like the entrance to a den.

We flopped down hard on our bellies, taking cover in low scrubby bushes. We'd been stupid to run up the hill like that. If the Greatwolves had been looking in our direction, they would have seen us. If the wind was different, they would have been able to smell us. Ruuqo and Rissa would never have done anything so reckless. I opened my eyes—I hadn't realized I had closed them—and lifted my head to look across the plain.

"The Greatwolf cache," I said. There was no yew tree, but with so many Greatwolves milling about, what else could it be? I couldn't believe we'd been so close to it during the auroch hunts.

"Is this the place you have you been looking for?" Jlela quorked, landing next to me. "It has always been here. Many Gripewolves always guard it."

Tlitoo alighted on Ázzuen's rump. The ravens must have followed us from Swamp Wallow.

"What are they guarding?" I asked Jlela.

"I don't know. Food? They have caches throughout the

valley, but only this one is guarded by so many. Ravens have tried to find if there is good food here and were chased away. Twice, ravens were killed. We do not go there anymore."

We watched the Greatwolves. Some sat beside the den hole, while several others took turns walking around the small hill. There was never a moment when at least one Greatwolf was not guarding each part of the hill.

"We have to think of a way to get them to leave," Ázzuen said, but I didn't think even he could think of a way to dispose of seven Greatwolves.

Then another Greatwolf emerged from the woods far across the plain from the hill. He moved slowly, as if it hurt him to do so.

"Zorindru!" I whispered. I wanted to go to him, but I couldn't let the Greatwolves know we were there. The other seven wolves watched as the ancient Greatwolf approached. He stopped a full fifty wolflengths from the cache. Five of the other Greatwolves went to him, greeting him as a leaderwolf. He then stopped and looked in our direction. I was sure he'd seen us, but he just turned and walked back the way he had come, and the five Greatwolves followed him into the woods, leaving only two Greatwolves behind.

"I have never seen so few Gruntwolves guarding the cache," Jlela said. "And they are young ones. Galindra and Sundru. They will be even stupider than other wolves."

I squinted down at the cache. Zorindru had looked right at us, I knew he had. But he hadn't alerted the other Great-wolves. I couldn't figure out what that meant.

The sound of soft, careful pawsteps behind me and the scent of wind-sage and willow made me turn. Pell was making his way cautiously up the hill behind us. Unlike the three of us, he had the sense to crawl up the hill on his belly, keeping low to the ground.

"You've found it?" he whispered.

"I thought Stone Peak wolves couldn't come here," Ázzuen said.

"It's only a problem if the Greatwolves catch me," Pell responded. "How do you know this is the place?"

"We don't," I said. "But there were five more Greatwolves here before, guarding it. They must be hiding something."

"Only two Greatworms left and five of us," Jlela said.

"I'll go down first," I said to Ázzuen and Marra. "I'm the one they care about. They'll chase me, then you two find out what they're hiding."

"No, wolf, not you," Tlitoo said. He gave a great cry, a call answered by a multitude of raven voices. Then, before I could argue, he and Jlela took flight. They were met halfway across the plain by at least twenty other ravens, all of whom flew screeching across the plain. The birds began diving at the two Greatwolves, pulling tails and ears, pecking them hard—not in play as they did with us but to draw blood. The Greatwolves snapped and snarled but did not leave the hill.

"It's not working," Ázzuen said.

"It will," Pell responded. He loped down the hill. When he was halfway across the plain, he stopped, planted his paws, and gave a great howl. Then he pelted full-speed toward the Greatwolves. The two Greatwolves—still under attack from the ravens—turned to stare at him, then took off down the hill to chase him. It wasn't that much different, I reflected, from hunting the aurochs.

"Is he crazy?" Marra asked, admiration clear in her voice.

"He's Stone Peak," Ázzuen said. "They're all crazy."

He was brave, anyway. The Greatwolves ran for him, and instead of running away, he kept going toward them. Only when they were almost upon him did he turn sharply to the right and run toward the woods. The Greatwolves followed, but they were so hindered by ravens that Pell was able to stay ahead of them. The three wolves disappeared into the woods followed by a dark cloud of birds.

"Now!" I woofed. We ran down the slope toward the Greatwolf cache. Ravens flew above our heads, back and forth from the woods to the cache. I kept my head low, to avoid getting clouted by wings or scratched by talons. Then I recognized one of the ravens. It was Nlitsa. She had returned to the valley. I tried to veer off toward her but had taken only a few steps when Marra tackled me. She was all muscle and bone, and it hurt.

"What are you doing?" she demanded.

"It's Nlitsa," I said. "She'll know where my mother is!"

"Later!" Ázzuen said. He had stopped when Marra had toppled me to the ground. "We won't have this chance again."

I was the dominant wolf. They should have done what I told them to do. But one look at Ázzuen's determined face and Marra's strong body atop me and I knew they wouldn't. Besides, they were right.

"Fine," I said. "Get off me."

Marra leapt to her feet, and the three of us sprinted across the plain. We ran until we reached the bottom of the small hill, and flopped down again on our stomachs so that we would not be easily visible to any other Greatwolves that might be nearby.

"You keep watch," I said to Marra. "Warn us if the Greatwolves come back."

Ázzuen and I crept to the opening in the hill that the Greatwolves had been guarding. Just as we reached it, a mound of dirt in front of it began to heave. We both froze. It could be anything: another Greatwolf left behind to guard the cache, a bear, anything. I looked back over my shoulder. Marra was still on guard, her gaze flicking from the heaving earth back to the forest that the Greatwolves had disappeared into.

"What should we do?" Ázzuen asked.

I was torn—half fascinated, half terrified. Then, as we stood there indecisive, the mound of earth erupted, sending dirt and sharp twigs flying. A stocky, light-colored wolf leapt from the dirt mound. It was no Greatwolf. It was just a young-wolf, a female. Her fur was nearly white, but filthy. She landed on all fours and immediately began growling at us. Then her ears lifted in surprise as she looked us over. We recognized each other at the same moment.

"Borlla," I said.

"Hey, Bear Food," she replied. "Why're you here?"

One of my earliest memories was of Borlla trying to kill me. I had been four weeks old, younger and weaker than the other Swift River pups, and Borlla had led two other pups, Unnan and Reel, to try to injure me so badly I would not be able to keep up with the pack. She had almost succeeded. Throughout our puphood Borlla had tried to bully me, tried to make Rissa and Ruuqo see me at first as weak, and then as a danger to the pack. I had hated her. Even after she was gone she caused me trouble; it was her disappearance that made some in the valley consider me drelshik. I would have been happier finding a starving bear or a horde of vipers in the Greatwolf cache. Ázzuen, Marra, and I stared at her in shock.

"What are *you* doing here?" I asked when I at last found my voice. Ázzuen and Marra were still staring at Borlla, their ears standing straight up on their heads. Marra's tail started to wave. Then she shot me a guilty look and stilled it.

"Leaving," Borlla replied. She looked past me to where the Greatwolves had disappeared, and quickly stretched her front and back legs, then her spine. She shook herself hard, then began to run.

"Wait," I said, following her.

"It took me five moons to get out of here," she said. "I'm not standing around until they come back for me. Which way is safest?"

Ázzuen and Marra scrambled to catch up with us.

"This way," Ázzuen said. He veered left toward the hill from which we had first seen the Greatwolf cache. "How come you're here? How did you get away? We all thought you were dead."

Borlla looked him over as we ran.

"Didn't expect you to survive the winter," she said to him. "Must've been an easy year. And obviously I'm not dead. Sorry to disappoint you."

She began to run faster. Borlla's legs were longer than Ázzuen's or mine, and we had to sprint to keep up with her. My mind raced, too. Could Borlla really be the Greatwolf secret? There had to be more.

"Borlla, is there something else the Greatwolves are hiding? We need to know."

She ignored me. I wasn't surprised; she hated me every bit as much as I hated her. I wanted to knock her over, pin her down, and make her tell me, but that would only make us all vulnerable if the Greatwolves returned. I looked at her and noticed that in spite of the fact that she was running well and quickly, her right foreleg was slightly crooked. Maybe I could get her to talk about the Greatwolves after all.

"What happened to your leg?" I asked, trying to sound as if I cared. We had reached the bottom of the poplar hill.

"They broke it," she said matter-of-factly, beginning to climb the hill, "the first time I tried to get away."

Marra exhaled sharply through her nose, and I stumbled a little in shock. Borlla's eyes swept over me. I had forgotten how arrogant, how insulting her gaze could be.

"You don't know anything about the Greatwolves and what they're willing to do, do you? Did you really think they'd let you be the humans' streck? I can't believe you're the one that half the council thinks might be wolfkind's savior. They must be pretty desperate."

Borlla was as arrogant and selfish as ever. The last thing I wanted was to have her back in my life. But she clearly knew something if she knew the Greatwolves had talked about me. I would have to keep trying.

"What did they say about that?" I panted. The ridge seemed much steeper on the way up. All four of us stopped when we reached the top. Borlla didn't answer me. She just looked from left to right, deciding which way to go.

"Borlla, it's important," I said. "The safety of the pack might depend on our knowing."

She whipped her head around, fury in her eyes. "Why should I care what happens to them?" she demanded. "They just left me. They left me with the Greatwolves for *five moons* without coming for me."

"They tried," Marra said, the only one of us not short of breath.

"Not hard enough," Borlla replied, looking coolly at Marra. Of the three of us, she was the only one that Borlla had some respect for—the only one she hadn't called a weakling when we were all smallpups.

"They looked for a long time," Marra said. "Minn looked for two moons, and Unnan never stopped trying to find out what happened."

Borlla winced at the mention of Unnan's name. I tried to imagine what it would have been like for her. Waiting for someone to come. If it had been me, I would have waited every day for Ázzuen or Marra to find me.

"It's important," I said again, starting to feel a little sorry for her. "It's life or death."

She swung her head back to me. She had spoken somewhat respectfully to Marra, but she had no use for me.

"Do you know what the Greatwolves said to me, when they broke my leg the first time I tried to escape? They told me they'd break all four of my legs if I tried to leave again. They told me they would tear off both my ears. You have no idea of what 'life or death' means."

My throat closed in disgust. I had known Milsindra was ruthless, but even so I'd never imagined the Greatwolves would do such things.

Borlla was looking at me with absolute contempt. "You don't know anything," she said.

She dove down the hill and dashed across a short stretch of grass and into a dense patch of forest. I lost sight of her. Then, almost instantly, I heard the impact of body upon body, a desperate scuffle, and a youngwolf's scream.

Ázzuen, Marra, and I bolted down the hill and into the woods. Borlla was in a small clearing, and she was being held down by one Greatwolf as another stood over her. She scrabbled frantically beneath the wolf who pinned her, but there was no way she could free herself.

"Together!" I barked, instinctively using the term Torell had used when he wanted us to leap as one at an auroch. It worked. Ázzuen, Marra, and I leapt at the same instant to slam into the Greatwolf who had Borlla pinned. I recognized both Greatwolves then. Galindra and Sundru, the two young Greatwolves who had been guarding the cache. Galindra staggered when the three of us hit her, and Borlla scrambled to her feet. I dove under Sundru's stomach, just as Torell had taught us to do with the aurochs. I saw Ázzuen and Marra darting around Galindra. Borlla took a deep and vicious bite out of Sundru's flank. The two Greatwolves were as angry as the aurochs, and almost as stupid, and we had them confused and off-balance. When Pell crashed into the clearing, followed by screaming ravens, the Greatwolves ran.

"Get out of here!" Pell said. "I'll keep them distracted."

Before I could protest, he had pelted after the Greatwolves, the ravens flying just above his head. I couldn't believe he was chasing Greatwolves. Borlla was already bolting from the clearing. I stood, stunned for a moment at the realization that we had fought a pair of Greatwolves and won.

"Come *on*, Kaala!" Ázzuen yipped.

I went.

The three of us followed Borlla's trail, catching up with her as the woods thinned. I noticed she was limping now and running more slowly than before.

We ran through the woods until even Marra was gasping for breath and we had to stop to rest in a copse of pine and oak. Ázzuen's ribs were heaving and his tongue hung halfway down to the ground. Borlla breathed in quick short pants. My own throat ached, and when I heard the sound of running water, I realized how thirsty I was. The day was cool, but we had hunted two aurochs and fought Greatwolves without even a chance to lap at a pond. The sound of water was just downhill from us. I could smell it now, the fresh, cool scent of a stream. Borlla had been leading us since we had run from the Greatwolves, but when I set off for the stream, she, Ázzuen, and Marra all followed.

The stream water was cool and savory with the taste of damp wood and fish. We gulped at the water, and I barely managed to stop myself from drinking so much that my belly would be too full to allow me to run. Then I looked around. I had been blindly following Borlla, trying to get as far away from the Greatwolves as we could. I realized that she had been leading us south, away from our humans and the pack. We would have to go back.

Ázzuen and Marra were lying down, still panting, still exhausted, but we had to keep moving. We had to let Torell know what we had found, and I wanted to make sure Pell was all right.

"Come on," I said. "We're leaving."

I didn't want Borlla to come with us, but I wasn't willing to live with the guilt of her being recaptured by the Greatwolves. She could follow if she wanted.

"Kaala, wait," Borlla said. Her voice shook. I remembered the terrified look on her face when Galindra held her down.

Reluctantly, I stopped and turned back to her. She was looking at me with dislike, as if she wanted to say something else insulting.

"You helped me," she said instead. "Otherwise I wouldn't tell you anything."

I waited. I heard an impatient rustling from above and looked up to see Tlitoo peering down at us from an oak tree. He had a tuft of light-colored fur in his beak.

Borlla growled softly. "Do you know why the Greatwolves took me?" she asked.

"Because they're dying and they need wolves to breed with," Ázzuen answered. "It's why they took the Wind Lake wolf, too, isn't it? Nothing else makes sense."

Borlla looked at him in surprise. She hadn't spent much time with Ázzuen. She didn't know how quickly his mind worked.

"They can't bear any more young," she said. "No Greatwolf pup has been born for over a hundred moons, and the Greatwolves of breeding age are growing older. Some of them want to mate with smallwolves to keep their bloodlines alive. Others think it might be time for the Greatwolves to die out. Some think only a few smallwolves should be kept alive to breed, and the rest should be killed."

It didn't surprise me that they were trying to breed a new race of wolves. Tlitoo had said the Greatwolves were dying, and Frandra and Jandru had wanted to take me from the valley at autumn's end so that they could mix my blood with that of other wolves. It did surprise me that some of them thought the Greatwolves should die out.

"What happened to the Wind Lake wolf?" I asked. It would be just like Borlla to escape and leave him there.

"His name was Ivvan," Borlla said. "They kept him with me for a few days, then took him away. I don't know what happened to him." She looked at me with distaste. "They talk about you all the time, Kaala. About whether you're a savior-wolf or a destroyer. They talk about how which one you are will determine whether or not smallwolves should live. Every half moon they have a ritual where they seek guidance from the Ancients. That's why there were only two Greatwolves guarding me. The rest have gone for the ritual. I heard Kivdru telling one of the younger Greatwolves about it—only the older Greatwolves are allowed to go, because whatever they do is too important for younger Greatwolves to know about. He said they chew the dream-sage and remember the time before time, the time of the Greatwolf Indru. He said they seek answers in the past."

She looked anxiously over her shoulder and began to speak more quickly. "They're waiting for some kind of traveler, who can see into the past. They say he will help them figure out how they can continue to survive and lead wolfkind. Until they find him, they look for guidance in memories of the ancestors."

"Where do they go?" I demanded. I could almost feel Tlitoo's beady gaze piercing the back of my head. The traveler could only be him, and Lydda had said the gift of the Nejakilakin could find the truth the Greatwolves guarded. I wanted to see those memories of the ancestors.

I thought Borlla might not answer, but she did so, grudgingly. "I don't know exactly. But they always come back smelling of dream-sage and of Swift River lands." Her ears and tail drooped. "They come back smelling of home."

"Did you hear anything else?" I demanded.

"They kept me there for five moons. What do you think?" she snarled.

"So what else can you tell us?" Ázzuen asked.

"Nothing. They could come back here any minute."

Again, the urge to pin her down and force her to talk overwhelmed me. But the Greatwolves could be upon us at any moment, and Borlla had as much right to do what was best for her as we did.

"Thank you for telling me," I said, controlling my anger. She didn't acknowledge my thanks, just turned to go.

"Borlla," I said, "Unnan is with the Wind Lake pack. He left Swift River and joined them. Because of what happened to you."

She hesitated for an instant, then turned back and touched her nose to my face.

"Good luck, Bear Food," she said, and bolted into the woods.

Tlitoo dropped from his oak, landing with a thump on the stream bank. He still had the tuft of fur in his mouth. He spat it out.

"The Stone Peak wolf is fine," he said before I could ask. "He returns to his pack to tell them of the hiding place. The two Greatworms have gone back to their hill and are very angry. We can go look for the other Gruntwolf place."

"Did Nlitsa say anything about my mother?" I asked.

"No, wolf. We must go *now*." He blinked at me and opened his beak to breathe in sharp, quick pants. His heart beat quickly under the smooth feathers of his chest.

I wanted to go just as much as he did. I had no idea how much time we had before the Greatwolves finished their ritual, and we couldn't wait another half moon.

"We don't have to be at Fallen Tree until darkfall," Marra said. "We still have time."

"Not much time," Ázzuen said. "As soon as Galindra and Sundru tell the other Greatwolves about Borlla, they'll want to talk to us."

"At least," I said. The Greatwolves wouldn't know we'd learned of their ritual, but they would know we had helped Borlla escape, and they wouldn't be happy about it. If we were going to find the Greatwolf ritual, we would have to start looking soon. I didn't want Ázzuen and Marra with me, though. I didn't want them seeing what Tlitoo and I did. I was about to suggest we split the territory to save time, when I saw Jlela flying fast above the stream. She landed in a skid and tumbled into Tlitoo.

"You need to come, Moonwolf," she said to me. "There is trouble."

"What trouble?" I asked impatiently. I needed to find the Greatwolf sleeping place, and ravens often had strange ideas about what was important.

"Trouble with your girl, wolf. You should come."

I didn't ask any more questions. I took off at a run toward the auroch plain. The Greatwolves would have to wait.

17

I took one look at the humans on the plain and saw what Jlela meant. Even from the top of the poplar hill I could tell that there was trouble. The humans weren't fighting or yelling, but there was something in the way HuLin was standing, in the set of TaLi's shoulders, that told me even from far away that something was wrong. The rest of the humans were standing around sleds already piled high with auroch, or cutting the remaining meat from the carcasses, as they would after any hunt, but they moved stiffly and did not take their eyes from HuLin and TaLi.

We ran down the hill, staying under the cover of the poplars and scrubby bushes as much as we could. When we reached our watching spot at the edge of the plain, I was surprised to find the Vole Eater youngwolf, Prannan, waiting for us at a spot where the woods met the plain.

"The ravens came for me," he said. "They said to guard the humans until you got here, and I did. One of the humans gave me firemeat!"

Still startled that he was there, I nosed his muzzle in thanks and looked more closely at the humans. I couldn't find KiLi or her mate, and all the other humans seemed to be doing their best to avoid HuLin and TaLi.

"What's happening?" I asked Prannan.

"The one called HuLin wants to take the tribe into a place called Aln territory tomorrow," he answered. "There's a small herd of elkryn there, and he wants to kill them all before the Aln tribe does. Then he wants to get all the forest pigs, walking birds, and smallprey in another tribe's forests—I can't remember their names—before the other humans realize the other prey is leaving. He wants to kill as much prey as he can before the other humans do. And he wants to use you to do it. Your girl is trying to stop him." He stopped to gulp a breath. "She says it goes against the teachings of the krianans. That it would upset the Balance."

Left to their own will, the humans would kill everything in the valley. TaLi's task would not be easy.

"They were called the Wen tribe!" Prannan said. "The ones with the smallprey. I have to go now, Kaala," he said. "I have to get back to my pack."

I just blinked at him, still not quite believing that he'd come to help us.

"Thanks," Marra said when I didn't answer Prannan.

Prannan ducked his head and loped into the woods. As his tail disappeared in the thick shrubs, I saw that Frandra and Jandru were back, lying with their heads in their paws, watching the humans. I wondered how long they'd been there, if they'd seen us running down the poplar hill. TaLi's voice drew my attention back to the plain.

"We can't kill all the prey," TaLi was saying, her voice even. Her back was to me, but the tension in her shoulders told me how difficult it was for her to keep her voice calm.

HuLin scowled. Unlike TaLi, he made no attempt to hide his displeasure.

"There is no time for this nonsense. We've followed the will of the krianans"—he spat the word—"for too long. Ton-Lin said he spoke directly to the Ancients, and they told him we could hunt wherever we wanted. DavRian says the same. The old woman wouldn't let us, but she's too old to stop us from it now."

"I will be taking on my grandmother's role," TaLi said. "You know you must follow the wisdom of the krianans. You know you must preserve the Balance."

"Not anymore!" he said. "Prey is scarce, and if we don't hunt as much as we can now, we'll starve."

"We'll have enough," TaLi said. "I will see to that with the help of the wolves." She looked over her shoulder at us. I didn't know when she'd noticed us. I walked over to her and pressed against her thigh. HuLin ignored me.

"If we kill everything in the valley it will upset the Balance for years to come," TaLi said. "If you kill so much now, there will be no young prey born. And it's wrong."

HuLin slammed the blunt end of his sharpstick into the ground. It broke off at the base. He swore and threw it aside.

"Rian tribe no longer follows the old krianans. Nor does Wen. They take what they want, and so will we. Tomorrow we take the elkryn. You will bring your wolves, TaLi, and they will help us."

"I won't," she said softly. "I can't."

"You will," HuLin said, losing patience with the girl. He leaned close to her and hissed in her ear, "If you do so, then you can call yourself krianan and choose your own mate. But you *will* help this tribe get the food that we need. You will bring the wolves to hunt with us in the morning, or I will bind you, carry you to Rian, and leave you there."

He turned and stalked back to the auroch-filled sleds, certain he would be obeyed.

"Come on, Silvermoon," TaLi said, backing quietly toward the woods where Ázzuen and Marra waited. I caught movement out of the corner of my eye and looked down the plain to see that Frandra and Jandru had stood. I went with TaLi. When she was hidden from the rest of the tribe by the trees, she sank onto her knees. Ázzuen, Marra, and I all pressed up against her to comfort her.

"I have to go back to Grandmother's," she whispered. "Come with me, Silvermoon."

She stood and took off at a run.

"We must go to the Greatwolf dreaming place, wolf," Tlitoo quorked, stalking over to me. "Before the Gruntwolves there awaken."

I knew we did. NiaLi's new shelter was more than an hour's lope, even for a wolf, from where we were, and it would take TaLi even longer. I needed to go find the Greatwolf ritual and to bring more meat to the pack. I needed to find Nlitsa and find out what she knew of my mother.

"Not until TaLi is safe," I told him.

I heard a rustling down the plain and saw Frandra and Jandru retreating into the woods. I thought about going to them to find out if they'd seen us on the poplar hill, but there was no time. If they wanted to talk to us, they'd find us.

"Hide the rest of the meat to bring back to the pack," I said to Marra, "then catch up with us."

Ázzuen and I loped after TaLi. The three of us ran as quickly as TaLi could until we were well away from the Western Plains and TaLi's tribe. Then TaLi slowed to a jog and spoke again.

"The Rian tribe and the Wens want to get rid of krianans," she said, "but Lan and Aln believe in the old ways. The other tribes are undecided."

She stopped and cocked her head as we all heard a rustling in the bushes.

"It's just Marra," I said, even though I knew she wouldn't understand me.

"It's not just me," Marra said, leaping over a juniper bush to join us. The scent of Rian male floated on the wind.

"DavRian's following us," TaLi hissed. "I know he is. He must have been hiding in the bushes like the snake he is. I don't want him knowing where my grandmother's new shelter is, Silvermoon."

I licked her hand to let her know I understood her.

Tlitoo landed on a low branch. "The clumsy human will be here soon, wolves," he said.

"Come on," I said to Ázzuen and Marra.

I pelted off in the direction of DavRian's scent, of his ungainly crashing through the woods. He was making a lot of noise, avoiding the path and trying to surprise TaLi. It only made it easier for us to find him.

We reached him just as he clambered over two trees that had fallen near the edge of a gentle slope that led into a lush ravine. He scaled both trees and leapt down, jumping higher than he needed to, as if showing himself he could. He was as strong and agile as any youngwolf, but he was clumsy. He landed off balance.

"Don't hurt him," I ordered. "Just stop him for a little while."

"I can do that." Ázzuen grinned. He leapt at DavRian's chest as Marra tangled herself in the young human's legs. DavRian toppled and landed hard on his rump as Ázzuen jumped clear of him. DavRian scrambled quickly to his feet. I prodded him in his back, and Tlitoo cawed loudly and flapped his wings just above DavRian's head. The human staggered, then slipped in the pine needles on the soft ground and slid almost gracefully down the slope. Marra leapt onto a pile of fallen wood and shoved it down on the boy. They were relatively small pieces of wood. They wouldn't hurt him much. Tlitoo stood atop the slope, tossing twigs and pinecones down at DavRian.

With a yip of triumph, I pelted after TaLi. The girl was running as quickly as she could when we overtook her. If she could maintain her speed, we would be out of DavRian's range by the time he freed himself. I worried that TaLi would not be fast enough, that she couldn't keep the fast pace, but her long legs took her flying through the woods. Even when she slowed to a trot, we made good progress until she stopped, panting, in front of NiaLi's shelter.

TaLi caught her breath, then lifted the deerskin flap and allowed us to precede her into the shelter. NiaLi looked up in surprise when we came in, but Trevegg had heard us coming. He was waiting right next to the entrance.

"What happened?" he demanded as TaLi flopped down next to the old woman and her fire. He began to sniff us all over. "You smell of Borlla!" he said, incredulous.

We told him—about the humans wanting to kill all the prey and about Borlla—as TaLi spilled out her own story to NiaLi. I could tell that the old woman was trying to listen to all of us at once. Trevegg was ecstatic to hear that Borlla was alive, and I could tell he had questions for us, but we all listened to NiaLi as she spoke.

"I am not pleased," she was saying to TaLi, "but I'm not surprised. HuLin was always thickheaded, even when he was a boy."

Tlitoo poked his head in through the smoke hole. "The Gruntwolves have followed. They are almost within hearing range. And we *must* go find the Greatworm sleeping place, wolf!" He cocked his head right, then left. "I will be right back." He pulled his head out of the shelter, and I heard the whoosh of wings.

"Frandra and Jandru said they would come to me tonight," NiaLi said. "They said they had something to tell me."

"They already know about HuLin wanting to kill all the prey," I said, "but not that we know about Borlla or the Greatwolf ritual." My throat clenched as I remembered them watching from the edge of the plain. "I hope they don't, anyway."

NiaLi tapped her fingers on the skins that covered her legs. "We'll know soon enough. You think this ritual of the krianan wolves is important, Silvermoon?"

"Yes," I said. "If they're so careful to hide it, then it must be important."

"And Borlla said that they never miss it," Marra added. "They go every half moon. We need to find out what it is."

"I agree," Trevegg said. "If they're hiding it, I want to know about it."

"As do I," NiaLi said. "Once you find what it is, come back to me. Whatever is happening, the krianans outside the valley must know."

She turned back to TaLi. The girl was looking back and forth between us and the old woman. She knew NiaLi could communicate with us in ways she couldn't. The old woman smiled at her.

"I need to teach you how to understand your friends," she said. "I should have done so before but didn't realize how little time we had." The old krianan turned back to us.

"If you're going to sneak up on the krianan wolves you will need to hide your scent. Get me the uijin, please, TaLi."

Raven feet scraped the top of the shelter. Tlitoo had returned. He dropped down from the smoke hole to land beside NiaLi.

"They are near," he quorked, and flew back out the smoke hole.

NiaLi dipped her head at TaLi. The girl stood silently and crossed to one of the shelter's mud walls. She stretched to her full height to get a dried gourd from a high wooden shelf. I recognized the scent of uijin, a salve made from chokeberries, herbs, and sap that could disguise a wolf's or a human's scent from others. TaLi had used it on me once before when we had spied on the Greatwolves.

I wanted to talk to Trevegg, to tell him that the Greatwolf ritual was somewhere in our territory, to get his advice on how to talk to the pack, but I couldn't if the Greatwolves were close enough to hear us. It was probably my imagination, but I could swear I could hear them breathing outside the shelter.

TaLi scooped some of the uijin out of the gourd and sat down next to me. NiaLi took the rest and called Ázzuen and Marra to her side. I stood still as TaLi rubbed the uijin into my fur, enjoying the feel of her hands stroking me. When all three of us were coated with the sticky stuff, TaLi set the gourd back up on the high shelf and sat beside me again.

"TaLi, I want you to stay here with me for a few nights," NiaLi said. "It will give HuLin time to calm himself. And time to realize that without you and the wolves he may go hungry. Then you will return and offer to help him—as krianan and in your own way. Don't be so foolish as to confront him directly again. It only makes him angry and defensive." She grinned. "I should know. If he still doesn't accept you, you will go to Lan and become their krianan."

I whuffed concern. That could take half a moon. We didn't have time.

"I know you're impatient, Silvermoon," the old woman chided, "but you have a promise to keep. If we can succeed in the challenge the Greatwolves have set you, we can leave the valley when we choose."

She didn't bother to talk about what would happen if we didn't succeed. We all knew. We'd be killed. I dipped my head.

"But I failed," TaLi said in a soft, shame-filled voice. "HuLin wouldn't listen to me, even after we hunted aurochs with the wolves. He says he won't follow the old ways anymore."

NiaLi held out her arms to the girl, and TaLi went to her. I followed, and Marra and Ázzuen made way for me, allowing me to push in between TaLi and her grandmother. NiaLi reached past me to stroke TaLi's hair. "You misunderstand the role of the krianan," the old woman said. "It is not about what rituals you perform or your status in your tribe. It is about doing what you must to ensure that those who follow you do not forget that they are part of the world around them. The krianans of the Wide Valley have long done so by listening to the krianan wolves and taking their messages back to our people. You and Silvermoon are finding a new way, and none of us knows what that will be yet." She pushed me gently out of the way so that she could take TaLi's face in her hands. "I do know this: being krianan has nothing to do with the title given by a tribe leader and everything to do with the choices that you make. You refused to go against the Balance, even when HuLin said he would make you krianan if you did so. That is not failure, it is the mark of a true krianan, and I am proud of you."

The tension went out of TaLi's shoulders, and she threw her arms around the old woman, holding her tight. NiaLi's face was in front of mine. I licked her cheek. The old woman laughed and sat back against her pile of skins and spoke to me.

"I think it is time for the three of you to go," she said.

"I'll stay here," Trevegg said. "When does the pack expect you back?"

"Darkfall," Marra said.

"Then you should go now."

I wanted to tell him not to trust Frandra and Jandru. I

wanted to ask him about what he thought the Greatwolf ritual might be. But I couldn't. Not if the Greatwolves might
overhear.

"I'm worried about TaLi," was what I whispered. "About
both of them. HuLin said he would force her to go to the Rian
tribe. I don't want to leave her."

"I know," Trevegg said, "but you must. I'll guard her life
with mine, Kaala."

"I know you will," I said, touching the oldwolf's nose with
mine. I could only hope it would be enough.

Ázzuen, Marra, and I emerged from the old woman's shelter
to find Jandru and Frandra already pushing their way into the
small clearing. Once again, they did not smell of wolf. I was
glad we hadn't spoken more about our plans or the Greatwolf
ritual; if not for Tlitoo, they could easily have snuck up and
heard us.

"How do you do that?" Ázzuen demanded. "How do you
disguise your scent?"

"It is a secret of the Greatwolves," Jandru responded, his
nose high in the air. "We speak to the Ancients and to the
trees, and they give us this gift."

"Ha!" Tlitoo said, hopping down from the top of NiaLi's
shelter. "You roll in the grouse-berry bush, then in the swamp
mud, and the yew bark, then in whatever dung you can find. I
saw you."

Jandru stared at him for a moment, then whuffed in annoyance and turned his attention to me. If he could smell the
old krianan's uijin on us, he didn't mention it.

"Walk with us," he said.

We followed the Greatwolves into the denser part of the woods. I was terrified that they had overheard us talking about the ritual, or that they'd seen us on the poplar hill and would know we'd seen the cache, but when they spoke, it was only of TaLi.

"The girl must be krianan, Kaala," Jandru said.

"I know," I said, relieved.

"The council is waiting to see what she does," Frandra added. "If she does not prevail, it may tip the balance against us."

"I know," I said, my relief quickly replaced by annoyance. And concern. I had been worried ever since NiaLi said she might send TaLi to the Lan tribe. Even if Lan was able to protect TaLi, and even if they let her train to be a krianan, it would take us time to teach Lan about hunting with the wolves, especially with BreLan away. Which meant that even if we succeeded, it might take too long for me prove to the other packs that we could do well with the humans. And too long for me to be able to get to my mother.

"She knows, Grumpwolves," Tlitoo said. The Greatwolves ignored him.

"You know that if the humans who wish to control everything triumph, nothing you or your pack may do will matter?"

"Yes." Even if the Lan tribe stayed true to the old ways, there would be three tribes in the valley no longer following the true krianans, and we would have to succeed in spite of them. The Greatwolves weren't telling me anything I didn't know. Why were they trying to make me feel worse about it than I already did?

"Good," Frandra said. "Then we have something to show you."

☐

They took us back the way we'd come, following almost exactly the path TaLi had taken to NiaLi's. When we reached the ravine where we had tripped DavRian, I hesitated.

"What are they going to do?" Ázzuen whispered.

I didn't know. I watched as Frandra's tail disappeared into the bushes, then followed. She stopped by the two fallen trees where we had tripped DavRian.

"Look, Kaala," Frandra said, pointing her nose down into the ravine.

DavRian was still there. He had not, as I'd expected, freed himself. Some of the sticks Marra had dumped on him were larger than we'd thought. He wasn't hurt, but he was trapped. Then I saw what Frandra was pointing to. The ravine, which I had assumed continued its gentle slope to the bottom, fell off sharply into a deeper canyon, just pawswidths from where DavRian lay.

"He's the one who convinced the leader of TaLi's tribe that she should not be krianan. If he did not live, your girl could still win out. She could convince her leader that she is best for the tribe."

Tlitoo flew down to stand above DavRian, then returned to us.

"He is not injured," the raven said, "but he cannot get out on his own. Other humans come, though."

"All you need to do, Kaala, is to push on the right side of the branch he lies upon. It will send the clump of dirt, and the human, down the hill. No one will know a wolf has done it. No one will know anything but that he fell in an accident."

I felt sick. I had only wanted to stop him from following us. Then the meaning of Frandra's words hit me. If DavRian was gone, he could not be a krianan. If he were dead, he could not insist on mating with TaLi, and she might have a better chance of being krianan of her own tribe. We could succeed quickly with the humans, and I could leave the valley to find my mother.

"Why don't you do it?" I asked the Greatwolves.

"It is not our place to do so. He is your enemy. The choice is yours."

DavRian looked up at me, and his eyes burned with hatred. I remembered him hitting TaLi. If the Lan tribe could not protect her, HuLin could force TaLi to be DavRian's mate and renounce her duty as krianan. TaLi would die before she would do that. DavRian's hate-filled eyes met mine, and I knew how easy it would be.

"No," I said. "I won't do it. It doesn't matter if no one knows. It's still breaking the promise of the Wide Valley."

Ázzuen exhaled sharply next to me.

"*Drelshan*," Jandru said softly.

"What? What do you mean?" I demanded. "What's drelshan?" I had been called drelshik before, but never drelshan.

Jandru didn't answer my question.

"Go to your pack, youngwolf," he said. "Get them to join with you."

He nodded to Frandra, and the two of them turned and bounded into the woods. By the time I had regained my breath and my wits, they were out of sight. We heard the voices of approaching humans.

"We have to go, Kaala," Ázzuen said.

"Too bad," Tlitoo grumbled. "I would have liked to taste this human's greslin."

I heard a commotion above me and looked up to see a raven shape in the trees. The ancient raven who had been following us was staring down at us. When he saw me watching, he gave a great cry and took flight.

Tlitoo stalked over to me and pecked my right forepaw. I yelped.

"*Now*, wolflet."

"All right!" I said, licking my paw.

"We have less than two hours left before darkfall," Marra said. "We'll have to split up the territory."

I was glad of it. I still wasn't ready to tell Marra and Ázzuen about what Tlitoo and I could do together. I told Marra to take the river's edge and Ázzuen to take the western part of the territory.

"If you find something, don't howl," I told them. "We'll meet at Fallen Tree by darkfall with the rest of the pack, and decide what to do then."

But they wouldn't find anything. I knew where the Greatwolf ritual was. Borlla had said it was in our territory in a place that smelled of dream-sage, and Lydda had spoken of an ancient yew. There was only one place in our lands where an old yew tree stood and dream-sage grew: Wolf Killer Hill.

18

olf Killer Hill had earned its name because wolves often fell from its steep cliffs onto jagged rocks below. There were stories that it was haunted by the angry spirits of wolves who'd died there, and none of us ever went there unless necessary. If it was a secret place of the Great-wolves, I realized, they might have made up those legends themselves.

It didn't take me long to get to Wolf Killer, but Tlitoo harried me the whole way, pecking at me if I slowed even a little, so that by the time I arrived at Wolf Killer just before dusk, I was panting. I couldn't help but remember the last—and only—time I had been there. Ázzuen, Marra, and I had been hiding deer meat atop the hill when we'd overheard the Stone Peak wolves plotting against the humans. That was the day I had been exiled from my pack and the day I found out that the Greatwolves were not to be trusted.

I knew where the patch of dream-sage was. I had seen it

340

the last time I was at Wolf Killer. I loped about halfway up the hill to where a path ran along a narrow ledge, then followed the path. To my left was the solid bulk of Wolf Killer Hill, to my right a grassy slope that led back down to the woods. I slowed as I reached a bend in the path, lowered myself to my belly, and began to edge forward. Tlitoo, uncharacteristically quiet, took small mincing steps beside me. I crawled around the bend and looked to my left, where the path fell away into a sudden drop that led to the sharp, lethal rocks below. It was as if some giant, starving beast had taken a huge bite out of the hill. A wolf running along the path could easily fall to her death.

Moving slowly, one pawswidth at a time, I crawled to the very brink of the cliff. I poked just my nose over the edge and smelled dream-sage. I lowered my muzzle and then the rest of my face over the ledge. The dream-sage grew in thick patches among the rocks, and, so close to the side of the hill that they would be hidden from a casual glance, the sleeping Great-wolves lay.

I took a huge, silent breath. A small part of me had hoped I was wrong, that I wouldn't find them. That I wouldn't have to lie down next to a sleeping Greatwolf and try to see its dreams. Now that I'd found them, I had no choice. Even if I wanted to leave now, Tlitoo wouldn't let me.

I looked more closely at the sleeping Greatwolves. Most of them were clustered together. I saw Milsindra and Zorindru, and many wolves I didn't recognize. Then I saw one wolf off to the side a little, in a particularly thick patch of dream-sage. It was Kivdru, Milsindra's mate. Not my first choice, but he would do.

Tlitoo had apparently come to the same conclusion. He launched himself from the ledge and landed several wolf-lengths from Kivdru. Raven wings can be loud, and he probably didn't want to risk waking the Greatwolf. He walked over to the Greatwolf and peered up at me.

I looked for a way down into the gorge. I could see large paw prints in the dirt wending a treacherous path between rocks and bushes. It must have been the way the Greatwolves had taken down. Slowly, carefully, I began to pick my way down the steep grade, following the Greatwolf trail as best I could. Their paw prints were too far apart, and I couldn't reach most of them. I'd managed to get about halfway down the hill when I had to leap over a rock a Greatwolf had just stepped over and landed in dry slippery dirt. As I began to skid down the hill, I dug my front paws into the dirt. That was a mistake. My rear end flipped over my front, and I found myself falling tail over head down the hill. It occurred to me that this was exactly how wolves died on Wolf Killer. As soon as that thought hit me, I splayed all four of my legs out, landing hard on my face and opening a deep gouge in my left front paw as a sharp rock sliced into it, but stopping myself before I rolled any farther. I gulped down several deep breaths, then got my paws under me. Out of the corner of my eye, I saw something move. A Greatwolf lifting its head. I froze and stared down at the Greatwolf. It was Zorindru. He turned his pale eyes toward me, and I was certain he would call out to the other wolves, or at least come over to me. But he just looked at me for several awful moments. Then what I could swear was a smile pulled at his muzzle, and he laid his head back down.

I breathed again. I was about twenty wolflengths from Kivdru and Tlitoo. I limped down to them. I expected Tlitoo to make some kind of remark about my graceless descent down the hill, but he just leapt onto Kivdru's back and blinked at me.

"Darkfall nears, wolf."

I didn't answer. There was no point in making more noise than necessary, and no point in waiting. I would have to trust the uijin to disguise my scent and Tlitoo to warn me if Kivdru started to wake up. I lay down next to Kivdru and carefully pressed myself against him. I was shaking so hard I was sure my trembling would wake him, but he slept on. Tlitoo walked across the Greatwolf's broad back, then lowered his head to mine.

I closed my eyes as the now familiar falling sensation washed over me. I let the cold flow over me and allowed my nose to become accustomed to the lack of scent. Then I opened my eyes, ready to see what Kivdru dreamt of. I saw only darkness and felt an overwhelming sadness and a deep, resentful anger. I pulled away and found myself back at Wolf Killer, feeling slightly nauseated by the despair and anger I'd felt from Kivdru. My throat was dry, and I swallowed several times, trying to moisten it. I looked up at Tlitoo. His eyes were narrowed in concentration, his neck ruff sticking straight out. I closed my eyes again, trying to see Kivdru's dream. Nothing. I prodded Tlitoo with my muzzle.

"It's not working," I whispered.

"I *know*, wolf," he rasped. The return of his acerbic manner comforted me.

I looked uneasily around the rocky dream-sage patch.

Zorindru had woken up already; what if another Greatwolf did?

"Maybe we should go," I said

"Quiet, wolf. I have an idea. Try again."

I closed my eyes once more, leaning hard against the Greatwolf. The darkness blurred, and my stomach lurched as I felt the world around me spin.

"Ha!" Tlitoo said. "I can so do it."

I opened my eyes. We were back the Stone Circle. We were back at the Inejalun. And a wolf was there, waiting for us.

He was a large wolf, not quite as big as a Greatwolf, but as big as the Stone Peaks. He had ordinary light gray fur, but his eyes were a bright silver unlike any wolf eyes I'd ever seen, and the tips of his ears seemed to disappear into the bright light above him. A raven stood next to him. It was the ancient raven who had been following me around, but he looked young and healthy and had silvery eyes just like the wolf's. The wolf opened his mouth in a smile, revealing large, sharp teeth.

"I believe I am what you're looking for," he said.

"Who are you?" I asked quickly, before the cold I knew was coming sealed my jaws.

"I am the one they dream of."

"Indru?" I asked.

He inclined his head. "I am Indru," he said, as if he were an ordinary wolf introducing himself to an equal. I felt my cold ears flattening against my head. "This is my friend, Hzralzu," he said, inclining his head toward the raven.

"But he is in both worlds," Tlitoo said. "How can he be?"

"How can you be?" Indru responded. "You have much to learn, Nejakilakin, but now is not the time. There is something this youngwolf must see, and you know she cannot stay here. Come along."

He turned and walked into the woods surrounding the Stone Circle. There was nothing to do but follow.

He stopped and sat in a copse of trees. When we caught up with him he lay down on his belly. "Come here beside me, Kaala," he said. Something in his manner made me want to trust him. I lay down next to him and followed his gaze. My nose was cooling, and I flinched, dreading the cold I knew would creep over the rest of me.

We were looking down on a snowy mountaintop. It was just below us, no farther away than the human homesite was from the bushes we hid behind to watch them. There was no such mountain anywhere near the Stone Circle, and I had to remind myself that this was not a real place. There were more than twenty wolves on the flat plain atop the mountain.

I recognized Indru, standing upon a rock above the other wolves, though his eyes were an ordinary pale yellow and his ears were as solid as mine. I looked in confusion at the spirit-wolf Indru lying next to me, his silver gaze intent on the wolves below. I didn't see how it could be possible that he could be in both places at once. There was a lot about the Inejalun I didn't understand.

Tlitoo pulled on my ear. It was so cold I barely felt it.

"Watch, wolflet. It's why we're here."

The Indru standing on the rock on the mountaintop was listening to one of the other wolves.

"It won't work," the large pale-coated male was saying. "We tried to help the humans, but all they do is attack us. It's not possible to help them."

"It has to be possible," the Indru standing on the rock said. "We have made a promise. And if we do not keep it, none of us will live."

"We tried," a stern-voiced female said. She was nearly as large as Indru. 'They tried to make us obey their every whim. They killed Savdra when she ate from the prey she brought down herself!"

"If you allow them to feel that they are in control, they are easy to handle," a small, soft-voiced male said.

"Then we're no better than slaves," the pale-furred male said. "That is not acceptable."

A lithe, wiry female leapt up to stand beside Indru. She pressed against him in a way that made me think she must be his mate. The spirit Indru beside me whined softly.

"We have noticed something," the female said. "Some of us are better able to be with the humans than others. Some of us fight with the humans, and some do not."

"So?" I heard a wolf say. I couldn't tell which of the many wolves on the mountaintop had spoken.

"So we must split the pack," Indru said. "Some of us to stay with the humans and some to shun them."

The cold had reached my lungs, and I coughed hard. The spirit Indru looked over at me in concern.

"There's not much time. Come away."

He led us back to the Stone Circle, where I stood shivering. For some reason I wasn't quite as cold as I had been the last time I was at the Inejalun. That time I was so frozen I couldn't even shake. I thought it must have something to do with Indru.

"Do you understand what you have seen?" he asked.

"I think so," I said through clacking teeth. I tried to hide my disappointment. I hadn't learned much.

Hzralzu raised his wings at me. "You do *not* understand, babywolf," he said.

Insulted, I glared at him. I had not been a babywolf for moons. Tlitoo pulled my tail as Hzralzu cackled a laugh. Then the ancient raven grew serious, and he spoke again.

> *"Wolves are of two clans,*
> *One large, one small, and to each*
> *A task is given.*

> *"Both took sacred vows:*
> *Smallwolves watch, Greatwolves sever,*
> *Guard all that is wild."*

I felt even more let down. Every wolf in the valley knew that by now. But Hzralzu had gotten it wrong.

"It's the Greatwolves, not the smallwolves, who've always been responsible for watching humankind," I said, shivering.

"No, Kaala," Indru said, "it is not."

He let that sink in. Let me understand it.

"It's us?" I said at last. "No, it can't be."

"What do you know about the origins of the Greatwolves, youngwolf?" he asked me.

"They came in the time of Lydda," I said. "She tried to bring wolf and humankind together, and at first it worked. But the humans and wolves fought, so the Greatwolves came to take over the promise. Because smallwolves are too strongly drawn to the humans. It's why Milsindra says I'll fail, why her followers say it's wrong for me to be with the humans."

The old raven gurgled rudely and spat a bug at me. Tlitoo warbled.

"It's another lie, isn't it?" I said.

"It's the secret the Greatwolves have protected for generations, a secret they have killed for," the spiritwolf Indru said. "I saw that some wolves in my pack were less likely to fight with the humans, and chose them to be the humans' guardians. Those who were quick to battle were entrusted with keeping safe the freedom of wolfkind. They promised to stay away from humankind. It happened that the larger wolves of my pack were the ones who fought the most and were the ones who were to stay away. They bred among themselves and grew larger than any other wolves. Then they took what was not theirs to have."

> "Wild-wolves, so jealous,
> Envied what the smallwolves had
> And so they stole it."

The old raven peered at me, as if waiting for me to say something. It made a strange sort of sense. I could see why Milsindra would do anything to protect that secret. Then I realized what it meant. If we were the ones meant to be with the humans, then the Greatwolves had no authority over us. No right to tell us what to do. And no right to say what happened with the humans. Once the packs in the valley heard about this, they would know I was right about the humans.

I tried to speak, but whatever Indru was doing to keep the cold at bay was no longer working. My muzzle was icy. I forced it open.

"Why do they keep watching what happened?" I managed to ask.

"I've wondered that myself," Indru said. "I have heard many of them say that I was mistaken, that I chose the wrong wolves to guard the humans, and they watch the past to justify that belief. And I think they bear a great guilt for what they did, and are trying to find a way to assuage it. Some, however, have begun to believe that it might be time to return responsibility for the humans to those who were first meant to bear it. Their leader, Zorindru, believes this. As do the two who watch over your pack. It is why they saved you when you were born, Kaala. But they have always been conflicted. They do not wish their kind to die out, or to be useless."

My muzzle was now frozen shut, and it was beginning to get difficult to breathe. *Why can't they come here to the Inejalun?* I wanted to ask. *Why do they want the Nejakilakin?* But I could no longer get any words out. I looked at Tlitoo, trying to get him to understand what I wanted to ask, but he just blinked at me in concern.

"She is cold," he said to Indru. "We must leave."

Indru touched his nose to my face, and warmth flowed through me.

"Take her," he said to Tlitoo.

Tlitoo flew to me and pressed against me.

The flapping of wings filled my ears, and I fell into darkness. An instant later I was lying next to Kivdru in the dreamsage patch. I was wonderfully warm and full of energy.

Somehow Indru had taken away the ill effects of the Inejalun. I felt as if I'd woken from a long midday nap, and my heart pounded at what I'd learned. We were the ones who were supposed to be with the humans. It could make all the difference. I whuffed in excitement.

"Quiet, wolflet," Tlitoo hissed.

But it was too late. Kivdru rolled over and blinked open his eyes. I froze. Tlitoo hopped agilely out of Kivdru's sight. The Greatwolf looked at me, and the skin between his eyes creased into a frown.

"What are you doing here?" he murmured. "Are you a dream?"

He placed a great paw upon my back, pressing me into the dirt. He sniffed at me. I held as still as I could, trying not to breathe. He sniffed and sniffed. When he raised his muzzle, his nose was covered in uijin.

"Nothing," he said, his breath heavy with the scent of dream-sage. "No one here. Why do you haunt my dreams, troublesome littlewolf? It will not help you. We cannot let you live."

He lifted his paw, which was now also covered in the uijin, and tucked it under his chest. He sighed, and his eyes closed slowly. I waited until I was sure he was fully asleep, and then crept backward away from him. As soon as I was half a wolflength from him, I bolted.

I charged up the hill, wincing at the pain in the paw I'd sliced on the rock. I reached the top of the cliff and pelted down the other side of Wolf Killer. I felt better than I had since Yllin's death. Indru had taken away all my fatigue, and once Ruuqo and Rissa knew the truth about the promise, they could convince Sonnen and the others that I was not unlucky. They might even join with the Stone Peaks in openly defying the Greatwolves. But even if they didn't, we had proven that we could hunt the aurochs with humans, and with the help of our pack and others we would be able to continue to do so, even without the Lin tribe. If Frandra and Jandru kept their word, I could set things right in the valley and then go find my mother. I ran through the territory as Tlitoo soared and dipped above my head.

19

I ran all the way back to Fallen Tree, but it was past darkfall when I arrived, and I was panting so hard I couldn't speak for a moment. Every wolf in the pack, except for Trevegg, who was still at NiaLi's, was waiting for me. Ruuqo stood atop a rounded rock. Rissa stood just below him in front of the rock. Minn and Werrna were just to their left. Ázzuen and Marra darted to me.

"What took you so long?" Ázzuen demanded. "We told them about Borlla and that we were looking for the Greatwolf ceremony. Ruuqo and Rissa have spoken to Sonnen, but wouldn't tell us anything until you got here." Then he noticed the expression on my face. "You found it?"

"I found it," I said, "at Wolf Killer Hill. I found out what they didn't want us to know."

"What did you find out?" Rissa asked. I thought she would scold me for being late, but her voice was kind, her tail waving. I was grateful that Marra and Ázzuen had brought the pack news of Borlla. It had evidently put them in a good mood.

I looked at my packmates, wondering if I should tell them what had really happened—that I had met Indru and seen into the past. I told myself that it would take too long, that I didn't have time to answer all the questions they would have. I quickly greeted the leaderwolves, Werrna, and Minn. Then I stood back to look up at Ruuqo. Tlitoo, quorking softly to himself, settled next to Ruuqo on the watch rock.

"The ritual was over, but I overheard the Greatwolves talking," I told them, ignoring the stab of guilt that lying to my packmates brought on. "It's not the Greatwolves who are meant to watch over humankind. It's us. It has been all along." As quickly as I could, I told them as much as I could about what I'd learned, without betraying the fact that I was able to see things no wolf should be able to see.

"Sonnen and Tree Line will have to side with us now," I said. "Maybe Pirra will, too."

I stopped, breathless, waiting for their response. I had waited since I was a smallpup to hear Ruuqo say that I was not an unlucky wolf. Since the day I'd pulled TaLi from the river, I'd wanted my pack to know that I was not drelshik for being with the humans. Now they would see that being with the humans had been the right thing to do and that having me in the pack was not a weakness, but a strength. I looked from Ruuqo to Rissa expectantly.

"Come over here, all of you," Ruuqo said to us.

Marra and Ázzuen came to join me at the foot of the watch rock. Rissa leapt up to stand beside Ruuqo, knocking Tlitoo off the rock. The raven grumbled and took flight, landing on the fallen spruce that split the gathering place in two.

"We have spoken to Sonnen again," Ruuqo said, "and we have come to a decision. We have decided to join him."

Join him in what? I thought, confused. We were the ones who were supposed to get Sonnen to join us now. We had information about the Greatwolves that every wolf in the valley would want.

"Milsindra and Kivdru have indeed extended their offer to us," Rissa said. "They came here themselves to tell us. And we have accepted."

I just blinked at them for several moments. Hadn't they heard what I'd told them?

"But we don't need to anymore," I said. "The Greatwolves have been lying to us. Again. We're the ones who are supposed to be with the humans. The Greatwolves stole Borlla and kept her for five moons! We just have to tell the other packs."

Rissa smiled. "We're glad Borlla is safe. And I wish the Greatwolves had not taken her. Milsindra explained to us that the Greatwolves need our blood to keep their line healthy. It is part of the agreement we have made with them."

Ruuqo and Rissa had made an agreement with Milsindra? I was shocked into silence. Ázzuen, fortunately, was not.

"What agreement?" he asked.

"We will support them in their battle for the Greatwolf council and will give them a pup every few years—as other packs will—so that their bloodline does not die out. We will have no more contact with the humans. In return, we will live—and our pups will live. The Greatwolves have promised they can bring back the prey, and they will help us eat until then."

It was so silent in the gathering place I could hear Tlitoo rustling his wings. I couldn't believe what I was hearing.

"But we're the ones who are supposed to be with the humans," I tried again. "Everything the Greatwolves have told us was wrong. We're *supposed* to be with the humans."

"It doesn't matter," Ruuqo said. "That was a long time ago. The Greatwolves are responsible for the humans now, and for us. We must follow their will, or die."

I shook my head, trying to clear it. It was as if once they'd made up their minds, they couldn't hear anything that didn't confirm what they wanted to believe was true. Torell had told me that Ruuqo and Rissa were weak, and I'd told him he was wrong.

"Even if we weren't the ones to take care of the humans, we wouldn't have to join Milsindra," Ázzuen said reasonably. "We can get plenty of auroch and elkryn meat, and Pirra and Sonnen will never attack us if the Stone Peaks stand with us."

"And we're succeeding," I said. I tried to sound as reasonable as Ázzuen did, but my voice shook. "We're bringing the best meat we've ever had. We can bring more now that we can hunt aurochs with the humans. We can show that Zorindru was right and can help him win against Milsindra. If we do, if Zorindru wins the council, we won't have to worry about Milsindra."

The leaderwolves said nothing. They just looked at us sympathetically.

"You decided a long time ago," Marra whispered. "It's what you wanted all along." I looked at her. I was surprised that she had been so silent until now. She was usually the first one to try to reason with the pack, to get them to see things her way. Now she was shaking with fury.

"We thought from the beginning that it was the right thing to do," Ruuqo agreed, "but didn't know if Milsindra would really allow us the opportunity. It's a better chance than we could have hoped for. You will cease your hunts with the humans and allow the Greatwolves to take over guarding them. You will avoid the humans, as you should have done all along."

"I can't," I said. "I promised Zorindru. And Frandra and Jandru. And I can't leave TaLi. And you promised, too. You can't go back on your word. It's wrong."

"We must do what is best for the pack, Kaala," Rissa said. "We must do what is best for the pack and best for wolfkind. We believe that Frandra and Jandru were wrong to let you stay with the humans, and that we were wrong to follow them."

I heard what she didn't say. That she thought Jandru and Frandra were wrong to spare my life when I was a small-pup.

"You are pack," she said. "You are a Swift River youngwolf, and we supported you at risk to the entire pack because of that. Now we have a duty to the valley and to save our pack. We will honor that duty."

"But what if Milsindra and Kivdru are lying to you?" I said desperately. "They lied before."

"They have admitted their mistake in doing so," Ruuqo said. "They believed it was necessary in order to protect us. Now they are allowing us to take part in the decision."

"It's just wrong," I said again. I remembered what Torell

had said about giving up what one believed in for the promise of safety.

"It's dishonorable," Marra spat. "It's shameful. It makes you no better than a grub finder."

"The decision has been made," Ruuqo said again.

"Grub finders," Tlitoo grumbled from his rock.

I felt so helpless I wanted to howl. I'd failed. I had assured Jandru and Frandra that I would gain my pack's support, and they had challenged Milsindra based on that promise. Zorindru had placed his trust in me, and I had failed him, too. I wanted to argue more, to speak against the pack's decision, but I was afraid that if I opened my mouth, nothing but a whimper would come out.

"And if we don't stop hunting with the humans?" Ázzuen asked. I was grateful to him for speaking up. "If we stay with them, what then?"

"You may stay with us and join us in this alliance," Ruuqo said. "Or you may choose to leave."

There it was, plain and simple. I had not thought they would state it so unabashedly. As if we had been given a choice between two perfectly sensible options. As if it were reasonable to betray everything that the Swift River pack had stood for.

"Will you give us romma if we leave?" Marra asked, jutting out her muzzle, as no youngwolf should do to a leaderwolf.

"We cannot," Ruuqo said. "If you fail to follow the rules of the pack, we cannot give you romma. If you stay with us, and follow our rules, then yes, you are all strong youngwolves and deserving of romma."

"We want you to stay," Rissa said. "We wish you would stay. We will need your help raising the new year's pups, as Yllin and Minn helped raise you. It will be difficult to feed them without you.

"Yllin died because of your actions," Werrna rumbled. "You owe us help with the new pups."

"They have the right to their own decisions, Werrna," Rissa said sharply. Maybe she really thought she was doing the right thing.

"Will you help Milsindra and Kivdru kill us?" Marra asked, her voice bitter.

"Of course not," Rissa said. "We insisted Milsindra agree to let you leave the valley unharmed, Kaala. You and any who would go with you."

"Like they let Yllin leave?" I asked. "They said she could go."

"We have told them our cooperation is dependent upon it," Ruuqo said. "So did Sonnen. He respects you, Kaala, even though he disagrees with you. And Milsindra just wants you out of her way."

"I'll bet she does," Ázzuen muttered.

"Think about it, youngwolves," Rissa said. "We would like to have all three of you stay with the pack, but we'll leave the New Cache meat for you, in case you decide to leave the valley."

Rissa and Ruuqo, then Werrna and Minn touched their noses to our cheeks, as they had done a hundred times before, as if today were no different from any other time we had parted, as if they were not leaving us to choose between the pack that had raised us and the promise we had made, as if it might not be the last time we were together as pack. Then they left us.

The cool evening breeze ruffled the fur between my ears. I was aware of Ázzuen and Marra watching me, waiting for me to decide what to do. Out of the corner of my eye I saw Tlitoo crouched on slightly bent legs, as if ready to take flight from the fallen spruce. I could only stand there, staring at the gap in the trees through which our pack had left. I was never sure we could win against Milsindra and Kivdru—I knew the risks we were taking. But I had always assumed that Ruuqo and Rissa would do the right thing, that Swift River pack was different from other packs, and that even if we made mistakes or failed, we would always do what was honorable. Now I didn't know what to believe. Those I depended upon most had betrayed me. Those I needed were no longer to be trusted.

Ázzuen scraped his paw in the dirt. "We have to change their minds," he said. "Once they think about it, about the truth about the promise, they'll change their minds."

"They won't," Marra said, disgusted. "They think it's safer to do what they're told. We have to find another way."

I looked at the two of them. Not everyone I trusted had betrayed me. I remembered what I had seen when Tlitoo had shown me Ruuqo's memories—how he had looked at Rissa when at last she was his, how he would do anything to protect her.

"No, they won't change their minds," I said.

Tlitoo flew from the spruce to land next to me.

"So what now, wolflet? Stay here and whine?"

I didn't know what now. I'd thought everything would be all right once I told the pack about the Greatwolves' secret. Now I realized how naive I'd been. Rissa had said that Milsindra would allow us to leave with our humans. Not a moon ago that was all I wanted. I still wanted it.

"We still have the Stone Peaks," Marra said when I remained silent.

"And the Lan tribe," Ázzuen added. "We can try hunting with them."

Their steadfastness made me ashamed of my own weakness. I couldn't run away when they were so eager to continue the fight.

"I'll go talk to NiaLi and Trevegg," I said. "They may have some ideas of what to do." The thought of their wisdom made me feel better.

Marra leapt to her feet. "I'll go to the Lan tribe and get MikLan. The old woman can tell him what's happening."

"And I'll tell the Stone Peaks," Ázzuen said just as eagerly.

"Good," I said, trying to match the enthusiasm in their voices. "Meet me back at NiaLi's as soon as you can. Howl that you've found good hunting when you're on your way."

They darted off. I looked at them. I envied their certainty. I couldn't help but wonder if I was making a mistake. If the reason the Greatwolves had taken over watching the humans was that we *were* too weak. I certainly felt like I was.

"I must go tell the raven clan, wolf."

He took off without waiting for my answer. I took one last look at Fallen Tree. I wouldn't be returning there. Then I took a deep breath and started toward NiaLi's.

⊞

Indru's rejuvenating effect on me was wearing off, and I was tired. I forced myself to run anyway; I didn't know how much time we had. NiaLi's new shelter was farther than I remembered from Fallen Tree, and my paw was hurting again. I slowed to a lope and then a walk. Finally I reached the tiny clearing that sheltered NiaLi's home.

I knew immediately that something was wrong. NiaLi's fire was out, and the scents of fear and anger seeped from the dwelling. I heard a deep-voiced shout and a higher-pitched shriek. Forgetting my fatigue, I bolted for the shelter. I dove under the preyskin at the shelter's entrance, pulling myself into the old woman's home on my belly.

At once, I saw three things. NiaLi lay crumpled in a heap next to her quenched fire, her neck bent at an unnatural angle and a deep slash oozing blood from her neck. She wasn't breathing. Trevegg stood growling in front of TaLi, protecting the girl as she hunched weeping over her grandmother. And DavRian stood over them both, his bloody spear raised.

I should have killed him when I had the chance.

The shelter was small, giving me little room to maneuver and no chance to get a running start. I leapt at DavRian just as he brought down his sharpstick in a vicious sweep, cutting deeply into Trevegg's chest and stomach. The oldwolf screamed and fell to his side, his legs kicking frantically, running from an enemy he could not escape and then going still. His breath began to come in short, harsh gasps. DavRian raised his spear again, ready to plunge it into Trevegg. An instant later, I hit him full force, knocking him against the side of the shelter.

We have rules about killing. Packmates are always warned before they are badly injured or killed. But there are things that are unforgivable, including killing a packmate for no reason other than greed or anger. The promise said we could not kill any human unless in defense of our lives. It did not mean we had to stand by and watch a human kill. DavRian had murdered NiaLi and probably Trevegg, too. When a wolf goes crazy and kills other wolves, when he breaks the rules of life, he is to be killed. DavRian had lost his right to be protected by the promise.

I would have done it. I would have killed him, but he had moved just as I leapt, and I hit him at an awkward angle. He dropped his sharpstick and shoved me. I landed on my back, and DavRian kicked me hard in the ribs. I twisted away and prepared to leap again, but I was slowed by fatigue and pain. By the time I had gotten to my feet, he had reached over Trevegg, who tried to snap at his arm, and seized up TaLi, gripping her tightly to his chest. She struggled against him, grabbing at his head and kicking at any part of him she could reach. He shifted his grip so that he pinned her arms tight against him and squeezed her so hard that she cried out in pain. I wanted to kill him more than I'd wanted anything in my life, but I couldn't get to his weak soft neck, because he held TaLi too close to it. Instead, I bit into his leg. His scream made my heart pound with the call to the hunt. His blood filled my mouth like the blood of any other prey, and I released his leg to bite the other. I saw the sharp stone blade the instant before it reached me. I twisted out of the way and the blade missed me. DavRian kicked me in the side of the head. I fell back, whimpering.

DavRian had let go of TaLi with one arm in order to attack me. The girl shrieked in fury, thrashing and fighting DavRian's now one-armed grip. She drove her elbow up into his face, and he dropped her. She tried to scramble to her feet, but he kicked her brutally in the stomach. She doubled over, gasping, and groped around the old woman's fire pit, seeking a weapon. As her fist closed around a large, sharp rock, DavRian grabbed his fallen spear and slammed the blunt end against TaLi's head. She sagged to the ground. I got my feet under me and leapt for DavRian again. I was too slow, and he stepped aside as I reached him and threw me so hard against the side of the shelter that for precious moments, I couldn't move. DavRian threw something over TaLi—it was the cloak he had given her and she had refused to wear—and picked her up.

I watched helplessly as he limped from the shelter, carrying her away. I tried twice to get to my feet and fell back, dizzy and nauseated. I had to go after them. I began to drag myself to the opening of the shelter. Then I realized that the labored breathing I heard was not my own. Trevegg was still alive. I dragged myself over to him and pressed my cheek to his.

"He came for the girl," Trevegg said. "He said he would take her as his mate and that he would be krianan for both Lin and Rian. The girl told him she would kill him before she would let him do so, that he was too stupid to be anything other than a rabbit hunter. I think he went crazy. All NiaLi did was rise to stand between them, and he killed her." Trevegg sounded so sad when he spoke of the old woman's death. He seemed to care more about that than about his own wound.

I looked at the old woman, pain and guilt welling in my chest. I should have taken better care of TaLi's grandmother. I looked at her bent neck and the clean cut at her throat. DavRian would pay for her death. The Lin tribe would not allow this.

"Kaala," Trevegg rasped. I shook myself from my thoughts. I could hardly bear to look at him. No wolf could survive such an injury. "What did the pack say?" he asked.

"They're going to follow Milsindra," I said. "They won't help me with the humans. They want things to be the way they were before."

The oldwolf's eyes clouded over with despair. "Then it's over," he said. "We gambled and we lost. It was all for nothing."

"No," I said, "it wasn't." Suddenly it was vital for me to make sure he knew that the fight wasn't over, that we still had a chance. I wanted him to know that. Before he died.

"It's not over," I said. "I found out what the Greatwolves have been hiding from us. We're supposed to be the ones to watch over the humans. Indru split his pack in two. The Greatwolves were supposed to stay away from humans, and we were supposed to watch over them."

"It's true?" he asked. "Frandra and Jandru told us that after you left. The old woman told the girl that they had to find the other krianans, to tell them. But I didn't believe them. How can you know that it's true? How do you know they aren't lying again?"

I looked into his dimming eyes. And I told him. "I saw it. Tlitoo can take me into the spirit world. He can take me into the minds of others."

"The Nejakilakin," he said. "I heard tales of it when I was a pup but thought they were no more than stories." He choked and lay panting, barely able to breathe.

"I'm sorry," I said.

"For what?" He looked up at me, the despair in his eyes

replaced by a gleam of excitement. "Don't you see, Kaala? Even without the pack, you can keep the promise. You must do so. Whatever else happens, you must keep the promise."

"I don't feel ready," I said. I should have been giving him comfort, not asking for it from him.

"It doesn't matter," he said. "You will have to make do with what skills and wisdom you have. You must make the best choices you can. So it is with every wolf."

My choices had not been good so far.

"I should have killed DavRian. I had the chance. I could have killed him and made it look like he had fallen. If I had, NiaLi would still be alive and you wouldn't . . ." I couldn't finish the sentence. "I'm sorry, I should have done it."

"No, Kaala, you should not have. It would have been the easy thing, the convenient thing, but it would not have been the *right* thing. You are able to keep everything in mind. All of the results and implications of every choice. It will make things harder for you, but it is what is needed now. Keep your courage and your convictions."

I lay next to him until his harsh breathing slowed and then stopped. I buried my nose in his neck so I could take his scent with me wherever I might go. Grief closed in on me and I shoved it away, as I had so many times forced away other grief. I would mourn for Trevegg, but I couldn't do so now. TaLi needed me, and I would go to her.

It took me twice as long as it should have to reach the human homesite. I should have been able to get there long before DavRian did, even though he was far ahead of me, but I was having trouble breathing, and with every step I grew more dizzy. DavRian had thrown me so hard against the wall of the shelter that my ribs throbbed with every step.

Despair pushed at me once again as I thought of Trevegg and NiaLi. I pushed back. I let anger roll over me instead, let it drive me forward as I followed DavRian's trail toward the human homesite. I remembered TaLi slumped in DavRian's arms and forced myself to move faster. By the time I crossed the river and staggered to the spiny tartberry bushes where I often hid to watch the humans, I was clamping shut my jaws to keep from whimpering aloud.

In spite of his head start and my slow progress, DavRian was just arriving at the human gathering place. He staggered into the homesite under TaLi's weight, limping from the bite on his leg. I hoped it hurt him. I hoped it festered and killed him. He pulled the cloak from TaLi's blood-covered head and set her down next to one of the fires that lit the night-darkened village.

All around the gathering place, humans stopped what they were doing and rushed to DavRian and TaLi.

"What happened?" RinaLi demanded, bending over the girl. For all she had been willing to mate TaLi to a man she hated, RinaLi seemed genuinely concerned.

"It was the wolves," DavRian said. "They killed the old woman and tried to kill TaLi. I slew one of them, but the other one got away. The one she's always with. Silvermoon. I wounded it, but it ran away."

He lied so easily, so convincingly. But they would find out soon enough. TaLi would take them to the old woman's shelter and they would see how she had been killed. RinaLi would see TaLi's head wound and know it could not have been made by any wolf.

TaLi, now half-conscious, was trying to speak. "Not a wolf," she mumbled. I heard her, but none of the other humans seemed to. Then RinaLi bent and covered TaLi's mouth with her hand. She had heard. She had heard and wanted to make sure no one else did.

"We'll find the wolves," HuLin said grimly as all around him humans picked up sharpsticks and blades. They weren't going to check DavRian's story. They just believed him. "We should have killed them long ago."

I had underestimated the humans' willingness to hate us. They wouldn't question DavRian, wouldn't believe TaLi when she told them. I had to get TaLi away. But there was no way. There were at least ten sharpstick-wielding humans gathered around HuLin and still more watching from other parts of the gathering place. It was one of the reasons they were so dangerous—there were so many of them. DavRian was hovering over the girl like a hyena at a kill. I couldn't get to her.

TaLi's eyes flew open. She looked directly at the tartberry bush. She knew it was where I often hid. Keeping flat on my belly, I crept forward just a few pawswidths so that my nose and the tips of my paws peeked out of the bush and so my eyes would reflect the light of the human's fires. A grim smile crossed TaLi's face.

"Stay there," she mouthed. But I wouldn't let her fight alone. Her hand tightened, and I realized that she had managed to hold on to the rock she had picked up at NiaLi's. In a motion as smooth and graceful as any wolf's she rolled to her feet and threw the rock at DavRian's head. Her aim was perfect. He staggered, blood flowing from his temple. TaLi scrambled on all fours to pick up the stone, which had fallen next to DavRian. She picked it up and hurled it at HuLin, who had the sense to duck. Two males grabbed TaLi's arms, holding her between them, and she cried out.

Fury overcame me. Before I knew what I was doing I tore from my bush and ran at the humans who held TaLi.

"There it is!" someone shouted, more fear than anger in his voice.

It seemed like every human in the homesite converged on me. Remembering what Torell had taught me, I thought of a hill dancer. I dodged and danced away from the humans. They stumbled over me, falling over themselves. I pounced on one of the males who held TaLi, slamming into him hard enough that he released his grip. TaLi bit the other one hard on the arm and pulled away. I tripped the human I had knocked into, and TaLi and I began to run to the woods. I kept TaLi in front of me, snapping and growling at any humans who came near. When one of the males tried to cut TaLi off, I ran in front of her and tangled myself in the human's legs. We both went sprawling as TaLi disappeared into the woods. I got my paws under me and started to follow her.

That was when I saw the sharpstick, the spear, in Dav-Rian's hand. Raised high above his bleeding head. Aimed at my chest. There were three humans standing next to him, and I couldn't get past them. As DavRian brought the spear down toward my chest, I twisted away. The spear pierced my right haunch, and I screamed. Then screamed again as DavRian ripped it from my haunch.

I began to drag myself away, only to be surrounded by humans.

"Kill it!" one of the males said. "Before it bites someone."

DavRian lifted his spear. I was glad TaLi had gotten away. I was glad that my pack would be safe, that they had been smart enough not to trust me when I said I could get the humans to live with us peacefully. I stared up at the spear, unable to take my eyes from its blood-covered tip.

"No, don't hurt her!" TaLi's voice made me want to howl. Why hadn't she kept running? "Don't kill her, and I will be your mate, DavRian."

The young man blinked a few times, then a slow grin spread across his face.

"I won't kill it," he said. "We'll keep it here. Then the rest of its pack will come looking for it, and we can kill them all at once."

A human grabbed each of my hind legs and began dragging me backward. My haunch hurt so much I couldn't stop whimpering, even though I knew it would distress TaLi to hear me. I turned and snapped at the hands that held me, but one of the humans yanked on my injured leg and I lay still. They dragged me across the village and to a dry, dusty grove just beyond it. Three of them picked me up by my hind end. I saw the pit a moment before they swung me into it. I fell and landed hard on what felt like a pile of sticks, rocks, and soft vegetation. TaLi's head filled the opening as she flung herself down at the pit's edge to see me. She was immediately dragged away.

I sat, panting at the bottom of the pit, wishing DavRian had just killed me. I had failed in every way. My pack would not keep their promise, and TaLi would not be krianan of her tribe. Milsindra had been right—we smallwolves weren't capable of watching over the humans. Trevegg and NiaLi were dead, and Ázzuen and Marra would be at risk when they tracked my scent from NiaLi's to the village. TaLi's tribemates would hunt the wolves of the valley, and there would be war. I would never find my mother. I whimpered.

A large black shape filled the hole at the top of the pit. Tlitoo flew down to me.

"There you are, wolf," he quorked. "It does not take you long to get into trouble when I am not here. Are you finished feeling sorry for yourself? There is still much to do."

I looked at him, incredulous. The pit was a little more than a wolflength wide and at least five wolflengths deep. There was no way I could get out of it.

"Your girl bit another one of the humans. On his ear. He now has half an ear. She has been spending too much time with wolves."

I had to laugh. My despair began to lift in spite of my sorrow and my concern for TaLi. I realized Tlitoo was right. We had work to do.

The Greatwolves had lied and lied again. My pack had betrayed me, and I knew they would not be the last to do so. The Lin tribe was no more trustworthy than a pack of hyenas. But TaLi had come back for me. Trevegg and NiaLi had died to defend the covenant of the wolves. Ázzuen and Marra had not given up, even when our pack had done so. TaLi had risked everything to do what was right when she refused to hunt Aln's prey. She thought of me as her packmate, so much so that she came back to save me when she could have escaped.

And in spite of what Milsindra had said, in spite of what Ruuqo had always believed, I was not a drelshik for wanting to be with the humans. We were supposed to be watching over them, and I had promised I would do so.

I heard Marra's distant howl, saying that she had discovered a herd of horses. It was the signal we had agreed upon to mean that she had found MikLan and would meet us at Nia-Li's. Ázzuen answered that he would join the hunt, which meant that he had found the Stone Peaks. Pell added his voice to Ázzuen's, saying that the Stone Peaks would run the hunt with us. They were all coming for me. Tlitoo could warn them to stay away from the human homesite, that the humans were coming to kill any wolf they could find. But I wanted them to know more than that.

I sat up and looked at the moon, shining above the pit. I held each member of my pack in my mind: Ázzuen, Marra, TaLi, MikLan and BreLan. Tlitoo, Jlela, and Nlitsa. I thought of how NiaLi and Trevegg had died to protect the promise, how TaLi had come for me. I thought of how we were pack. I thought of the task we had taken on, and what it meant for wolf and humankind. Sitting up in the dank pit I looked up at the moon that I knew every member of my pack could see, and I howled to them.

I, for one, would keep the promise I had made.